Ravenscliffe

Also by Jane Sanderson

Netherwood

Ravenscliffe

jane sanderson

WILLIAM MORROW

An Imprint of HarperCollins*Publishers*

RAVENSCLIFFE. Copyright © 2012 by Jane Sanderson. All rights reserved. Printed in the United States of America. No part of this book may be used or reproduced in any manner whatsoever without written permission except in the case of brief quotations embodied in critical articles and reviews. For information address Harper-Collins Publishers, 10 East 53rd Street, New York, NY 10022.

HarperCollins books may be purchased for educational, business, or sales promotional use. For information please e-mail the Special Markets Department at SPsales@harpercollins.com.

First published in Great Britain as a paperback original in 2012 by Sphere, an imprint of Little, Brown Book Group.

FIRST U.S. EDITION

Library of Congress Cataloging-in-Publication Data has been applied for.

ISBN 978-0-06-230037-9

14 15 16 17 18   OV/RRD   10 9 8 7 6 5 4 3 2 1

For my parents, Anne and Bob Sanderson

Acknowledgments

I began the acknowledgments in *Netherwood* with my mum and dad, Anne and Bob Sanderson, and I'm going to do the same again. Once more, they have helped so much with detail and information, with books and photographs, with memories and anecdotes. Added to this, their interest and encouragement continue unabated and for this I'm deeply grateful. Thanks also to my mum for her one-woman campaign to sell my books throughout—and far beyond—the Worsbrough Bridge Bowling Club. Her commitment to this task is unswerving.

My wise and steady agent, Andrew Gordon, has been a fount of sound advice from the beginning, and I'm truly happy to have him on my side. At Sphere, Rebecca Saunders made my whole year with her response to *Ravenscliffe*, and I thank her not just for her generous praise but also for picking up the baton last summer in such a reassuring and enthusiastic way. Thanks to Zoe Gullen at Sphere for her face-saving forensic approach to the edit, and to Louise Davies, for tempering with compliments her notes and queries: an unexpected kindness and much appreciated.

To my three beloved children, Eleanor, Joseph, and Jacob, I'd like to say thanks for remaining so resolutely and endearingly yourselves: keep up the good work. And to Brian, my most ardent and loyal champion: your love and support underpins everything. Thank you.

PART ONE

Chapter 1

High on the northern side of the mining town of Nether-wood was a windblown swathe of common land—not vast, certainly not a wilderness, but wide and varied enough for a person who walked there to feel unfettered and alone. It wasn't much to look at: coarse grass more yellow than green; pockets of unchecked scrub; spiteful, unruly gangs of hawthorn; the occasional craggy outcrop hinting at a wild and different geology before man farmed the earth, or mined it. An ancient bill of rights gave the people of the town license to graze their livestock here, but in this community of miners it wasn't much of an advantage. Instead, the grass was kept down by a herd of retired pit ponies, stocky little Shetlands that had survived the rigors of their long, underground life and been given the freedom of the common in return. Once in a blue moon some-one managed to acquire a pig, but the common was unfenced, and while the wary ponies never strayed, pigs seemed driven by curiosity and wanderlust: even a sturdy pen built by Percy Medlicott a few years ago had failed to contain his Tamworth sow. She had rubbed her snout against the latch until it slipped open, and the liberated sow had met an early end on Turnpike

Lane in a collision with a coach-and-four. The driver, unseated from the box by the accident, was compensated in pork; he had traveled home to York the following day with a fractured collarbone and a bag of loin chops.

So Netherwood Common, not being of any great practical benefit to anyone, was simply enjoyed by the townsfolk for what it was: a natural open space—rare enough in this gray industrial landscape—where children could play out of earshot of their mothers and a workingman could smoke a Woodbine in peace. The common in its present form had evolved over the past hundred years and it owed its existence to the three collieries that dominated the town, because as coal production replaced agriculture in Netherwood's economy, the fertile land became less useful than the stuff beneath. The area's farmland origins could still be seen in the hedgerows and ancient field boundaries that crisscrossed the common, but it was over a century now since the soil there had been tilled or crops planted.

Like everything else in the neighborhood, the common fell within the vast acreage of the Netherwood estate, and from its highest point, and facing south, an observer could map the principal features of the earl's Yorkshire dominion. New Mill, Long Martley, and Middlecar collieries—positioned respectively north, east, and south of the town—dominated the outlook, their muck stacks, headstocks, and winding gear stark against the sky. The residential terraces, long rows of doughty stone houses, stood like stocky bulwarks, built to withstand the worst of the four winds. Victoria Street, Market Street, and Mill Street claimed precedence on the south side of town and formed its modestly prosperous commercial center, where small shops, stalls, and barrows plied their trade and vied for customers with the Co-operative Society, whose premises, like its profits, seemed to grow annually. One town hall. One town hall clock tower. Three public houses. Three churches—one high, two low. And then beyond Mill Lane and Middlecar Colliery, but still visible from the common, the road gradually narrowed and dipped, following the contours of a shallow valley and leading to a gate—one of four—to the ancestral home of Edward Hoyland, Sixth Earl of Netherwood, and his wife, Clarissa. The great house itself, Netherwood Hall, was tucked away out of sight: a remarkable feat, given its size, and a fortuitous one. Not only was great privacy accorded the aristocratic family within, but also they were spared the unlovely sight of the scarred landscape of the Yorkshire coalfields. But beauty is in the eye of the beholder. Eve Williams and Anna Rabinovich, standing on this clear August day on the highest point of the common, saw nothing to offend the eye as they regarded the familiar vista before them.

"See?" Anna said, her arms spread before her in a proprietorial way, as if she was personally responsible for the view. "World at your feet." Her accent, her hybrid dialect of Russian and Yorkshire, made most of her statements sound comical. She had no end of colloquialisms at hand, but still wasn't mistress of the definite article.

Eve laughed. "Always knew it was only a matter of time," she said.

"But imagine, Eve. All this, ours."

"Aye, ours and three thousand other folks'. It's a common, y'know, not a back garden."

Anna shrugged. Mere detail, and detail was the enemy of an adventurous spirit. She had brought her friend up here, dragging her unwillingly from all the things she should be doing, to look at a house. It was the only property on the common, a large, detached villa, deeper than it was wide, double-fronted with generous bay windows and its name and date carved in stone over the door: Ravenscliffe, 1852. Like everything else, it belonged to Lord Netherwood, though it had been designed and built by the same architect who was responsible for most of the dwellings in the town. Abraham Carr had sought and been granted permission from the present earl's father to erect a house for his own use and at his own expense, and had named it for the Yorkshire village of his birth. Then, just five years after taking up residence, he had passed away: born in one Ravenscliffe, died in another. The house was bought by the Netherwood estate, absorbed into all its other possessions, and instantly put to work. Various tenants had taken it in the forty years since Mr. Carr's demise, merchants, mostly, or people from the professional classes whose wages stretched further than those of the miners. Now, though, it was empty. Unfurnished. Unloved. And Anna wanted to live there.

Something about the house spoke to her, and you should listen to a house, she believed. She wasn't in any other way a fanciful person, never looked for meanings or omens in everyday happenings, never tried to interpret her dreams or fathom the patterns of the stars, but a house was another matter: there were good ones and bad ones and the two could look identical, but while one would bring happiness, the other would bring only misery. As a child in Kiev, in another life and time, she had lived in an imposing mansion with around towers and six wide steps up to the front door. It was her father's statement to the world that he was a successful man, but for all its fineness Anna knew, even as a little girl, that it was riddled with misery, from its foundations to its roof tiles. She never understood why: some houses were afflicted, that was all. When her parents disowned her for marrying a Jew, when they spat on the floor at her feet and told her never to return, she had thought, it's the house speaking: you two have been here too long.

This house on the common, though, this Ravenscliffe, held the promise of happiness. Its hearths were empty and cold, but there was warmth here. Anna had stood before it, looked it in the eye, and recognized this at once. So her mission in persuading Eve that the rent—though more than four times what they currently paid—was of negligible concern compared with the ease and comfort it would bring, came directly from the heart. She felt compelled to win this battle, overcome her friend's reservations, press her point. In any case, from a purely practical point of view, they were bursting at the seams in Beaumont Lane. And when Eve and Daniel were wed, he would be there too, because Eve and the children couldn't live in that doll's house they'd put him in at the Hall. And then babies might come. No. There was simply no other course of action.

They walked back down toward the house, and Anna could tell from the silence and her friend's unfocused gaze that Eve's mind had drifted elsewhere.

"Bedrooms for us all," Anna said, to pull her back to the matter in hand. "Space for your children and my little Maya. Fresh air."

"Mmm, as fresh as it gets around 'ere, anyroad."

"And kitchen big enough to dance polka. And bathroom, Eve. No tin tubs and outdoor privy."

"Yes, Anna. I know. It's just . . ."

"I know. Beaumont Lane was Arthur's home," she said, with the slightest hint of weariness, as if she'd heard it once too often.

"Don't say it like that, as if it's not rational of me to think of it."

Eve, provoked, stopped abruptly so that when Anna turned to face her she had to trot back up the slope a little way.

"That's not what I meant," Anna said, though it was, in part. "What I meant was, I understand how you feel, how leaving Arthur's home would feel."

"It's not just me," said Eve, setting off again. "I mean, I'm not only worried on my account."

Anna sighed. "Seth?"

"Aye. 'e's already 'ad too much to take on."

No more than Eliza and Ellen, thought Anna, but she held her tongue. Eve's eldest child made heavy going of life, in her view, and was as rude and withdrawn with Daniel as he had been with Anna herself when she first moved into Beaumont Lane eighteen months ago, after Arthur was killed. It was a long road ahead for Daniel, if her own experience was anything to go by. All of this ran through Anna's mind as the two women walked in silence down the slope, then rounded the bend toward Ravenscliffe. Her heart lifted at the sight of it.

"Eve," she said, quite urgently, so that they both halted again. Her friend turned to her, questioningly.

"When you and Daniel marry," said Anna, "wouldn't it be better for everyone if you made new home, and left one you had shared with Arthur?"

Eve sighed, looked at the ground. This conversation, kindly meant, was nevertheless unsettling. "Probably," she said.

"Arthur lives on in your children, you know, not in bricks and mortar."

"Aye. I know that." And she did. But still, she thought, it was a link with him. She didn't want her love for Daniel to eclipse her memories of Arthur: that would be wrong and less than he deserved. While she lived in her little terrace in Beaumont Lane, she could still picture him at the table wolfing his dinner, or in the tub sluicing off the coal dust. Where would he be in Ravenscliffe?

They went in, though; like burglars, through an unfastened sash window discovered by Anna on a previous foray. She opened it now and ushered Eve through it, holding up her skirts and giving her a gentle push into a large square entrance hall.

They stood for a moment in the profound stillness of the empty house.

"You'll get us arrested," Eve whispered. She was half impressed, half scandalized at her friend's resourcefulness. Anna, her eyes bright with purpose, grinned at her. She looked more twelve than twenty-two, Eve thought.

"No need to whisper," Anna said. She spoke with bold confidence, and in the empty house her voice rang out like a challenge. "Come. This way," and she set off through the ground floor with a certainty of direction that suggested she'd been here before. There was no resisting her, so Eve dispatched her disapproval and allowed herself to be led from one large, impressive room to another. Abraham Carr had done a fine job. There was a fair amount of dust, and the spiders had claimed all the corners, but there was no getting away from the fact that this was a glorious house, flooded with natural light, substantially built and sure of itself, adorned with Victorian flourishes—lavishly tiled floors, plaster cornicing, marble fire surrounds, a sweeping, mahogany staircase—and positioned to make the most of the views of Netherwood Common, from the front and from the back. How odd it would be, thought Eve, as she gazed through one of two windows in the large kitchen, to look out every day on grass and trees. Anna joined her, and Eve said: "Makes a change from looking at Lilly and Maud's drawers on t'washing line, doesn't it?"

"At least when their drawers are up you can't see privvies."

They laughed, then Anna wandered across to the other window and Eve turned to study the range. It was rather fine, a Leamington Kitchener, twice the size of her range in Beaumont Lane and with no visible faults that a pot of black lead and a rag wouldn't solve. It was set into a recess, which was bordered on its two long sides by carved columns and across its top by a handsome mantel in the same classical style, as if it were a prize exhibit, carefully positioned by a curator. Eve placed her hands on the top of the stove. She wondered how long it had stood cold.

Anna said: "You could watch Seth play knur and spell from here, see?"

Eve turned back to the window and joined her friend, who pointed up the hill outside toward the wide clearing of trampled grass where men gathered most Saturday afternoons with their pummels and knurs. Seth had watched his father play ever since he was old enough to be taken along to matches, and now he used his dad's pummel, which was too big for him, really, but try telling him that. If the competition wasn't too fierce or if they were a man short, Seth was asked to join in; along with the allotment, it was the one thing that could make him smile.

Eve moved to Anna's side: saw the same long, wide slope and the same clearing. But she didn't see Seth there. She saw Arthur. Jacket discarded on the ground, shirtsleeves rolled above the elbows, facing the spell and its finely balanced knur, his eyes never leaving the ball as the spring launched it up and he swiped it long and true with the pummel his own father had made for him. That's where Arthur would be at Ravenscliffe, she thought. Not in the house, but up there, on the hill.

She turned and walked out of the kitchen so abruptly that Anna was sure she had taken against the idea of the move once and for all, and as they clambered back out of the window Eve was silent. But then she pulled open the front gate, which hung lopsided, its top hinge having splintered away from the post, and she said: "That'll need fixing for a start."

Beside her, Anna smiled.

Chapter 2

Clarissa Hoyland, in bed, draped in Flanders lace, propped up on three fat pillows, turned a petulant face toward her husband. It was the same expression her youngest daughter used when early signs indicated she might not get her way: brows puckered, bottom lip jutting, the suggestion of tears in her eyes. But of course, Isabella was only twelve. The child was away from home for a few weeks, staying with cousins in Suffolk, but Teddy Hoyland felt her presence now in the bed before him.

"I simply can't see the difficulty," said the countess. "And I wonder at you, Teddy, presenting me with obstacles at every turn, when already there is so much to be organized."

"Obstacles! I hardly think so."

The earl, standing at the foot of his wife's bed, was already dressed and replete with breakfast, ready for the day's business, while Clarissa still lay disheveled and rosy in a tumble of bed-clothes. She was slow to surface in the mornings, unfurling delicately each new day like a fern, while her husband woke like one of his black Labradors, bounding with gusto from sleep into wakefulness. His rude health and sturdiness seemed almost

11

an affront here, in his wife's room. The countess was tiny, bones like a bird, wrists you could encircle with room to spare between index finger and thumb. Lying there under the satin counterpane she looked fragile and vulnerable, and though he knew that any suggestion of weakness was an illusion—that she was, in fact, armed with a will of iron and nerves of steel—still she made him feel like a cad, a tweed-clad brute, denying his charming wife the smallest happiness. This was how she triumphed, always.

"Very well," she said now, arranging her face into a mask of brave resignation. "We shall put him off."

She picked up her novel and began to read, though it was upside down. For a short while he watched her, more amused than annoyed. Then he said: "Now, Clarissa. That won't be necessary."

She looked up.

"Oh, you're still here! Well, I beg to differ, Teddy. Far better the king doesn't come to Netherwood at all, than to come and find us lacking."

The Earl of Netherwood knew well enough what the royal visit meant to his wife. As Prince of Wales the monarch had visited three times: as king, not at all. Now that he was at last expected, Teddy knew how important it was, in Clarissa's opinion, that Bertie should leave with the impression of having enjoyed limitless hospitality at the finest, most gracious country house in the whole of England. But still. To insist upon a program of complete and lavish redecoration was one thing: to declare the bathrooms—all of them—as unfit for use was quite another. And this, just four weeks before King Edward and his entourage were due. Lord Netherwood decided to make one last appeal to reason.

"My dear, the house has never looked so spruce. You've done a magnificent job"—this to appeal to her vanity—"and your instincts in matters of style and taste are unsurpassed."

12

She looked at him askance now, because even she detected flattery and flannel. "But there is neither the time nor the need to tear out perfectly good bathroom furniture for the benefit of Bertie. A lavatory he sat on as Prince of Wales will serve him just as well as king."

"Teddy!" she said.

"Well, it's true. We entertained him in grand style before, without any real upheaval at all. I'm perfectly confident we shall do the same again."

She put down her book.

"I'm sorry, Teddy. New baths, new basins, new lavatories, or I shall declare us indisposed. Something dreadfully infectious, perhaps. A polite letter to the horrid Knollys warning of a risk to the king of scarlet fever."

Of course he knew, as she knew, that the ultimatum was preposterous. Clarissa would sooner run naked through the streets of Netherwood than write such a letter to the king's man. In any case, if it suited Bertie to visit Netherwood Hall— and it did, as he was coming from Doncaster and the St. Leger—then visit he would. An outbreak of scarlet fever, real or imaginary, would be of no account. He pleased himself, did Bertie, and on this occasion he had done as he always did by blithely announcing his intention to visit, entirely at his own convenience, leaving the honored hosts to a tumult of anxious preparation. However, standing before his beautiful, pouting, manipulative wife, Teddy decided—not for the first time, nor for the last—to cave in. It was certainly his quickest route out of the countess's rooms and into the fresh air and it wasn't as if they couldn't afford the work. And if Clarissa was happy, generally speaking, they all were happy. She had, after all, already been forced to concede the vexed point of Dorothea Sterling's invitation to Netherwood Hall. No small concession either, given her initial opposition to that particular scheme.

"Very well," said the earl. "Talk to Motson. If he believes the work can be achieved in the time available, go ahead."

"Thank you, Teddy," she said, briskly now that her mission was accomplished. She blew him a kiss by way of dismissal so he took his cue, exiting his wife's room just as a housemaid arrived with lemon tea. The girl stepped back and bobbed a respectful curtsy, and the cup rattled in the saucer in her trembling hand. She should save her awe for a figure of actual authority, thought the earl wryly as he strode off down the long corridor. Underfoot, the pile of the new carpet felt soft and rich—not that the old one had ever seemed unsatisfactory to him. New bathroom furniture indeed. He wasn't sure who was the bigger fool: his wife, for inventing the project, or himself for sanctioning it.

In her room, the countess lay back on the pillows and picked up a writing pad and pencil that she kept at all times on her nightstand. She had many of her best ideas in bed, in those unstructured moments just before sleeping or just after waking, when the mind loosens itself from the shackles of daily routine. In bed, she had imagined any number of wonderful dresses for herself and the girls that had subsequently been realized by her dressmaker in chiffon or satin or cotton lawn. In bed, too, she had visualized garden schemes—the famous wisteria tunnel, the pagoda in the Japanese water garden, the precise combination of blooms in the white border—and last night, just before she succumbed to sleep, she had seen in her mind's eye the exquisite rope of tightly plaited orchids in magenta and cream that must grace the table for the forthcoming royal party. She had sat up at once and sketched these and would hand them on later today to Mrs. Powell-Hughes, the housekeeper. Now, though, she took up the pad and wrote "Motson" to remind herself to send word that he should begin work immediately on the main bathrooms of the east wing. She had every faith in him and his small army of workmen to

14

complete the work swiftly, and, in any case, everything they needed was ordered already; stylish pieces with sleek, modern lines in white porcelain with chrome accessories. For while she felt it was only polite to seek her husband's permission, the process was, in fact, just a formality; she had not had even the smallest doubt that her wish would be granted.

Henrietta was waiting for the earl at the bottom of the main staircase, where the graceful curve of the banister concluded its journey with a flourish in the form of a fine, intricately carved newel post. She was leaning against it with her back to her father as he began his descent. Unnoticed by her, he paused. His eldest daughter was dressed for riding: habit, gloves, and boots on, her thick blond hair caught up in a knot, and he knew at once that the fact she hadn't yet gone meant she must have something to say—to him, doubtless. Something pressing. Something that would either complicate his morning or reflect badly on his character. The shameful notion crossed his mind that he might yet retreat and take the servants' stairs instead. He didn't, though, dismissing the idea even as it was conceived and, as if to make up for the unrealized slight, he called cheerfully to her as he bounded down, two stairs at a time as always.

"Morning, Henry!" He almost sang the greeting.

She turned and smiled, but it was tight and brief, with no accompanying twinkle, which meant—as he had feared—that she had something in particular on her mind and, indeed, she wasted no time on pleasantries but launched straight into the first item on her agenda.

"I have to say, Daddy, the very least you might have done is read it."

Merciful heavens, he thought to himself, would his womenfolk give him no peace? He tried a rueful smile but she regarded him sternly without a hint of forgiveness; this young woman—forceful, determined, robustly argumentative—would make a splendid governess, he thought, if ever they fell into penury. She waggled under his nose a wad of papers loosely bound in a buff-colored folder, which had sat on his desk for three days now, growing ever less visible under the gradual accumulation of newspapers and other matters pending, but which Henry had obviously ferreted out this morning. He did wish she wouldn't make quite so free with his study: like his club and the outside lavatory, it was no place for a woman.

"Here," she said, handing over the document. "Look at it now. It's fascinating."

He flipped it open and held it out at arm's length, which was the only way he seemed to be able to read anything these days. "The West Riding Colliery Center for Training Men in Mines Rescue—bit of a mouthful," he said. He looked at his daughter. "And who is this chap, did you say?"

"Mr. Garforth. The safety-lamp man. He's quite local. We could meet him, visit the center. People do, you see. Mining engineers and whatnot."

"Whoa, now," said the earl, as if steadying his hunter. "Let's not run ahead."

"Daddy, what possible argument could you have against making our mines safer?"

None, of course, when she put it like that. But life was never as simple as Henrietta liked to make out. First of all, the king's visit was imminent and, while the earl baulked at using that as an excuse to his principled daughter for postponing this particular issue, it was nevertheless a consideration, and a major one at that. Second, he doubted if any of the miners at his collieries would take kindly to going back to school and on their own time, too. Third, he was in any case skeptical about the need for any kind of extra training for his men when all they really needed to know was how to extract coal. In this they were expert practitioners.

"Thank you, Henry," he said, reining her in firmly. "Please don't begin one of your moral monologues. I will read this, but in my own time, if you please, because just at this moment I have other more urgent business to attend to."

She made as if to speak, then thought better of it. She knew her father well: no progress would be made if he felt harried. But this fellow, this Garforth, he sounded simply splendid. It seemed to Henrietta a foolish, backward-looking thing to resist innovation in their own field of industry.

Behind her and with a decisive clunk, the oak door of her father's study swung shut, and Henrietta, taking her cue, strode through the hallway, seized her riding crop from the umbrella stand, and left the house for the uncomplicated pleasures of the saddle.

Downstairs in the kitchens, the hubbub caused by the preparation of breakfast had subsided. All that remained were the mingled smells—grilled meat, poached haddock, fried tomatoes, coddled eggs—and the dirty skillets, crockery, and cutlery now piled high on the board by the sink. These, however, were no concern of Mary Adams, who had years ago been done with tedious jobs such as dishwashing. As cook, it was now her perfect right to take the weight off her swollen legs and sit down on the carver—her throne, the scullery maids called it, out of range of her hearing—and eke out what little gossip there was with the nearest available body. Unfortunately for Mrs. Adams, this morning it was Elizabeth Powell-Hughes, who had a habit of nipping an opening gambit smartly in the bud. The cook's defensive tone and thwarted expression suggested that this frustrating process was already under way.

"Well 'islop never made a moment's trouble, that's all I can say. Nob'dy easier to please than 'im."

"Now, Mary. Hislop could be a cantankerous old devil, and well you know it."

Mrs. Powell-Hughes regarded the cook sternly over the top of her gold-rimmed spectacles; she was a cut above Mrs. Adams in breeding and status and was the only person in the household—other than the family, though they rarely used the privilege—who got away with calling her Mary. She herself, however, was Mrs. Powell-Hughes to everyone—had no memory, in fact, of the last time anyone called her Elizabeth, as these last thirty years had been spent in service at Nether-wood. There was no Mr. Powell-Hughes, of course. Never had been. But Miss wouldn't do for a housekeeper, so Mrs. Powell-Hughes she was. Mrs. P-H to the family and, very occasionally, to Parkinson the butler, but only when he'd had a sherry at Christmas, and even then he felt he was probably overstepping a line.

"Aye, but that was out there, on 'is own territory." Mrs. Adams swung a fat arm toward the garden. "In 'ere, 'e was as quiet as a mouse."

The cook was rewriting history again, thought Mrs. Powell Hughes. She did this when it suited her story. No matter what the evidence was to the contrary, she would concoct her own version of events and present it as gospel. In fact, Hislop, the retired head gardener, had been—and still was, no doubt—a sharp-tongued, ill-mannered gnome of a man, too easily rattled and too ready to curse. His replacement, a tall, good-looking fellow with a Scots burr and an easy manner, was a more than satisfactory exchange. And the newcomer's crime, in Mary Adams's book of kitchen law, had been to reject the cup of tea he'd been given because he preferred to drink it without milk.

"Pushed it away, like it was poison," said the cook, working herself up all over again, though it was two weeks, now, since the atrocity took place.

Mrs. Powell-Hughes said: "Mary, I was there at the time, so think on," and Mrs. Adams, while determined to cherish and nurture the offense, nevertheless held her tongue. She would save her indignation for a more receptive audience, since it was clearly wasted on the housekeeper. Still, she huffed a little, inwardly. Tea without milk. Who could trust such a man?

Mrs. Powell-Hughes reached for her fob, checked the time, let it drop. She wore it like a medal on her chest, with a black grosgrain ribbon to hide the pin.

"Linens," she said, standing up. Always the first to finish a sit-down, thought Mrs. Adams, truly out of humor now with her colleague. Always leaping to her feet as if she was the only one with work to do. The kitchen door swung open and a pink-cheeked housemaid entered, carrying the now-empty china cup and saucer she had taken upstairs, full of tea, to the countess ten minutes ago.

"Slowly, Agnes," said the housekeeper. "The next cup you chip through carelessness comes out of your wages, remember."

The girl said: "Sorry, Mrs. Powell-'ughes. Mrs. Powell-'ughes?"

"Yes?"

"'er ladyship gave me this, for Mr. Motson."

She passed a note to the housekeeper, a sheet of thick vellum paper, folded in half but without an envelope. There was no doubting for whose eyes it was intended, since it had "Mr. Motson" written on it quite clearly in Lady Hoyland's distinctive hand, but who wouldn't sneak a look, in those circumstances? Certainly Agnes had, in the privacy of the back stairs, and now she and the cook watched as Mrs. Powell-Hughes flicked open the writing paper and quickly scanned its contents. Her expression was inscrutable. She folded it back, and placed it in the pocket of her skirt.

"Well?" said Mrs. Adams. "What is it?"

"More work for my girls, that's what," she said, tight-lipped, and left it at that. Mrs. Adams watched in deep umbrage as the housekeeper swept from the room, all dignified restraint and self-importance. The cook turned to the girl.

"Well?" she said, again.

"All t'bathrooms are coming out. Before t'king comes," she said.

Mrs. Adams smiled. Comeuppance, she thought to herself with immense satisfaction. Comeuppance. That's what that was.

Chapter 3

Runners, peas, lettuce, caulis, onions, plums, raspberries, and gooseberries. Where do you want 'em?"

Amos Sykes stood in the open doorway of the kitchen, bearing in his arms with visible effort a large, muddy box of newly harvested produce. His handsome, craggy face, ruddy from the sun, had rivulets of sweat running in lines from under the brim of his cap, and he blinked in an effort to redirect them away from his eyes. It was a long walk from the allotment, and hot enough outside to crack the flagstones. A drink wouldn't go amiss, he thought, and flashed a bright, winning smile at Nellie Kay. She was chopping onions as if she bore them a personal grudge, and she didn't look up from the task but said, "Somewhere folk won't fall over 'em."

She said this grimly, as if it happened all the time, as if Amos carelessly depositing his veg boxes in people's paths was a regular occurrence. He rolled his eyes at Alice Buckle, who blushed and looked away, afraid of taking anyone's side against the formidable Nellie. Alice was stationed this morning at the sink, peeling potatoes with the swift efficiency that came from years of practice, and Amos walked over to leave the vegetables on her side of the room.

"Eve in?" he said.

"Aye," said Alice. "Upstairs." She tilted her head upward, to underline the point, but she didn't look at him or stop peeling. The big sink was full of potatoes, and there was another sack on the floor. Leek and potato soup was on the menu today, though they were calling it by a strange foreign name she couldn't remember and serving it cold, which seemed like an odd business to Alice. The weather would never be so hot that the Buckles didn't warm their soup on the stove, but Eve had come back from her spell in London with new ideas, and not just chilled soup, though that was probably the most outlandish. You could still order it warm if you wanted to, though, and Alice was comforted by this nod to normality. There were fishcakes today too, new for the summer menu but reassuringly familiar. The cod was waiting for her in the cold store, wrapped in the fishmonger's blue and white paper; when the potatoes were done, the fish had to be skinned and pin-boned and Alice's nimble fingers seemed better suited than anyone else's to this delicate task. She would work like a blind woman, gazing ahead while her fingertips ran swiftly up and down the fish fillet feeling for the tiny bones, thin and flimsy as eyelashes, and whipping them out with a surgeon's precision. These jobs—the peeling, the skinning, the boning—were always performed with a single-minded dedication that left no room for chitchat. She knew, for instance, that everything in the dinnertime service would be skewed if the present job wasn't done by half past ten and she would rather plunge the paring knife into her heart than fail at the task. Alice, plucked last year from domestic obscurity and placed here, in the working hub of Eve's Puddings & Pies at Mitchell's old flour mill, would do anything for Eve Williams, and would rather die than let her down. True, in coming to work for her she had simply swapped one kind of drudgery for another, but here, in this professional kitchen,

Alice felt more valued than she ever had at home, where her taciturn husband, Jonas, was king and her own place in the family hierarchy was some way beneath the children, the dog, and the racing pigeons that Jonas kept in the back yard. More than that though, Alice somehow felt that Eve had made her part of a great venture, a new chapter in Netherwood's history. This wonderful idea—too grandiose and self-regarding ever to be shared with anyone else—was what sustained her as she peeled her way through the potato mountain.

Amos knew he'd get no small talk out of Alice Buckle. In any case, it was Eve he was after, so he climbed the stairs, puffing in the heat. The summer, which everyone had thought was done, had come once again to Netherwood, its fierce, debilitating heat hitting the town with a heavyweight punch, so that people in the street went about their business with stunned expressions and a lead-limbed lethargy, all the time longing for shade. In the upstairs dining room at the mill, all the windows were open, but the muslin curtains, drawn against the glare, were absolutely still, and Eve, sitting at one of the tables with Ginger Timpson, fanned herself with a menu as they spoke. She had her back to Amos, so it was Ginger who saw him first.

"Amos Sykes, as I live and breathe," she said. "Never too warm to leave your cap at 'ome, is it?"

He winked at her and pulled it off. His hair was damp and flattened, and he ran a hand through it so it stuck up in spikes. "Nice bit o' shade under this brim," he said.

Eve turned, and smiled with pleasure. He was a rare sight at the mill these days.

"You're a good man, to bring us a delivery in this 'eat," she said.

"Some beautiful produce down there," he said. "Raspberries like this." He made an oval with his thumb and index finger. The fruit cage had been his own idea, and he and Seth had built it themselves out of canes and chicken wire. It sagged here and there, but kept the birds off the berries, and had distracted Seth, for the time being, from building a melon pit. "And gooseberries like this." He made another shape with the other hand, a circle this time, and implausibly large. Ginger raised an eyebrow, but kept her mouth shut. Fresh produce was fresh produce. No point offending the gardener. She looked at Eve.

"Crumbles, then? Or pies?" she said.

"Meringues, I'd say. For t'raspberries anyroad. Serve 'em with whipped cream. And gooseberry fool. Or set some aside for jam, if there's plenty."

Ginger nodded and stood up. "I'll go an' get cracking," she said. "Twenty booked in for dinner, and who knows who'll drop in unannounced." She nodded at Amos as she left, and he returned the compliment, then turned to Eve. She was a fine-looking woman, he thought: warm smile, dark eyes. But he had taught himself not to care.

"Busy as ever then?" he said, casual, neutral.

"Busier, if anything. We've been run off our feet this week and next month that Fortnum's order starts. I shall need more staff at this rate. 'ow's things with you?"

"Champion," he said.

"Work all right?"

"Aye, grand."

"Allotment doin' well?"

He wagged his head, made a little downturned arc with his mouth. "So-so," he said. "Could do wi' rain, but Seth manages to keep it all watered."

"Seth loves that garden. It's 'is chief pleasure in life."

"Aye, well. Seth's a grand lad. Grand worker an' all."

Their conversation limped a little, still hampered by a lingering awkwardness between them. It wasn't quite a year since Amos had offered Eve his hand in marriage and been immediately, kindly, emphatically declined. It had taken all his courage to voice his feelings—he was no poet, and was out of practice in matters of the heart—and the wound from her rejection had been slow to heal. Now, of course, she was engaged to another man. This fact, as much as anything else, had closed his mind to any further thoughts of romance with the lovely Eve Williams. He wasn't fool enough to give chase when she was already caught.

"It was Seth I wanted a word about, as a matter of fact," he said now.

"Oh?"

"Nowt to worry about. Not yet, anyroad. Just, 'e's been on about going down t'pit after 'e turns twelve. I've told 'im what I think o' that plan, but you might want a chat with 'im yourself."

Amos delivered his news casually, without drama, but Eve's face fell. Her boy, the eldest of her three children, would be perfectly well aware of the explosive effect this information would have on his mother, and undoubtedly this new development was calculated to wound. Seth was angry with her most of the time these days; the arrival in Netherwood of Daniel, the suspicion that they were planning a life together, the shift in the normal order of things that, for him, had anyway only recently settled into an acceptable pattern—all this had sent the boy into a dark mood from which he only really surfaced in the company of Amos. Eve knew, of course she did, that the boy missed his father every day, and she tried to take account of this when his behavior overstepped the mark. But here was Amos, innocently delivering Seth's bombshell, quite unaware that only yesterday, over dinner, Eve had talked to the boy about college in Sheffield, about all the different, wonderful directions that an education could take a man, and though he had sat there wordless, she had thought he was taking it in, was even, in spite of his sullenness, interested. He was a clever

25

boy, a reader and a thinker, and he knew very well that there was no need for him to scrape a meager living underground, but now it occurred to her that he would perhaps do it, just to hurt her.

"Seth doesn't say a lot to me," was all she said, though, to Amos.

"No, well, like 'is father. A man o' few words."

Like Arthur, and not like, thought Eve. Her late husband never made her feel, as Seth did now, that all her decisions were selfish ones. He was a carbon copy in appearance though, and—just like Arthur—a devil for clamming up when something troubled him. Even now, nearly eighteen months after his dad had been killed in a rockfall at New Mill Colliery, Eve was certain that somewhere within Seth, buried like the coal under its protective layers of rock and shale, lay an untapped seam of grief.

"Do you think 'e wants to do it for Arthur?" she said, hope suddenly springing forth that Seth might be motivated by love for his father rather than by resentment toward her.

"Aye, 'appen so."

Amos replaced his cap as he spoke, a signal to Eve, subtle but unmistakable, that his involvement in the problem was ended now that he had passed it on to her. This, Eve had found, was the price she had paid for turning him down. There was a time he would have done anything for her and her small family. Now, and not unreasonably, there were limits to his generosity and concern. But he still worked the allotment with Seth as often as his new job at the miners' union allowed, and for that Eve was grateful.

"Well, thanks, Amos, for lettin' me know. And for t'fruit an' veg. It's what folk keep coming back for, y'know, that homegrown produce."

He smiled. "I think it might 'ave more to do with what you do wi' it after I've picked it," he said.

She stood to go back downstairs with him. "Well, take summat 'ome with you. There's plenty ready."

They walked together across the dining room. The windows, six of them, elegantly arched and draped in soft muslin, flooded the long room with light and the polished wooden floor gleamed honey-colored underfoot. There were jugs of sweet peas on the tables, and blue and white cloths made from old linen flour sacks that Anna had found stashed in a chest in a forgotten corner. The effect was charming.

"You've worked wonders up 'ere," said Amos. He remembered its beginnings, when the earl first proposed it as the place for Eve to expand her business: an abandoned storeroom in the disused flour mill, the floor thick with bird droppings, the beams chock-full of roosting pigeons.

"It's Anna's work, mostly," Eve said. "She 'as an eye for this sort of thing. She's a demon with that sewing machine."

Ginger, standing at the foot of the stairs, called up: "Eve, there's a wooden crate been delivered. Is it summat we're expectin'?"

They joined her downstairs, their progress at the bottom impeded by the large crate in question. Its lid was nailed shut and across the top, stamped in black ink, it said MRS. A. WILLIAMS, NETHERWOOD, YORKSHIRE. That was all. They stood for a moment, staring. It had the look of a crate that had traveled some distance to be here.

"Now then," Eve said, puzzled. "Amos?"

"Nowt to do wi' me," he said. But he was curious enough to linger while Nellie—this was her kind of job—prized off the lid in short order with a sturdy steel knife. A thick layer of straw hid the contents and Ginger stepped back, as if something alive, or explosive, might be revealed beneath. Alice, still peeling, watched from the safety of the sink.

"Go on," said Eve to Nellie, who didn't need asking twice and pulled with two hands at the blanket of straw.

They all stared.

"Well, I'll be blowed," said Nellie.

"Bananas," Ginger said.

And they were. Hand after hand of yellow bananas, each layer protected from the next by more straw. At the sink Alice, overcome with mute astonishment, dropped her knife and it fell with a discordant clatter, disturbing the respectful silence.

"Can't grow them in Netherwood soil," said Amos.

Eve looked at him, then back at the bananas, then back at Amos again. Her face was unreadable and the color seemed to drain from it so that he was afraid she might be about to faint away. He put a hand out, rested it on her arm.

"You've gone white," he said.

"Silas," she said, and she seemed to be offering this enigmatic pronouncement as an explanation. The others, Amos, Ginger, Nellie, and Alice, looked at her uncomprehendingly.

"My brother, Silas," she said.

Still they stared.

"A long time ago, when 'e wasn't much more'n a bairn, 'e said that one day 'e'd send me bananas," Eve said. She was smiling now, her eyes bright with the beginnings of excitement. She looked down at the crate at their feet, at the exotic cargo, incongruous in this Yorkshire kitchen. Looking up again, she laughed at the miracle of it.

"And now 'e 'as," she said.

Chapter 4

Patient observation. This, Daniel knew, was what was required to make a new garden. Wait and watch over the course of a twelvemonth, see what comes up and how well it looks, or how incongruous. Walk the acreage daily, and let it slowly reveal its secrets to you. All very well in theory, he thought, but nigh on impossible in practice, when there was clearly so much to be done. He looked at the majestic gardens of Netherwood Hall, of which the countess was so fond and so proud, and he saw not a fine and finished product, but the greatest challenge of his life. There was no geometry to the plan. Indeed, he thought to himself, coming up once again from the ha-ha that separated the gardens from the park, there was no plan at all. Instead there were great swathes of undulating, tree-dotted lawns, interrupted here and there by the realization of Lady Netherwood's various whimsical fads and fancies. The Japanese water garden was monstrous, risible, and its days were numbered. The circular maze of yew could stay, but it needed regular close cropping if it wasn't to resemble a shaggy, mythical beast. The wisteria tunnel was doubtless attractive for its three weeks of joy in late spring, yet it stood like a folly, without purpose, leading nowhere. Before it and beyond, there would have to be created entirely new garden rooms with paths and beds and stonework, in order that the tunnel might then make sense and lead from one place and into another.

There must be more water. A garden with lawns this size cried out for the shimmering, glassy counterpoint of a Grand Canal. There must be parterres. There must be knot gardens. There would still be flowers, and many of them, but there must also be clipped box and precise gravel paths and flowerbeds with perfect specimens selected for their rare and delicate qualities. He had made a start; the ruler and set square were, to Daniel, as crucial to gardening as a spade and a hoe, and he had already begun his drawings for Netherwood. These loose lines and undulating curves, the hallmark of the landscape movement, would not do. Gardening, to him, was the control and the manipulation of nature, not an attempt to mirror it. Let Capability Brown turn in his grave. This English garden— now *his* English garden—would, when Daniel was done with it, rival Versailles.

Behind him, a soft footfall became suddenly apparent and, just as he registered the sound, Eve appeared at his side.

"Found you," she said, slipping an arm through his.

He smiled down at her. His Eve, his love, the reason he was here in Netherwood. She smiled back.

"So," she said, looking away from him and at the garden. "What's t'verdict?"

He grimaced. "It's just as I expected," he said. "Dull as ditch water. No vision, no imagination, no flair."

She laughed, quite sure he was joking. To her the gardens of Netherwood Hall looked magnificent, even now in the dog days of summer when the sun had leached the colors from the plants and the earth was baked hard like a potter's clay in the kiln.

"I'm serious," he said. "That's coming out for a start."

He pointed at the pagoda, centerpiece of the Japanese water garden and just visible from where they stood.

"Not before t'king's visit, I 'ope," she said. "And 'ave you broken it to Lady Netherwood? I mean, I could be mistaken, but I think she might be very partial to that particular corner."

"I'll win her around," he said. "She had all sorts of ideas for Fulton House, and I managed to ignore those too."

This was true. The garden of the family's London residence in Belgravia was a small masterpiece, but it was all of Daniel's making. In twenty years in her service, he had contrived a way of agreeing with the countess yet all the while pursuing his own obsessions. Curiously, she seemed to detect no discrepancy between what she suggested and what she got; indeed, she happily claimed credit for all improvements, however far they strayed from the original brief. So while he knew he'd have to consult Lady Netherwood before too long, he also knew his vision would be realized. Money wasn't an issue, because the higher the cost of a scheme, the more Lady Netherwood seemed to regard it. The skill would lie in persuading her, without giving offense, that the garden in its present form did no justice to the house.

They turned and began to walk together, though Eve released his arm. Hardly anyone knew how things stood between them—it was barely three weeks since he'd arrived here. In any case, there were stringent new rules, apparently, now that he had come to Netherwood for her. In London, in May, when Eve was at Fulton House to cook for the countess, she had fallen into Daniel's arms with an abandon that filled him with delight. But now—and until they were married, she had said—they would behave with absolute propriety. It wasn't easy when he knew full well exactly how her naked body felt against his; there wasn't an inch of this woman he didn't know, and yet here she was, walking along beside him as prim as a Sunday-school teacher.

She folded her arms across her chest, to keep from taking his hand.

"Anna showed me t'house," she said.

"And?"

"Big."

"We need big, don't we?"

"Mmm."

They walked on in silence for a few moments. He didn't want to rush her on this, or on anything else, but he hoped he wouldn't be too long in the gardener's hut. Custom-built for Hislop forty years ago, it provided nowhere, other than on the staircase, that Daniel could stand entirely upright. It would be comical, except he kept cracking his head on beams and lintels. As he went about his ablutions in the morning, he felt like Gulliver making his way around a Lilliputian guesthouse. If Ravenscliffe was big, it would get his vote.

"I liked it, actually," she said now. "It needs some work—y'know, cleaning, decorating—but Anna reckons she can tackle that. Then there's t'bairns. They know nowt about it."

"Then tell them, Eve," he said. "Really. Give them time to get used to the idea of change, of our marrying, of moving house. They've probably guessed, anyway. Seth and Eliza, certainly."

"Aye, you're probably right." Her face was very grave, as if the difficulties she faced were numerous and insurmountable.

He smiled down at her. "Don't present it as a dark development," he said. "Keep it light. Make sure they know you're happy."

It was good advice and it was possible, she had come to realize, to tread too carefully around the children, to muddy the waters with veiled hints and allusions rather than clarifying with cheerful facts. When Daniel had first arrived she had made a proper hash of things, introducing him to them in a vague and foolish way: he was a friend, Mr. MacLeod from

32

London, come to Netherwood as head gardener down at the big house, wasn't that lovely? The older two had looked at her with knowing eyes and it was immediately clear to Eve that only little Ellen had no inkling of the full story. The others correctly interpreted the situation at once, and nine-year-old Eliza, in her frank manner and piping voice, had said, "Mam, are you an' Mr. MacLeod courting?" so that Eve had been forced to stammer out a yes. Eliza had stared at Daniel with new interest and Seth had turned away blackly, exuding hostile resentment. Even before his father's untimely death in the colliery, the boy's happiness had been a fragile thing, easily knocked off course: now he seemed to walk through each day with something akin to dread, as if misery lay in wait in all the most unexpected places.

"It's all 'appened so fast for them," Eve said now to Daniel. "We're a good few steps ahead of t'bairns, me an' you."

"I think they've caught on," Daniel said. "And they're going to be just fine. Even Seth." Privately Daniel wondered if a more robust approach to Seth's famous feelings might be in everyone's interests. However, he wouldn't say so.

"I'll talk to 'em later," she said decisively, making an effort. "And I'll take Ravenscliffe. That's if Mr. Blandford lets me 'ave it."

She said this with a smile, but in fact she wasn't speaking in jest. It was only three months ago that she'd spurned the unwelcome and wholly unexpected advances of the earl's bailiff: Absalom Blandford, a fastidious guardian of his own dignity, would hardly be inclined to accommodate the wishes of the woman who had so recently humiliated him. Mercifully, she was rarely in his orbit, but when she did see him, he regarded her coldly and his nostrils seemed to flare and twitch as if the air around her offended him.

"Send Anna," said Daniel. "She'll sort him out. In any case,

what kind of bailiff would he be to refuse to let Ravenscliffe? I don't see a line of potential tenants forming, do you?"

She didn't answer, because the great bell in the clock tower chimed a quarter past the hour and she exclaimed at the time, leaving him standing there watching as she walked briskly away up the avenue toward the house to meet Lady Netherwood and Mrs. Adams in the morning room to discuss Yorkshire puddings for the king.

Strictly speaking, Eve's Yorkshires were King Edward's principal reason for visiting Netherwood Hall. An extraordinary fact, but there it was, and try as she might to suppress that information, the countess found it had traveled far and wide, not least because when the king had fallen for Eve's cooking—specifically, for the tiny Yorkshire puddings filled with rare roast beef—it had been at a crowded party during the London season, where the guests, hanging on his every word, missed nothing that the monarch had to say. However, this humiliation was a small price to pay for the sheer relief of securing a royal visit; the honor had been long overdue, even to the point that society had been holding its collective breath in delicious anticipation of an out-and-out snub. But the Hoylands had been spared, his visit was imminent, and now Clarissa's time was spent planning every detail of every day he would be with them. She wasn't sure, at first, to what extent Yorkshire puddings should feature. Should they appear, wittily, in a different guise at every meal? The earl had tactfully advised against this approach, persuading her that one magnificent offering would have greater meaning than several, and that there was no better occasion to serve it than on the evening of his arrival. So it was agreed: ten courses of old-fashioned, plain fare of the type Bertie—from time to time—delighted in. There would be three subsequent evenings on which to ply him with cream and truffles, but for his first dinner at Netherwood Hall, Mary Adams could produce her near-legendary roast rib of beef, with Vichy carrots, stewed peas, and claret gravy, while Eve would be drafted to do her bit, by royal appointment.

"Quite an honor for you, my dear," said the countess now to Eve, as they faced each other across the luster of the morning room table. On Eve's left sat Mrs. Adams, spilling over the edges of the Chippendale chair and listening closely for slights. Clarissa held her pocketbook open in front of her.

"And a little silly," she continued diplomatically, "since Mrs. Adams makes lovely Yorkshire puddings. But we did promise Bertie he could have yours."

This was the line she was taking, for the sake of the cook's dignity and her own: that Eve's presence in the Netherwood kitchens was indulgent nonsense and, though requested by the king, was still entirely at the say-so of the countess. Eve quite understood. She knew Lady Netherwood well enough now to expect and accept these small rewritings of history. Eve didn't much mind, either, that there'd been no mention of payment. None of it was of any account, in the wider scheme of things. She let the countess prattle on about details, and allowed her mind to wander, because she had been in this room before, just where she sat now, not much over a year ago. She had come, tongue-tied and mortified, to ask the earl to invest in her business, and—inexplicably, it had seemed to her—he had thrown himself with unbridled zeal into the project. It had been a spectacularly successful partnership, Lord Netherwood's money helping to convert the former flour mill in town where Eve's Puddings & Pies now flourished. His faith in Eve's talents had paid dividends; more than that, though, it had forged a warm regard of each for the other, rooted on one side in profound admiration and on the other, profound gratitude. Also, it had given Lady Netherwood the mistaken idea that Eve Williams was theirs, to be called upon at the drop of a hat.

"So. Wednesday the fourteenth," said the countess now. She was looking down at her list in the confident assumption that Eve's mind, like her own, would be wholly focused on the king's Yorkshire puddings. "Dinner is to be half past seven for eight. You may decide when you need to report for duty. We shall be thirty altogether."

She looked up and Eve, a little caught out and rather wooly on the exact details, was nevertheless ready with a smile.

"Grand," she said. "Thank you, your ladyship."

Mrs. Adams harrumphed. She admired Eve Williams; her talent for pork pies and her skill with pastry had already been tested and proven. But batter was a different matter. Batter had always been Mrs. Adams's speciality: that is to say, one of them, for she felt she had plenty. Respect for the countess forced her to hold her tongue, but there was enough she could have said and it showed in her face.

Lady Netherwood, quite aware that the cook's feelings were running high, took pity and regarded the cook warmly.

"Dear Mrs. Adams," she said. "You are most obliging to allow Mrs. Williams into your kitchen." Then she leaned across the table toward both of them and lowered her voice confidingly.

Mrs. Keppel's coming, of course. She hasn't been here before and some people won't have her at all, you know. The Norfolks at Arundel, the Cecils at Hatfield." The countess paused, and sighed. "I do hope we're not upsetting the queen. One would so detest to be in her position."

Eve, entirely flummoxed at this unexpected turn in the conversation, had absolutely nothing to say. Mrs. Adams, on the other hand, had an opinion for every occasion and she opened her mouth to pass a remark, but was prevented from speaking by the countess who, it seemed, was merely thinking aloud.

"I suppose one simply suspends one's judgment," she said. Particularly—this thought she kept to herself—as her own record with regard to marital fidelity was hardly unblemished. But still, she had never indulged in corridor-creeping at other people's country homes. Her *liaisons dangereuses* had always been conducted in London, in the respectable hours of daylight between three and five o'clock.

"Anyway, none of this need concern you," she said, briskly now and in a tone that rather implied someone other than herself had raised the subject in the first place. Eve bridled a little.

"No, indeed, your ladyship," she said. "Yorkshire puddings are where my involvement starts and ends."

And though Eve was entirely serious, the countess laughed merrily.

"Poor you," she said, then she clapped her slender hands together to conclude the meeting and snapped shut her pocketbook, and at this slightest of signals the door was opened by one footman, her chair pulled back by another, and she swept gracefully from the room, leaving behind nothing of herself but an invisible cloud of rose-scented cologne.

Eve and Mrs. Adams looked at each other.

"Strange times," said the cook.

Eve stood to leave. "Aye," she said. "You can say that again."

Mrs. Adams collected herself in readiness for the effort of standing up, bracing her hands on the arms of the chair. A large shoehorn might have been useful.

"If I were you," she said. "I'd practice them puddings."

This was said not kindly but ungraciously, though Eve let it pass because she had no wish to lock horns with Mary Adams. Instead she nodded civilly at the cook, though as she crossed the room to leave she rolled her eyes heavenward. Practice, my eye, she thought indignantly. She had no more need to practice Yorkshire puddings than she had to practice breathing. What's more, she reckoned Mrs. Adams, currently wholly occupied in the task of heaving her bulk out of the chair, knew this to be true.

Chapter 5

When the Global Steamship Company employed Silas Whittam as not much more than a midshipman fourteen years earlier, he alone had known himself to be on the cusp of greatness, a latter-day adventurer, fearless explorer of dark and dangerous lands, albeit in the guise of a malnourished boy of sixteen with only his wits to live on. He had set out from Grangely the very day that Eve married Arthur: he stayed for the wedding, but only just, sitting at the back of the chapel and slipping out during the "Ode to Joy." His haste to leave was misinterpreted by many, but not by his sister: she understood perfectly. Like Silas, Eve felt that their real life was just beginning, as if a long and undeserved prison sentence had been suddenly revoked and the door of their cell flung open. Silas had fidgeted on his bony backside on the chapel pew until he could stand it no longer. He had to get to Liverpool and he couldn't waste another minute. He didn't even manage to catch Eve's eye before he fled, so his empty seat was her first indication that Silas was gone. But she knew where he was off to: he had told her often enough.

His journey to the Liverpool docks had been frustratingly slow for a boy with his sights set on the West Indies. He looked a complete ruffian; not the sort of boy you'd want to offer a lift to, skulking along the edges of the county's main highways, sticking out his thumb for a ride. He had walked for days and days—he had no idea how many—before he remembered the railway, after which he began to make better progress. Freight trains were the easiest—there were no passengers on board to blow his cover—but even then there were setbacks, as freight-train drivers had an awkward habit of unexpectedly retracing their journey, having no obligation to announce their intention to a series of empty wagons. More than once Silas found he'd fallen asleep in a hidden corner of a cargo train, only to find himself traveling east again after the load had been shed. By this erratic, snakes-and-ladders method he made his way west, finally arriving in Liverpool in some style, courtesy of the Lancashire Railway Company, having crept unnoticed into an empty Pullman car and slept deeply, gratefully, dreamlessly, all the way from Crewe.

From the station he followed the seagulls to Albert Dock, then wandered for a while enjoying the stink and bustle and purpose of the place. There was a towering unbroken run of red-brick warehouses and shipping offices, and he thought about trying for a position at one of these, but changed his mind when he saw how people were looking at him; even in this insalubrious ragbag of humanity, he seemed to stand out as undesirable, and people gave him a wide berth, skirting around him, checking the contents of their pockets as they passed. In any case, thought Silas, it was more in the spirit of his big adventure to stow away in one of the great vessels anchored at the harbor side.

He watched for an hour or so as cases were disgorged from the ships' holds and opened for inspection at the foot of the gangplanks by port officers bloated with self-importance. Brandy, cotton, tea, ivory, sugar, silk: Silas was looking for bananas, but found none.

"Is that your ship?" he asked a seaman, who stood among a pile of crates close to the water's edge, sucking hard on a grubby, hand-rolled fag. The sailor regarded him coolly and nodded.

"Where's tha bin?" said Silas, and the seaman took another long drag, weighing up whether or not to trouble himself, then he said, "Jah-maay-caah," in an accent he clearly intended as parody, though it was lost on the boy, who only knew pure Grangely. Silas absorbed this interesting fact—that the ship docked just beside him had sailed from the very island he had once read about at school, the very island where he happened to know that bananas grew on trees. Someone barreled down the gangplank and shoved Silas roughly out of the way, so that he stumbled backward over a crate, perilously close to the harbor's edge. Below him, black water slapped the wall and behind him, the seaman laughed.

"Mister?" Silas said, when he was standing again.

The seaman dropped the stubby damp end of his cigarette and ground it out with the toe of his boot. He didn't answer.

"Are there bananas in any o' these cases?" asked Silas, undeterred.

The seaman gave a brief, dismissive laugh. "No, soft lad," he said, in his real accent now, his Scouse one.

"Why?"

"Because there's not." He pulled a tin from his pocket and, opening it, pinched a nub of tobacco and popped it in his mouth.

"Where I come from," said Silas, "miners chew baccy an' all. Can't light a fag down a mine."

"Is that right? So where you from?"

"Grangely," said Silas. The seaman laughed.

"Grangely," he said, imitating the boy's Yorkshire brogue. "An' where the fuck's tha'?"

"I reckon you can't carry bananas cos they'd rot, comin' over," said Silas, who knew that the seaman had no real interest in exactly where in England Grangely might be. "But they grow 'em, in Jamaica. I've seen it in a book."

The seaman, losing what little interest he'd had, shrugged and strolled away into the throng. Silas stayed put, gazing at the vessel with calculating eyes, watching the rhythm of the activity on the gangplank, waiting for his moment. The steamship had one great, fat chimney at its center, white with a band of blue around its top. There were two masts festooned with a complex cat's cradle of rigging, and the broad hull looked newly painted, glossily blue to match the trim on the flue. In white lettering along the bow was painted *Adventurer*, which Silas took as final proof that this ship was where his life would begin.

By nightfall he was on board, squeezed into the top third of a barrel of apples, munching contentedly on the fruit. And by the time he was discovered forty-eight hours later, the ship was steaming at full tilt for the Indies, already too far out of Liverpool, too far from land, to bother doing anything but put the little blighter to work.

He was thirty now. A success in the world, you could see that. His suits were Henry Poole and his hats were Locke & Co. He had a small townhouse in Mayfair, a plantation house in Kingston—Jamaica, that is, not Surrey: he always had to explain this, laughingly, because no one ever thought he could possibly mean the West Indies—and the end property in a Georgian terrace in Clifton, because much of his time was spent in Bristol, where his small shipping company was based. He wasn't tall but neither was he short: he was lean still, but not painfully so, as he'd been as a lad. His clothes hung well on him: he was, said his tailor, a pleasure to dress and these past eight years his measurements had stayed the same, for all his love of good wine and food. He was handsome, no doubt about that. Eyes that undressed you and a smile—crooked, engaging—that got him what he wanted. There was no Mrs. Whittam, and wouldn't be anytime soon. He liked to be free, unshackled, at liberty to jump on one of his own ships whenever he pleased.

His accent, his flat, broad Yorkshire vowels, had long gone, eradicated by years of traveling the globe, of trading with foreigners, of mixing with successful merchants and men of business. He had found it easy to reinvent himself, because he hadn't really known what he was in the first place. But he knew what he was now all right: Silas Whittam, a gentleman of means, with his own name on a brand-new warehouse full of half-ripe bananas at Bristol docks, and a fleet of steamships— the *Dominion*, the *Trinity*, the *Emperor*, and the *Antonia*— cutting through the oceans between England and Jamaica on his behalf. They were fine vessels, models of their kind, all of them fitted out with the latest innovations in refrigeration: when the bananas were lifted out of their packing crates to hang in the warehouse, they were cold to the touch, no further on in the ripening process than when they were picked. It was a marvel, really, as if time stopped for the duration of the voyage, starting again only when the cases were unpacked. There were vertical iron poles in the warehouse, hundreds of them, their surfaces studded with hooks, and onto these hooks the cold, green bananas went, losing their chill in the mild Bristol climate, clinging to their man-made trees and slowly, obligingly, turning yellow, even though they were so very far from home.

They had made Silas a fortune, these bananas, and they continued to do so. Extraordinary that it had all started with a picture in a schoolbook. He was fond of saying this, elaborating and embellishing as people do a small, insignificant detail of childhood and making it into something portentous. The story went that he had seen, aged seven, a picture of a banana palm, and it had ignited a spark of ambition in his youthful self that, burning ever stronger, took him across the world in pursuit of his dream. The full account of the past fourteen years was, of course, rather less romantic: a man couldn't get as far as Silas in so short a time without recourse to ruthlessness. But, still, there was much to admire about the man, and all of it was on the surface, the better to appreciate it.

His train arrived at Netherwood Station one week to the day after his crate of bananas had been delivered to Eve at the mill. He'd sent them on an impulse from Bristol, hoping she'd remember what he said to her in those last few days before they both left Grangely. When I get to t'West Indies, I'll send you a bunch of bananas. Well it wasn't a bunch in the end, it was a crate, because he was a wealthy man and fond of a flamboyant gesture. He wished he could have been there to see her face.

He stepped off the train in the clothes of a gentleman so that people turned to look and the stationmaster asked if he needed a carriage.

"Thank you, no. I shall walk," he said. Then he remembered that, of course, he had no idea where in Netherwood Eve and Arthur lived, so he added, "But could you tell me where I might find Mr. and Mrs. Williams?"

The stationmaster's face reddened a little and turned grave.

"Mr. Williams passed away some time ago, sir, sorry, sir. An accident like, down at New Mill. But Mrs. Williams, now," he said, his expression brightening with the relief of imparting good news, "she's at Beaumont Lane. Number five. Anyone'll show you, once you're in town."

Arthur dead, thought Silas. The fact aroused no emotion in him: he hadn't really known Arthur, and it was so long ago. But he was sorry for Eve; he wondered how she'd fared without her husband's wage. He wondered, too, whether he might have helped, in this regard. It was so very long since he'd seen her and he could, in truth, have come sooner. And yet, and yet, life had a habit of swallowing time, and in any case, thought Silas, there had never been a good, sound business reason to come to Netherwood until now. He was not a man governed by emotion; he would not have come for Eve alone. Neither was he a man given to regret, so his spirits remained buoyant and he smiled as he strolled up Victoria Street, cutting a dash in his linen suit, white and tan spectators, and a panama hat at a rakish tilt: people stared. Lilly Pickering, Eve's neighbor in Beaumont Lane, was buying scrag ends at the butcher's and she said: "That'll be one o' t'king's men," with such authority that Mavis Moxon, behind her in the line, believed her, even though King Edward's visit was still three weeks away.

He found Beaumont Lane without asking: the town wasn't so large that an hour's exploration wouldn't reveal its basic geography. There was a small posse of children at a spigot in the street, larking about, turning it on and ducking their heads under. He had half a mind to join them. The day was devilishly hot, even for a man familiar with the Jamaican climate.

"Any of you belong to Eve Williams?" he said. They hadn't noticed his approach, being too busy squealing and splashing, so they were astonished at his voice, which cut through their play with cultured tones. They stopped, abruptly, and took a step away from him. For a moment none of them spoke, then: "Me, I do," said a young girl, prettier than her friends, with chestnut plaits and wide eyes that stared at him audaciously.

"Shurrup," said a boy, scowling first at her, then at the new arrival.

"Well, I do," she said without taking her eyes off the stranger. "You do an'all."

"Right," said Silas. "Well, I don't know who you two are, but I'm your Uncle Silas."

It was the first time he'd uttered that—the first time he'd thought it, even—and he liked the way it sounded. It had an amusing, cozy ring to it, a sound of belonging. It had little visible effect on the children, however; they seemed quite unmoved. The girl looked at the scowling boy now, as if for guidance, though he offered none.

"It's a pleasure to meet you both," Silas said, unfazed. "Could you take me to your mother—" He hesitated, thought again, corrected himself. "I mean, to your mam?"

"She's up at t'mill," said the girl. "Anna's in, though."

"'e dun't know Anna, does 'e?" said the boy contemptuously.

"Come on," said the girl, ignoring him. "It's over 'ere." And she set off with an encouraging smile at Silas, crossing the street and disappearing up a wide, covered entry. He followed, closely tailed not by the boy—who held his ground and his scowl—but by another little girl, much smaller than the first: this one sucked on her thumb and met his smile with neutral solemnity. The entry opened onto a cobbled yard and a series of back doors, all of which stood open on this summer afternoon.

The girl, the older one, called out, "Anna!" and almost immediately a woman appeared at one of the doors, her fine blond hair plaited in the same style as the child's. She looked as if she'd been interrupted in some effortful domestic task, her sleeves rolled up to the elbows, her face flushed with exertion. Silas wondered if his sister had a maid of all work until she spoke, in a confident, authoritative voice that dispelled any thought that she might be a servant.

"Silas, I suppose?" she said, smiling crisply like a society hostess and extending a hand still damp with suds from the sink. "Mystery banana man. You'd better step inside."

Two hours later and unforewarned, Eve came home. Anna had been all for sending Eliza up to the mill with the news, but Silas had argued persuasively in favor of surprising his sister; it would be diverting, he said, to witness her reaction. In the event, though, both he and Anna thought Eve might die of shock when she walked in and saw him sitting at her kitchen table. She froze and stared at him as at a ghost: a ghost from her past, her lost brother, clad in finery yet looking at her with the same face, the same features, that she had held clearly in her mind through all the years of his absence. Silas stood up abruptly, feeling some alarm. The sight of her—her lovely face, their mother's face—had ambushed him, and a rush of emotion threatened to undo his composure. He stepped toward her and wrapped her in an embrace, and this seemed to break the tension because she began to laugh and to cry at the same time, quite swamped by her mix of emotions.

"Evie," he said. "The bananas were meant to be a visiting card. I thought you'd be expecting me."

"And I was," she managed to say, though she was weeping properly now because no one had called her Evie for fourteen years and the shock and the joy of it were greater than she

47

could have imagined. She stepped backward out of his arms to look at him properly.

"You look so grand," she said wonderingly. She sniffed, fumbled for a handkerchief, blew her nose. "You were such a ragamuffin in Grangely."

He smiled at her. "Evie," he said. "It's so good to see you."

Chapter 6

There was a very strong case for moving to Barnsley. A very strong case indeed. Amos leaned on the handle of his spade for a breather and silently ran through the familiar argument yet again. One: the Yorkshire Miners' Association employed him, and he now had a desk at the regional office in Barnsley. Two: Netherwood marked the farthest boundary of Amos's remit, so most of the collieries he now found himself responsible for were closer to Barnsley than not. Three: the time he spent on the train traveling to wherever he needed to be was beginning to amount to several hours each week.

Plus, he liked Barnsley. Not quite three months with the YMA as against three decades down New Mill Colliery, but already he felt comfortable in his new environment. He had taken to walking through the town when he'd been too long at his desk and he needed to move his limbs and fill his lungs. He had favorite places: the noble bulk of the Methodist Church in Pitt Street, the cobbled expanse of Cheapside, the grand frontage and laudable purpose of the Harvey Institute, with its exhibitions of art and recitals of music for the working classes. And his office, his place of work, was in itself a joy to behold, built with towers and turrets, as if it was the Barnsley residence of a Bavarian prince. There were plenty of rooms to let on Huddersfield Road: he could take one of those, and step across to the YMA without even bothering with a coat.

"But there's no seeds, so I can't see 'ow we could grow 'em."

Seth's voice cut into Amos's thoughts and reminded him that, be there ever so many reasons for leaving Netherwood, here was one very good reason to stay. Arthur's lad.

"What's that, son?" Amos returned to his digging. The ground was hard and dry, the soil baked solid into red-brown clumps. He chopped at them savagely with the edge of the spade, making a noise that jangled the nerves, as if he was digging on a shingle beach. He had winter cabbages to plant out, but he might as well scatter them on Victoria Street as in this bed. They'd fare no worse.

"Bananas," said Seth, patiently. "There's no seeds that I can find."

"Tropical fruit, them. They need warmth."

"Oh aye, an' it's freezin' 'ere," said Seth.

Amos looked at him, at his young face attempting a mature, sardonic smile.

"Yes, smart aleck, it's 'ot now, we all know that. But come December, tha'll 'ave forgotten what sunshine feels like. Bananas need to be warm all year around, see?"

In fact, Amos had no idea what bananas needed; he just knew he didn't want to try to grow them. Seth's mind was like a fertile vegetable plot itself, with new ideas shooting up on an almost daily basis. As it was, the produce in the allotment was so abundant there was barely room to squeeze in another beanpole. Bananas indeed. Why not try for sugar cane, and perhaps a tea plantation at the back of the potting shed?

"I'm not sayin' we should grow 'em," Seth said, still in a voice of exaggerated patience.

"Good," Amos said, still digging.

"I'm just sayin' it's odd. No seeds, like."

"Ask your Uncle Silas. 'e grows 'em, doesn't 'e?"

Seth nodded, but fell silent. There was nothing he'd like to do more than quiz his fascinating, newly acquired uncle about the banana plantation, but he hadn't yet recovered the lost ground from their first encounter. Eliza, on the other hand, had galloped on as she'd begun and was already and predictably firm friends with Silas. Last night she'd sat on his knee while he told a story about a sea voyage in an apple barrel. It sounded farfetched to Seth, but Eliza had hung on to his every word, Ellen too, though she couldn't really have understood much. Even Seth's mother and Anna had listened, leaning either side of the fireplace with their arms folded, giving Silas their precious time. Seth had been there as well, but on the fringes, lurking between the front room and the kitchen, pretending to be busy with his penknife and a stick, wishing he could just sit down with the others instead. He hated this about himself: these helpless, headlong plunges into bad moods and ill manners from which he could never find a dignified exit. He knew what they all thought—that he was difficult and troublesome— just as he knew everyone loved Eliza for her willing smile and sunny nature. Sometimes he even thought they'd all made him the way he was, just by expecting nothing different from him. He wasn't including Amos in this, not at all. Amos was the only person in the world who seemed to understand that he, Seth, was actually a very nice lad.

"You've not spoken to 'im yet, 'ave you?" Amos said now. He ceased the digging and stood to look the boy in the eye. "You want to put that right, for a start, else there'll soon be more folk walking this earth that you're not talking to than them you are. Get off 'ome and strike up a conversation. You'll be sorry when they're all sat around t'kitchen table talkin' and laughin' and you're stuck there with a face like a wet weekend an' everybody ignorin' you."

The picture was so vivid and familiar that Seth laughed. Amos resumed his digging.

"We mun turn some compost through this before we plant owt," he said.

"There's still some in t'barrow. I'll fetch it," said Seth, but he hung about for a while, watching Amos work. In the neighboring plot, old Percy Medlicott arrived and raised an arm in greeting, and Seth saluted him in return.

"Warm enough for you, lad?' said Percy, who came to the allotment as much for the company as for the gardening. Amos thought him an old windbag and tried never to catch his eye, but Seth liked him.

"Too warm, Mr. Medlicott. A spot o' rain wouldn't go amiss."

"Not much chance today."

"Right enough."

"It'll come soon mind, mark my words."

"We'll see," Seth said, with the gloomy fatalism of the seasoned gardener. He loved these exchanges; loved to feel on a par with Percy Medlicott; loved to sound like a man who understood the seasons and the soil.

"What about that compost then?"

This was Amos, still stabbing at the earth with a spade. Seth, pushing his luck, said: "If I talk to Uncle Silas, will you talk to Mr. MacLeod?"

Amos looked up.

"I'll fetch that compost," said Seth.

Tobias Hoyland was playing croquet, not—as one might reasonably expect on a summer afternoon—on the designated lawn outside, but up in the Long Gallery of Netherwood Hall, where the heavy-handed or the uninitiated could too easily send the balls skidding wildly across the floor to rebound from the skirting boards with a crack of wood upon wood. Indoor croquet: a game requiring great skill and finesse and invented by Tobias ten years ago using strategically positioned furniture for hoops, since even he could see that to ram metal spikes between the polished floorboards would be going too far in the pursuit of fun. The center peg was always a Wedgwood vase, one of several dotted about the Long Gallery: not priceless, but valuable enough. It added a certain frisson to the contest that the vase—ideally—should remain intact, but at the same time must be struck by a ball in order to win the game.

The hoops—three occasional tables, two elegant chairs with slender, bowed legs, and a Chinese rosewood plant stand—were already in position when Henrietta found her brother. His various haunts were familiar to her and the Long Gallery was a particular favorite, as its dimensions gave it great scope for entertainment. Why design a room like a gigantic skittle alley then expect people to behave in it with decorum? This was Tobias's view at any rate.

"Just in time," he said, when he saw Henrietta. He smiled and held out a mallet. "Dickie said he'd play but he jibbed. Any idea what he's up to?"

Henrietta took the proffered mallet. "Indoor croquet is a strictly wet-weather activity," she said reprovingly, in the instantly recognizable, slightly joyless tones of Mrs. Powell-Hughes. The housekeeper's length of service had given her occasional scolding rights over the Hoyland offspring; they were young adults now—apart from Isabella, of course—but still they were not always beyond reproof.

Tobias placed his ball and sized up the distance to the first target. "Time was when you could read him like a book," he said. "But these days I just can't say what he's thinking. Have you stepped outside, Henry? Mad hot. Even Mrs. P-H couldn't tell me we're not better off indoors."

"I think he might be in love," said Henrietta.

She spoke just as Tobias took his first shot, and she timed it to perfection, causing him to look up in astonishment at the critical moment. The ball veered off ineffectually to the right and Henrietta laughed.

"Mimi Adamson. She's staying with her uncle, a short canter away," she said. "Botched it. Bad luck. My shot."

"Mimi Adamson? What would that gorgeous creature see in our Dickie? And that was sabotage, by the way. Your triumph— if triumph you do—will be hollow."

The game petered out in the end, the contestants defeated by the heat, which, indoors, had a different quality from outside—less intense, more cloying, but equally debilitating. They sat down and Henrietta rang for lemonade. She blew a jet of air from the corner of her mouth up into her face, and a tendril of hair lifted briefly from her damp forehead, then settled again.

"I'm dying," she said. "Literally."

"Don't do that," said Tobias. "Who would I mock with you gone?"

"We could swim," she said, ignoring him. "Down at the ponds."

"Two days, then Thea will be here," said Tobias. He sat forward, all animation. Behind him, on the wall, an oil painting of their father as a young man showed the same lively expression, the same shock of sandy hair, the same suggestion of perpetual and carefree irrepressibility. Dickie, their younger brother, had it too: the male line were peas in a pod. No one knew whom Henrietta resembled. Not her mother, certainly: on this the countess often remarked, with a special, sorrowful smile. Not that she needed waste any sympathy on Henrietta, who liked her own height and strength and robust, outdoor constitution. Born for the saddle, not the chaise longue: this was her father's fond assessment, and Henrietta took it as the compliment he intended. She smiled now at the thought, and Tobias, mistaking it for Thea-related encouragement, smiled back and said: "Henry, I'm a goner. I can't remember when I last felt this excited."

"Oh Toby, you're always excited about something. You have the personality of a puppy."

"Topping idea, a swim," he said. "Shall we? Except all the town'll be down there."

Henrietta pulled a face. "Not the town ponds, idiot. The one down at Home Farm. I'm not taking a dip in public view. Unseemly enough in private."

Agnes, the housemaid, tapped on the door and entered, bearing a silver tray with two glasses and a jug of iced lemonade. She walked with scrupulous care, as if on a tightrope.

"Just the ticket," said Tobias. "Thank you, Agnes."

The girl blushed, bobbed, and left, and brother and sister were silent for a moment as they each took a deep draft of the cold drink. Henrietta, her thirst slaked, held the glass against first one cheek and then the other. She closed one eye and scrutinized Tobias critically.

"So," she said. "Thea Sterling."

"O, be still my beating heart," said Tobias, theatrically.

"Don't fling yourself at her feet the minute she turns up. You'll frighten her."

"I shall behave with perfect chivalry and decorum, all the while waiting for my moment."

"Your moment?"

"To ask her to be my wife. Thea Hoyland, Countess of Netherwood. It sounds well, doesn't it?"

Henrietta smiled. "Thea Sterling sounds well too. She's a modern young woman. She may not be looking for a husband."

"Oh, come off it," said Tobias. "Aren't you all?"

"Speaking only for myself, no."

"Odd girl. Well, there'll always be a place for you here

when Thea and I are earl and countess. You can be Mad Aunt Henry in the West Wing."

Henrietta nodded graciously. "Thank you," she said. She held up her glass and Tobias clinked his own against it to seal the deal.

"Mama will be raging, of course," she said. "She can't stick Americans, especially attractive ones who're out to snare her sons. Not that Thea has the least notion of snaring anyone."

"Mama must overcome her prejudice. In any case, she'll be entirely diverted by the presence of the king," said Tobias, then, changing tack: "Lovely Mimi Anderson and Dickie. What an unlikely match."

Henrietta snorted with laughter. "Toby, mind what you say against your brother. He's the image of you."

"Minus my charisma and irresistible charm," said Tobias.

"Minus your staggering self-regard, you mean."

"That too," he said, and grinned. "Right. Last one in the pond's a rotten egg."

And he was up and off, leaving Henrietta to trail in his wake and wonder at her brother's simple and limitless appetite for frivolity.

Chapter 7

You'd think a man might take off his jacket and loosen his tie when the thermometer on the wall outside the estate office showed seventy-two degrees. Jem Arkwright, the earl's land agent, had his sleeves rolled up past the elbows and no collar on his shirt, and he made no apology for it. But there was Absalom Blandford, sitting behind his desk, buttoned up tight to the Adam's apple and still wearing the immaculate black worsted jacket he favored for work. Jem stuck his head around Absalom's door and the bailiff looked up as if affronted by the intrusion. His eyes were the interesting burnished brown of new chestnuts and on anyone else they might have been a winning feature; but now they alighted on Jem with their customary cold indifference. Miserable little sod, thought Jem, but he said: "Morning, bailiff. Those leases on t'Harley End fields expire next month, isn't that so?"

"Michaelmas Day," said Absalom immediately, without recourse to any paperwork.

"Aye, as I thought," said Jem. He could have looked this up quite easily but why bother when the human compendium of estate facts occupied the neighboring office?

"If t'master asks after me, that's where I shall be, then."
He waited for a second, wondering if he might elicit a response,
but Absalom was back at his ledger, scratching figures in columns, his lips moving as he wrote, but without making a sound.
Jem left him to it and whistled for his terrier, which came bar-
reling out of the stables with joyful alacrity.

"You been eating 'orse muck again?" said Jem cheerfully,
and the little dog responded in the affirmative with a short
series of excited yaps. It came to summat, thought Jem, when
a man's dog was a better conversationalist than his colleague.

He sauntered out of the courtyard and Absalom listened
with satisfaction to the sound of Jem's boots receding on the
cobbles. It pleased him to know he was alone now in the estate
offices. If he had appeared affronted by Jem's appearance at
the door, it was because he most certainly was. The land agent,
with his bluff manners, disconcerting directness, and incurable
habit of never knocking, was an irritation at the best of times,
but today—disheveled, informal, coated in perspiration—he was
beyond the pale. Absalom sniffed the air cautiously for traces
of body odor and his worst fears were confirmed. He trailed
his fingers through a bowl of potpourri that he kept on the
desk for just these emergencies, and brought them up to his
nose. Bergamot and citrus filled his nostrils. He breathed deeply,
in and out, and he savored the aroma and the silence: his
equilibrium, so grievously disturbed by Jem's visit, began to
settle back into place.

An hour passed. Two hours. Accounts were cross-referenced,
inventories amended, figures adjusted. Once, years ago, the earl
had suggested that his bailiff have an assistant to share the ad-
ministrative load, but this idea was repellent to Absalom. His
office was his sanctuary: he would as soon share his bathtub.

Presently a new footfall became audible outside. There were
no appointments in his diary and few people—other than Jem,
or perhaps the earl—dropped in on Absalom unannounced, so

he sat poised, his pen aloft, his head cocked, waiting for the footsteps to move on but they did not. Instead they stopped by his door, and there came three sharp raps. Oh well, he thought: at least this individual knew how to seek admission in the proper manner.

"Come," said Absalom with chilly authority.

The door opened and a man entered, well dressed and debonair, a stranger, who carried himself with graceful authority. He smiled and approached the desk with his right hand extended, which rather forced the bailiff to take it and shake, an activity he preferred to avoid unless he was wearing gloves. When he spoke, the stranger's voice was pleasant without being obsequious, and there was no trace of a Yorkshire accent. This immediately elevated him beyond the ordinary: the bailiff's own origins were in Hertfordshire and every dropped aitch and flat vowel he was forced to listen to in the course of a day reminded him of his own superiority in this county. Absalom listened attentively as the man, urbanely and without unnecessary preamble, introduced himself and explained his business: he would be a few months in Netherwood and needed a permanent base.

"There's a house set apart from the town," he said. "A little neglected, perhaps, but its size and location are very much to my taste."

Absalom nodded. "Indeed. I believe you mean Ravenscliffe. A fine dwelling, currently empty. Would you like to view the property?" He spoke with calm professionalism, which disguised a rising swell of grim satisfaction. Here was an opportunity indeed. He had two days ago declined an approach from Mrs. Williams for the said property and this fact had since weighed heavily on his mind. Not because of any sense of unfairness on his part, not remotely: Mrs. Williams had forever forfeited her right to fair play at his hands. But it ran counter to all his bailiff's instincts to keep a house empty when it could be filled, and it was not beyond the realms of possibility that Mrs. Williams might take her application to the earl, with whom she was on distressingly friendly terms. Absalom had imagined a hideous scenario in which he must attempt to defend his position to Lord Netherwood while Mrs. Williams looked on, triumphant. He had given her the power to humiliate him when he offered—and she rejected—his suit: he had feared, when he lied and told her Ravenscliffe was taken, that he had made himself vulnerable again. Now, however, it seemed she was to be denied the pleasure of belittling him professionally as well as personally. A lease could be arranged with this impressive gentleman, Mrs. Williams would be thwarted, and Absalom's integrity could not be called into question.

"Actually, I don't think so. I've seen all I need to and I'm happy to proceed," said the man now. "I can make a down payment on the rent immediately, if you wish, and supply references as to my character and liquidity."

"Well, payment in hand would be desirable but as to references, no, no, I think that won't be necessary," said Absalom, barely able to credit his good fortune and anxious to hasten the completion of this timely transaction. "How long do you wish the tenancy to run?"

"Shall we say twelve months, renewable, from the end of September?"

"Twelve months. Renewable." The bailiff opened a drawer and withdrew a pristine new tenancy agreement on which he wrote, in his impeccable hand, Ravenscliffe, Netherwood Common, and alongside it the date. He signed it—Absalom Blandford, Bailiff, Netherwood Estate—then slid it across the desk and offered his tight, unsettling little smile, which the stranger returned, but warmly.

"You'd like my signature?" he said.

"If you wouldn't mind. Just above my own."

The man signed. Silas Whittam, he wrote. Then he smiled again.

"What a very great pleasure it has been, Mr. Blandford."

"Indeed, Mr., er"—he looked at the signature—"Whittam."

"Does this conclude the paperwork?"

Absalom nodded. "Indeed," he said again. He was still a little stunned at this fortuitous turn of events.

"In that case," said Silas, "here's a down payment against the rent." He produced a soft calfskin wallet and slid a slim fold of banknotes across the desk toward the bailiff. "Perhaps I might have a key, in return? I'd like to have a look inside; acquaint myself properly with the property."

"Certainly," said Absalom. He stood, and from a wall-mounted wooden box he took four keys. "Front and back doors, two sets," he said. "Always wise to have a spare."

"Thank you," said Silas. "I shall inspect it directly. Just as soon as you've had it cleaned, that is." He laughed lightly, and Absalom, appalled, attempted to do the same. How to say, without giving offense, that it was customary for incoming tenants to clean their own property?

"Ah, well, now let's see," he said.

Silas looked at him inquiringly and said: "Shall we say by the end of the week?"

The bailiff, helpless, caved in. "End of the week. Absolutely. Even if I have to do it myself," he said, in a rare attempt at humor.

Silas acknowledged the jest with a generous laugh, bid the bailiff farewell, and beat a retreat. He crossed the courtyard just as Jem returned from Harley End and the two men nodded a greeting as they passed each other, then, as Silas disappeared from view, Jem opened Absalom's office door—infuriating fellow—and said: "I see you've met Silas Whittam, then?"

The bailiff, piqued that Jem seemed to know the man, agreed grudgingly that yes, he had indeed met Mr. Whittam—had in fact just agreed the tenancy of Ravenscliffe, the vacant property on—

"—Netherwood Common," said Jem, interrupting. "Interesting. Next thing you'll find is that number five Beaumont Lane is being vacated."

"The Williams' property? I hardly think so," said Absalom.

"Oh aye," said Jem maddeningly. "Sure as eggs's eggs."

A black dot of dread swam across Absalom's vision. "Because?" he said, in a voice that betrayed his discomfiture.

"Because," said Jem, "you just let Ravenscliffe to 'er brother."

"So it's ours?"

"Well it's mine, strictly speaking. But I shall graciously let you live there."

Anna was sitting with Eve and Silas at a table in the courtyard of the mill. She was perched on the edge of her chair as if poised to spring; her hands were clasped together, her face and eyes alive with pleasure. She may have bounced a little, in her effort to contain her excitement. Eve laughed.

"You look like Eliza on Christmas morning," she said.

"I feel it!" said Anna. "Ravenscliffe is gift for us all. Just you wait to see."

"*And* see," said Eve automatically. "Wait *and* see."

"Slimy little toad, that bailiff," said Silas. He looked very at home, his legs stretched out and crossed before him, his hands clasped behind his head. Around them was the hum and bustle of the lunchtime service. People traveled some distance to eat here these days; Eve's café, from its humble beginnings in Beaumont Lane, had by degrees raised the tone of the town, bringing to Netherwood a steady supply of affluent outsiders. This café, in the charming surroundings of the old mill, was where they came when the possibilities of Victoria Street and the marketplace had been exhausted. There was a continental feel to the courtyard: the round iron tables and lattice-backed chairs had been painted pale green, and there were cream canvas parasols casting a modicum of shade over the customers. Silas, in his linen suit and fine shoes, seemed to complete the picture; he looked like an advertisement for the French Riviera.

"Cheek o' t'man," said Eve. "Sat there as cool as a cucumber and told me it wasn't available."

"Couldn't let it to me fast enough," said Silas.

"I wonder if he knows he's had wool pulled over eyes?" said Anna.

Silas roared with laughter.

"What is funny?" she said.

"Sorry, sorry," he said, though he looked quite the reverse. He adopted her heavy Russian accent: "Vool pulled over eyes. You don't sound much like a local."

She shrugged. "I like to stand out," she said.

She did, too. Anna, haughty, diminutive, bright as a button, had come to Netherwood as a charity case, moving into Eve's house in Beaumont Lane when she and her baby daughter had nowhere else to turn. And yet, as Netherwood folk often put it, to look at her you'd think she was somebody. It wasn't that she was unfriendly, not at all. Anna would pass the time of day with anyone—liked to, in fact, since she saw any conversation as an opportunity to brush up her command of colloquial English. But she had an air about her, an assuredness, and she'd had it since the day she arrived. There was no patronizing Anna: she wouldn't suffer condescension.

It wasn't just self-confidence, though, that set Anna Rabinovich apart from the crowd: it was the way she looked, the way she dressed. She set no store by convention—quite the opposite, in fact. Today she had on a sky-blue, slim-cut cotton skirt, which barely skimmed her ankles, and a white poplin sleeveless blouse, which managed to be daring and prim in equal measure. She made everything herself at the Singer—for Eve and the children too—and she could look at the weather at eight in the morning and be wearing the perfect, seasonal outfit by ten. Today's garment was an earlier model, adapted for the Indian summer: the leg o' mutton sleeves now lay folded in her bag of scraps, waiting for their certain reincarnation. She'd offered to do the same for Eve, but her friend had demurred: skirts cut on the bias and scoop-necked blouses were quite avant-garde enough without unpicking and removing sleeves as well. She looked at Anna now, her bare arms turning pink in the sunshine, and she smiled.

"You should watch yourself," she said. "You're pink as a boiled shrimp."

Anna shrugged. She didn't mind the heat of the sun on her skin: soon enough, she'd be wrapped up against the autumn cold.

Silas delved into a pocket in his jacket, which he had slung over the back of the chair. "Keys," he said, and he passed them across the table to Eve, though it was Anna who took them.

"When can we move?" she said.

"Just as soon as Mr. Blandford has finished cleaning it." Silas's face was a study in solemnity, but at his words Anna and Eve erupted into noisy hilarity, so that the ladies at a neighboring table turned to stare and Ginger came out from the kitchen wondering what on earth she had missed.

Chapter 8

The secret—or one of them—to entertaining the king was to create an illusion: that the levels of comfort and luxury he encountered were entirely standard and, had he dropped in unannounced, there would have been no discernible difference in hospitality. This was Lady Netherwood's belief, but two days before the monarch's arrival it seemed less than certain that her aim could possibly be achieved. On the upper floors the detritus of recent renovation—the paint pots, brushes, ladders, wallpaper remnants, and dust sheets—were still in the process of being removed, and the great house's interior was redolent with the smell of freshly applied paint. Mrs. Powell-Hughes was near demented with the demands being made upon her and her staff; the countess had taken to her room with a cold compress and had made it clear that by the time she emerged she expected perfect calm and order to have been restored; and now one of Mr. Motson's team of lads had carried his equipment out of the house from the upper floors with white paint on the sole of one of his clogs. The evidence of his crime—a regular series of ever-diminishing stains from a second-floor landing to the main staircase—was currently being attacked by an underhousemaid armed with a turpentine-soaked rag and this method, though effective, did nothing to improve the prevailing aroma.

Mrs. Powell-Hughes had the unpleasant and unusual sensation of being not quite in control. Her reputation for running an immaculate house hung by a thread: if Edward VII arrived to paint fumes and dark patches of turpentine, then she might as well hang up her keys, pack her trunk, and go and spend the rest of her days with her sister in Filey. She was rushing through the kitchens on her way to the stillroom when she ran full tilt into the butler. The shock of the impact threatened to overcome her as if here, finally, was the last straw she'd known was coming. She stared at Parkinson white-faced and wild-eyed and he was profoundly moved by her evident plight.

"Now, now, Mrs. Powell-Hughes, come and sit down for a moment," he said, responding to the extraordinary with the ordinary. Then, turning to the nearest kitchen maid, he mouthed "tea" at her, before opening the door to his sitting room, his inner sanctum, and ushering in his unlikely charge. In itself, this act of kindness underlined the gravity of the situation. Mr. Parkinson's private quarters were so rarely breached by anyone other than himself; the trappings of his solitary leisure hours—a pipe, a tobacco tin, a Bible, a bundle of letters—lay about the place, and even the housekeeper, exalted among the staff, felt a little awed.

He sat her down in a brown plush chair, pushing her gently by the shoulders, as she looked likely to resist. "Now," he said, "Lottie will bring us a cup of tea—no, Mrs. Powell-Hughes, it's ordered, it's on its way, it's useless to protest—and we shall take five minutes together to take stock."

"But I really don't have the time, Mr. Parkinson, though I appreciate your concern." Her voice was strained from barking orders at the girls under her command.

"A cup of tea and a moment to order your thoughts will make all the difference," said the butler. He was a good man and he acted through genuine kindness. If Mary Adams had stood here ministering to her, or Florrie Flytton, the countess's lady's maid, they would have certainly, somehow, betrayed a consciousness of their own ordered existence and a smug satisfaction at the housekeeper's distress. Both women were capable of kindness, but their kindnesses came with a subtext: you have deserved your present misery, yet I shall be magnanimous and comfort you. Mr. Parkinson was different. His pale blue eyes were full of real concern, his face, oddly unlined for a man in his mid-fifties, a study in sympathy. He had always looked younger than his years: once, in the early days of service, he had thought he would be forever a footman, hampered in his ambitions by his well-formed calves—as essential in a footman as his discretion—and an adorably cherubic face. Even now his looks didn't quite suit his position: his wavy blond hair refused to thin or to turn gray, his face had no severity or pallor. He looked rosy and amiable: when he addressed his ranks he had their absolute respect but still it wasn't hard to picture him in a cassock and ruff.

Lottie tapped on the door and entered as she was bid. She tiptoed across the room with her tray as if this was a hospital ward and the housekeeper a patient. It was too much, thought Parkinson.

"Thank you Lottie, no need to creep so."

"Sorry, Mr. Parkinson," she said, though in a whisper and still, when she left, she crept. The butler smiled at Mrs. Powell-Hughes.

"Poor Lottie," he said. "She's quite unequal to any occurrence beyond the strictly predictable. Now. Let me pour, and while I do, tell me your concerns."

The housekeeper, already soothed to some degree by Mr. Parkinson's calm manner, was beginning to feel like herself again. "Oh, well. I feel a little silly now. I don't quite know what came over me."

"We're all entitled to mild panic every so often," he said and he smiled warmly. "What are the specifics of the case?"

"Oh, the smell of paint and turpentine, mostly," she said. "Nothing that can't be dealt with, I expect."

"Ah, that sounds like the Mrs. Powell-Hughes I know so well. We shall open all doors and windows to admit what little breeze there is, and I'm sure you've asked Ruth for more of her stillroom concoctions? Potpourri can work miracles."

"That's my next job," she said. "That's where I was going." She blew across the top of her cup of tea and steam briefly clouded her spectacles, giving her the misleading appearance of utter helplessness. "Really, Mr. Parkinson, the new sanitaryware has been the principal difficulty. If it had only been installed a little sooner—"

"Indeed," he said delicately. "The timing was challenging."

This was tricky ground and the two loyal servants trod carefully, for neither of them wanted to openly criticize the countess, whatever private thoughts they might each entertain regarding her excessive demands.

"The redecoration of the bathrooms, you see, had to wait until Mr. Motson had replaced everything. And a job that size can't be rushed."

"But I gather the result is—"

"Oh, absolutely splendid," said Mrs. Powell-Hughes, eager to return to safer territory. "Quite magnificent. I can't imagine the king will have anything better at Buckingham Palace."

"Almost certainly not," said Parkinson. "But being the king, he doesn't have anyone to impress, does he?"

Mrs. Powell-Hughes understood him perfectly. The king's penchant for visiting his society friends at their own country homes had begun a frenzy of expensive restoration by the aristocracy: Lady Netherwood's rigor in refurbishing throughout had been matched many times over by those who had already played host to Bertie and his entourage.

"You know, people have ruined themselves entertaining the king," said Mr. Parkinson, speaking low and with a grave expression on his angelic face.

Mrs. Powell-Hughes tutted and shook her head sadly. She sipped her fortifying tea.

The butler leaned in confidingly. "The chap he stays with during the St. Leger is feeling pinched, by all accounts," he said. "Quite spent up."

"My word, what a business. At least that's not one of our worries," she said, as if she and Mr. Parkinson were personally footing the bill.

"Well, quite," he said. "And by the end of today I imagine you'll find you and your staff have brought perfect order to the upper floors. If there's anything I can do to assist you . . . ?"

The housekeeper placed her cup and saucer carefully on the side table next to her. She might be stretched beyond all possible reason, but she wouldn't have footmen and valets deployed in areas of the house where they had no business.

"Oh, no, thank you," she said, with a small laugh to indicate that not only was his offer unnecessary but that she could find amusement in it. "We shall soldier on until we triumph."

"That's the spirit," said Parkinson. "Now, back to the battlefield?"

Parkinson's prediction was quite correct. By the time the countess emerged from her darkened rooms, refreshed from the effects of the compress and a restorative afternoon nap, she found there wasn't a corner of Netherwood Hall that wasn't fit for the king's inspection. Even the smell of turpentine had been all but obliterated by the fragrant combination of dried orange blossom and damask roses, and still there was all day tomorrow to clear the air completely.

Alone, feeling contemplative and with a vaguely unsettling sense of fragile calm, Lord Netherwood wandered through his home. His wife's disregard for expense was evident in every room he entered. The royal quarters had been cleverly arranged in the East Wing from a series of interconnecting rooms that the king would share—according to a discreet communication regarding protocol—with Mrs. Keppel: they were magnificent. The dark Victorian wallpaper had been replaced with pastel stripes in rose and cream, and elegant furniture—modern pieces, newly commissioned—now replaced the heavy dressing tables and age-spotted mirrors. Pale buttermilk satin adorned the royal four-poster and at the windows hung new drapes in rose-colored shot silk. There was a chair by the bed, low and wide and upholstered in the same silk as the curtains: this was for the king's fox terrier, Caesar. The dog, it seemed, enjoyed the same privileges as Mrs. Keppel: certainly they had shared a protocol memorandum. Lord Netherwood wondered if anyone had yet told Mrs. Powell-Hughes that Caesar was to be allowed the run of the place.

Downstairs he found Clarissa.

"Well?" she said.

"Tip-top."

"Even the new bathrooms?"

"Especially the new bathrooms. We're better appointed than the Savoy."

The countess smiled. She was pleased with her husband: not a single purchase had been queried, not a single expense spared. He had even conceded—briefly balking but swiftly capitulating—the necessity of giving up his study because the king demanded a telegraph room wherever he stayed, in order that he might be in touch with his government.

"I'll wager he never sets foot inside," said the earl now, opening his study door and looking rather glumly at the sight of his own desk cleared of books and papers to make room for the contraption that now occupied it.

"Well, anyway, you wouldn't have been able to slope off here yourself," said Clarissa. "The host must be always on hand. So, you see, your study is perfect for the job."

Just what he expected. His wife had added an eleventh commandment to the original ten: thou shalt not admit to inconvenience caused by the royal visit. He sighed. Speaking personally, he would be jolly glad when it was over.

Chapter 9

Whatever hit the mine owners hit the miners harder. This was and had ever been a fact of life. If supply outstripped demand and the market price fell, if cheaper coal was being sold on the Continent, if a colliery began to dry up and become less productive—always, always, the men suffered more than the masters. This, Amos said to Anna, was the principal injustice he wanted to see eradicated. There were others—widows' pensions, sick pay, greater investment in safety—but these could follow when the basic human right of a fair day's pay for a full day's work had been enshrined in British law.

They were sitting together on the wiry grass of Netherwood Common, looking down on Ravenscliffe. Eve had postponed the moving in until after the king's visit—that is, until after the first dinner. She couldn't, she said, think about the upheaval of moving until the royal puddings were behind her. Anna spent time at the new house all the same, measuring windows, walking the rooms, imagining them furnished and peopled and the sounds of family life ringing throughout. She'd coaxd Amos in today, though he couldn't shed the uncomfortable feeling of trespassing. The house had seemed to him implausibly large: all he could think was how much coal they'd get through in the winter. But he smiled and nodded because he could see what it meant to Anna that he liked it.

The two of them were making a habit of walking together, so their presence high up on the common wasn't unusual, though there were plenty of people who considered it irregular. It didn't take a lot to get tongues wagging in Netherwood: if you were five minutes late opening your curtains, somebody would notice and pass a remark. So Anna Rabinovich and Amos Sykes, strolling together toward Bluebell Wood or Harley Hill or Netherwood Common—well, there was a topic you could get your teeth into. It wasn't just the strolling, either—it was the way they talked, heads together, lost in conversation, trading words back and forth between each other as if there wasn't the time in the world for all they had to say.

Of course, if the gossips had been privy to what passed between Anna and Amos, they would have been disappointed. No tender words or compliments, no flattery or flirtation. They talked, as they did now, about politics, economics, and the lot of the workingman.

"Y'see, t'earl looks at a miner and 'e sees a man who owes 'im a debt of gratitude," Amos was saying.

"And perhaps they do," said Anna, the devil's advocate with capitalist leanings. "Without earl, they would not have job or wage. They would starve."

"Aye, 'e employs 'em, granted. Then they risk their lives every day in a coal mine to create 'is wealth. If anyone should be grateful, it's Lord Netherwood."

"Well, and perhaps he is," she said, determined to see the other side. "From what I hear, he is good man. Only you, it seems, think he should be horsewhipped."

Amos laughed grimly. "Do you know what, Anna? I'm sick to death of 'earing what a good man t'earl is. A good man would listen to what 'is men 'ave to say. Lord Netherwood is only good by comparison wi' some of those bastards 'e calls 'is friends."

"Language."

"Beg pardon. But as far as goodness goes, you 'ave to admit there's nowt by way o' competition."

She frowned at him. Sometimes he spoke too quickly for her to grasp his meaning.

"Sorry," he said and he continued more slowly. "What I mean is, t'standard set by landowners and employers in this country is so abysmal that Lord Netherwood looks like a saint by comparison. And yet 'e sits back and says nowt and does nowt in support of 'is men. I don't call that good. I call that cowardly and complacent."

"But there are union members at his collieries now. Perhaps you ask too much too quickly. Perhaps you should slow down, give him time to adapt."

"You're talking pigs will, if you don't mind me saying. It's taken nigh on an 'undred and fifty years to unionize New Mill Colliery. Slow down? I don't think so."

"Pigs will," she repeated slowly. "So that means nonsense?"

He grinned at her and nodded, then turned serious again: "There's change in t'air, Anna. Real change, not just small pockets o' triumph. Balfour's looking weak over tariff reform, t'Liberals are listenin' to Labor, and Lord Netherwood is a fool if 'e doesn't know it. We 'ave workingmen in Parliament these days and there's plenty more where they came from."

"You, for example," she said.

"Come again?"

"You. Amos Sykes, MP. Doesn't that sound fine?"

He threw back his head and roared with laughter at the

74

absurdity of the idea that he should take himself off to West-minster at the behest of the voting public. Anna, however, was entirely serious and she looked at him with an unsmiling face.

"What?" she said.

He didn't answer, but his laughter tailed off in the face of Anna's stony disapproval. Then he said: "Enough of this. There's work to be done and I'm sat on my backside in t'sunshine." He picked up a sheaf of papers from the ground by his side then, standing, offered Anna a helping hand, which she took, though she was still displeased with him. Vision and ambition were dearly held tenets to Anna Rabinovich: to waste one's talent, to limit one's horizons—these, to her, were cardinal sins. She had much more to say to Amos on the subject, but he seemed in a hurry, so she put away her mental ammunition for another day and restricted herself to pleasantries.

"Busy, then?" she said, standing and brushing the dry grass from her skirt.

"Aye. Meeting at New Mill. What about you?"

She delved into a pocket of her skirt and produced a rolled-up tape measure.

"Curtains," she said.

They set off down the hill, walking slowly. Anna wore a straw hat against the sun but she pulled it off suddenly and shook her head, letting her hair fly about her. She'd had it cut shorter in this hot weather and it fell only to her shoulders now: it made her look younger than ever. He had a good fifteen years on her, although her wisdom and experience often closed the gap. Today though, by her side, Amos felt positively ancient.

It still felt like going home, walking the cinder track to New Mill Colliery. Since boyhood he had trodden this route: he remembered his fear as a lad among grown men on the day he started. He remembered, even, the feel of the new snap tin that banged against his chest in the inside pocket of his old wool jacket. Two slices of bread and dripping and when the time came to eat it he felt sick to his stomach. There had been a big, simpleminded boy, a few years older than Amos, working next to him on the screens. At his age he should have been down the pit, but he wasn't all there: picking rock and shale out of the coal as it passed on conveyor belts was all he was deemed fit for. Anyway, this boy had watched to see if Amos, the new lad, was going to be able to manage to eat and, when it became clear that he'd gone into first-day shock, he helped himself, delving uninvited and bold as a magpie into Amos's jacket where it hung on the peg. Through his fog of misery Amos thought, he can't be all that daft, then.

This memory, for some reason, came back to him as he approached the pit yard. The big lad's name was Bert Wilson and he'd died of typhoid fever, along with about twenty-five others from the same row of houses. They said the water from the spigot in their street was coming through the midden first, and folk were dying like flies. Bert Wilson. He had loomed large—literally—in Amos's first dreadful days at the pit, then had, just as suddenly, disappeared. It was probably twenty-five years since the lad had even crossed Amos's consciousness, but he reckoned he could still pick Bert out in a crowd.

"Now then, comrade."

A familiar voice broke his reverie and Sam Bamford fell into step beside him.

"Sam," said Amos. "'ow do."

"If you've come to incite us to revolution, you've wasted your time," said Sam. "We've all got t'day off tomorrow to wave flags at t'king, so you'll find no malcontents 'ere."

Amos laughed. "Very glad to 'ear it," he said. "'ow's things?"

"Middlin'. Another rockfall by Wharncliffe seam, no casualties, but it's still not cleared. 'ow's things wi' thee?"

"Busy. More members every week. Strength in numbers, as they say."

"Did you know Sparky were killed?" Sam said.

"Ah no, don't tell me that." Amos stopped in his tracks, wholly distracted from the working-class struggle by this bleak news. It was always a black day at a colliery when a pony had to be destroyed; grown men had been known to cry like babies. Sparky must've been near retirement age, he thought now: poor old soul, denied his last few years out to grass in the daylight.

"Aye, bad do," said Sam. It wasn't news to him and he spoke in a brisk, matter-of-fact voice. "Isaac Chandler 'ad 'im settin' new props, shiftin' old uns. Summat went awry, not sure what. Sparky got trapped under a piece o' timber, broke 'is back."

They were in the yard now, inhaling the sharp, sulfurous smell of the pit, standing by the time office, which was full of men clocking on for the afternoon shift, and Amos felt a pang of something like regret, though it wasn't that exactly. That he hadn't known, until now, about Sparky's death suddenly seemed inexpressibly sad because time was when nothing happened at New Mill without Amos Sykes knowing about it. He watched Sam walk into the office, exchanging a word here and there with his colleagues; he heard the rise and fall of miners' voices and the occasional bark of laughter and he felt on the very periphery of what had once been his world.

But the melancholy didn't last. Don Manvers, the colliery

manager, hailed him from his office and Amos crossed the yard, papers tucked under his arm, for their meeting. And the miracle of this—that he was here at the Earl of Netherwood's colliery in the interests of democracy and socialism—was more than enough to put a spring back in his step.

Chapter 10

The luggage arrived at Netherwood Hall ahead of the guests so that by the time they, too, made their stately progress up Oak Avenue, their belongings would be waiting upstairs for them, ready to be unpacked by the visiting valets and ladies' maids. Mrs. Powell-Hughes had rallied superbly after her brief collapse and the house was in a state of perfect readiness. Twenty-two guest rooms would be in use in addition to the king's apartments, and each one was supplied with fresh flowers, new writing paper and ink, a basket of exotic fruit from the hothouses, and colognes and toiletries from the stillroom. The names of the guests had been handwritten on cards, which were placed in brass frames on each door. As usual, Mrs. Powell-Hughes, in consultation with the countess, had made a skillful job of allocation, her decisions on this occasion based on diplomacy and tact as much as on hierarchy. The Duke of Knightwick, for example, was billeted in comfortable quarters in the East Wing, while his wife the duchess was some distance from him but conveniently—and significantly—close to the dashing financier Sir Wally Goldman. Similarly, Lady Hartwick, widowed last year at the heartbreakingly tender age of twenty-nine, was merely a hop, skip, and a jump from the very eligible Frank Ponsonby: there were high hopes that one more weekend in close quarters might produce the longed-for proposal of marriage. It had all been beautifully managed by the peerless Mrs. Powell-Hughes: a question, quite simply, of the judicious and discreet application of inside information.

The guest list was just as the king liked it: a lively mix of courtiers, politicians, businessmen, society beauties, and wags. An exotic diplomat or two was usually desirable, especially at winter house parties, when shooting was the main event, and Johnny Foreigner—who, anyway, couldn't be trusted with a gun—would often agree to sit at home and entertain the ladies. The closest this latest Netherwood ensemble had to exotic was the American ambassador, though from what Teddy Hoyland had gleaned when they met, the chap was probably rather more down to earth than most of the other guests. Still, being so little known, Joseph Choate was considered the wild card: could he, for example, play cricket? This question was the cause of some consternation to the earl and he put it now to Henrietta, as they sat together on a bench overlooking the main lawn. This was hardly the thing to be doing with the arrival of the first guests imminent, but they had found each other in the garden, both with the same idea of stealing a few moments of quiet before the frenzy. Neither of them relished the prospect of the next four days: being wildly amusing could be such a bore.

"Thea says he plays baseball," said Henrietta. "I think they all do at the embassy."

She gazed across the lawn to where Daniel MacLeod and a small posse of undergardeners were fine-tuning the white border so that only the freshest blooms remained on their stems. It still seemed most odd to see him here in Netherwood, thought Henrietta: he was so very much part of their London staff.

"Baseball?" said Lord Hoyland. "What on earth?"

"Not sure, but it involves a bat and a ball, like cricket."

"Well then, I expect he'll pick up the gist. What about tennis? Do they have that in America?"

Henrietta snorted with laughter. "Daddy, you're quite ridiculous. Of course they do. Thea's a dab-hand, actually. She ran me all around the court last time we played."

"You two sound awfully chummy."

"Mmm, I've seen her in London a couple of times since we first met. I like her a lot. Too bright by half for Toby."

"Keep your voice down," said the earl, looking over his shoulder, genuinely anxious. "Your mother's at breaking point as it is."

Dorothea Sterling, bright, witty, vivacious, and one hundred percent American, had caught the eye of Tobias to the extent that he fancied himself in love. His announcement that he intended to marry the girl—an honor of which Thea was still entirely ignorant—had been treated with contemptuous disbelief by the countess. It wasn't that she disliked Americans per se: they were an amiable breed and enlivened many a London soirée. But Thea Sterling was not and could never be marriage material for her son. She didn't care how many charming American women had married English aristocrats; on this the countess was unequivocal. The earl, on the other hand, admired the girl enormously. Simply the fact that she had struck out from home on an ocean liner to spread her wings in England was impressive in his view. Thea was Connecticut-born though she lived in New York, and she had come to London to stay for a few months with Joseph and Caroline Choate, who were friends of her parents. She had told Teddy when they met that she had the offer of a place at Cornell University, but she hadn't decided yet whether or not to accept. Lord Netherwood had been rather bowled over by her sparky independence.

81

"Has Toby seen her again? In London, I mean," the earl said now to Henrietta. He was speaking low, as if Clarissa might be listening from inside one of the vast stone urns that flanked the bench they sat on. The Choates and Miss Sterling were due to arrive with the rest of the house party later this afternoon; Clarissa's early objections to their inclusion had been vociferous, but then the king had expressed an interest in seeing them again, and that was that.

"Once, that's all. We went down together, remember? End of July? Mama was too busy here to notice much what Toby was up to. We went dancing, which is mostly what Thea likes to do when her head isn't stuck in a book. She's a darling. Tobes was most unlike himself. He could hardly think of a thing to say. He just gazed at her, looking a perfect fool."

"I wish your mother wasn't so set against her. A girl like that could be just what Tobias needs."

"Yes, well, I shouldn't have to remind you that Toby has a knack of getting his own way. Anyway, don't worry—Mama has to be on her best behavior like the rest of us. And she might relent when she sees that everyone else loves Thea. Which they will. Oops, there we go—I believe I can hear a motor."

Henrietta was right. A covetable little red two-seat run-about was bowling down the avenue toward the great house, throwing up gusts of gravel dust as it came.

"Wally Goldman," said the earl. "Look at that little beauty."

They stood and walked together up the wide steps to the carriageway at the front of the house, arriving there at the same time as Sir Wally, but in less of an uproar. He waved at them flamboyantly with a gloved hand, then shed his goggles and a voluminous linen duster before vaulting athletically out of the car.

"What ho!" he said. "First to arrive again? How shaming. Henry, darling, you look utterly ravishing. Teddy, my dear man, so do you."

The earl laughed. "And you are as full of bunkum as ever, but enough of this—introduce me to your motor: what is she?"

"Ford. Model A. Newly minted, shipped her over last month." He nodded at the nearest footman, who stepped forward eagerly to take the wheel. "Cracker, isn't she? Ten horsepower, imagine that? Seven hundred and fifty dollars' worth of pure motoring poetry."

It was like Wally Goldman to mention the price. Bankers, thought the earl, could be depended upon to demonstrate the distinction between being of society and being merely in it.

"Come indoors, Wally, and slake your thirst," he said and the three of them walked under the portico, through the heavy brass-studded front door, and into the blessed cool of the marble entrance hall.

By three o'clock the rear courtyard was full of every possible variety of vehicle, from Wally's Ford Model A to the Duke and Duchess of Abberley's ancient landau. The king had yet to arrive, which of course was exactly as planned: he would stroll, with the rest of his traveling entourage, into a houseful of waiting friends as if the gathering was spontaneous and all the more delightful for that. Until he appeared, something of a hiatus had descended: the guests sat in small groups talking quietly as if to conserve their energy for the antics ahead. The Choates and Thea Sterling had arrived without incident; when Parkinson entered the room and announced them, Lady Netherwood had behaved with such faultless good manners that even Tobias was lulled into a warm feeling of false security. In any case, she had no objection whatsoever to the ambassador and his wife: gracious, urbane, instantly likable, they had been long enough in English society to fully understand the advanced etiquette required to see them through a country house party, even one with a king attached. Thea, on the other hand, was still a little unclear about the rules; she appeared gauche and rather loud by comparison with her chaperones and it occurred to the countess, as she submitted to a vigorous handshake and a ricochet of enthusiastic declarations from Thea, that her presence here might be no bad thing. Give her enough rope, thought Clarissa, and she might well hang herself. It was clear for all to see that here was no great beauty. It was only the second time that Clarissa had laid eyes on her, and in her mind the countess had created an enchantress, a siren. But this was a girl with a vulgar drawl, a weak chin, hair too short for a chignon, and the silhouette of an adolescent boy. From what Clarissa could tell—without looking too closely—Thea wasn't even wearing a corset. Certainly there was no waist to speak of, and no bosom; instead, she was straight up and down, and scrawny. As she smiled a gracious welcome, the countess felt it was merely a matter of time before Tobias lost interest and looked elsewhere, and her heart lightened at the thought.

The weather broke as the king stepped from the royal train. So swiftly and silently that no one had really noticed, the vivid blue sky had become crowded with pewter clouds and three weeks' worth of rain was released from the heavens. Flunkies rushed about him with umbrellas, but Bertie dismissed them, finding the downpour a great joke, so all the party followed suit, squealing and roaring with laughter as soft, drenching raindrops fell onto their fine hats, coats, and dresses. A fleet of three Daimlers—two of them newly purchased for the occasion—waited to convey them to Netherwood Hall, and they all piled in, loud and rambunctious. Atkins, the earl's chauffeur, was drenched too, as were the drivers of the two other motorcars: rain splashed as if from an open tap from the peaks of their caps and collected in deep puddles at their feet. This was their finest hour and the weather had made a mockery of it. They stood with what dignity they could muster while the king and Mrs. Keppel, both of them hooting with merriment, settled into the first car with Caesar the fox terrier. The rest of the party went behind and the royal progress began—a short drive from the earl's private railway station to the great house, but a difficult one through the new pools and eddies that blocked the way on the roads. This wasn't a state visit—the king had made that clear—yet the route to the hall was lined with loyal subjects. The miners had the day off, the schools had closed for the afternoon; it wasn't every day that a monarch passed within touching distance, and this small matter of a biblical downpour wasn't going to drive them away from the spectacle. The king rewarded their stoicism and good humor by insisting that Atkins lower the roof; stopping the convoy, the chauffeur hauled back the canopy and the Daimler began immediately to fill with rain as effectively as a water butt, its pale cream leather seats darkening so rapidly in the torrent that Atkins wondered if they could possibly ever be restored. But never mind, because there was King Edward VII, somehow larger than life, beaming, waving, and—if anything—wetter than the crowds that hailed him, and by his side the beautiful Alice Keppel, bold as you like and soaked to the skin in blue chiffon that clung to her contours like a bathing suit.

Chapter 11

E ve had been down to Netherwood Hall and come back
again by the time Silas arrived home with the children.
He had taken them to Victoria Street to watch the king drive
by and they burst into the kitchen, sodden, breathless, grinning
at each other at some shared triumph or private joke. They
dripped on her clean floor and she had to bite back a reprimand;
the novelty of having her brother here had somehow altered
the normal way of things, and rules that were once set in stone
were flouted daily.

"Mam!" said Eliza. "We saw Mrs. Keppel and 'er dress was
soppin'."

"King!" said Ellen, pushing to the front, muscling in on
the conversation. She had progressed these days from simply
mimicking others to volunteering her own contributions to
conversation: her vocabulary was small still, but was growing
by the day. She had no idea what a king was, of course, or
which, of all the fine people she had seen, he might have been;
but the crowds and the atmosphere and the thrill of the run
home in the rain had all contributed to her sense of occasion.

"You saw the king?" Eve said to her youngest child. Ellen nodded gravely, eyes wide with the wonder of it.

"Could hardly miss him, with that belly," said Silas and he shared a grown-up wink with Seth, paying him the compliment of this irreverent aside. Seth's frostiness toward Silas had melted over the past few days under the onslaught of his uncle's warm attention: his stories of world travel and derring-do were hard to resist. Seth had shifted from a position of chilly suspicion to cautious interest and finally to unbridled admiration in a few easy anecdotes. Also, Silas was the talk of the town—not least because his crate of bananas had been donated by Eve to the school and every child had run home with a share of the booty—and Seth had quickly realized that the cachet of owning such an uncle was immense. Time must not be wasted sulking while this glamorous stranger was among them. They sniggered together now, best of friends, and Seth said: "I 'ope you've made plenty o' batter, mam. I reckon 'e looked 'ungry," and everyone laughed.

"Less o' your cheek," said Eve, and then, to Silas: "Enough from you an' all," but she was smiling, so the party atmosphere among the excited children lingered on and the girls squealed and giggled at each other as they peeled off their wet stockings, then ran barefoot upstairs to change, leaving wet prints on the linoleum. Seth hung about, reluctant to leave the company of his uncle, but Eve said: "Get on wi' you, you'll take a chill standin' in those wet things," and the boy, temporarily compliant, did as he was bid.

"You're a good influence on 'im," Eve said.

"Thank you," Silas said, and bowed.

"Bad influence on Eliza, mind. She's a right giddy kipper when you're 'ere."

"Oh well, can't have everything." He stretched out an arm to pick up a piece of parkin from a plate behind his sister and began to munch on it unselfconsciously. With every word and deed, he radiated ease and familiarity: extraordinary, considering how recently arrived he was. Eve, happy to have him, was nevertheless occasionally thrown by his casual manner. She had to draw back now from the impulse to slap the back of his hand, as if he was an impudent child. He wasn't staying at Beaumont Lane—there was nowhere for him but the parlor floor, and anyway Silas preferred the privacy afforded by the rooms above the Hare and Hounds—but he let himself in and out of the house as if it was his. Eve encouraged this but Anna didn't like it: he kept making her jump, walking in uninvited. Why couldn't he at least knock? There was something to be said for standing on ceremony, in Anna's book.

"How come you're back, anyway?" Silas said now. "Don't you have kingly puddings to make?"

"I made t'batter already. It 'as to stand for a while."

Silas pulled a skeptical face. "And how can you be sure the wicked fat cook won't sabotage it in your absence?" Eve had sketched a verbal picture for him of Mrs. Adams's build and temperament; she found herself wanting to make him laugh, so had exaggerated the cook's less attractive traits and now he imagined her a villain. "What if she adds a few drops of arsenic and you're hauled off to the Tower?"

Eve laughed. "She's not that bad. Anyroad, she looked too busy to be messin' about with my batter." She had too: tomato red in the face and the wrong side of frantic. In the sultry heat the kitchens were like Turkish hammams and the usual pleasant hum of conversation had been replaced by a tense silence, broken occasionally by an ill-tempered outburst from the cook. Eve had considered offering to stay and help with other things, but she thought again when Mrs. Adams flung a basin of spoiled hollandaise at the wall. It wasn't characteristic of the cook, this irrational, hysterical behavior, and it wasn't going to help put a ten-course banquet on the table either. A small posse of kitchen maids, cowed into silence by the horror of the smashed bowl and the slick of pale yellow sauce sliding down the tiles, shrank back as one to let Eve pass when she left them all to it. She hoped that by the time she returned at half past five, a semblance of order would have been restored.

"Where's Anna?" Silas said. "Didn't see her in the crowds."

"No, you won't find Anna anywhere near King Edward. She doesn't rate 'im."

Silas laughed, but he wasn't really amused. Personally, he found Anna's disapproval too liberally distributed; he had realized from her tight smile that he wasn't always welcome at Beaumont Lane when Eve wasn't there. It didn't surprise him now to hear that the king was on her blacklist too.

"She thinks 'e should 'ave brought t'queen, for a start. And she doesn't like what she's read about 'im. Y'know, t'way 'e carries on."

Silas shrugged. "He can do as he pleases."

"Aye well, and so can Anna. She's with Amos, I think."

"Ah, yes, Comrade Sykes. Another one unlikely to cheer the king, I should imagine."

This casual derision played uneasily with Eve; Silas knew so little about any of them that to mock seemed hardly appropriate. But she let it pass, because he was smiling and seemed to mean no harm and because his presence in her kitchen still seemed nothing short of miraculous. They looked at each other for a moment, seeing in each other's faces the similarity to themselves. With his fine clothes and well-modulated voice he might have been called an imposter, except for this startling resemblance to his sister. They could have been twins, Eve and Silas, everyone said so, and once there'd been five of them, all with the same fine features and dark eyes: Eve, the oldest, then Silas, then the little ones, Clara, Michael, and Thomas. Not much more than babies really, when they died, all of them under three years old. Looking at Silas now called them to mind: Clara would have been seventeen in November, Eve thought. She could see the little girl in her brother, though by the end Clara had been drawn and hollow-eyed with hunger and sickness. How good life had been to Silas, and to her: how bitterly cruel the fate of their siblings. The unfulfilled promise of those three little souls, the injustice to them of a life denied, weighed heavily on Eve now as she contemplated her own advantages, and those of her affluent, debonair brother.

"Do you think about Grangely?" she said. "Do you think about t'bairns?"

Silas shifted slightly, folded his arms. The past was hostile terrain, best left alone; he hadn't expected the question and didn't much like it. No, never, would have been the honest answer, but he knew how that would sound.

"Do you?" he said instead.

"Aye. I wish I could have another chance. Now that I'm not a child myself."

"You did your best. We both did."

She dismissed his platitude with the wave of a hand. "We knew nowt," she said.

"Evie, we were orphans. We're lucky to be here to tell the tale ourselves. And it's gone now, it's the past." Truly, he was bewildered at her train of thought. "What's got into you?"

She couldn't say for sure. The sorrows of Grangely were long ago, the wounding sharpness of their memory dulled by the passing of time; she remembered the past, of course she did, but only rarely and not in detail. But then along came Silas, and she saw in his face the faces of the little ones and she recalled the horror, the misplaced faith in their eyes, that she, their big sister, would help them get better. She'd spoken to Daniel about this but she couldn't, she now found, talk to Silas. She wondered if he found it painful, recalling the past; she wondered if his memories were the same as her own. But there he stood in his natty linen suit and hat, soaked to the skin but caring nothing for it, and he seemed the very image of insouciance. Eve suppressed the stirrings of disappointment and smiled at him: least said, she thought, soonest mended.

"Let's 'ave a brew. Then I'd best get back to work."

"Now you're talking," he said.

At five o' clock Parkinson came downstairs with a request for beef tea for the ladies of the royal party. They were chilled, he said, after the drama of their drenching, and the countess was concerned that they should ward off any ills to which extreme dampness might make them susceptible. The tea was to be served warm, not hot, and in glasses, not cups, and they should be taken upstairs to the ladies' bedrooms. It wasn't an unreasonable request, although the kitchen was at full stretch and in something of a panic because Mrs. Adams hadn't been seen for who knew how long. Parkinson had no patience with the garbled explanations of a kitchen maid; she should leave off podding peas, he said, and busy herself with the broth for upstairs. He had too much to be getting on with himself, he said, to worry about what was happening in the kitchen. Mrs. Powell-Hughes and five ropes of plaited orchids were waiting for him in the dining room. He left, the soles of his immaculate black shoes clip-clopping briskly up the back stairs. Eve met him at the top, narrowly missing a collision with the baize door, which swung open with violent purpose just as she reached it. He strode past without seeming to see her: it was unlike him. Parkinson, gravely formal as his position demanded, nevertheless usually showed a glimmer of good humor and kindness beneath his butler's veneer. Not today, however. It boded ill, thought Eve as she descended to the kitchens and, indeed, she was accosted the moment she walked in by the kitchen maid still dithering at the foot of the stairs.

"Mrs. Adams can't be found and I've them peas to pod but Mr. Parkinson said I must make beef tea," said the kitchen maid, throwing herself on the mercy of the first available authority figure. Eve knew some of the kitchen staff here, but not this one. The girl had the blank, helpless gaze of a sheep, and she held it steadily on Eve as she waited to be told what to do.

"What do they call you?" Eve said.

"Ivy Ramsbottom, ma'am."

"Right, Ivy. You'll find beef tea in a jar at the back of t'cold store and it's a job of only minutes to warm it through and send it upstairs. Get on with it. T'peas'll wait while you're done."

Grateful for the direction, Ivy trotted off toward the cold larder. Eve passed through the kitchen to her own corner, which she found as she'd left it, wiped down and orderly, the pudding tins stacked together in a heap, her own beef dripping brought from home in a jug and her apron hanging on a peg alongside the thick white oven cloths. Eve took it down now and put it on and as she did so the kitchen rang out with a spectral wail, an unearthly sound that stopped the busy kitchen like a sorcerer's spell; undercooks, kitchen maids, and scullions ceased their peeling, chopping, and stirring and listened, appalled, to this certain harbinger of tragedy. Into the frozen tableau stumbled Ivy, perhaps of all the staff the least equal to what had now befallen her. Her ovine face was drained of all color and horrified panic lit her eyes, which darted about the assembled company in search of sympathy, alighting finally on Eve.

"Mrs. Adams," said Ivy, in a small voice.

"Speak up, Ivy," Eve said. "And tell us what you mean to say."

"She's—I think she's—"

"Where's Mrs. Adams?" Eve said, with more patience than she felt. This did not seem, to her, to be a kitchen that was ready to serve the king.

"In t'larder," said Ivy, more clearly. "But I think she's dead."

Chapter 12

Mary Adams was down on the stone floor like a felled oak, face up, arms outstretched to the sides, legs straight and modestly covered by her voluminous skirts, which seemed tidily arranged as if she'd been laid out for public viewing. Eve, squeezing in beside her, bent down and gently touched the cook's cheek: cold. How long had she lain here? Her face, jowly and bloated as it ever was, had lost its crimson complexion and had a ghastly pallor, the color of wet snow. Ivy's keening had been joined by that of others, inspired more by duty than emotion, because Mrs. Adams had few actual friends below stairs. She was too sharp too often, and always forgot to temper the vinegar with honey. Eve stood. Next in line in the kitchen hierarchy was Sarah Pickersgill, undercook, who stood at the front of a small crowd at the larder door. She and Eve looked at each other.

"What will we do?" Sarah said.

Eve frowned. "We?" she said.

"I can't manage without Mrs. Adams. She did everything."

"But, Sarah, it's nigh on 'alf past five. You must be all but ready?"

Sarah shook her head, sorrowfully, an apology forming in her eyes.

"She never let me do all that much," she said.

This, Eve knew, was true. She'd worked in these kitchens before, had seen how things were; Mrs. Adams did the lion's share, delegating only menial or tedious jobs to her staff. Eve could well imagine that Sarah Pickersgill had spent her years here peeling, blanching, and parboiling. It wasn't so much that Mary Adams had no confidence in anyone else: more that she knew she could always do better. Eve had watched her in action and had recognized the symptoms; relinquishing control was an art she had had to learn herself and it didn't come easily to capable women, however busy they might be and however much they might stand to benefit by delegating tasks.

"Well, this is a pickle," she said. "What's on t'menu?"

Being there only for the Yorkshire puddings, she hadn't paid much attention to everything else. Sarah, allowing herself to take enormous hope from Eve's question, said: "It's ten courses, but nowt too fancy. Mrs. Adams said it was a rum do, giving curd tarts and such like to t'king."

Eve was feeling a little faint. Ten courses, the king upstairs expecting to sit down at eight for dinner, and no one in the collection of anxious faces before her who seemed willing or capable of taking the helm.

"Right. Mrs. Adams must've written it down somewhere. Find it and show me. Then we need to find out who's done what and what's still to be done." She caught the eye of a kitchen lad skulking about the margins of the room. "You," she said, startling him witless, "run to t'coachman with a message from me. Tell 'im Mrs. Adams 'as died"—she paused momentarily and swallowed—"and we need Ginger Timpson, Nellie Kay, and Alice Buckle. Tell 'im it's urgent and 'e must fetch 'em as soon as 'e can."

The lad darted off. This was drama indeed, and here he

was, at the heart of it. Eve, still in the cold store with Mrs. Adams, reached across her and took up a jar of beef tea, which she passed to Ivy.

"Get on with this, Ivy. Stand it in a pan of 'ot water until it's warmed through, then find an 'ousemaid to take it up. Step lively."

Ivy turned, clutching the jar against her chest with two hands as if she had the cook's remains in her safekeeping, and the small crowd parted to let her through.

"Mrs. Adams, may she rest in peace, is goin' to 'ave to stay 'ere until we get this dinner on t'table," Eve said. "I know it's a bad business, but she of all folk would understand. Now, get back to whatever you were doin' an' I'll be around in a minute with more jobs for you all."

They dispersed as one; if Mary Adams had dinned anything into their heads, it was to respond quickly to an authoritative voice. Eve picked up the two large jugs of pudding batter that she'd left there to rest earlier in the day, then she stepped gingerly around the corpse and closed the door on her, as quietly and respectfully as she could.

Upstairs the family and all the guests were safely in their rooms bathing and dressing: cocktails at half past six, the countess had said, and no one should dress too formally since this was their home for the next few days and she wanted everyone to be comfortable. No one would pay any heed to her advice and nor would she expect them to: comparing diamonds was as much a country sport as hunting, shooting, and fishing. Henrietta explained this quietly to Thea as she accompanied her up the staircase.

"What an absolute gas," said Thea. "So we all agree to dress down, then go upstairs and do just the opposite?"

It struck Henry that a handbook should be written in order that innocents like Thea might learn to extrapolate what was meant from what was said on evenings such as the one before them.

"Quite. And ordinarily my mother would sparkle brighter than everyone. But tonight we have the fascinating Mrs. Keppel, and who knows with what jewels she'll be adorned." Henrietta lingered outside Thea's door and lowered her voice to a barely audible whisper. "Was it just me, or was her wet chiffon transparent?"

Thea giggled. "Put it this way, we saw more of Mrs. Keppel than she saw of us," she said and they fell together, joined by mutual mirth, shaking with silent laughter.

News of Mrs. Adams's demise was still not widely known. Parkinson and Mrs. Powell-Hughes were blissfully ignorant as they went about their business, which for the time being was applying finishing touches to the dining room; the dinner menu might be old-fashioned Yorkshire fare, but there was nothing plain about the table, which might have been set by forest sprites, such was its sylvan charm. The orchid ropes ran not only down the center of the table but also around its outside edge in a fragrant abundance of purple and cream. White roses dripped from the fluted lips of slender silver vases and the audacious, surprising blue of delphiniums adorned a central candelabrum. They worked in silence, but the butler and the housekeeper were still able, by the merest occasional twitch of the features, to share with each other their mutual disapproval of the extraordinary arrival of the king and his cohorts—the gentlemen roaring with laughter, water running from the folds of the ladies' dresses, and the little dog Caesar tearing about as if his ambition was to leave footprints on every square inch of the floor. Mrs. Powell-Hughes hated Caesar already. He wore a silver tag that declared: "I am Caesar. I belong to the king," but he barely needed the identification. Here was an animal upon which no discipline had ever been properly imposed. Your home is my home, he seemed to say, and if I wish to cock my leg against your furniture, I shall.

The disarray had been dealt with, but it was impossible—and unthinkable—to audibly articulate the complex mix of punctured excitement and injured pride felt by the Netherwood staff who had assembled in two respectful lines to greet the king, only to be entirely overlooked in the pandemonium that accompanied his arrival. No hands were shaken, no curtsys acknowledged: the very moment the king burst in, Lord Netherwood began snapping his fingers at the valets and housemaids, urging them to fetch this or take that, until the receiving lines were entirely dismantled and the servants had to hurry about their extra duties in the most disappointing, deflating fashion.

"Staff dinner almost an hour late now" was all Mrs. Powell-Hughes would allow herself to say to Parkinson as together they left the dining room and took the servants' staircase down to the kitchen. And then, of course, she learned that a delayed dinner was the least of the difficulties below stairs, because there was Eve Williams where Mrs. Adams generally stood, expertly seasoning three five-rib roasts with pepper and thyme, while the cook lay quite dead in the cold store.

The cavalry arrived in the form of Ginger and Nellie but not Alice; Jonas had forbidden his wife to come—his own tea wasn't on the table yet and he reckoned that trumped the king's dinner—so Ginger had the coachman stop at Watson Street for Nellie, then hotfoot it back to Netherwood Hall. They were ready for action in their pinafores, Eve's right-hand women, sitting in one of the earl's carriages with an aura about them of great importance. In the kitchen they were greeted with a smile and a nod, but there was too much to do to give any time to pleasantries. The beef was in, and there were plum puddings rattling on their trivets on the range. A scribbled menu in Mrs. Adams's near-illegible hand was now in Eve's possession, though she had made a small alteration to the running order; her Yorkshire puddings would be served as a course in their own right, before the rib of beef and after the pea and bacon soup. It seemed only fair, thought Eve, that they should take center stage, since they had lured the king to Netherwood in the first place. A good, thick onion gravy would accompany each pudding, served in sweet little individual brass pitchers that Eve had found, dusty and forgotten, stacked in a cupboard. Ivy, shaking slightly and still pasty with shock, was currently preparing them for use, rubbing them with rock alum, buffing them until they shone with the brilliance of solid gold. Nellie was making custard for the plum puddings and had taken over the claret gravy for the beef, too. Ginger was on hollandaise for the salmon fishcakes, and had moved in on the curd tart: Sarah Pickersgill, who had been about to make a start, had been happy to give way, fetching fresh curds from the dairy for Ginger, then busying herself soaking currants in rum, the sort of simple task she enjoyed most. No wonder Mary Adams had dropped down dead, thought Eve: the miracle was that it hadn't happened sooner. There wasn't a dish of food left this kitchen that Mrs. Adams hadn't had a hand in. Perhaps the strain of performing this feat day in, day out—and, ultimately, terrifyingly, for the reigning monarch—had in the end proved fatal.

"Do you think a woman could cook 'erself to death?" Eve asked Nellie, who had just enveloped them both in meaty steam by adding wine to a pan of bubbling beef juices.

Nellie sniffed judgmentally. "It were fat killed Mary Adams, you mark my words," she said. "She fair fills that larder floor. I 'ope t'undertaker 'as plenty 'o timber because she'll take some boxing."

"Always a good spread here. House of plenty, this one."

The Duke of Knightwick, sitting next to Thea Sterling, patted his pot belly with both hands as if to show her where the food was going.

"Y'see, you can't always rely on these great houses," he continued. Thea, not very fascinated, glanced at Tobias to see if he was still watching her. He was. "At Chatsworth one year"— the duke lowered his voice now as if the Devonshires, who were safely at home in their Derbyshire pile, might be straining to eavesdrop—"the snipe ran short and there were no apologies. None at all. I was given half a bird. Imagine!"

Thea smiled, shook her head in a parody of astonishment, and tried to imagine half a snipe but found she couldn't even picture a whole one. She added "snipe" to her mental list of things to look up in the English dictionary back in her room.

"I mean to say," said the duke, "I'll share most things with any man, even my wife, but I won't be made to share a snipe!" He roared with laughter at his own wit while opposite and along, the Duchess of Knightwick raised a knowing, saucy eyebrow at Sir Wally Goldman. Extraordinary, thought Thea. She cut another glance at Tobias, who caught it and smiled at her. He would be accused of neglecting his neighbors at this rate. She was pleased, though, even as she looked away.

Parkinson stepped into the room, followed by a slick procession of footmen bearing in each of their hands a silver-domed platter. The king sat up in his chair with a boyish enthusiasm for what was to come, and conversation, while not entirely ceasing, dropped to a few murmured exchanges. The footmen slid soundlessly around the table, sharing themselves one between two, and then in perfect synchronicity they placed the platters in a precise and measured fashion onto the table before the diners. A barely discernible tilt of the head from Parkinson, and the domes were raised in beautiful unison, revealing small tureens of the sort of pea and bacon soup that was commonplace all over Netherwood town, but an extraordinary novelty here.

The monarch, watched in varying degrees of fondness by the whole table, dipped his great head like an inquisitive bear and took a deep, impolite, appreciative sniff of the vapors that rose from the bowl. His face registered great pleasure and the countess allowed herself a small frisson of satisfaction: triumph was in the air. The king smiled at Clarissa, lifted his spoon, and began to eat.

Chapter 13

Anna regarded Silas coolly. He wasn't looking at her, but was reading the newspaper she'd bought earlier, scouring the business pages for, he said, news of his investments. He whistled as he read, the implication being that his shares were high or—perhaps—that high or low, it was all the same to him. Anna didn't ask. There was a quality about Silas that she found hard to define but which made her determined to resist him. It was late, and she wished he would go. She sat at the sewing machine and concentrated on the fabric in her hands; it was a new bolt of cloth, a jacquard weave, richly patterned in shades of blue from cornflower through to dove gray, the different colors of the summer sky. Anna spent more time in the draper's than in any other shop in Netherwood. The smell of new fabric lured her just as surely as others were drawn to the aroma of baking bread. She loved the possibilities, the potential, of the cloth: the linens, silks, chintzes, brocades, velvets, and damasks. In the shady privacy between the shelves of fabric rolls she imagined Ravenscliffe draped and upholstered, enhanced and embellished by the curtains and covers she planned to make. The cloth she held now was destined for a large window on a half-landing where the staircase turned an elegant forty-five-degree angle before making its final flight. Anna raised a corner of the cloth to her face and inhaled surreptitiously, smelling its newness, feeling the texture of the weave against her cheek, and when she lowered it Silas was watching her with a smirk on his face.

"What?" she said, feeling caught out, defensive.

"Nothing." Silas returned his gaze to the newspaper. He knew Anna's story—the eviction from her miserable home in Grangely, the death of her wretched Russian husband, the kindness of the meddling Methodist minister who brought her to Netherwood to lodge here in Beaumont Lane—but he didn't quite understand why, when she was clearly back on her feet, she was still living cheek by jowl with his sister. He'd asked Eve, and she'd looked puzzled by the question. It's her home, Evie had said; she lives here. Her tone, though friendly, invited no further discussion and Silas had let the matter drop. Odd business though, he thought: there wasn't a person on God's green earth with whom Silas could share such close quarters without being driven to madness or murder.

He was waiting, now, for his sister to come home. Anna wished he would go, but word had spread—as word always did—that the cook had dropped dead and so Silas wanted the full story before returning to his rooms. It maddened Anna that suddenly Eve—what she did, what she said, where she was—was Silas's business. She suspected herself of childish jealousy and tried hard to fight it, and yet here was this stranger, landed among them with tales of the world and his own wonderful success, and Anna—who, goodness knows, had been a stranger to Netherwood herself not so very long ago—found him hard to believe in. Not the reality of him, or his claim on Eve; no one could look at the two of them together and doubt they were siblings. Rather, it was a subtle, unsettling concern, hard for her to express in English, though she'd tried, earlier this afternoon, sitting in the allotment with Amos, sheltering from the downpour under an old green umbrella that for the past three weeks had been needed solely for shade from the sun. The two of them had been avoiding the royal arrival—Amos thought the king a scandalous drain on the nation's coffers, Anna thought him merely scandalous—but it had been Silas Whittam on Anna's mind as they bided their time in the deluge.

"He's too . . . too sure of himself and too . . . ah, what is word?"

"Good to be true?" said Amos, who didn't mind Silas but could see that the wonder of him might wear thin if you were too long in his company.

"That, yes. But also he is too often blowing his trumpet."

Amos didn't laugh or correct her because he could see how serious Anna was. It troubled her, he knew, that her response to Silas was so different from Eve's.

"Aye well, 'appen folk'll tire o' listenin'. No point blowin' a trumpet when you've lost yer audience."

Anna picked up a twig and began to draw it through the earth. Much as it craved the rain, the sun-baked soil was slow to absorb it; water collected in the track she made, forming a miniature canal as it followed the trail left by her stick.

"When he first came, he seemed interesting. Not many people I meet here have seen anything of world."

"No. Bit short of globe-trotters in our little corner," said Amos.

"But always he comes and tells stories of his great adventures and always he is great hero. It makes me . . ."

"Suspicious?"

She nodded. "Sort of. And sad," she said, "because Eve is so happy to have him here. But I don't think he's kind man, and always I'm thinking, what is it you want? Why is it you're here?" She looked at him glumly and Amos wondered, not for the first time, what she would do if he put an arm around her shoulders.

104

"Look," he said, instead. "Silas Whittam won't be around for too long if 'e's t'big shot 'e reckons to be. A man like that 'as to keep an eye on 'is business."

"This is what I think," said Anna. She fell silent for a moment, drawing now a small nine-square grid in the earth with her twig. Then she looked at Amos again.

"Unless it is business which brings him here," she said enigmatically. Then, with a conversational segue that threw him entirely, she said: "Noughts and crosses? Here,"—she gave him the twig—"you begin."

Alice Keppel entered a room as if she was walking onto a stage. When the ladies retired from the table and left the men to their port and cigars, she contrived to hang back until she could enter a drawing room that already held an audience, and when the gentlemen joined them she stood again, crossing the room to claim her king, dazzling the group, her neck adorned with diamonds, her earlobes dripping with them, and her voluptuous curves close-clad in a shimmering silver gown. The king watched her with his lascivious, hooded eyes and it was clear to everyone that Mrs. Keppel was indispensable to him; she anticipated his needs, chivied him out of a sulk, prompted his best anecdotes, and, leaning in toward his ear, could make him either roar with laughter or glaze over with lustful desire, depending on the tone of her whispered confidences. Everyone was mesmerized by her, the women as much as the men. Lady Netherwood had been quite prepared to loathe her out of loyalty to Alexandra. But now, the very evening of Mrs. Keppel's arrival at Netherwood Hall, she and the countess were cozy together on the chaise longue, exchanging compliments and court gossip and the queen was quite forgotten: in any case, murmured Hermione Hartwick to Frank Ponsonby, Alexandra was far better off at Sandringham, where it didn't matter a jot that she was as deaf as a post, because there was no one there with anything to say worth hearing.

Bertie, on the other hand, was in fine fettle, everyone said so. Credit had to be laid at his tailor's door for his appearance; his corpulence was skillfully contained, so that his general appearance was of noble stoutness rather than obesity. He was in a cheerful frame of mind too, helped along by two good days at the races in Doncaster—not only had he backed the triumphant Pretty Polly in both the St. Leger and the Park Hill Stakes, but also all his friends had backed the wrong horses and lost their money. And now, here he was, in the bountiful home of the Earl and Countess of Netherwood, where dinner had turned out to be a sort of childhood fantasy of hearty northern fare and nursery classics. The memory of Eve's Yorkshire puddings had remained with him since he'd last eaten them, back in May. If anything, the memory had been surpassed: plain, simple, perfect. He remembered Eve, too. Flushed and harassed at the stove when he complimented her, but quite beautiful in a humble sort of way. Naturally, one wouldn't expect diamonds and décolletage in the kitchen.

"I say, Clarissa," he said now, acting on impulse and fueled by the earl's fine claret. "Let's have the little Yorkshire pudding chef up for an ovation."

"Oh, I don't think—"

The countess faltered. Summoning Eve was a foolish plan; below-stairs staff should remain so, in her view. Yet the prevailing credo of Bertie's circle was that he must not be denied, contradicted, or allowed to grow bored. Clarissa laughed lightly, playing for time.

"Come, come," said the king, not yet vexed. He looked about the drawing room and found Parkinson, respectfully alert and standing by the door. The king spoke directly to him.

106

"Fetch her up here, there's a good fellow."

Parkinson bowed. "Certainly, Your Majesty," he said. He turned and left the room, then, in the hallway, he waited. Moments later the countess appeared, as he had known she would.

"Parkinson," she said urgently. "I see no way out of this, but what on earth will Mrs. Adams think, when she was responsible for most of the dinner? It's too bad."

"I really don't think Mrs. Adams will mind, your ladyship," said Parkinson neutrally.

Lady Hoyland tutted, exasperated. "Well of course she will. You know very well how cross she's been. I saw her only this morning and she had a face like thunder."

Now is as good a time as any, thought the butler. He coughed, then spoke: "Mrs. Adams has passed away, your ladyship."

The countess stared at him, uncomprehending. He nodded somberly, keen to impress upon her the truth of his words.

"Impossible," she said, then, illogically: "When?"

"The time of death isn't entirely clear, your ladyship. Some time after afternoon tea, we believe. Certainly before dinner."

Unchecked, the countess's face registered annoyance, not sorrow.

"How utterly inconvenient. So who . . . ?"

"Mrs. Williams, your ladyship. And her fellow cooks from the old flour mill."

Lady Netherwood processed this information for a moment. Then she remembered the three evenings ahead of her, and irritation darkened her face again.

"All very well," she said, as if Parkinson deserved a reprimand. "But we can hardly let Mrs. Williams loose on the *oeufs brouillés aux truffes* and *pavé de saumon* tomorrow evening, for heaven's sake."

"Mrs. Powell-Hughes has dispatched a telegram for Monsieur

Reynard," he said. "We hope he will be with us before lunchtime tomorrow."

The butler's genuine distress at the demise of his old colleague was very evident in his expression and it was this, as well as the resolution of her immediate difficulties, that finally prompted an appropriate response from the countess. She laid a small bejeweled hand upon his black worsted sleeve.

"Dear Parkinson," she said. "How terrible this must have been for you all. And poor Mrs. Adams, lying there cold—oh goodness!" Lady Hoyland's hand came up to her mouth as another unwelcome thought occurred to her. "Where is she?"

"Currently still in the cold store, I'm afraid, your ladyship. But Jeremiah Hague has been sent for and she will be restored to dignity within the hour."

There was much that could still have been said: both of them knew it. Mary Adams had worked in the Netherwood kitchens for forty-five years, twenty of them as head cook. She had watched the earl grow from boy to man, and knew the preferences and dislikes of every member of the Hoyland family. Her death was shocking: it would shift the foundations of the way of life here. But both countess and butler understood perfectly that time was pressing; the hostess had been absent from her exalted guest for too long. Parkinson, dismissed by a silent nod, took the back stairs down to the kitchens to deliver the unwelcome news to Eve that she was wanted by the king, and Lady Netherwood returned to the drawing room to find that in fact she hadn't been missed at all. On the contrary, she entered the room unnoticed because the king had Caesar on his lap with Mrs. Keppel's diamond choker around the dog's neck, which would have been entertaining enough, but there was Mrs. Keppel, feigning outrage and demanding in exchange the leather collar with its silver name tag. The countess slipped easily into the body of the merry throng. She felt calm and composed, in spite of the tragedy below stairs, and this, she knew, was because Parkinson and Mrs. Powell-Hughes were such pillars of dependability. How blessed she was, she thought, in her household staff: how very well they served her. She began to laugh merrily at the antics of the king and his mistress, along with everyone else: to appear conspicuously solemn would have been unforgivable, a dereliction of duty. Clarissa Hoyland could never be accused of that.

Eve endured fifteen minutes in the gilded drawing room, the center of attention of everyone in it. She accepted the compliments heaped upon her by the king, blushed furiously—to her enduring annoyance—when he remarked on her beauty in the most condescending terms to the room in general, then she found herself listening, appalled, to his insistence that she travel with them in the royal train in order to continue to cook for him in the royal palaces. There was a heavy silence when he ceased speaking. It was not at all the thing, even for a monarch, to pluck staff willy-nilly from the homes of his friends. The king, however, looked expectantly at Eve. He was drunk, but still cheerfully so, and the room held its breath: the wrong answer from this young woman before them could alter the whole tenor of the evening.

"Thank you, Your Majesty," she said. "You're very kind, and I'm very flattered. But I can't accept, I'm so sorry."

She was looking directly at him and she spoke clearly, quite unafraid. He gave a short bark of laughter.

"I see. And why not, pray?"

"Because Netherwood is my 'ome, Your Majesty. And I'm soon to be married."

The earl and countess exchanged a look: this was news to

them. Lady Netherwood leaned into her husband and whispered: "Has she asked our permission?" and he said: "She doesn't need it, Clarissa, she's not ours." Meanwhile the king, pouting a little, was looking perilously close to falling out of humor. Eve, aware that denying a monarch's request was a hazardous business, continued to speak.

"But I shall cook for you, Your Majesty, whenever you visit the earl and countess, if it pleases you, Your Majesty."

This was well said, respectful and earnest. Lord Netherwood felt a wash of pride in Eve that was almost paternal. Like a break in a bank of gathering clouds, the king's countenance cleared and he allowed his attention to be diverted elsewhere. Eve, no longer required, backed from the room feeling a little as if she was retreating, miraculously unscathed, from a bear pit.

She rode home in the carriage with Nellie and Ginger; they spoke very little, all of them exhausted and somewhat stunned at the evening's course of events. Eve, sitting opposite the other two women, could see in their faces the triumph of a job well done, burning bright beneath their weariness. Herself, she felt deflated and dispirited. Seeing the king, rosy and loose-tongued with wine, petulant as a spoiled child, had seemed to Eve to somehow reduce their valiant efforts in the kitchen to the mere indulgence of the already over-indulged. She pressed her forehead against the cold glass of the carriage window and, as she did, she saw they were rattling past the gardener's cottage, Daniel's house. There was the ethereal glow of yellow lamplight in the bedroom window, and Eve imagined the bliss of joining him there now, and losing herself in his arms. She was suddenly struck at the cruel injustice of him lying alone in his bed while she sped by on her way to her family. She hadn't done right by him since he came all this way to Netherwood for her, she thought now with a sudden pang of conscience. She treated him as the last in a long list of more pressing concerns. He deserved better, she told herself, remorsefully. She would make amends. She would begin tomorrow.

Chapter 14

"What do you say to a trip down one of your mines, Teddy, old boy?"

This was the king, mouth full of roast woodcock, catching the earl completely unawares. Sarah Pickersgill, after a sleepless night, had proved herself capable of more than she thought and had cooked twenty woodcocks, twenty veal chops, and fifteen smoked herrings on a spit while supervising the preparation of eggs—scrambled, fried, and coddled—bacon, and tomatoes. It was all delicious and Parkinson warmed her heart by saying that the famous Monsieur Reynard would find a capable second-in-command when he arrived later in the day. Currently, the king was gorging himself on meat and sharing it occasionally with Caesar, who sat on the floor by his master's chair; it was a mercy, thought Lord Netherwood, that the terrier didn't require his own seat. The earl bit into a piece of toast in a ruminative way, then chewed and swallowed before replying to the question, giving himself time to collect his wits. He would have liked to say that a colliery was a place of industry, not a destination for idle sightseeing; however, he didn't.

"Certainly, sir." He had found himself unable—and even,

112

somehow, unqualified—to call the king Bertie, and no one said Edward. One or two of the royal party referred to him affectionately as Tum-Tum, but this was a familiarity too far, in the earl's opinion. Clarissa, at their mutual debriefing in her rooms last night, had told him he sounded obsequious with his "Your Majesty" this and "sir" that, but truly the earl could take no other path: he felt he barely knew the king, and what he did know, he didn't much admire. Now he had to attempt to talk him out of a preposterous suggestion without giving offense. Conversation with the king, he was finding, had something of the dangerous quality of a high-wire act: one wrong step spelled disaster. "Although," he continued carefully, "I know Clarissa has a full day's sport planned for the gentlemen. A grouse drive for the shots among us. Cricket. Tennis. A little croquet. However, if you prefer . . ."

"Tomorrow then," said the king brusquely. "It's settled. Anyone care to accompany?" He looked around at his fellow diners, who were very few at this hour. Lady Netherwood rarely emerged from her room before eleven in the morning, preferring to take breakfast in bed, and she had encouraged the female guests to do the same, although Thea Sterling and Henrietta were at the table, having agreed to ride out with Tobias and Dickie before nine. Joseph Choate, the American ambassador, was present, as was Frank Ponsonby and the Duke of Knightwick. His Duchess was absent and, one couldn't help but notice, so was Sir Wally. Poor show, thought the earl.

"Oh sure," said Thea unexpectedly. "Count me in."

The earl looked aghast but the king beamed. He loved a tomboy, and this young woman seemed game for a good time. She'd been somewhat the star of the show last night; she had produced a gramophone record and popped it on just as the gathering was beginning to droop. It was an extraordinary, foot-tapping, syncopated something-or-other, music from the wrong side of the tracks, Thea had said. The king had danced with her, doing exactly as she told him; then Alice had cut in and Thea had hauled Tobias to his feet and the pair of them had cut quite a dash, dancing as if they'd had a bit of practice together.

"Splendid," the king said to her, and she nodded at him pleasantly as she carried on eating, balancing bacon on a piece of toast and carrying it up to her mouth without recourse to cutlery. Watching her, the earl wondered if she knew quite in whose company she was breakfasting. She was more at ease than anyone else in the party, and she flouted the rules of English etiquette with such supreme grace and style that Teddy suspected they'd all be copying her before the visit was over.

"Me too, please," piped up Henrietta. Her father cut her a disapproving look. She was taking advantage of the situation, having begged him, often and to no avail, to take her in a cage down a mineshaft.

The king laughed. "Just the girls and myself, then, eh?" at which cue, Frank Ponsonby declared himself available, as did Tobias, eagerly and with great gusto; he had shunned countless entreaties from the earl to show an interest in the collieries, yet now, this morning, he simply couldn't wait. The earl and Henrietta, united—if only briefly—in their derision, shared a smile across the table.

"Well," said Lord Netherwood, determined still to impose some order and authority on this plan, "I'll see what can be done. Ladies, you can certainly visit the colliery yard, and, Your Majesty, I shall arrange for a—"

"Oh no you don't," said Thea perkily, wagging a forefinger at him. "We go where the boys go, don't we, Henry?"

"Certainly we do," said Henrietta, nipping in before her father could stop her. "Helmets all around; can't see a problem."

Dickie said: "It'll be dark, noisy, and dull, I'll wager. I shan't go."

Henrietta smiled fondly at him.

"Dear Dickie," she said. "Such a spirit of adventure! Such curiosity about the world!"

He looked at her with placid eyes. There was never any baiting him.

"I'd rather shoot, that's all," he said mildly. "I'd always rather shoot than almost anything else."

The king signaled for more woodcock. Two, he found, were never enough.

"One can shoot anywhere," he said, to the gathering in general. "But only in Netherwood can one mine for coal."

Silas Whittam was on his way to the railway station when he encountered Jem Arkwright, heading in the same direction. They nodded at each other and Silas fell into step with him, pleased at the opportunity to talk to the earl's land agent: he was a useful man to know, Silas had worked that out within a day or two of arriving in Netherwood. It was a skill of his, weeding out the wheat from the chaff, and part of the secret of his success. Silas couldn't care less if someone was decent, kind, honorable, honest; the only quality he looked for in a new acquaintance was the extent of their usefulness to him. Jem, with his knowledge of land prices, his understanding of the market, his instinct for a good deal, was very much Silas's kind of chap.

"Off again then," said Jem, and it was a statement, not a question.

"Briefly. Back to Bristol for a few days. The fleet's due in tomorrow and I need to be there to check the cargo."

This was untrue, in fact: not that the ships were due—they were—but that he had to be there. Hugh Oliver, his deputy at Whittam & Co., was more than capable of managing without him, but Silas had decided that a few days back in Bristol would be preferable to being obliged to help Eve with the dreary upheaval of moving house. Let the Scotsman do the heavy lifting: he himself had no wish to be involved in any of it. Rather, he thought he'd like to return when she was nicely ensconced in the lovely house up on the common. Her sharp-tongued shadow, Anna Rabinovich, had given him a sideways look when he made his sorrowful apologies, and he had smiled pleasantly at her, which was his favored method of attack.

"Bananas, in't it?" said Jem pithily.

"It is. Fascinating trade, and demand's increasing all the time. I say, are you heading for the station too?"

Jem shook his head. "New Mill," he said.

"Shame. We could've talked on the train."

"Oh aye? About what?" The land agent eyed Silas cautiously. He was wearing a three-piece suit and a Homburg hat and by his side, in breeches and a collarless shirt, Jem felt very much the workingman. He doubted they had anything much in common.

"Well." Silas looked about him before he continued. "I was thinking of sinking a mine."

Jem hadn't known what he expected this dandified brother of Eve Williams to say, but it certainly wasn't that. Not that he betrayed any surprise in his response. "Oh aye," he said, as if Silas had said he was thinking of buying a loaf of bread.

"I need my own supply of bunker fuel for the ships. Makes no sense, dealing out hard-earned money to feed the beasts when I could be producing my own. And with the proposed expansion of the fleet . . ."

He tailed off, expecting some interest from Jem, but the man strode along silently beside him. Unless a direct question had been asked, Jem Arkwright saw no reason to speak.

"So," said Silas, as this fact dawned on him. "I'm after a prime piece of land where a shaft might be sunk. Wondered if you might have some suggestions. Have you heard of anything likely? On the grapevine, as it were?"

"No," said Jem bluntly. He didn't much like the volley of questions, or the familiarity implied by them. Also, the earl's interests—always paramount in the thoughts of his land agent—seemed vaguely under threat from this newcomer. Jem, devoted to the earl and the preservation of his prosperity, was inclined to throw him off the scent.

"No," he said again. "An' there's no point pursuin' it, if you want my view. This part o' Yorkshire's bristlin' wi' windin' gear as it is. There's been no new mine sunk for nigh on forty years. You'd be wastin' your time an' your money."

"I see." Silas felt rather deflated. Jem had a dour and final manner of speaking that could make a man feel a proper fool.

"What about, perhaps, buying, just for the sake of argument, an existing colliery?" Silas spoke cautiously, as if his proposal was hypothetical: some self-protection was necessary, he felt.

"Aye, well. Different story, that," said Jem. "Course, you'd want to know why it were for sale in't first place."

"Of course," said Silas, encouraged. "Of course. There'd be no rushing into anything. And do you know of anything? For sale, I mean?"

"Aye, one or two."

"And they are?" Good God, thought Silas: blood from a stone.

"Ashton Vale's lookin' for new owners. Out by Monk Bretton, Barnsley way. An' Dreaton Main's coming up, just through Netherwood, out on Sheffield Road."

Jem lapsed back into silence. Silas, needing more, said: "So, Ashton Vale any good?"

"Terrible. Poor coal, 'ard to extract."

No harder surely, thought Silas, than it was to extract information from Jem. He chipped away with another question.

"And Dreaton Main?"

"Aye," said Jem. "Decent colliery, productive. They'll be after a good price."

Suddenly, without ceremony, Jem swung a right turn onto the track that led down to the pit yard of New Mill Colliery. Silas, surprised and more than a little put out, watched him go, then called out: "Good-bye then, Mr. Arkwright," with a noticeable edge to his voice, a slight, ironic reproof. Jem, if he picked it up at all, ignored it.

He hadn't intended any sort of slight; it was simply that when Jem's path diverged from that of the other man, he saw no reason for formalities. This was Jem's way. He had a job to do, a message to deliver to Don Manvers in the pit office, and therefore he took the New Mill road when he came upon it. Other folk might have time for farewells, but Jem never wasted his breath on them. So he thought nothing of it, and no more of Silas Whittam, as he entered the yard. It was midmorning, three hours before the end of the day shift; he could see the lads at the screens in the far shed, a few more at the mouth of the pit unloading wagons, and Wilf Barrow nodded a greeting through the open doorway of the stores, but otherwise there were few people about on the pit top. Jem thanked God, as he always did when the earl's business sent him to one of the collieries, that he wasn't a miner, that his work was outside, on the land, in daylight; he'd rather spend twelve months digging ditches in driving rain than spend a single day in a tunnel underground.

Don was at his desk, head down, poring over price lists. Best coal, seconds coal, top coal, slack, riddled slack, screen slack: all separately priced, all changing—sometimes up, often down—by the week. Whether Netherwood coal held its price at the Coal Exchange was the estate's concern, not his personal one, but Don felt the fluctuations as if his own carelessness might be the cause. So his brow was furrowed when he looked up, and he kept his place on the column of figures with an index finger, firmly planted.

"'ow do," he said, and then: "What's up now?" because Jem Arkwright rarely darkened his door, and only then when there was some kind of problem.

"Message from Lord Netherwood," said Jem, holding open the door but not coming in. "You've to smarten up t'pit yard and t'shaft bottom. T'king 'as a mind to pay a visit."

Don laughed. "Very funny."

Jem smiled grimly.

"I'm not coddin'," he said. "Tomorrow, before t'afternoon shift goes down, you'll 'ave a royal visit and 'e wants to go down t'pit. So, daft as it sounds, you mun get them lads off them screens, and give 'em a broom each. There's tins o' white-wash coming' up on a cart, and some planted tubs. Set tomorrow's day shift on wi' it an' all. T'earl says do what you 'ave to do, but get it done."

Jem retreated, closing the door on Don, and began to cross the pit yard, then stopped, came back, and stuck his head around the door again.

"There's a pile o' timber needs shiftin' out there by t'stores and summat needs to be done wi' all that rustin' iron. It's a right mess."

"It's a pit yard," said Don, but he said it to a closed door because Jem was gone.

Chapter 15

The day they moved house from Beaumont Lane to Ravens-cliffe, Seth couldn't be found. This came as no surprise to anyone, but still, the boy had to be located and Eliza was dispatched to all his usual haunts: the allotment, the railway track, Harley Hill. She stood at the top, panting with the effort of running all the way and, like a lad in the crow's nest of the sort of ship she imagined for her Uncle Silas, she turned a full circle, one flat hand shading her eyes, scanning the terrain beneath and beyond. She meandered then toward home: forgot, for a while, her mission and joined a skipping game in Allott's Way, then, remembering again, she hurried back, bursting into the upturned household with the message that Seth was nowhere.

Anna, her face obscured by the crates she carried, said: "You mean you can't find him."

"That's what I said."

"No. You said Seth was nowhere. This makes no sense."

Eliza was used to Anna's lectures in the uses and meaning of language, but even she could see that now was no time to engage in a debate. There was a high-sided dray in Watson Street by the entry, and the contents of the house were being carried out and piled onto it. Everything looked smaller outside the house than it had when it was inside, and much less comfy, thought Eliza. She watched in a detached manner as the narrow single beds and Maya's cot were brought out by two bulky men whose arms, thick as hams, made light work of their humble sticks of furniture. The painted frames of the beds were chipped with age and use and the coiled springs of their bases dropped flakes of rust as they went. Eliza pulled a face and Eve saw it.

"I 'ope t'wind doesn't change," she said, and Eliza immediately, obligingly, rearranged her features into a smile. Eve deposited a bundle of braided rag rugs and smiled back at her daughter.

"No sign o' Seth then?" she said.

"No."

"Oh well, 'appen 'e'll show up when all this lifting's done." She kept her voice deliberately bright and cheerful so as not to frighten Eliza.

"Mam?"

"Yes?"

"Will Mr. MacLeod be living with us?"

"I think you should call 'im Daniel. And yes, of course, after we're wed, 'e'll be living with us." Eve had sat her children down at the kitchen table the night before and told them that a date had at last been set for her wedding to Daniel and that she knew—she would make sure of this, she said—that they were all going to be very happy. Seth had taken the news surprisingly stoically: unsmiling but without fireworks. Still, thought Eve, his absence now would almost certainly be connected. The boy had known for weeks about the wedding, but without a date it had perhaps seemed more of an idea than a reality. She wouldn't get off lightly, that much she knew.

"Good. I like 'im," said Eliza with her blessed, uncomplicated enthusiasm. "And will I be a bridesmaid?"

"Well, of course. And Ellen and Maya." She lowered her voice and leaned close to her daughter's ear. "Anna looks busy now," she said confidingly, "but actually she's thinking about the beautiful dress she's going to make for you to wear."

Eliza shone with joy. The little girl was as light as her brother was dark, thought Eve. She bestowed her approval readily, welcoming new people into her circle of friends with an ease and an interest that kept them there, out of love for her. When Anna and Maya had first come to live with them, Eliza had been instantly glad: the more the merrier, seemed to be her life philosophy. If she had to share her bedroom with a perfect stranger and her fretful baby, it may as well be done with good grace, was Eliza's view. Now she had made room in her affections for Uncle Silas with no more fuss than if she had bunched up on a tram seat to let him sit down: and Daniel, whom she had barely had chance to get to know, was accepted too. He had given her a flower press and stolen her heart. It was that easy with Eliza.

Seth, though: Eve was close to accepting that he was beyond her influence. He liked Silas—well, he was hard to resist—and he loved Amos, but fiercely, defensively, privately. Daniel, on the few occasions she had managed to keep Seth in the same room, was treated with open hostility, breathtaking rudeness, the sort of behavior, really, that deserved a clout, but how would that help? You couldn't beat a lad into liking someone, and anyway Eve understood that Seth was clinging to his dead father's memory, as if by admitting Daniel into the family, Arthur would be forgotten. She felt a fool for thinking that because Daniel was a gardener, Seth would be all lively interest: a picture of them in her mind, working side by side at some planting scheme or other, seemed fanciful now. Seth had taken his gift from Daniel—a beautiful, illustrated book about the travels of John Tradescant—and placed it on the kitchen table, pointedly, without opening it. It had stayed there, too, until Eve had packed it with Seth's things this morning.

"Ignore him," was Anna's counsel to Eve and Daniel. "He was same to me—cold, cross, always with scowl. But now he is right as rain. Worst thing is if you try too hard with Seth. Treat him like wild animal. Let him come to you."

This was sound advice, borne out by experience; time would overcome Seth's reservations, Eve was sure of it. But still she wished he didn't have to make things so difficult. She walked back up the entry to the back door of her house to collect another load, passing Anna, who staggered in the opposite direction with a crate of crockery. They exchanged a look, eyebrows raised, smiles rueful; they had their work cut out today. Silas had been called away on business—dreadful timing, but unavoidable, he'd said; Daniel, Eve knew, would come when he could. She had splurged on a moving firm from Barnsley to shift the heavy furniture, and the silent men they'd sent on the dray were making quick work of all that, but she insisted that the trappings of the kitchen were packed and loaded by herself and Anna; what would two men with more brawn than brains know about the importance of keeping like with like from the kitchen cupboards and shelves? And those hands: fingers like butchers' sausages that could crush a teacup and barely feel it go. She nodded at Lilly Pickering and Maud Platt, side by side on Maud's back doorstep, watching with pursed lips and folded arms the spectacle of Eve Williams officially getting above herself. She could've used Sol Windross's rag-and-bone cart for her few bits of furniture, but no—Chandler's Removals, no less. And her departure from Beaumont Lane was insulting, in their view: a slap in the face to her neighbors. They glowered as they sat in judgment, united in their verdict, but Eve, used to ignoring their naked disapproval, found she had no difficulty in doing so again. You could spend your whole life trying to please the likes of Lilly and still get nowhere. Give her a gold pig, Arthur used to say, and it'd be the wrong color.

The countess was sitting in the rose garden alone when Daniel appeared. He had come to assess the damage inflicted by three weeks of unabated sunshine followed by a torrent of rain, which had fallen on the flowerbeds and shrubberies like the wrath of God. The roses, at least, were already nearly over anyway. There were more than two hundred varieties here; the collection had been started by an earlier countess whose French ancestry had led her, rather scandalously, to visit Josephine Bonaparte at Malmaison. The ambitions of the empress, the scope of her famous rose gardens, had thus traveled back across the English Channel to Netherwood.

"You've kept a secret from me," the countess said to Daniel, with no preamble or pleasantry. She had been looking for him since yesterday morning in order to effect a chance encounter.

He was startled to see her at this early hour. She looked fragile and pale, not out of place among these tired roses; her fine cotton lawn gown, gauzy layers of pale pink, seemed insubstantial against the chill. The temperature, since the rain, had dropped to something more typical of the time of year. Lady Netherwood looked at him; her tone had been jocular but her expression was accusatory.

"Och well, I keep a fair few secrets from you, your ladyship," he said, unfazed. "Which of them have you discovered?" He had never developed the habit of dipping his head in the company of greatness. He looked her directly in the eye when he spoke, as he did to all members of the family. They had a gardener in Daniel MacLeod, but they did not have a servant.

She pouted at him. "You know very well," she said. "You're to marry Eve Williams. And since you've been here barely a month, I can only assume that was already your intention when you accepted my offer of employment here."

"Correct," he said. "I came here to be your head gardener and to marry Eve."

"You should have told me."

"Should I? Forgive me, but I do think whether and to whom I get married is my business."

"You're very impertinent. No one speaks to me as you do."

"I don't mean to be rude, your ladyship. But I love Eve Williams, and she loves me. We're to be married in October. I hope I have your blessing, but we'll go ahead without it if we must. None of this could possibly affect my abilities as your gardener."

"Oh Daniel." She wagged a hand at him, brushing away his indignation. "You must do as you wish. I'm just sad you didn't feel able to confide."

She was such an artiste, he thought, such a performer. In this brief conversation she had moved seamlessly from sulky child to haughty aristocrat to injured confidante. She looked at him now with another expression and one that made him uncomfortable: a sort of longing, but not quite that. More a wistful regret. There had never been anything between these two but a love of gardens, and it would ever remain thus, at least as far as Daniel was concerned. But he had underestimated—and so, perhaps, had the countess—the extent to which she regarded him as her own possession. And she had discovered, to her annoyance and surprise, that she didn't want Daniel MacLeod to be married in the least. She turned her face away from him, the better to display her famous delicate profile.

"I suppose you have all sorts of plans for me," she said, deliberately ambiguous.

"For the garden, yes, I do," he said, deliberately unambiguous. "They're beautiful, and they're all rolled up safe and sound in my wee cottage."

"Well, when all this has died down"—she waved an arm, slender as a sapling, in the direction of the house, meaning to indicate the king—"we shall sit down together, you and I, and discuss them."

"I should like that, your ladyship," he said, and smiled at her.

She wished she could say, "Call me Clarissa." Instead, she smiled demurely and rose from the seat to drift away up the stone steps and along the gravel path toward the hall, conscious that her figure, still that of a girl and skimpily clad, would look charming from this angle, in this light.

Chapter 16

He found Eve alone in the house. She was upstairs, in the bedroom she had shared with Arthur and, latterly, with Seth and Ellen. He had left his boots at the door; they were encrusted with mud from his morning's work in the rose garden and he knew she wouldn't thank him for treading any of it into the newly cleaned, empty house. He stepped into the kitchen and admired the evidence of her labors; the flagstones were glossy from a recent encounter with a mop and the wooden surfaces, dented and bruised from years of use, were scrubbed and polished to a high, proud shine. The smell was of scouring powder and fresh air. In his stocking feet he climbed the stairs and, unheard by Eve, had the luxury of watching her for a moment where she stood, her back to him, looking out through the bedroom window over Beaumont Lane. She held a chamois leather in one hand, though she wasn't cleaning the glass, but simply gazing out through it, as if committing the view to memory. Her long brown hair was tied up with a pale blue scarf, and that contrast—the blue, the brown—as well as her absolute stillness in the clear light of the window, gave the scene the appearance of an old master.

Daniel reached instinctively for the doorframe. Whenever he saw her, his breath momentarily failed and his heart pounded; he was floored, like a hapless, love-struck lad. He was looking forward to a time when she would seem ordinary to him, when his familiarity with the look, smell, and feel of her would give him some immunity and the mere sight of her wouldn't flood him with lust. Today she wore a drab serge skirt in serviceable brown and a white, high-collared blouse that hid her arms and her throat, and yet she appeared to him a vision of desirable loveliness.

"Eve," he said, and she jumped and turned, his voice clearly having interrupted a deep reverie. He went to her and caught her up in an embrace, though she stepped clear of the panes before he reached her, even now wary of being seen by prying eyes with this man, her intended. With her face in his neck she kissed the hollow above his collarbone and inhaled deeply.

"I love t'smell of you," she said. "Sweat and toil."

He said nothing but held her hard and moved against her hoping—without any real hope—to reduce her to wanton desire, to have her here and now on the scarred linoleum floor of her old bedroom. She pushed away from him, although her breathing, rapid and shallow, gave her away.

"Don't," she said. "Not 'ere."

"No," he said. "So where, then?" He spoke lightly, looking about the room and grinning as he did, expecting at worse an indignant clip around the ear, but to his horror she began to cry and he gathered her up again and held her, this time with no motive other than giving comfort.

This move from her old, beloved, familiar home was momentous for her, he knew that; she used the local word for it, called it flitting, but it seemed too light and easy a term for the great leap of faith she was taking. He understood, really he did; she was bidding farewell to her past.

"I was nearly eighteen when Arthur brought me 'ere," she said finally, through her tears. She sniffed, hiccupped, shuddered. "I loved this 'ouse from t'minute I set foot in it: it saved me. An' Arthur did an' all—Arthur saved me. He seemed like a miracle."

"I expect you were the miracle, to him," Daniel said feelingly.

"Aye, well." She sighed. "If I was, 'e never said."

"Y'know, if I'd loved you first, then died, I would've wanted only happiness for you, Eve. I'm sure Arthur would too."

They didn't speak for a while but stood together in the slanting afternoon light, Eve lost in her memories, Daniel lost in Eve. After a time her sadness seemed to be abating and he gently suggested that perhaps it was time to follow the others up to the new house. She looked at him and said: "I can't leave. I can't go," and her words filled Daniel with sudden, cold dread.

"Eve, Eve." He took her face in his hands and tilted it upward, kissing it again and again, tasting the tears. "I just want to make you happy."

"I shall be," she said, controlling the sobs as they threatened to rise in her again. "I am. You do. But I can't leave, because Seth has gone and I can't 'ave him come back to an empty 'ouse."

Ah thank God, thank God, he thought, that was all. He had thought she meant she couldn't do any of it—move house, love him, change her name from Arthur's to his. Relief made him giddy and he had to keep himself from laughing.

"Should I look for him?" he said. "While you wait here?"

She shrugged. "Eliza looked before. But you could."

"He might be up at Ravenscliffe already, I suppose?"

"Never in this world," she said bitterly. "That's t'last place 'e'd go."

"Well then," he said, patient, soothing. "Where d'you suggest I start?"

"Never mind," she said, her voice weary. "You go up to t'house. I'll just wait 'ere."

Seth had spent a pleasant morning. True, it hadn't started well: the industrious bustle of packing the house, the chaos of too many people intoo small a space, the prospect of a move he didn't want to make and—hanging above all of this like a great shadow—the fact of his mam's marriage to a stranger. A stranger, moreover, who offered him, like the answer to everything, a book about a botanist: as if that was all it took to make things right. So the mutinous boy had left them all to it, slipping off without eating breakfast—to heighten his own misery and generate maximum concern—and making sure he visited none of the places they would be likely to look. He wandered across the common, cutting switches of hawthorn and witch hazel and whittling them into arrows with his knife until he had enough to fill a quiver; he tied them into a tidy bundle with a stalk of dry yellow grass, and hid them in the hollow of an oak. They could wait there for him until he had managed to make a bow. Then he spent some time with the old ponies: they loved a bit of a fuss—they missed the miners, Amos said. He'd told Seth their names, but they all looked alike and their names were confusingly similar too, all single syllables—Sal, Jack, Patch, Flash—and he could never remember which was which. The ponies had gone after a while when their investigations had conclusively proved there was no stash of apples or carrots. They turned from Seth all of a sudden, trotting away with some urgency, as if they'd just remembered a previous engagement and were already late for it. It had made him laugh and he had been surprised at the sound: surprised he could laugh, when he was so miserable. This, in turn, made him determined to revive the misery, so he headed for Ravenscliffe and sat on a wide hummock of pale, sharp grass overlooking the house. He thought about his dad and how much life had changed since he died, and the tears rolled easily then. He wanted his dad more than anything in the universe: wanted him more, now he couldn't have him, than he ever had when Arthur was alive.

And it was thinking about Arthur that reminded Seth of something he had entirely forgotten. In all the drama of Uncle Silas arriving and his mam wanting to move house, Seth had forgotten about his plan to sign up at New Mill. He would be twelve in a week and a half, and at twelve, he had promised himself, he would become a miner: the living torchbearer for his dead father's memory. Everyone was against it, Seth knew this—Amos, Anna, his mam, they'd all told him he should stay at school, he was a clever lad, he could use his brain and do something better with his life. He'd heard their words, he'd even looked at them as they spoke, but he hadn't listened. He couldn't do better than follow in his dad's footsteps; it would be an honor and a privilege. In his mind's eye, he saw himself: young, inexperienced, but bravely setting forth into a man's world with a dudley and a snap tin. He would come in from work every day too tired to speak, the whites of his eyes bright against the coal dust that caked his face. He would be like the ghost of his dad; he would remind his mam of what she'd lost.

"Bloody Nora, lad. You pick yer moments."

This wasn't the warm reception Seth had anticipated from the colliery manager. Early signs had been so promising, the pit yard a much jollier place than he'd been led to believe; men that he knew hailed him cheerfully as he passed, there were red geraniums in wooden tubs, and carefree boys with brushes larked about, flicking each other with whitewash as they painted the brick walls of the workshops. Seth had expected something much grimmer and hard-edged, but here was a place where he already felt at home. The scene had warmed his heart and his suffering spirits had soared with the joy of his noble mission. And then he had encountered Don Manvers, who glared at him as if he was a thief, caught red-handed and made to account for himself.

"Arthur Williams's lad, right?"

Seth nodded. "Aye," he said. His voice was small, but he stood proud.

"Tha couldn't be any bugger else wi' them ears," said Mr. Manvers. He laughed briefly, then resumed his crossness.

"What's tha want? Tha's got ten seconds."

Seth wasted three of them, then managed to stutter out that he wanted to come and work at New Mill, like his dad.

"'ow old are you?"

"Twelve, Mr. Manvers. Well, I shall be, a week Wednesday."

"Oh aye?" He spoke with a slow, skeptical drawl. "An' what does yer mam 'ave to say about it?"

"She doesn't mind," said Seth. "She thinks it's a right good idea."

"Does she now?"

Seth nodded, proud of his cunning and the quick-thinking lie.

"I'll tell thi summat for nowt," said Mr. Manvers. "There's

not a mother in this miserable world who's ever thought it a 'right good idea' for 'er son to start at a pit. Only them that 'as no choice comes 'ere, lad. An' I reckon you're not one of 'em."

Seth—crushed, humiliated, wrong-footed—stood his ground.

"All right," he said, red-faced and defiant. "Me mam doesn't like it, but it's what I want."

"Look," said Mr. Manvers. "Arthur Williams were a fine worker an' there's a place 'ere for thi, if tha really wants it. But best talk again to thi mam. I don't want Eve Williams comin' down 'ere to play merry 'ell wi' me for signing you up. All right?"

Seth contained his triumph in a brief manly nod. Then Mr. Manvers cocked his head as if to size him up and said: "What's tha up to now, lad?"

"Nowt, Mr. Manvers," said Seth.

"In that case, get thissen a paintbrush and lend an 'and. We've t'king comin' in three hours. Go on—make thi'sen useful."

So Seth had spent a happy few hours with a tin of white-wash and a crowd of lively boys not much older than himself. Thoughts of Ravenscliffe, Daniel, his dad—all were banished in the collective endeavor to make New Mill pit yard fit for a royal visit. Seth felt foolish for having thought the paint and the flowers were the normal way of things: he was grateful—profoundly so—that he hadn't given away this misunderstanding to Mr. Manvers. That was the sort of stupid blunder that could dog a person for years. And then, before he'd been made to leave—"Are you still 'ere? Get thi'sen gone!" Mr. Manvers had said, but with a smile, not angrily—Seth had stood in a line with the others along the cinder track as the colliery band played a welcome overture and the king drove into the yard in Lord Hoyland's Daimler.

By the time he walked back to Beaumont Lane it was nearly two o'clock and the house, when he pushed open the door and stepped inside, was completely empty of furniture, though he could hear Eve's footsteps on the floorboards upstairs. Funny, he thought, how you always knew a person from their footfall. His mam's was brisk and clipped. Eliza skipped or ran. Amos strode, so that the next step was always a little longer coming than you expected. Seth looked about the kitchen and was aware, as he did so, that he felt fine: calm, not distressed. Now none of their things were here, he could see that a house was something you could walk away from. He decided he'd leave his mark, though, before he left for the last time, and he went through the kitchen and into the parlor and, crouching low in a corner of the room, he scratched SETH into the brown painted wood of the skirting board with the tip of his penknife. It was a poor effort, the letters scrappy, the word on a tilt. He wished he could start again and make a better job of it, but Eve's boots were clattering down the stairs now so he stood, slipping the knife into a pocket out of her sight. She started speaking before she reached the bottom and her voice was bright but brittle: familiar to Seth, who knew when she was being careful with him.

"Is that you, Seth? Where've you been, love? Everybody's worrying about you and nob'dy more than me—and what's that on you?" She was in the parlor with him now, looking at the flecks of white paint that speckled the gray of his shorts. He could have told her everything, of course: that it was whitewash from New Mill on his clothes and he'd had the time of his life this morning and seen the king to boot, and how he didn't mind the move so much anymore. He could have told her all that to ease the blow of his other news—but he didn't. Instead he set his face into a scowl and said gruffly: "I've been up to t'pit to sign on. I start a week on Thursday." He didn't know why. He simply couldn't help himself. And he watched with a sort of odd pleasure at the pain he had inflicted: at the wounding power of words.

Chapter 17

Half a mile underground five men gathered at the foot of the mineshaft. They'd swept the floor as well as they could and strung Union-flag bunting along the first few yards of the walls on either side of the main roadway. They hadn't had time to whitewash anything down here so, apart from the flags, it was its usual dismal self, and just as well, thought Sam Bamford. Speaking personally, he couldn't see the merit in making the pit out to be something it wasn't. Bad enough to do up the yard like a church garden party without starting on the pit bottom as well. If the king wanted to see a working pit in action, then that's what he should be shown: not geraniums and flags and painted brickwork. The headstocks had been painted yesterday, too—the first time in anyone's memory—by a couple of youngsters who, carrying ropes, canvas, and buckets of paint, climbed them like monkeys, rigged up a couple of rudimentary harnesses, then casually swung their way down, daubing the wooden beams with black paint, which had dried to a high glossy shine. There was a flagpole, too, bearing the Royal Standard, which was currently tied tight and couldn't be unfurled until the king arrived. The white pole rose sixty feet up at the entrance to the pit yard, incongruously grand, sent up to the colliery from Netherwood Hall. It was a blessing, thought Sam, that they hadn't been given more notice, or else Don Manvers would've had them waxing and polishing the cobbles and laying red carpet up the steps to the pit bank.

It was Sam, though, who'd had the bright idea of involving the pit ponies in the underground reception committee and two of them—Ace and Queenie, chosen for their good manners and irresistible, heavy-lashed eyes—now formed part of the guard of honor. They stood placidly in line with the waiting men, red rosettes and ribbons tied to their newly blacked harnesses, enjoying the attention and the novelty of coming out of their underground stables, not to haul wagons of coal but simply to stand and be petted.

"What a bloody carrying-on."

Sidney Cutts, plucked from the time office and placed with the others at the foot of the shaft in recognition of his long service at New Mill, was skeptical about the extent of the honor. "I feel a right daft sod, stood 'ere."

"I'm all for it, me," said Lofty Vickers amiably. "Makes a change."

"What is it we say again? If he talks to us, like?" Frank Ogden was just a boy, not long fifteen. He'd been picked to represent the youthful contingent of the workforce and he felt burdened by the responsibility. His mam hadn't helped, fussing over him in the kitchen that morning, plastering down his disobedient hair, eyes welling with maternal pride.

"You say, 'Nah then, Bertie, 'ow's tha bin?' then you sing t'national anthem, solo," said Sam.

"Get lost," said Frank. He scowled at Sam, who laughed at him.

"Tha says nowt unless tha spoken to," said Albie Gilford, Don Manvers's humorless deputy. "An' then tha says, 'Yes, Your Majesty,' or, 'No, Your Majesty.' Depending on t'question, like."

"Oh aye?" said Sam. "An' if 'e says, 'What's your name, young fellow-me-lad?'"

But he stopped short because the empty upward cage suddenly began to creak with the early signs of life, preparing to head toward the pinprick of daylight at the top of the shaft: this could only mean that the visitors were on their way down.

Albie said: "I 'ope they know what they're in for."

"They don't," said Sam.

"I can't credit it, me," said Lofty. "A king in a pit cage. It's not right."

"If it's good enough for us . . ." Sam began to say, but he stopped again because the flow and slide of the cables told them the royal party was now plummeting in their direction.

There were seven of them, in the end—the king, the earl, Tobias, Frank Ponsonby, Henrietta, Thea, and Joseph Choate, who had no real enthusiasm for the scheme but whose wife felt their wayward charge needed a chaperone. She was proving more of a handful than the ambassador had expected; he felt his old friend Elliot Sterling had ill-prepared him for the girl's evident boundless enthusiasm for every unsuitable activity. Yesterday, while the other ladies played croquet and drank tea, Thea had walked out with an impromptu shooting party and, borrowing Toby's gun, had bagged a respectable five birds with a series of cracking shots. She had shrugged off the praise: easier than killing rats and rattlesnakes, she had said.

"Watch her today," Caroline Choate had murmured to her husband as they left for New Mill. "Don't let her get her hands on a pick ax or shovel."

They were met by Don Manvers, rigid and dry-mouthed with anxiety. He looked, thought Lord Netherwood with sympathetic amusement, as if he might cry. The earl had consulted the king's private secretary about the correct protocol concerning a sovereign visit down a coal mine: there was none, Francis Knollys had said with an oily smile, because there was no precedent. His best advice for such a scheme would be to cancel it, he had said, unhelpfully. So, unassisted by the courtier-in-chief, the earl had decided on a course of action: Don Manvers—capable, steady, pedantic Don—would take the royal party through the usual pit-top routine before descending the mine.

"You mean brass checks an' helmets an' lamps, your lordship?" Don had said, incredulous.

"Exactly, Don. Might as well show His Royal Highness how it's done, what!"

"The ladies as well?"

"Ladies as well."

So Don Manvers, uncomfortably conscious of the way he sounded and the frayed edge of his shirt collar, had led them to the time office, doled out two brass checks per person—one round, one square—chivied them respectfully along to the lamp room, fitted them out with helmets, then led them up the wooden steps and introduced them to Stan Clough, who waited at the pit bank to take their downward checks and settle them into the cage.

"You mun keep your square checks fo' t'trip back up," he said plainly, much as if he was speaking to a group of lads promoted from the screens to work underground and heading down now for the first time. "Dunt lose 'em, else we'll not know if you're safe." They stood, an unlikely pack of apprentices, listening attentively.

"Thank you, Mr. Clough," Henrietta said.

"Aye," said Stan, looking at his clogs. He hadn't expected womenfolk. Womenfolk at a colliery were a bad business, in his opinion.

"In we go, then," said the earl cheerfully. He had made

this journey before and he knew what none of the rest of his present party did—that the cage would drop like a stone down a well when released. He was looking forward to seeing Henrietta's face when it did. She had had an aggravating air about her, a triumphant jauntiness at succeeding where he had been determined she should fail. They stepped onto the iron grille of the cage floor, stooping slightly in the confined space, and Stan hauled the door into place.

"You might want to 'old on," was all he said by way of advice. He pointed at the safety bar and they all reached for it, obediently. "Ready?"

Two miles away on the east side of Netherwood, the afternoon shift at Long Martley was under way. No bunting or fresh paint here: this was the least presentable of the earl's three collieries, and the men who mined it knew it would never be graced by a visit from the king. There was a unifying resentment, the camaraderie of shared indignation, among the Long Martley miners at their poor-relation status in Netherwood. It was, by a very small margin, the least productive of the three pits and its appearance was more than usually shabby, but then—as the men there would robustly maintain—it was always the last to benefit from investment or innovation, always the one waiting longest for repairs. There was no rhyme or reason for this: it was just that, rightly or wrongly, Long Martley had become known as the runt of the earl's coal-producing litter. There were even rumors that he was running it down ready for closure, but the same story had been peddled around town for the past ten years and yet there Long Martley still stood, scruffier and more neglected in appearance than New Mill or Middlecar, but still yielding tubs of first-quality coal every working day of the week, and still providing a living for six hundred men and boys.

They were a partisan lot, as well. There was no cross-pollination between pits, and once you started somewhere, that's where you stayed, for good or ill. Alfred Kay had worked at Long Martley for twenty-eight years; his father and grandfather had worked there before him and now his sons were there too, all three of them. They were doing nicely, the Kays. Four wages from Long Martley and Nellie's income from her work at Eve's Puddings & Pies up at the old flour mill. They'd never felt so flush. There was talk of a few days in Bridlington in August.

Alf and his lads kept the same shift patterns: Nellie preferred it that way, and wherever possible her menfolk tried to keep her happy—or, at least, keep her not unhappy, which was the closest to happy that Nellie generally got. This week they were on afternoons, starting at half past one, finishing at half past ten. Alf and his boys, William, Richard, and Edward—distinguished names, never shortened by their parents—walked the short distance to Long Martley together, though at the pit they dispersed among the couple of hundred men gathering there at the foot of the pit-bank steps. The day shift was up, but half of them were still in the yard listening to Amos Sykes, who stood like a lay preacher on an upturned crate, hurling words at the gathering of workingmen. He was good, too: convincing, passionate. Alf liked to listen to him. There were skeptics, still, and plenty of them, but shorter hours, more pay, protection from the workhouse for miners' widows—what was there to take issue with? That was Alf's view, anyway. He raised an arm in salute at Amos as he passed, and Amos saluted back without breaking his verbal stride.

It took a while to get the afternoon shift down, but by half past two Alf was underground and heading for the Crookgate seam with his own lad Richard and Victor Pickering. They were to lay a new road there: easy work, compared to hewing coal. Three abreast, they negotiated the busy main roadway, where trammers, faceworkers, and boys with ponies were mill-ing about at the start of their shift, and then, turning off into a narrower passage, they dropped into single file, Alf at the head. Their lamps threw bouncing light onto the wet walls of the tunnel as they walked. Victor whistled a cheerful tune. Ten more minutes and they'd be there. And then the warm air that until this moment had blown steadily against their backs suddenly stopped, reversed, and came at them in a hot gust from the opposite direction so that now they were walking into it. A thick and silent cloud of foul-smelling dust whipped up and swam about their faces and the flames in their lamps were reduced to a thin plume of sickly blue. The change was soundless, sinister, and absolute, and all three miners knew instantly what it meant: somewhere in the pit there had been an explosion.

To their eternal credit they continued on to Crookgate to investigate.

Chapter 18

Extraordinarily, Sam Bamford and Lord Netherwood heard the explosion. Heard it and felt it: a raging, furious roar of ignition, then a profound, sickening, prolonged vibration in the bowels of the earth as they took the impact. The king, along with the rest of the group, had been led a few hundred yards along the main roadway by Albie Gilford, who was relishing his role as oracle and answering their questions with an articulacy that no one had known he possessed. The tour group had emerged submissive and humble from their short adventure in the cage and even Thea had nothing to say for a full five minutes after disembarking. Now, like mountaineers adjusting to conditions at base camp, they were all perking up, venturing farther afield and making sensible inquiries about the purpose of different pieces of equipment and the logistics of hacking coal from a seam and carrying it up to the surface of the earth. Ace and Queenie, proudly led by Frank and Lofty, flanked the little posse and batted their lashes at the ladies. Sidney Cutts, struck dumb by the presence of the monarch, brought up the rear. So Sam, his presence not immediately required, had elected to stay by the shaft bottom and wait for their return, and the earl, who had no wish to steal Albie's thunder, stayed with Sam. This was why, in the silence of the near-empty pit—its normal business paused for the duration of the king's tour—the two men heard the distant but unmistakable boom of catastrophe underground.

Sam was far more familiar than the earl with the subterranean geography of this colliery: he knew that this spot, at the bottom of the shaft, was the closest of any point in New Mill to the underground workings of Long Martley and his experience told him from which direction the sound had come, so when the earl looked at him, bemused, he simply said: "Long Martley. Firedamp, most likely."

"God damn it," said the earl, beads of sweat suddenly lining his brow. He stumbled fractionally: felt, for the first time, the terrible proximity of danger in these mines of his, the volatility of their moods. "What the hell do we do now?"

"Get back up," said Sam. "T'show's over."

There was nothing to say that she hadn't already said, thought Eve: she was sick of the sound of her own voice. So she and Seth, their spirits defeated by each other, left Beaumont Lane together in a heavy, despondent silence. For a final time she pulled her old back door shut and heard the lock snap into place, closing them out for good. They walked down the cobbled entry and out into Watson Street and then suddenly, before and behind them, like birds driven by beaters from a copse, women began to emerge from their houses, running grim-faced and oblivious to one another in the direction of Long Martley. She and Seth halted in the sudden wave of activity around them. She saw Lilly Pickering fleeing with an infant under each arm and Eve reached out to her, pulled at her skirts, forced her to stop.

"Leave 'em with me, Lilly," she said, and Lilly, without speaking a word, bundled her children into Eve's arms, then resumed her swift pace. Beside his mother, Seth was white-faced. She hoisted Lilly's little ones, one on each hip, then she turned a livid face on her son.

"Do you see now what you've done?" she said, her voice hard and loud. "I 'oped never again to suffer like these women are suffering. Do you see? To hear t'sound of a poker on t'fireback, to run to t'pit without knowing if your man or your lad's been carried up dead? That's what you'll give back to me if you go to New Mill next week. Fear, Seth. Terror. Do you see?" The pitch of her voice grew urgent, frantic, as if their lives depended on his understanding her. One of the children, Lilly's youngest, began to cry.

For a few beats Seth said nothing; Eve could hear him breathe, in and out through his nose, his mouth clamped shut to keep from crying too. Then he said: "You make me sick, you do," and his voice matched hers in anger. "It's all 'ow you feel, what you think, what you want, in't it?" He looked away from her, then back, and said again: "You only think o' yourself. You make me sick."

She was stunned. This child, this boy, this precious being of hers and Arthur's, for whom she would walk through fire if she had to—he was staring at her with contempt and she didn't know how they had come to this or what she should do to mend it.

The first of the dead were up and laid out in rows on the floor of the wages office by the time the earl's convoy drove into the pit yard at Long Martley. Their journey had been slow through the crowd of women who were pushing their way down the narrow lane to the colliery and standing in a silent mass in the yard, waiting for news. There were hundreds of them. It was like a scene from the fringes of hell, thought Thea: the damned awaiting admittance. Like Henrietta, Thea had refused to be driven back to Netherwood Hall, insisting instead that she could be of some use. Frank Ponsonby and Joseph Choate had returned, but Tobias had come to the colliery and the king was with them too. It was a rare thing, he had said, to be among his subjects in a time of need. Henrietta had wondered how welcome he would be amid the grief and horror, but there was no one in the party with the influence or authority to steer his inclination in another direction. Certainly her father seemed unequal to the task; he had somehow emerged from the New Mill pit shaft a lesser man than the one who went down. One wouldn't expect ebullience at such a time, but one might expect authority and command. She wondered if the cause of this change was fear at the sound of the explosion, or shame at the onset of fear. Either way, the earl was pale and quiet, and it had been Henrietta who had allocated motorcars and directed chauffeurs. Lord Netherwood, as was proper, rode with the king, and their vehicle had made its way through the ranks of wives and mothers in a sad parody of the usual royal progress: crowds lined the road, but there were no Union flags, no smiles, no sound at all. It seemed hardly possible that such a multitude could maintain so profound a silence.

The Daimlers crawled into the pit yard and came to a halt, but for a few moments it was impossible to get out because the sea of humanity, which had parted to let them through, closed again around the stationary vehicles as more people pressed into the area, looking for loved ones, desperate for news. Atkins, who drove the earl and the king, managed to prize himself out, then held back the tide for his distinguished passengers. Harry Booth, the colliery manager, had seen them arrive and he pushed his way toward them. He was an angry

146

man: angry and distressed. He hadn't expected to see King Edward VII, but he took it in his stride. Tragedy, he thought afterward, was a great leveler. Men and boys were dead and dying: deference was a nonsense at such times.

"Explosion out by Crookgate district," he said to the earl, cutting to the chase the moment Lord Netherwood levered himself out of the car. "It's bad. Rescue team are down, but we're short o' breathing apparatus. We've sent to New Mill for more. I don't suppose you 'ave it?"

Of course you don't have it, he might have added, for what use are you to us now? He kept his voice steady, but there was evident accusation in it. The earl heard this but replied evenly. "We must all do what we can with what we have, Mr. Booth. What's the tally so far?"

"It's not a bag of pheasant, m'lord," said Harry Booth. He knew he had probably just lost his job with this remark, but he found, at this moment of crisis, that his loyalty and respect for his colleagues was far greater than that he felt for his employer. He turned away and walked back through the crowds to the pit bank. The wheel and cables of the winding gear were moving and the cage very likely held more corpses. The earl faced Henrietta, who he knew was watching him.

"I meant death toll," he said. His face was stricken and he looked suddenly pitiful.

"I know you did," she said consolingly, as if to a child. She was acutely aware of the picture they presented: cosseted, protected, untouched by the pain of personal loss. And there was the king, observing her father with a look of incomprehension. The famous royal face showed his thoughts as clearly as if he had spoken them aloud; these were the Earl of Netherwood's serfs and yet they moved about him as if he was invisible, and spoke to him as if he was a fool. Henrietta saw it all and she took immediate control.

"Tobias," she said to her brother, who was only here because of Thea and who had never looked more out of place in his life. "Accompany His Majesty—if it pleases you, Your Majesty—" she added quickly, to the king's evident relief, since in this pandemonium his status seemed to have been all but forgotten—"to the manager's offices. I can see injured men in there whose spirits may be lifted by a meeting with the king. Father, you must go up to the pit bank with Mr. Booth. These are your men and they need your support. Thea, you and I—"

But Thea was gone and when Henrietta scanned the crowd she saw her, kneeling on the stones of the pit yard, her arms supporting an old woman who had fallen to the floor in an agony of grief.

There were obvious signs of an explosion, even before Alf, Richard, and Victor got as far as Crookgate: splintered tubs, damaged, twisted supports, and the foul stench of gaseous air. Alf called out into the darkness but his shouts were met by silence. They ventured a little farther and found the first body, and beyond that, another, lying broken and badly burned beside the corpse of a pony. Alf sent Richard back to the pit bottom for rescue assistance and he and Victor crept forward, feeling their way with the feeble assistance of their lamps. In the crepuscular light it was hard to identify anyone, but it was plain to both men that there were many more bodies on the tunnel floor, and not a breath of life between them.

Behind them, Richard reappeared, sooner than they'd expected.

"Rescue team's on its way, they say. They've sent to New Mill for more breathing equipment, but they're coming down with what we 'ave."

Unprotected by safety gear, the three men made a start themselves. They were hampered by the dust and the stink, but they ripped off their vests and used them as rudimentary masks, covering their noses and mouths, then began carrying the dead out of the tunnel. More men joined them. Alf saw his two other lads, William and Edward, among them: he nodded his approval. If he'd taught his sons anything about this life underground, it was their bounden duty toward their colleagues. The time would come, he always said, when they would be the ones in need. To date, they had never been found lacking and he was proud of all three of them; they were a credit to him and Nellie.

"Mind out," Alf said brusquely now to Edward as he passed him, pulling the body of a young pony boy out toward the wide main roadway. There were wagons there, and the corpses were being placed tenderly, respectfully, into them, for their last journey out of the pit. Ahead, a small platoon of rescuers hove into view, monstrous in the heavy metal helmets that gave them some immunity to the dust and the gas. Alf and the rest of them stepped aside; they could return to the pit bottom now that the professionals were here, but already they had hauled twelve bodies from the scene. Alf turned, signaled to Victor that he was heading out, and Victor signaled back. Then Richard, just ahead of his father, spun around and shouted: "We need to shift," but even as he issued the warning, a slam, like the heaviest of doors shutting, reverberated through the tunnel and Richard's lamp flew from his hand, knocked away by the searing wave of hot air that barreled like a solid mass, unstoppable and inexorable in the confined space.

"Down on your faces, lads," Alf shouted. He dropped to the floor, saw Richard do the same, hoped to hell that Edward and William were clear. Then a ball of fire, monstrous and pitiless, came hurtling toward them down the tunnel like a comet flung by a vengeful god. There was no time to move:

barely time to pray. Richard reached out toward his father and took his hand and with their faces pressed to the cold tunnel floor they gripped each other firmly, their fingers locked together. It was the first time they'd touched each other in affection for fifteen years, and they both felt the deep comfort of it before they were engulfed by the flames.

Chapter 19

Do you believe in omens?"

"I don't."

Eve looked at Daniel. "You sound very sure."

"I am. I believe we make our own fate."

"Then you don't think that what happened yesterday . . ."

"Bodes ill for us here? No, I really don't."

Daniel wasn't going to concede an inch on this point. He was as shaken as any of them, but he wasn't going to have Eve reading anything more into yesterday than what it was: a terrible accident, an appalling tragedy, which for a while must cast a long shadow over Netherwood, but not forever, and not over Ravenscliffe. The house was very fine, he could see that now: in the fragile light of early dawn it seemed to stand strong and sure like a citadel, a refuge from the vagaries of the world, a place of safety for its inhabitants. Apart from Eve, they all slept, but she was up and dressed when he arrived and she made him tea in a kitchen that was in chaos, crates piled upon crates, because nothing had been accomplished yesterday beyond the basic act of moving belongings from one dwelling to another. This was the first time Daniel had set foot in Ravenscliffe—since arriving at Netherwood Hall he had barely left the garden, apart from two rather formal occasions when he ate an evening meal with Eve and the children, all of them grateful for Eliza's stream of questions and observations. Now he sat in a room that itself was perhaps as big as the ground floor of the little house in Beaumont Lane. Because they were alone, Eve sat close. She looked drawn, dark shadows bruising the tender skin below her eyes. He put out a hand and cupped her cheek.

"There wasn't any sinister meaning," he said. "You're going to be happy here. We all are."

She nodded, and sat in silence for a moment, but then she said: "Years ago, when we first moved into Beaumont Lane, Arthur found a dead crow in the stovepipe."

"And?"

She shrugged, unwilling to continue in the face of his skepticism, but he knew exactly what she was getting at.

"The dead crow was a dead crow," he said. "Unlucky for the bird, but not for you."

Eve looked away, too sorrowful to be reassured. But life was already moving on, the morning gathering strength and momentum from its pale beginnings and growing swiftly into a full-blown day. Outside, far beyond and below them, miners walked the roads to their pits. Long Martley was open for business again today. The Crookgate district would be closed while the roads were cleared and the scorched timbers replaced, but there was no reason why the rest of the pit shouldn't be mined, and none of the dead would expect a man to lose a day's pay out of a misguided sense of sorrow or respect.

Seventy-six men and twelve boys had perished yesterday. All of the rescue party died in the second explosion, and the first had killed everyone in the vicinity of Crookgate. It was the worst accident in Netherwood's mining history and the first editions of the *Chronicle*, dumped in tied bundles outside Fletcher's paper shop, blared out the tragedy in a series of headlines that filled the front page:

TERRIBLE PIT CALAMITY AT NETHERWOOD
HORRIFIC EXPLOSIONS SWEEP LONG MARTLEY
EIGHTY-EIGHT LIVES LOST
KING VISITS BEREAVED AT COLLIERY

[Pen picture of the scene of the tragedy.]

OFFICIAL LIST OF DEAD
RELIEF FUND OPENED FOR BEREAVED WIDOWS

Daniel had picked up a copy on his way over to Ravenscliffe, exchanging platitudes with Ted Fletcher because it was hard to say anything original or meaningful about a catastrophe of this scale. There was a list of the dead inside the paper and Eve had read it and wept with horror and astonishment at the barefaced cruelty of death. All of Nellie's menfolk were gone: Alf, William, Richard, and Edward, dead within an hour and a half of starting their shift. Lilly's Victor had perished too. Her little ones were still with Eve, sleeping the untroubled sleep of infancy in a room with Eliza. Eve had taken them back to Lilly last night and found her whey-faced and unresponsive, catatonic with fear for her future and that of her children. She'd never held Victor in much esteem when he lived, but now he was dead she saw that he'd stood firm between her and the open door of the workhouse. Eve had sat in Lilly's dismal kitchen for a mostly silent half hour, then had picked up the children, two boys, both of them sorry little scraps of humanity with no meat on their bones or color in their cheeks, and had carried them back to Ravenscliffe, where she'd fed them and put them to bed. It was the least she could

153

do and even so it still left five more looking to Lilly for comfort.

Daniel stood. His fob watch showed him six o'clock and it was half an hour's walk back to Netherwood Hall. Eve said: "Shall we see you later?"

"Aye," he said. "This evening, if you like."

"I would like," she said, and she smiled wanly. He stooped over her where she still sat and pressed his mouth to the top of her head, keeping it there awhile so that she felt his hot breath through her hair. Fleetingly, like a dream remembered, she felt a sense of how fortunate she was, and how happy, and then it passed.

"I need to go and see Nellie today," she said. "I can't think what I might say to 'er."

"Did anyone say anything to you, when Arthur died—y'know, something that comforted you? That you remember still?"

She gazed at him, taking herself back to that time: not so very long ago, but she felt as if it was another life she recalled, a different woman. "No," she said, after a while. "There was no comfort. Then Anna came, and she made all t'difference. But not because of anything she said. I don't think we talked about Arthur at all. She just, well . . . she just shared t'burden, somehow or other."

"Well then. Try to do the same for Nellie."

Ah, she thought, but you don't know Nellie.

The house party was affected, of course it was, but there was no reason for it to disband entirely, thought Lady Netherwood, who had risen early out of a sense of crisis and now sat at her desk in the morning room feeling virtuous and serious-minded. Mixed doubles tennis, lunch in the summerhouse, fishing for carp in the ponds, an archery contest: no reason why these activities shouldn't still take place, so long as hilarity and high jinks were kept under control—obviously—out of respect. Teddy, morose and quiet since he had come home yesterday, thought everyone should go. Clarissa thought absolutely that they shouldn't. In any case, the king must decide what the best course of action was for himself, and so long as they didn't all mope about the house looking miserable, the countess was confident that Bertie would stay put. Also he would be swayed by Alice—as Clarissa now blithely thought of Mrs. Keppel—and since Alice hadn't been at the wretched colliery, hadn't witnessed the dead or ministered to the injured, she was still as full of high spirits as she had been since arriving. She must be called upon to assist, thought Clarissa: she must be given the job of helping gee up the party as it teetered on the brink of the doldrums. After all, only a minority of those present had involved themselves in yesterday's disaster—the rest had had an extremely pleasant afternoon. And also—and this surely was the key point—no one here had actually suffered any personal loss. They had returned yesterday as if bereaved, the Daimlers driving at funereal pace and the passengers apparently shattered by what they'd witnessed. But for heaven's sake, thought Clarissa: if an accident at the colliery was going to spoil their fun, then what was the point in planning anything, ever?

However. She drummed her lovely fingers on the mellow rosewood of the table, her brow knotted in concentration. If Thea Sterling felt she really couldn't stay, that wouldn't be at all a bad thing. There was, she knew, a plan to take the Americans to Glendonoch for the shooting, but they could surely be persuaded that this was no longer appropriate. And then they could all sneak off to Scotland after they'd gone. Tobias was traipsing about after the girl like a hopeless case, and Clarissa didn't mind admitting she had misjudged the depth of her son's infatuation. A corsetless beanpole she may be, but

Thea seemed to possess magnetism. Even Clarissa had found herself being drawn in; she had always admired spirit in a girl. This, far from reconciling her to the object of her son's ardor, only made her doubly anxious to get Thea off the premises. If a marriage couldn't take place, then where was the sense in tormenting Tobias in this way, dangling Thea before him like a carrot before a donkey? No, let her return to London, where she might snare a banker or some such. So, the question was this: how to persuade the Choates and Miss Sterling that their early departure would be acceptable, while holding on to everyone else? This was the sort of social conundrum that Clarissa rather enjoyed. She rang a small brass bell on her desk and the door opened immediately, revealing a footman awaiting instruction.

"I'll take another cup of tea, please, Robert. Lemon."

"Of course, your ladyship." He closed the door softly and with great care, as you might close the door on a newly bereaved woman or a patient with no hope of recovery, and Clarissa felt a flash of irritation. Really, this was too silly. She must speak to Mrs. Powell-Hughes. The drama was over and she must be able to rely on the household to set the tone.

It was midafternoon, the day after the explosions. Investigations had begun into the cause, the district coroner had opened an inquest, and death certificates had been signed for eighty-eight souls so that the funerals could be arranged. Not all of the bodies had been easily identifiable, because of the charring. Billy Somerscale, a fourteen-year-old pony boy, had been recognizable to his mother only by the soles of his boots; a broken metal cleat, which had caused him to complain to her—on the very morning of the day he died—that he rocked a little to the

156

left when he walked, was still evident when all the rest of him was burned black. He had been found dead with his arm around the neck of his pony, and this detail, while heartbreaking in itself, at least gave his mother the comfort that her boy hadn't been alone when he passed.

In the Netherwood Methodist churchyard, eight sextons were working diligently on a large plot of ground for the graves of the dead. The Archbishop of York, moved by the scale of the tragedy reported in the day's national newspapers, had offered his assistance with the service, but Wilfred Oxspring had declined the help; Netherwood's Methodist minister, who had known every one of the victims personally, would be conducting the funerals. A relief fund had been opened; there were sixty-one widows as a result of the accident, but when the girls and boys who had lost their fathers were counted, the number of dependants totalled one hundred and ninety-four. The whole town was in mourning, it seemed to Eve as she walked to Nellie's. There were more curtains closed than open and the streets were empty but for the occasional arrival of a horse and cart taking coffins from the colliery to the houses.

Nellie was baking when Eve arrived. She had a housecoat on and a hairnet over her gray curls. The kitchen was spotless, the flagstone floor newly swabbed, the range newly blacked. Sarah, Nellie's daughter, was nowhere to be seen: usually by now they'd both be at the mill, busy with cooking and customers.

"Nellie?" Eve said cautiously.

"Oh, it's you," Nellie said without turning. "Come in if you're comin' in. I can't be doin' wi' that draft."

Eve stepped into the kitchen and closed the door. For a moment she watched Nellie in silence, and Nellie didn't turn. She dipped a finger into the bowl, licked it, then added a shake of sugar. Eve felt surplus to requirements.

"Nellie, I'm so sorry, love," she said.

"God's will," said Nellie, pounding at the cake batter. Eve stepped closer, reached out a hand, and placed it on Nellie's shoulder, but the gesture wasn't acknowledged.

"Is there anythin' you need? Anythin' I can do?"

Nellie stopped beating and looked at Eve for the first time since she'd arrived.

"You can open t'mill and give me a reason to get out of bed in t'morning," she said. She turned back to her bowl.

Eve stared for a few beats, then said: "Yes, I see. Well, I shall. It's only closed today because, well . . ."

"Yes, I understand why it's closed today. But if I can get up there tomorrow and get on with things, I shall feel a lot better."

Eve's hand still lay useless and unwanted on Nellie's shoulder, but she didn't know how to remove it now it was there. "Thank God you have Sarah," she said, though she wished the words unsaid at once: she meant to comfort, but instead felt she'd merely emphasised Nellie's loss.

Nellie regarded her for a moment. "I should never 'ave sent 'em all on t'same shift," she said. She looked at the wooden spoon she held in her hand as if, for a moment, she had forgotten what its purpose was. "It were easier for me, to 'ave 'em all down t'pit together."

"You weren't to know, Nellie."

"No 'appen not. But now I do."

She resumed her beating and Eve understood that the subject was closed. She lifted her hand from Nellie's shoulder and folded her arms, feeling awkward and suddenly chilled. How those young men and their father must have filled this house, she thought. How very empty it seemed now.

"I'll see you tomorrow then, Nellie?" she said.

"Aye," Nellie said. "Pull that door to on your way out."

Chapter 20

Far from curtailing his visit, the king extended it, staying until the day after the funerals, which he had respectfully asked leave to attend. He had sat humble and sorrowful with the earl at the front of the chapel, and spoke afterward to many of the mourners who were so numerous that they spilled out into the churchyard and beyond to the road. A cynic, Amos thought, might suspect the monarch of conducting a brilliant popularity campaign. Certainly his stock was very high in the town by the time he swept through the streets to Hoyland Halt, from where he would be traveling to London and on from there to the spa in Marienbad. Not that anyone turned out to wave him off. It was more that if his name was mentioned, it was always warmly, fondly, almost familiarly; the king had shared Netherwood's sorrow, and these matters were binding.

What Amos wondered was why, if the king was so moved by the town's plight, the relief fund had to date received nothing from the Crown.

"'appen 'e's 'ard up," said Enoch Wadsworth, tamping tobacco into his pipe. "All them palaces, but no ready cash."

"'ard up, my eye," said Amos.

They were in their shared office at the YMA, Amos on a chair, Enoch perched on the corner of a desk. He was a tall man by local standards, and lanky. He had a beaky nose and round, wire-framed spectacles, which together gave him the look of a bird, a long-legged wader. Enoch was a trade-union official who had served his time in the mines. But he was also an intellectual, a thinker; he read Marxist literature, corresponded with Sidney Webb, wrote essays for the Fabian Society, and fired off generally unpublished letters to *The Times* about the nationalization of the land and the abolition of the House of Lords. He was younger than Amos, though he looked older; the pits took their toll on all miners, but six years after he'd left the colliery, Enoch's lined skin still had an underground pallor because, unlike Amos, who felt the sun on his face in the allotment, Enoch spent all his free time indoors with his books. He had bad lungs, too, and from time to time he would be seized by a fit of coughing that left him quite debilitated; his narrow shoulders were permanently hunched with the effort of breathing.

He was fascinated by Amos. He'd heard him in full flight at a union meeting, and it was as if Enoch's own ideas and principles were being given voice. Enoch had none of Amos's powers of oratory: not for him a soapbox in a pit yard. His own strength was with pen and paper—the mechanics of union work, not the drama of it. While Amos was never happier than when he was in front of a crowd promising to change the world, Enoch's preference was for paperwork—the hard physical evidence of the fact that their union was growing in size and power. They valued each other's skills, each recognizing in the other man qualities that he didn't have himself, and they complemented each other; the two of them combined made one perfect recruiting agent. However, this symbiosis didn't stop Enoch from badgering his colleague this morning—not for the first time—to look beyond the YMA and stand as an Independent Labor Party candidate in the forthcoming Ardington by-election.

"It's not too late, by t'way," he said now, casually, as if they'd just been talking about nominations of candidates.

Amos looked at him questioningly.

"To stand," said Enoch.

"Oh give it a rest, man," said Amos. "It's Liberal territory, Ardington."

"Aye, it is," said Enoch. "But if you stand for Labor you'll give 'em a run for their money. Politics isn't always about winning. It's sometimes about making a stand."

This was true, and Amos knew it. In Parliament Labor still danced to the tune of the Liberals, relying on their numbers and their money to forward the cause of the workingman. But outside Parliament, in the country at large, the Labor cause was growing apace and not just among the miners: dock laborers, railway engineers, textile workers—they were all beginning to see the possibilities of an Independent Labor Party with its own clear voice. Enoch firmly believed that in this changing climate, Amos's rabble-rousing talents deserved a wider audience.

"What about funding? We can't run a campaign on fresh air," Amos said, which was encouragement indeed for Enoch.

"If you'll stand, I'll find t'funding," he said. "I know more folk than you do. Friends in 'igh places." He winked knowingly, but Amos regarded him coolly. There were, it was true, wealthy men with socialist leanings, men who liked to divide the Liberal vote by bankrolling Labor candidates, but Amos hadn't realized that Enoch had access to their wallets. Clearly, there was more to his colleague than he had imagined.

Amos still hadn't replied, but Enoch sensed a weakening in the silence and he closed in.

"When Keir 'ardie stood in Mid Lanark, did 'e win? No. Did 'e care? No, because 'e knew 'e couldn't win that seat, and 'e knew 'e'd win another somewhere else, some other time. But 'e cut 'is teeth on those early campaigns and put t'Labor cause on t'ballot papers. That, my friend, is what you should be doing."

He smiled at Amos, who he knew was pondering his words. And indeed, Amos was thinking that his colleague had a point. There was currently no Labor candidate in the Ardington by-election. The Liberals would hold it, the Tories would be second. But perhaps, thought Amos, victory shouldn't be the only goal.

"I'll think on it,' Amos said, noncommittal. But Enoch felt a surge of hope anyway.

A rich, sweet tomato sauce simmered in a cast-iron pot on the back of the range, and side by side at the worktop Alice Buckle and Eve stood in an easy silence, both of them engaged in the same task: wrapping the largest leaves—blanched until soft enough to fold—from the outsides of eight Savoy cabbages around small, soft balls of uncooked sausage meat. They flew from the kitchen whenever they made these pig parcels, an innovation from Anna's native Russia, but a mainstay on the menu for over a year now. Occasionally, just to break the monotony of making them, they'd experimented with the filling: cooked rice and peas, minced lamb, even—disastrously—mashed potato, which Eve had thought might be a creative nod toward bubble-and-squeak, but turned out to be nothing of the sort. They were bland and sloppy and they didn't even go on sale; instead, Alice had taken them home for Jonas's pigeons. In the end, Eve had abandoned all attempt at variation, returned to the original recipe, and stuck with it, innovation being deemed less important than contented customers.

Eve always enjoyed working with Alice: she was such a peaceful individual and had been trained through fifteen years of marriage to a demanding husband to do exactly what was required of her, exactly when it was required. Also, she didn't need to chat or sing, like Ginger, or complain about anyone, like Nellie. Alice just peeled, chopped, stirred, whisked, or—as today—folded, with an expression of contentment on her sweetly plump face.

So they were each lost in their own thoughts when Lord Netherwood rapped on the window and nearly scared them both out of their wits. They looked up simultaneously and saw the earl outside in the courtyard, indicating with a pantomime of gestures and grimaces that he couldn't come inside because his boots were too muddy. Alice looked down again, immediately bashful: she would never, she thought privately, be able to look the Earl of Netherwood in the eye and greet him as if he was nobody special. Eve, though, gave him a casual wave.

"Back in a mo'," she said to Alice, then she stepped outside to talk to him.

"Sorry to distract you from your endeavors," he said as she emerged. "Came up through Bluebell Wood with the dogs and hit a bit of a bog, what."

He smiled at her. He looked tired, she thought: paler than usual. Beside him two black Labradors, also caked in mud from the haunches down, sat panting solemnly, gazing at Eve without any particular interest.

"Not at all," Eve said. "It's nice to see you. Business is quiet, mind, at t'moment. It 'as been since . . ."

Eve blushed and tailed off. There was talk that the earl's position of privilege might not protect him from censure, a suggestion that he might be somehow culpable this time. This wasn't something Eve was willing to believe—he could have no stronger advocate than her. But she felt awkward now at having raised the specter of the accident, and it hung momentarily in the air between them.

Then he said brightly: "No, no, I'm not here to keep an

eye on my investment. I'm here on another matter entirely, Mrs. Williams. Your marriage to my head gardener."

He spoke mock-sternly and Eve smiled at him, relieved that the moment had passed.

"I 'ope you don't mind," she said.

"Mind? I think it's absolutely splendid, my dear. He's a lucky chap. I think the countess may take another view if you distract him from his work, however, but that's by the by. No—I couldn't be more delighted. And I wanted to offer you our own chapel for the service."

"At Netherwood 'all?" said Eve, touched by his warmth and enthusiasm but a little thrown by the suggestion.

"That's the idea, yes. It's a beautiful little church, and, well, the Methodist chapel . . ."

He faltered, sounded uncharacteristically unsure of himself, but she took his meaning immediately. Bleak and painful memories—Arthur's coffin being lowered into the hard earth, Eve blank-eyed with trauma, the Methodist graveyard crowded with mourners—rose up between them like a cold wind. She appreciated his impulse to protect her from the past.

"Thank you," she said, and though she spoke simply, her eyes conveyed a fuller meaning. "I shall talk to Daniel."

"I think he would happily marry you in a pigpen if that's what you preferred, my dear," said the earl. "Now, I gather you're living in Ravenscliffe?"

"Yes. Just moved in."

"Interesting property. I expect Mr. Blandford is pleased to have let it. He doesn't like my houses lying idle."

"Yes, I expect 'e is," she lied. How to begin expressing her misgivings about the bailiff? She really wouldn't know where to start.

"Quite an adventure for you. New house, new husband, what? I must say, my dear, your news has been a welcome bright spot in a rather gray few days."

164

He smiled, but sadly, and she felt terribly sorry for him; if he'd been anyone other than Lord Netherwood she'd have given him a hug.

"Can I tempt you to a pie? For t'journey 'ome?" she said, alighting on the one way she could offer comfort without taking liberties.

"Do you know, I think you could," he said, his face brightening. He leaned in and spoke confidingly. "We have a Frenchman in the kitchen now, you know. The countess has always rather longed for it and now it has come to pass. But I doubt he has a recipe for pork pie."

Eve laughed. "Well, that's something you need never go without," she said and she stepped back inside to fetch one for him. Like the dogs, he watched her go, then he turned to survey the courtyard with its ironwork tables and fountain centerpiece, where a soft jet of water played over the old gray stone of the former grist mill. The dogs, denied anyone to stare at, wandered across the cobbles to lap disconsolately at the wet stone, more out of boredom than thirst. Teddy remembered the same stone when it was inside, two floors up and caked in bird muck. Then, all that stood here was an abandoned and overlooked old flour mill fit for nothing but roosting pigeons and eventual demolition. Now, it was a thriving professional kitchen and café. But more than that, it was also a face-lift for this corner of Netherwood, a new meeting place for townsfolk, a draw for people from farther afield; in short, an unqualified success. Something to be proud of, in fact, and this small triumph was consoling, he found. By the time Eve emerged with a pie wrapped in waxed paper, the earl was feeling already a little restored.

He lifted the flap of his jacket pocket and slipped the parcel inside. "The secret," he said, "is to make the pie last the journey home, yet to finish it before the countess catches me."

"Watch out for crumbs, then. Dead giveaway."

He smiled at her and she returned it. Then he cheerfully saluted a mortified Alice, who was peeping out of the window, and walked at a lick out of the courtyard. The dogs galloped joyfully after him.

The walk up to Ravenscliffe was a bit of an effort with a climbing rose under each arm, so Amos was puffing with effort by the time he cornered the track that led to the house. Anna was out at the front, in what would one day be the garden but for now was simply an extension of the common hemmed in by a picket fence. She welcomed him with a smile and a wave. Her hair was tied back from her face and the sleeves of her white blouse were rolled up above the elbows. She looked rosy, fresh, newly minted: she was beautiful, he thought, although he knew he never used to think that, and this puzzled him.

"'ow do," he said. "These 'ere need a drink afore they're planted.'

She opened the gate for him.

"Roses?" she said.

"Ramblers. Pink. They'll do champion over there."

He placed them down carefully, one on either side of the front door, then looked at her for approval. She smiled, stepped forward, and kissed him, once on each cheek, and he had to look away to hide his confusion and pleasure. He wished he could do that, just step up to her and kiss her, but it wasn't how people here went on. Anna, though—she had foreign blood coursing through her veins and had doubtless grown up bestowing kisses. He knew it didn't mean anything, didn't make him special to her.

She walked into the house and he followed her through to

the kitchen. Eve was in there, stirring something on the range, and Seth sat at the table with his head in a book. Tomorrow was his twelfth birthday; there was a cake already baked, and a small pile of presents already wrapped, but there was little being said on the subject because the day after he would start at New Mill. Amos had given him the benefit of his advice, but the lad was pressing ahead with the plan. So be it. Let him learn the hard way, was Amos's view.

"Now then," he said, by way of greeting.

Eve smiled and Seth said: "It says 'ere that veg that grow above ground, like peas an' such, should be planted in t'mornin' an' veg that grows underground should be planted in t'evenin'."

"That, my lad, is what's commonly known as an old wives' tale," Amos said.

"It's summat to do with sunrise and sunset." Seth had read it in a book and the written word, to him, was sacrosanct.

"It's nowt o't'sort." Amos sounded brutal, but he'd learned from experience that unless the boy's more fanciful notions were nipped in the bud, they had a habit of becoming enshrined in allotment law.

"Tea?" Anna said.

"Grand."

He sat down by Seth, who had resumed his reading. Anna placed a mug in front of him and sat down too.

"So?" she said, meaning, What do you have to tell me? She had known the moment he arrived that he wasn't just here for the roses. He laughed.

"Well. As it 'appens I do 'ave a bit o' news."

"I know you do," Anna said. "What is it?"

"I'm standing for Labor in t'by-election."

Seth looked up from his book, Eve stopped stirring, Anna nodded. She sighed a deep sigh of satisfaction.

"This is good news," she said.

"I can't win t'seat," he said.

"You might," Eve said.

"No." He shook his head. "It'll go to t'Liberals. But still . . ."

"I'm proud of you, Amos," Anna said. They looked at each other across the table, held each other's gaze, and smiled.

PART TWO

Chapter 21

The drawing room window of the house at the western end of Caledonia Place provided a perfectly framed view of the Clifton Suspension Bridge, and this had been the principal reason Silas had bought the property. He liked a striking view: insisted upon it. His plantation house near Port Antonio was high in the hills overlooking the startling turquoise waters of the Blue Lagoon; his London house in Mayfair had an unrestricted view of Hyde Park. This was his favorite, though, this view of the bridge across the Avon Gorge, and what it lacked in glamour it made up for in symbolism. The sheer ambition of Brunel's vision; the triumph of endeavor and brilliance over the facts of the case; the realization of the seemingly impossible. These things appealed to Silas. These, and the endless comings and goings of people on foot, in carriages, in motorcars: life—and sometimes death—running its course. Once, on a summer's evening, standing at this window, he had watched a young man in evening dress walk from the Clifton end to the center of the bridge then, without even a moment's hesitation, vault over the iron rail and plummet into the broad brown waters of the Avon below. He had jumped with insouciance, as if he was clearing a five-bar gate in a field. Silas hadn't been horrified by this spectacle: rather, he was thrilled by it. He told his friends in Bristol, why pay to visit the Theater Royal when real life is played out in such entertaining fashion through his own drawing room window?

It was a long walk from here to the docks: an even longer one back. Bristol's hills were steep and unforgiving and Clifton was up at the top on the edge of the downs where the air was sweeter. But Silas always preferred to walk. He didn't enjoy the trams—too much proximity to fellow passengers—and he didn't own a motorcar, because from what he could see, a motorcar made a fellow fat and lazy. So always he would walk, whatever the weather, and his brisk pace down through the teeming streets of Bristol toward the warehouse and dock kept him connected to the boy he once was: lean, sharp, energetic, ambitious. He had a strong sense of himself and this was because he was aware of being watched by others. If he was convinced of his superiority among men, he could hardly be blamed; he saw himself as they saw him: uncommonly handsome, moving through them with the strength and grace of a cat, elegantly fashionable in his London tailoring.

"Whittam! Hey there!"

The voice hailed Silas from across the street, but the pavement was crowded and it took him a while to identify its source: a tall, thin, sallow man, the only stationary person in the tide of humanity, who waited patiently for Silas to spot him.

"Trencham," Silas said when he finally picked out the familiar face. His greeting lacked enthusiasm, though he waited while the other man crossed the street, which he did incompetently, with scant regard for his own safety. Wilberforce Trencham was Bristolian born and bred, but he walked about the city like a bewildered newcomer.

"One day," said Silas, "you'll be hit by a tram or a horse and that'll be the end of you."

"Wishful thinking, Whittam?"

"Not at all, Trencham. You add spice to my life, and it would be the blander for your demise."

Wilberforce laughed.

"Are we traveling in the same direction or are you merely trailing me?" Silas said pleasantly.

"Both, as a matter of fact. I've an article to write on Fyfield's new ship from Swan & Hunter. Lovely vessel, don't you think?" The question was clearly intended to rankle, so Silas remained stoically unruffled. Wilberforce Trencham, shipping correspondent of the *Bristol Mercury*, was determined to uncover pernicious professional rivalry between Whittam's and Fyfield's, even if he had to fabricate it, which he wasn't at all averse to doing.

"Haven't seen it. I'm just back from Yorkshire," Silas said mildly.

"Business?"

"My business, yes. Not yours."

There was no shaming Trencham. He merely changed tack and returned to the subject of Fyfield's latest investment: "Purpose-built carriers, gross tonnage three thousand eight hundred, thirteen knots, and the whole cargo space insulated. They reckon sixty thousand stems a trip, comfortably."

Silas shrugged. "Nothing very innovative there. If you're trying to imply that they're nipping at my heels, I say, good luck to them. Nip away."

"Your own plans in this regard are bigger, are they?"

Silas smiled. "This is where we part company," he said, indicating the small tobacconist that supplied his favorite slim cigars. He sprang nimbly up the three stone steps and entered the shop while Trencham, unperturbed, strolled on toward the docks. He knew Whittam was up to something: he always was.

In any case the harborside, always a fertile hotbed of gossip, was alive with the rumor that he'd negotiated a government contract to carry passengers to Jamaica on a new fleet of banana boats. Trencham mulled it over as he continued on his way: Whittam was well in with the Colonial Office—had been since he collaborated with them on commercial shipments to England from the Caribbean. Well. He'd have another crack at this particular nut later in the day: the harder its shell, the sweeter the kernel.

Silas didn't care what Wilberforce Trencham did or didn't know about his plans for expansion, but it amused him to watch the journalist rooting around for information like a rat in a garbage can. Trencham had been on his tail for one reason or another for years, ever since Silas emerged from the sale of the Global Steamship Company with three-quarters of a million pounds, a ready-made fleet of ships, and the drive and flair to go it alone. He was an industry phenomenon: a ship's lad turned managing director and major shareholder—and when the spoils were divided, Silas hadn't had to pay a bean. The shares and the ships were a gift from Sir Walter Hollis, the Global chairman; whether for services professional or personal, no one was entirely sure, and even now, years later, there was speculation on this score. But however he had come about his generous haul, there was no denying his judgment in business matters. It was Silas who predicted the decline of the cane-sugar industry just before it damaged the company's fortunes; it was Silas who made the case for increasing the banana trade, creating new business for the company and giving Jamaica's failing economy a timely boost. The Colonial Office, alert to Jamaica's difficulties, had funded Global's early investigations into the feasibility of shipping bananas to England, then subsidized the first refrigerated shipment; the benefits at home and abroad were legion if this new trade should prove profitable. When the *Dominion* returned from its maiden voyage—steaming into Avonmouth to a rapturous reception and a band playing "Under the British Flag"—it bore in its hold eighteen thousand stems of bananas and forty crates of mangoes for good measure. Silas was on board, all breeze-blown hair and noble dignity, like a Crusader returned victorious from the Holy Land. At a gala dinner that evening, where Bristol's merchants sampled the fruit before it was packed onto railway wagons and sent to grocers and fruit vendors up and down the country, Silas addressed the assembled company: "The *Dominion* is returned, the *Trinity* and the *Emperor* are ready to sail," he said. "We are poised, gentlemen, on the brink of a new prosperity, once more leading the world in innovation and discovery. Let us be upstanding and raise a toast to the glorious fruits of the British Empire."

"The glorious fruits of the British Empire!" they boomed at once and as one, acknowledging by their mass compliance the unassailable position of Silas as the savior of Jamaica's economy, the linchpin of the Global Shipping Company, and the king of the banana trade. Small wonder that he thought so well of himself.

He was in his warehouse now, taking the stairs two at a time to the office accommodation above. His clerks hadn't expected him back today, and a shiver of alarm disturbed the room as Silas crossed it. Not that standards slipped while he was away or that they had anything to hide: simply that it was pleasant to work without his presence from time to time. They sat at their Davenport desks, pens poised above silver inkwells, and watched warily as he strolled between them. When he reached the door of his own office he turned, surveyed the room, and said, "Brigstock?"

"Sir?" A startled young man stood at once, as if he was in a schoolroom.

"What can you tell me about the new Fyfield's vessel?"

Brigstock, not long in the employ of Whittam & Co. and new to the joys of tonnage, knots, and hold capacity, trembled visibly and there wasn't a man in the room who didn't pity him.

"Sorry, sir," he said—and he sounded truly contrite—"I haven't seen it yet."

"Then your presence here is surplus to requirement. Please leave your desk as it is so your replacement knows exactly where he is to begin. Now . . ."—he gazed about the room placidly—". . . Jones. I put the same question to you."

Another man stood while behind him Brigstock made as small a performance as possible of leaving the room.

"She's called *Port Morant,* sir, room for twelve passengers, insulated hold for sixty thousand stems, not quite as fast as ours, sir, at thirteen knots."

"Thank you," said Silas. "Now, Jones, alert Mr. Oliver to my presence here and ask him to join me in my office."

He closed his office door on the room and saw, from the small stack of papers on his desk, that there was business to attend to, but for the moment he ignored it and instead stood at the window and stared down at the teeming dockside. The water was crowded with vessels, but he could pick out the *Port Morant*—could even pick out Trencham sizing up the new ship while a Fyfield man boasted to the journalist of its special qualities. Silas could see nothing very extraordinary: certainly nothing to worry about. Behind him the door opened and Hugh Oliver walked in.

"Brigstock passed me on the stairs. Looked pretty hangdog," he said.

"He's a fool."

"He had potential. Would have made a good clerk if you'd given him longer than five minutes at it."

"The competition takes delivery of a new ship and Brigstock either doesn't know or doesn't care," said Silas. "I don't call that good. I call it incompetent."

"Still, he was a capable lad. You know your trouble"

"Of course I do. You tell me every time I dismiss someone."

"Well, I'll tell you again. Everyone has to be like you. No good being an excellent clerk, if you don't live and breathe boats and bananas."

"Quite," said Silas. "Brigstock can find employment in a company where boats and bananas don't figure. Now. Two things you need to know: one, we're buying a coal mine in Yorkshire and two, we're diversifying."

Hugh Oliver looked anxious. The coal mine came as no surprise; the diversification, however, was news to him. He was second-in-command at Whittam & Co.—the "& Co.," he liked to say, on the painted fascia of the warehouse front. And yet always, always, the boss was several steps ahead of him.

"Diversification into?" he asked, and his thoughts were of pineapples and passion fruit.

"Travel," said Silas. "Luxury travel. We don't have a ship in the fleet that carries more than fourteen passengers, and yet we travel back and forth to paradise on a regular basis."

Hugh said: "I see. Liners then?"

"Small luxury liners, first-class cabins only. Same capacity for cargo as the present fleet but with, shall we say, added value."

He smiled at Hugh. Contrary to the impression he gave, Silas held his colleague in high esteem. He didn't need Hugh's approval of the scheme, but he would very much prefer it. For his part, Hugh was thinking that once, just once, it would be pleasant to be consulted rather than told. What he said, though, was: "And where will they stay? These first-class passengers of ours?"

"In the first-class hotel we're going to build," said Silas. "Now, what do you know about mining?"

Chapter 22

The king, his mistress, and his confounded dog had gone; the guest rooms were vacated, cleaned, and aired; the earl's study was no longer a telegraph room; Mrs. Adams was respectfully buried in the same plot as her mother and father in the Methodist churchyard; and in her place at the head of kitchen operations was Claude Reynard, patisserie chef extraordinaire and man-of-the-moment below stairs. No one wanted to be the first to say it, but he was much easier on the ears than Mary Adams had been, and easier still on the eyes. Sarah Pickersgill, so often in the old cook's firing line and formerly pitied by all, was now the envy of the kitchen staff. It was all "Sarah, a moment, *s'il vous plaît*" or "Sarah, where is *le bain-marie?*" in his fabulously French accent, and Sarah was as soft and pliable as the pastry that he rolled and folded in his dexterous hands. Monsieur Reynard had the sleek manly beauty of a matinee idol: dark eyes, darker hair, a carefully cultivated mustache following the curve of his top lip.

"When 'e looks at me," Sarah whispered to Ivy and Agnes, "I feel like I'm meltin' or summat."

The kitchen maids were agog. Sarah melting? Whatever did

she mean? But they hovered on the fringes of Monsieur Reynard's orbit, and hoped to experience for themselves his warming influence. They would stand in their respective corners carving carrots into matchsticks and potatoes into marbles, and they would steal furtive glances across the kitchen at the new cook—the chef, they were to call him—whose dashing good looks, tall hat, and white jacket with silver buttons were the most interesting things they had ever seen. Apart, that is, from Mrs. Adams dead in the cold store.

Parkinson was less ready to admire. The "man-cook," as he persisted in calling him, had had an unsettling effect on the girls in the household. Some of them seemed to be loosening their buns so that tendrils escaped from their caps and the staff dinner gong these days sparked a shameful stampede to Monsieur Reynard's end of the table. The chef himself only seemed to encourage them in their infatuation. He appeared to adore them all: he had their names down pat and the way he pronounced them sounded like seduction. Even Agnes, such a plain, everyday sort of name—well suited to the plain, everyday sort of housemaid attached to it—sounded exotic and beautiful after Monsieur Reynard's translation. *Ann–yes*, he said it, losing the ugly "g" and elevating the spirits of little Agnes Nichols every time he singled her out for a mention. It was too bad, thought Parkinson, but his chilly disapproval had thus far gone entirely unnoticed, so he had a word with Mrs. Powell-Hughes, who suspected her colleague of old-fashioned jealousy but spared him the discomfort of telling him so.

"The man has no innate sense of the dignity of his position," Parkinson had said to her. "He's vain as a peacock. All style over substance."

"I'm sure it'll all settle down, Mr. Parkinson," said Mrs. Powell-Hughes soothingly; his feelings clearly ran high, she thought, if he could be so patently unjust about the new chef. "It's all still a great novelty for everyone, you see. And you have to admit, he's sending some beautiful food upstairs, from what I've seen."

Parkinson nodded minimally. It couldn't be denied; the food was superb, and the kitchen girls were working hard at their tasks between regular peeps at Monsieur Reynard's Gallic profile. But the butler was still very far from accepting the new status quo.

"The problem is," he said, "that our man-cook is French."

Mrs. Powell-Hughes waited.

"And the French," Parkinson went on, "have no respect for hierarchy."

"Well, I don't think they're still beheading aristocrats, Mr. Parkinson."

He looked a little crushed; she remembered his many kindnesses to her and felt contrite. "But I imagine you and I can lead by example," she went on. "We can show Monsieur Reynard how we go on in a correctly run English house. And I'll speak to the girls; remind them of their positions. But we should bear in mind that the countess is very pleased with the appointment."

He nodded. "Indeed, indeed, a point of crucial significance. Thank you, Mrs. Powell-Hughes. You're a most dependable friend."

"As are you, Mr. Parkinson. We shall address the situation together. We must both be on our guard for irregularities, while demonstrating traditional English courtesy and respect to Monsieur Reynard."

The butler smiled. He liked that idea. He could adapt, he thought, to being a moral and social compass for the Frenchman, embodying standards of etiquette toward which the man-cook might aspire, if not actually attain.

Whatever Parkinson's reservations, Netherwood Hall was fortunate to have Monsieur Reynard and it might never have come about had not the timing of the emergency telegram been so fortuitous. He was a Parisian chef of the very highest pedigree; he had trained with Escoffier, and worked in the kitchens of the Ritz in Paris and the Savoy in London. From time to time he would make guest appearances in the great houses of noble families: his elaborate patisserie—his clever ways with spun sugar, his miraculous petal-thin pastry—elevated the tone at a banquet and even the redoubtable Mrs. Adams had stepped aside on occasion to make room for him and his staff. When the plea for assistance from Netherwood had reached him, it was just two days after he had flounced dramatically away from the Savoy for the very excellent reason— in his view—that because the hotel continued to make such an excessive ritual of afternoon tea, none of the guests were hungry come dinnertime. A small triangle of bread and cucumber, a slender slice of Madeira cake, a finger of shortbread: one of these delicacies taken with a cup of tea was one thing. But a multitiered cornucopia of creamy confections was quite another. He felt most strongly on the subject, to the point that the countess, on the very day he arrived at Netherwood Hall, had had to agree that no one's appetite would be willfully spoiled at four o'clock in the afternoon now that he was master of the kitchen, although until the king left for London there could be no such rule, obviously. Even Claude Reynard wouldn't dare to deny Bertie a plate of cream scones—which, in any case, didn't seem remotely to diminish the relish with which he would then eat his dinner. Monsieur Reynard had cooked for the king before and knew it to be a fact that the great man was impossible to fill. The night before he left Netherwood Hall the king had ordered a plate of oysters before retiring and then had a cold roast chicken sent to his apartment in case he—or perhaps Caesar—felt peckish in the night.

There was some relief in the house that the king was gone, and below stairs it was palpable. Without him, mealtimes were properly sedate, bedtimes were properly respected, and Mrs. Powell-Hughes found that she could once again beat the dust from a chaise longue without returning half an hour later to find Caesar curled up on it, embedding wiry white hairs into the plum velvet while he slept. Soon it would be quieter still in the great house, since the family's departure for Glendonoch was imminent—they would be in Scotland for ten days, and Mrs. Powell-Hughes felt not a shred of disloyalty at the relish with which she anticipated their temporary absence. Indeed, these periodic lulls were essential in preserving the house-keeper's staunch goodwill and sterling service: if she had to live and work without any respite from the demands made by her employers, she believed she would have packed her trunk years ago.

The countess had singularly failed in her stratagem. The Choates were gone, yet Thea remained, a situation that was actually worse than the one she had been trying to avoid in the first place. How this had come about was still something of a mystery to Clarissa, who was unused to failure in her manipulation of other people and had yet to comprehend fully the extent to which Thea Sterling did as she pleased.

"So now we have the American girl without an official chaperone," the countess said to Teddy. She had tapped on his door and entered his bedroom at an extremely inopportune moment, but instead of retreating until he was at liberty to speak, she had planted herself on a leather ottoman and was speaking loudly to him through the locked door of his bathroom. "And having seen what she's capable of under the watchful eye of Mrs. Choate, I dread to think what she might get up to unobserved."

"I do think we might discuss this at another time," said the earl waspishly. He felt grievously harassed, helpless in the face of this blatant assault on his basic human right to lavatorial privacy.

"Don't you think I wouldn't rather be elsewhere?" said Clarissa sharply. "But this is a matter of some urgency and I'd like you to at least acknowledge that."

"Actually," he said defiantly, "I like her."

"Well, of course you do. So do I, come to that. But liking or not liking doesn't enter into it. She must be kept away from Tobias."

He sighed, resigning himself to the conversation. "Your antipathy to Dorothea is passé, my dear. An American daughter-in-law would bring us bang up to the minute."

"An American countess at Netherwood Hall?" Clarissa's voice wavered melodramatically.

"Just the ticket," he said lightly, deliberately provocative. "What's more, she's not an heiress. All she'd bring by way of a dowry would be a few gramophone records and a jolly good head on her shoulders."

From inside the bathroom came the rush of flushing water, and the countess was obliged to wait until the cacophonous pipe symphony had subsided. He took his time washing his hands, then drew back the bolt, opened the door, and came out to face her. As he'd expected, her expression was reproachful.

"And how, pray, does her relative poverty add to her appeal?"

"It makes her interesting. Rich Americans are so proliferous as to have become downright dull."

The countess, finding no support where she had counted on it, was furious. She stood in order to bring her baleful glare closer to his maddeningly placid face. "Your flippancy does you no credit," she said icily. "Do bloodlines mean nothing to you?"

"Not beyond the stable yard, no," he said, and he realized with a flash of pure and unusual understanding that he really meant this. A curious, uncharacteristic defiance had settled upon him. He always backed down in the end, both of them knew it: but this time, he really thought he might not. Even the tears now springing to his wife's blue eyes—always, until this moment, a reliable last resort—left him unmoved.

"I believe it's a matter of perspective, Clarissa," he said. "I believe there are things in life more important than whether Tobias marries Thea Sterling."

She looked at him in utter disbelief. "Such as?"

"Such as the loss of eighty-eight lives in one of my collieries."

"Teddy! Have you lost your mind? The two matters are entirely unconnected!" She felt genuinely aggrieved that he had—eccentrically, perversely, pointlessly—invoked the wretched explosion, and now stood looking at her as if he was personally responsible. Really, it was beyond her understanding: he had lost all his famous vim and vigor the day of the disaster, and he was a much lesser man without it, in her view. Perhaps a few days on his Scottish moor would lay this business to rest. She said as much, trying hard to keep her disappointment in him out of her voice. He stood silent for a moment, then shook his head.

"I may not be joining you," he said levelly.

"What new nonsense is this?" She laughed brightly to disguise her discomfiture.

"It's time I began to make amends," he said, and he walked to the door, where, just in the nick of time, he remembered his manners and paused, turning to Clarissa with a civil smile. "Will you excuse me?" he said.

"Where are you going?" She felt disorientated and a little queasy. Never had Teddy resisted her so completely and so coolly.

"To talk to Henry," he said and he left her standing there, incongruously slight and delicate amid the dark green and burgundy of his bedroom, but aware that all her feminine wiles had failed her and she was powerless for the first time in their marriage to influence him.

Chapter 23

The night before Seth started work at New Mill Colliery he had woken Eve in the darkness, just like he had sometimes done as a little boy. He had his own room at the new house, which was supposed to be—and in many ways was—a wonderful thing, though he minded more than he would ever say that he couldn't still hear his mam breathing while she slept. But it wasn't that he was missing her company on this occasion: simply that he was missing his dad's scarf, the one Arthur had always worn to work on cold mornings, the one Seth now believed he needed for his own walk to New Mill in three hours' time. He had been up for over an hour—turning his room upside down looking for it—by the time he burst in on Eve: and then, because he himself was wide awake and agitated, he had walked bold and forthright into her bedroom, making no attempt at softness or quiet.

"Mam! Wake up," he said urgently, stabbing at her unconsciousness with his words.

She sat upright instantly, immediately alert to her child's presence. There were no curtains at these windows yet and the moon in a cloudless night sky washed her room in an ethereal silver light.

"Seth, love," she said. "What is it?" Her heart pounded in her chest but there was no reprimand in her voice: to have him come to her in this way seemed like progress.

"My dad's scarf," he said in the challenging tones he saved for her. "It's not 'ere."

"Yes, it is," she said evenly. "I put it in a trunk myself."

"Which trunk, then?"

"T'brown one. It's still downstairs—but Seth, I'll fetch it out in t'morning. Get some more sleep." Still she held her voice steady, as if there was nothing she expected more than to be dragged from the depths of sleep and asked the whereabouts of Arthur's plaid scarf.

"No. I want it now and I'll get it mi'sen." He tried to be gruff but his voice still had the piping pitch of a young boy in spite of the fact that today he was a workingman. He lingered, though, at the perimeter of her room and she held his gaze, willing him to say that he'd had second thoughts about his decision; that he wanted to go to school today, where he belonged. But instead he clamped his mouth against soft words and left her looking at an open doorway. For a few moments she stared at the space where he'd been, then she lay back down on her bed to stare at the ceiling and listen to the sounds of the night out on the common. She wouldn't sleep again tonight, that much she knew.

In the kitchen, two hours later, Eve and Anna stood side by side with their backs against the range waiting for the kettle to whistle. It had taken the Kitchener two days to make the journey from stone cold to piping hot, but now it radiated warmth and this simple fact was remarkably cheering, immensely reassuring: a sign that this big, old, empty house could in due course be tamed and transformed into a home. Everything they'd brought with them was too small: this was the principal problem at the moment. The scrubbed pine table, a tight fit in Beaumont Lane, seemed spindly and insubstantial in its corner of this new kitchen. The two armchairs and the couch were spread out in the parlor, lonely and awkward-looking, like unfashionable first arrivals at a party; and in the bedrooms the chests of drawers, the beds, the wardrobes—all of them were diminished by their surroundings, none of them able to fill their new positions with the solidity and permanence that they'd accomplished perfectly well in the old house. Anna had plans, of course—she was never without a plan of one sort or another—but the view she took was to go slowly in these matters: Ravenscliffe was theirs, this was the main thing. The house was clean and bright and—thanks to the range and the newly swept chimneys—warm enough for comfort. If the furniture lacked heft and girth, well, what did it matter? There was still a chair for everyone to sit on, and enough cups in the cupboard to hold the tea when it was poured.

"Have you definitely woken him?" Anna said. She meant Seth, who, after half the night prowling the house, had fallen into a profound sleep from which Eve had struggled to rouse him.

"Mmm," Eve said. "Like raising t'dead, though." He'd been wrapped in the scarf as well, his mini-Arthur face poking out of the tunnel of wool that he'd made around his neck: as comical as it was devastating. She would be glad when today was over: it was too weighty, too full of morbid significance. Her head ached with it, and there was a constant threat of tears, a lake of them, biding its time, waiting to spill. On top of all the bigger worries—Seth's wasted intelligence, the dangers at New Mill, his enduring fury with her—was the smaller one of how the boy would feel walking alone to the colliery among all those miners. He should be walking in the lee of his dad's broad shoulders, thought Eve, although if Arthur was still here to accompany him, Seth wouldn't be going to the pit today at all. He'd be getting up with Eliza and looking forward to nothing more frightening or hazardous than a chestnut fight in the school playground.

"D'you think I could walk with 'im?" Eve said.

"No," said Anna emphatically.

"Well, it's only that I need to be at t'mill by half five and it's not much out o' my way to go by t'pit."

Anna looked at her askance. The kettle began its shrill serenade and she picked it up off the stove to fill the brown teapot, inhaling like a connoisseur the pungent vapor released by hot water on the loose leaves.

"You'll make him look fool," she said. "Walking to work with his mother, like child on first day at school. It's out of question."

"I know," Eve said. She did. Seth wouldn't let her, anyway. But she had a persistent mental image of Seth's skinny little frame picking its way sadly across the common in the dawn light, then trailing through the streets of Netherwood to the pit yard. In her vision, no one spoke to him or even nodded hello, and a bitter wind blew against him as he walked. She shook her head to dispel the picture and the boy himself walked into the kitchen, looking more robust and a good deal less tragic in the flesh than in her imagination.

"Eggs?" said Eve mock-brightly.

Seth screwed up his face. "I'm not 'ungry," he said, but he sat down at the table anyway. It was too early to leave, even for a new boy.

"You should eat something," Eve said automatically.

Seth nodded at the spanking new snap tin that Eve had crammed with bread and beef dripping. "I can have a slice o' that later," he said flatly.

"Can I just say . . ." said Anna, from a safe distance, ". . . you really don't have to go, Seth. If you want to, you could change your mind." She spoke not so much out of concern for Seth—who she believed would learn best from his own mistakes—but out of concern for Eve. She spoke the words she knew Eve would like to say but daren't, because she couldn't risk a row on this of all mornings. Coming from Anna, the statement lost its inflammatory potential and Eve flashed a swift, grateful look at her friend. Seth said: "Aye, well, I'm set on it now."

"So. Fair enough," said Anna. "This is good thing, to know your own mind."

A silence descended. Seth stood, picked up the snap tin, and tucked it in the pocket of his jacket. He looked so small, so vulnerable, that Eve had to press her hands between the range and her backside to stop herself from falling on him in maternal distress. Anna glared at her: "do not cry" was the message.

"Right," Seth said. "I'll be off, then." His voice cracked marginally because at this moment of departure he suddenly felt the burden of trying to be a man when he'd only turned twelve the day before: and, after all, it was a lonely prospect, walking to work without your dad. But just as he made to leave there came a sharp, startling rap at the front door and the three of them stared at each other, because a knock at quarter to five in the morning surely heralded disaster, or—at the very least—unwelcome news. No one moved. Again, the rap at the door and this time Eve, Anna, and Seth moved as one from the kitchen and across the hallway, and Seth, newly conscious of being the man of the house, pushed forward to lift the latch. He opened the door to reveal Amos, flat-capped and overcoated, grinning down at the boy whose face now broke into a genuine smile of sheer delight.

"Thought I'd missed you," Amos said. "Can't 'ave thi walkin' on thi own to t'pit. I thought I'd offer my services."

"Amos," said Eve feelingly. She was humbled by his thoughtfulness, speechless with gratitude. He looked at her, smiled pleasantly, then looked across at Anna.

"We need to talk," he said. "I need some 'elp rallying voters if I'm not to be a right washout come polling day."

"Later today?" Anna said. "I'll be here."

He nodded at her, pleased: she was as important to his campaign as Enoch. More important: she was the reason, if truth were told, that he was running.

"Right, young fellow-my-lad. You come wi' me and I'll give you t'lowdown as we go."

Seth, back straight, head held high, gave his mother and Anna a cursory, manly wave as he sauntered off with Amos. From the doorstep they watched them go.

"Amos is so kind," said Anna. "So lovely." Her cheeks were pink and Eve laughed and nudged her knowingly.

"What?"

Anna turned, tossing her chin and stalking back through to the kitchen, but her indignation meant nothing; she knew exactly what Eve was getting at.

Later, in a quiet house, Anna stood at her sewing table—now housed in its own sewing room, such was the space at her command—and let the fluid weight of the ivory satin slide between her hands. She had designed the wedding dress herself, sketching ideas again and again in the face of Eve's discouragement, until finally she presented her friend with a drawing of a dress that didn't provoke an instant rejection. It wasn't that Eve had ideas of her own: rather, the opposite. If Anna had allowed it, Eve would have married Daniel—and he wouldn't have raised an objection—in her navy serge skirt and Sunday blouse, so the parade of beautiful gowns that sprang from Anna's imagination provoked in the bride-to-be a sort of bashful, horrified recoil from showiness that had proved a challenge to overcome. In the end, and because she really couldn't bear to see Eve married without a bridal gown, Anna had managed to come up with a design that combined modesty with low-key elegance, and Eve, worn down by Anna's persistence, had pointed to it and said yes. It was still in the earliest stages: still more a swathe of loose fabric than a dress. Anna had a tailor's dummy that shared Eve's dimensions and now she lifted the satin up and over, pinning it at the back so that it clung to the contours and fell to the floor in sleek ivory ripples. The neckline was crucial: Anna wanted a wide, shallow line, which she would trim with antique lace, delicate and intricate. More of the same lace was destined to adorn the sleeves too: Medieval sleeves, which followed closely the length of the arms then ended in a soft pointed flare just below the wrists. She worked without a paper pattern because she held the image in her head and she would never make such a dress again. It was to be unique: Anna's gift to Eve, her homage to their friendship, a token of her love. These were weighty themes and Anna knew, if she tried to express them in words, they would embarrass Eve or come out wrong. So the dress was important: the dress said everything she wanted to say. She beetled away at it like the Tailor of Gloucester, sewing and snippeting and piecing out the satin, and this is how Amos found her, entirely absorbed in the task at hand and her mouth clamped tight around six pins that, one at a time, were being carefully placed in the yards of fabric from which, like a butterfly from a chrysalis, a dress was beginning to emerge. She didn't hear him come in, but she acknowledged him calmly when she realized he was in the room. For his part, he registered a detached interest in the fact that he could look on what was clearly to be Eve's wedding dress with no particular emotion, no pang of regret or twist of the heart. It was the little seamstress, her sweet fresh face intent on the job at hand, who held all his attention, and this, too, he registered with the same detached recognition. The storm of emotion Eve had once provoked in him had truly broken and been replaced, as storms so often were, by a bright, clear calm.

Anna couldn't speak because of the pins, but she gave him a little wave.

"Them bairns look 'appy," he said, thumbing toward the front door, which Anna had left wide open for Ellen and Maya to come and go. The little girls had a pail each and wooden spoons, and were mixing soil and water to make a chocolate cake: this is what Ellen told him, when Amos stopped to ask what they were up to. Maya, ineptly slapping her spoon about in the bucket of thick mud, had looked at him with her mother's eyes and said "yum yum" with the accent of a true Yorkshire tyke. It had made him laugh.

Anna took the pins out of her mouth and set them down on the sewing table.

"So," she said and clasped her hands together in a gesture of eagerness. "Let's talk politics."

Chapter 24

If William Garforth was surprised to discover that his two o'clock appointment was with not only the Earl of Netherwood but also Lady Henrietta Hoyland, he showed it in neither his face nor his conduct. He shook her hand as firmly as he shook her father's, and in the ensuing conversation he was scrupulously fair in the division of his attention as he spoke, sharing equally between the two of them his wise and steady gaze. An ex-army man with a gentleman's manners and an engineer's brain, Mr. Garforth's perfect composure sprang from a reliable and sustainable source: his unwavering belief in the common good of the pursuit of greater mine safety. If these fine folk standing before him shared that goal, they were and would ever be welcome at the West Riding Colliery.

They were here to witness in action his Mines Rescue Center, a simulated accident scene in a sealed-off chamber by the pit bank, where his men regularly endured the same smoke- and dust-filled conditions they would encounter after an underground blast or collapse while shifting tons of rock and rubble that had been placed there for the purpose. It was the only such center in the world, and there were plenty in the industry who had William Garforth marked down as a crackpot for spending money on training for an event that might never happen. But he cared nothing for naysayers. His interest was in people like the Earl of Netherwood and his forthright daughter: forward thinkers, with a large budget.

Mr. Garforth assessed them shrewdly as the three talked in general terms about the Netherwood Collieries, the recent explosion, the lamentable number of fatalities. He noticed that while the earl did plenty of talking, the young woman often quietly prompted her father, reminding him of details or steering him back to their purpose if he seemed liable to wander off the subject. She clearly had some authority in this relationship, though he could see she was making strenuous efforts to take a back seat, for the sake of appearances. Mr. Garforth wondered if this visit had in fact been at her insistence; certainly Lord Netherwood seemed less well acquainted than his daughter with the purpose of the rescue center. Which wasn't to say the earl was uninterested: quite the reverse. He had a battery of questions for Mr. Garforth, who answered in minute detail, acutely aware that here was a man with a good deal of clout— a colliery owner, not a colliery manager like himself. If the Earl of Netherwood went home convinced of the value of safety and rescue training, then three more pits in Yorkshire would become less dangerous places to make a living.

"So. The West Riding Colliery is one of Pope and Pearson's?" said Lord Netherwood. He was fascinated by this; that this distinguished man with military bearing, impeccable in a stiff white collar and monogrammed necktie, was merely an employee.

"It is, m'lord, yes."

"And are they involved in your innovations?"

"Not directly. The training school is my initiative, based on my own experience of running collieries. I've been at this

196

game for over three decades. But the owners do stand to gain, of course." He spoke well, like a man used to hearing the sound of his own voice and using it to good effect.

"Gain? Financially, do you mean?"

Henrietta rolled her eyes skyward.

"Daddy," she murmured, "there are benefits other than those of increased profits."

Mr. Garforth smiled: a warm, generous smile that implied he wasn't taking sides, though he hoped his own daughters would never speak to him with the same cool disdain.

"We all stand to benefit—the miners, the management, and the owners," he said. "Advances in underground safety and rescue mean fewer fatalities, higher morale among the men, greater productivity, higher profits."

"And the mines rescue center—do you expect your men to attend in their own time? Unpaid?"

"Yes. I've never encountered unwillingness."

The earl laughed. "Lucky chap," he said and turned to Henrietta. "I can imagine how such a proposal would be received in Netherwood." He expected a smile, but she looked stern, as if his levity was an embarrassment to her.

"I think our miners have the same respect for one anothers' safety as Mr. Garforth's employees. You underestimate them."

"I think," said Mr. Garforth carefully, "that we three have never lain waiting for help on the wrong side of a rockfall. Improvements in mines rescue aren't something miners quibble over. I asked for thirty-five volunteers when we first started. Every man who works here put his name forward."

The earl nodded. He felt incapable of saying the right thing. He had come here with his daughter out of a creeping and uncomfortable awareness of his failings, a realization—late in life, admittedly, but better that, he supposed, than never at all—that he didn't quite measure up to the man he had thought he was. There had been a moment at the foot of the mine shaft

197

at New Mill when he had thought his life was in danger and an emasculating liquid rush of fear had coursed through his system: it had shocked him, brought him up short, as if an unwelcome home truth had at last been spoken out loud and to his face. In his own eyes, on that day, he had lost confidence in his standing and did not yet feel quite recovered. Now, facing this earnest, educated colliery manager, he felt even slighter, even less of a presence in the world of honorable, serious men. There were certificates and diplomas all about the office walls displaying Mr. Garforth's excellence and endeavor: president of the local Mining Institute, vice president of the national body, fellow of the National Geological Society, an expert practitioner in aspects of mining engineering that the earl hadn't even known existed. On the desk between them stood a brass safety lamp that the man had invented himself, for heaven's sake. And yet, in the pantheon of great, titled colliery owners, Teddy Hoyland had always stood tall as a man with his employees' best interests at heart. It was at once inspiring and disorienting, this dismantling of certainties and reordering of priorities: he had a notion that he might never be the same again, and that this might be no bad thing.

Thea was trapped again in a corner of the drawing room with the Duke of Knightwick, whose blatantly adulterous wife left him alone for great stretches of time and who therefore craved alternative female company on whom to inflict his wide range of opinions. Thea Sterling was an obvious target; he fancied himself a mentor to the young American woman and was forever seeking her out to continue his program of instruction in the ways of the English aristocracy. She hadn't yet devised an effective method of cutting him short, being altogether too amiable for her own good. She pitied him his situation, though—his wife's all-consuming liaison with the dazzling banker Wally Goldman, the pair's careless and inappropriate intimacy, seemed to Thea intolerable and inhumane. So, instead of taking her cue from the duke's more seasoned acquaintances and turning away as he approached or remembering a pressing engagement when he was midsentence, she would listen obligingly to his long, bewildering monologues and even, sometimes, submit to a short test at the end. Today's lesson was at least topical, being a digest of the shooting season, prior to their departure for Glendonoch; she found she needed all her powers of concentration to follow the complex subtleties of what one might shoot when.

"The whole shebang commenced on the twelfth of August—the Glorious Twelfth, you might have heard that said? No? Well, I'll be blowed! You really are an innocent abroad. Anyway, grouse shooting from the twelfth in England, Scotland, and Ireland. Partridge shooting starts on September the first, ends on the first of February. Pheasant shooting starts October the first, also ends the first of February. Are you with me? Hares may be shot until March the first, rabbits can be shot at any old time of the year. Rooks, May the twelfth and all through the summer."

"I see," Thea said. "Rooks. Who would shoot rooks?"

"Good in a pie," said the duke, obliquely. "So. Start of the season is . . . ?"

"The Glorious Twelfth," she said obediently.

"Pheasant?"

She grimaced charmingly. "Golly. What was it? September first?"

He gave a patronizing smile, pleased that this favorite subject of his was not so easy to master after all. "October the first. September's partridge.'

"Right," she said, in a voice so obviously flat with lack of interest that even the duke couldn't miss it. "So, what is it about you guys that you need to keep shooting birds out of the sky? You seem kind of crazy about it." Her New York drawl still seemed incongruous in the context of this English stately home. "Shooding birds," she said, and "kinda crazy": her accent was one of the things about Thea that either attracted people or repelled them. The duke fell into the former group, but nevertheless he bridled at this casual slight against the sporting prowess of a nation; in a few easy words, she had managed to reduce a noble pursuit to an eccentric aberration. Unprepared for the challenge and unused to justifying his pastime, he briefly fell silent while a defense formulated itself in his head, but it proved to be a critical pause and one he instantly regretted, because Tobias strolled into the room and hailed Thea from the opposite end.

"There you are, you elusive creature," he said, and she leaped to her feet at once, seizing the chance to make an escape without appearing rude. She blew Knightwick a kiss and winked at him: saucy behavior, but not untypical, and it at least brought a frisson of pleasure to the duke's poor, neglected breast. If he was but twenty years younger, he thought to himself wistfully. He watched her shimmy across the room to Tobias in her startling gown—bold girl, wearing red satin on a Wednesday morning—and thought she had something of a bird's qualities about her, though an exotic one, not the type one would take a shot at. Tobias watched her too, with the minutely focused attention of a connoisseur of women. He would have liked to place his hands on either side of her waist to feel the satin slide under his fingers; he would have liked to press her against the wall of the drawing room and bruise her lips with his own. An effort of will was required simply to stand and smile in a casual manner, but his will prevailed and he managed, again, to keep his hands from her.

200

"Tobes," she said. Her smile was direct, straight into his green eyes. He had grown on her, this English earl-in-waiting. He was fun.

"Thea. You look extraordinary. Have you finished teasing poor Knightwick?"

She looked back at the duke in alarm, but he was deeply involved now with the *Sporting Life*. She shot Toby a chiding look.

"Don't be mean. And I don't tease him, I listen to him."

"You can't help being irresistible. Nobody blames you."

"Quit the flattery. What's the plan today, then?" There would be something, she knew that much. Tobias was wooing her with activities, keeping her mind off thoughts of returning to London or—worse—America, where she still thought she might take up the place at Cornell. Toby would follow her there if he had to, though he hoped it wouldn't come to that. Far better, he thought, that he captured this rare North American specimen and kept her here.

"Netherwood Common and all my boyhood haunts. There's a tree with a hollow trunk. You can climb it, but only by going up the inside."

She smiled again, that wonderful, piercing, direct smile.

"Henry and Dickie too?"

"Sadly no," he said, not sad at all. "Just dull old you and boring old me."

Her peal of laughter caused the duke to look up briefly from details of the three-thirty at York but the sight of Tobias and Thea on the other side of the room radiating bright beams of youth and desire and energy sent him instantly back to the pages of the *Sporting Life*, a landscape he understood and where he felt he belonged.

Chapter 25

The first indication Amos had that he was considered a threat was an offer from the Liberals of a safe seat at the next general election and a substantial salary from the party if he withdrew from this forthcoming contest as Labor candidate. He would, he was told, be a well-paid Liberal MP with a real voice in the House of Commons if he would but take his name off the Ardington ticket. Amos said no, decisively and bluntly, without taking time to think or talk it over with Enoch or Anna, who between them had become his political inner circle; if he was to enter politics, he told himself, he would be led by his heart first, then his head, but never by his pocket, and no one would convince him otherwise. Enoch backed him entirely; the Labor Party would never amount to anything if it continued to simply shore up the Liberals at every election. Anna agreed too, though she put him through his paces first, playing devil's advocate to be sure he knew his own mind.

"Perhaps better a Liberal MP than not an MP at all?" she said.

"No," Amos said emphatically. "Better a principled failure than an unprincipled victor."

"Everyone says Liberals will win at next general election. Think of it—you could be part of government, not opposition."

"Oh aye—an MP in a government I don't believe in? Not me. There's workingmen in Parliament already who're only there because they toe t'Liberal line—they can't speak for t'likes o' Stan Clough or Sam Bamford because t'Liberal whip won't let 'em. It's like 'aving a guard dog, then clouting 'im for barking. If I'm to be an MP, I want to be an MP who can stand up and say exactly what I would say at a miners' meeting in New Mill pit yard."

"Very good, very nice. And who will hear your fine, principled opinions if you don't first get elected to Parliament?"

"My views are 'eard every time I raise a crowd at a colliery and if it never goes farther than that, so be it. I shall fight as a Labor candidate, or not at all. The working poor of Ardington need a poor workingman to represent 'em. That's me."

She was proud of him, proud of his fierce integrity, but she worried, too, that in spurning the Liberal Party so wholeheartedly, he had gained as many powerful new adversaries as he had admirers. And then one evening in Ardington, on the steps outside the Pheasant Inn in front of a crowd of locals, Amos burned his bridges, promising his audience that the Labor Party would one day replace the Liberals and hoist the working classes from their present place as an afterthought in the Liberal manifesto to true prominence in Parliament.

"That's torn it," said Enoch afterward.

"Good." Amos, slow to get started, was fast developing his radical public persona. He had always known how to use words, and now he honed the skill, speaking with passion and fury at the betrayal of the ordinary man by the Liberals in Parliament who claimed to speak for them but forgot their interests at every critical vote. Labor had to cut its ties with the Liberals and plow its own political furrow, he said, so this was the message that Amos, Enoch, and

Anna—and a small, loyal posse of supporters—took from door to door in the few days before the by-election. Anna walked so far, knocking on doors and preaching the Sykes gospel, that her voice was reduced to a pitiful croak and her feet bled; in the evenings, back in the kitchen at Ravenscliffe, she wincingly forced them into a bowl of warm salt water in the hope that the cruel stinging meant the weals and blisters would heal by morning.

"You should consider a bicycle," Eve said, peering into the bowl and flinching in sympathy. She was back from the mill, back from a day of making and baking a hundred and fifty miniature veal and ham pies for Fortnum & Mason, and she was dog-tired herself, though her feet, at least, were still in one piece. Amos's political ambitions were taking a heavy toll on her friend: taking a toll, too, on the state of the house. Eve inadvertently let her gaze stray over a pile of unwashed linen, a sink full of dirty pots, and Anna, seeing her, said: "It's only until Thursday."

"I know," Eve said. "It's fine." But, anyway, she set to work on the washing-up because she couldn't bear to sit down while there was work to be done.

"Is Seth back, then?" Eve liked to be home to see him, but sometimes it just wasn't manageable and, in any case, she hardly got two words out of him. It was through Anna and, occasionally, Amos that she had gleaned the few scraps she knew about her son's first days at New Mill.

"Mmm. He's upstairs with his vegetable book."

"Good. I'll go and say g'night then. 'ow did 'e look?"

"Same. White where he wasn't spotted with black. He said his ears are ringing."

Eve shook her head in dismay. Seth was on the screens, and stood his entire long shift at a rattling conveyor belt picking useless rocks and shale out from the moving mass of coal. The work was mindless and hellishly noisy, so that when the lads were allowed to sit outside and eat their snap they took a few moments to adjust and continued to yell at each other as if they were still trying to be heard above the clank and grind. You could train a monkey to do what Seth was doing, thought Eve. She abandoned the pots in their sudsy water, left Anna to her salt footbath, and climbed the grand wooden staircase to the first floor. Along the landing she paused at the little girls' bedroom and looked inside. There were two iron beds side by side, but Ellen and Maya were curled up together in only one of them, facing each other, foreheads grazing, their angel faces deadly serious in repose. Next door was Eliza, who, though on the edge of sleep, waved from her bed and asked Eve if she'd had a nice day.

"Busy. You?"

"We did geography and I stood at t'front and talked about Jamaica. Blanche Marsden said I was making it up."

Eve smiled.

"Blanche Marsden doesn't 'ave an Uncle Silas, so don't be too 'ard on 'er."

"I'm not. Minnie Pickering cried again and went 'ome early."

"Oh dear. T'Pickerings are all very sad at t'moment."

"When my dad died, it were only 'im, weren't it?"

Eve nodded.

"I cried an' all."

"Today?"

"Aye. With Minnie. She set me off. But it was for my dad, not 'ers. I'm right as rain now, though." She smiled, to prove it. "I saw your wedding dress."

"I 'ope you didn't touch it wi' mucky fingers."

"No. Anna said she'd chop 'em off if I did."

"I should say so."

"I wish she'd finish it and make mine."

"She's saving t'best for last. Get some sleep now. You're a devil for keeping me chatting."

Eliza smiled ruefully. "I can't 'elp it. There's such a lot to talk about," she said.

"Night night."

"Night. Shall you be in t'kitchen when I get up?"

"I shall. We can walk to school together tomorrow."

Her daughter, sublimely easy to please, sighed with pleasure at this happy prospect, then settled back down into her pillow, which clouded up on either side of her face, obscuring her from Eve's view. In here, Eliza's bedroom, Anna had used three different paint colors on the wooden floor so that it was pastel-striped like a bathing hut or a deck chair: pale blue, pale pink, pale yellow on each consecutive floorboard. At the window she had hung simple cambric drapes with side-ties of broad navy blue ribbon. The bed had blue and white bunting strung along its length, and Eliza's clothes were folded into a wooden chest onto which the child's name had been stencilled in dancing capital letters. Her few books and toys—a bear, Mabel the china doll, whose face was fixed like Eliza's in an expression of wide-eyed wonder, a xylophone, and the flower press from Daniel—were arranged in a line along the floor, waiting for a shelf to go up on the white walls. The perfect plainness of these was lifted by Anna's delicate handiwork: a painted garland of pink, blue, and yellow daisies, which looped and twisted around the four walls until it met its beginning. It was all so utterly charming that Eliza had burst into joyful tears when Anna allowed her to have her first peep. It had given the little girl the impression that Anna, already very high in Eliza's estimation, had magical qualities, fairy powers, a mysterious ability to turn an ordinary bedroom into an enchanted place. Eve, who had never in her life wielded a paintbrush or properly mastered a sewing machine, was inclined to agree.

Further down the hallway Seth's bedroom door was ajar and a slice of soft light extended from it onto the landing, which meant his lamp was still burning. Eve, encouraged, pushed the door wider and looked inside. In here Anna had spread more magic and begun a mural of a tree whose branches were going to bear an unlikely menagerie—monkeys, parrots, lemurs, hummingbirds, owls, squirrels. This special project was—unbeknownst to Eve—the subject of considerable behind-the-scenes bargaining. Anna had told Seth that her work on the mural was connected directly to his own behavior toward his mother and Daniel, and this explained its faltering progress: some days even the prospect of a spider monkey hanging by its tail from a branch wasn't enough to keep a civil tongue in Seth's head, and on these days, Anna's paintbrushes would remain in the jar of turpentine. Eve, ignorant of this and standing at the threshold of the room, saw the tree and marveled at it, as she always did, because to use a wall as a canvas seemed to her such a bold, inventive thing to do. The tree was a great oak, a version of the one that stood outside on the common, perfectly framed by Seth's bedroom window. He was sound asleep, his vegetable book fanned out on his chest and moving slowly up and down as he breathed. He had washed his face but his hands, spread like two starfish on the counterpane, were filthy, coal dust packed into his bitten fingernails and in the creases of his knuckles. This would once have raised a flash of annoyance in Eve: now, all she felt was sadness. She picked up the book, closed it, and placed it on his bedside table, then snuffed out the lamp. She would see him in the morning before he left for work. Leaving the bedroom, stepping softly across the floorboards—unpainted as yet, though they were to be the same bright green as spring grass—she paused again to admire Anna's oak tree, a shadowy image now in the lampless gloom. From an uppermost bough a wise old tawny owl gazed with amber eyes directly at Seth in his bed as if trying by the force of its avian will to make the boy see sense. Good luck to you, thought Eve.

Silas was downstairs when she reappeared in the kitchen and he was sitting at the table nursing a cup of tea between both hands, with his customary comfortable ease, as if he had been there all along, waiting for her. He'd sent no word of his impending return, preferring the mild drama of an unexpected appearance. But it was late for visiting; this, anyway, was what Anna's expression said. She was cross to have had her salt soak interrupted, cross to have padded to the door with wet, bare feet to find Silas waiting for admittance, when they hadn't even known he was back from Bristol, and though she was performing the motions of hospitality, slicing cheese and buttering bread for a sandwich, she banged down the things—the loaf, the plate, the knife, the Cheddar—on the worktop a little louder than was necessary.

"Good grief," Eve said. "It's you, out o' t'blue again."

He smiled his best, crooked smile. "Hello, Evie," he said. "You look—" He paused, and she jumped in.

"Tired? I am."

"Very lovely, I was going to say. A little pale, perhaps, but it suits you. You look like the Botticelli Venus."

"Chutney?" Anna said brusquely, from where she stood across the kitchen.

"No fear," he said, without looking at her. "Never had a taste for vinegar."

Eve sat down opposite him at the table. "So, what do you think?" she said.

"About?"

"Ravenscliffe. 'aven't we gone up in t'world?"

208

"It's very fine," he said, in a voice that conveyed the weight of his experience of beautiful properties, the difficulties inherent in trying to impress him.

Anna placed his sandwich in front of him and sat down too, next to Eve.

"Thank you," he said, then: "They tell me at the Hare and Hounds that Amos is running for Parliament."

There was a small smile playing about his mouth: it might have been friendly, or it might have been the opposite; Anna couldn't tell, though she could have made an educated guess. She ignored the question in his statement and said: "So, you're staying there again?"

"Plenty of room 'ere," Eve said, hope and encouragement evident in her voice. Beside her, Anna tensed. They seemed to see him through different eyes, she thought.

He dipped his head apologetically. "I'm used to being alone," he said. "My habits are irregular and I don't enjoy the restrictions of other people's domestic timetables. And also I rather like the Hare and Hounds. I like the way the noises and smells of the snug filter up to my quarters."

Eve, nose wrinkled, said: "That's a good thing?" and Anna, heady and generous with relief, said, "More tea?"

He held up a hand to indicate no, then said with studied casualness: "So, I'm buying a small colliery. Dreaton Main." He allowed himself a moment to enjoy the looks on their faces before continuing. "Coal for my ships, you see. Makes sound sense."

There was silence, and then: "Aren't there mines closer to Bristol than Dreaton Main?"

This was Anna, who was making a very good point, although he ignored it. His haste and drive to buy a colliery so close to his childhood home was indefensible in business terms. Wales would certainly suit better, geographically speaking; but he wanted one here, where he'd started from nothing. Thumbing his nose, he supposed, at what destiny had once had in mind for him, at what his life could have been.

"A pit? You're buying a pit?" Eve was utterly bewildered. She hadn't realized this was possible; did pits come up for sale? Did they change hands, like motorcars or horses?

"I am indeed."

"You'll be a colliery owner, then?" She sounded simple, she knew that. But in her experience, colliery owners were dukes and earls, not boys from Grangely. His confidence—the sheer brassiness of him—was breathtaking. She had no idea what she felt: pride, anxiety, amusement, shock. All of these.

"Mmmm. Amusing, isn't it?" he said, mightily pleased with the effect of his announcement. "Penniless trapper at twelve, and look at me now."

Together, facing him across the scrubbed pine, they looked. Looking back at them, Silas laughed, to fill the silence.

Chapter 26

An ugly gash, a broad, brown scar, cut through the perfect green of the lawn from its uppermost beginnings to its farthest end and Daniel—the architect of this outrage—walked its perimeter with an air of supreme satisfaction. He had his hands shoved deep in the pockets of his corduroy work breeches and he sauntered with a jaunty, carefree gait along the length, across the width, and all the way back up toward the house again, and the scar was so wide and so long that it took him a full fifteen minutes to make the journey. He was imagining, as he walked, the brilliant future of this Grand Canal: a regatta, perhaps—a small flotilla of handsome yachts scudding prettily across the water; or gondolas and gondoliers at a Venice-themed event; or fireworks blazing into the night sky above the canal, their brilliance exquisitely reflected on the surface of the black water. But these things were hard to visualize for anyone who wasn't Daniel, and to a man, his thirty-four undergardeners thought their new boss was addled in the brain. They had, after all, spent the years of Hislop's tyrannical reign paying slavish attention to the quality and condition of the grass, feeding it, laboriously mowing it, aerating it with the tines of a fork, scrupulously checking it for foreign bodies: fallen leaves, rogue daisies, defiant buttercups, the insidious beginnings of moss. From a distance this lawn had, under their vigilant care, taken on the appearance of the green baize surface of an enormous billiard table. Now, at Daniel MacLeod's insistence, the baize had been slashed and torn, and for what? For a canal, apparently; a word that invited an image of the oil-slicked stretch of gray-brown water that ran from Barnsley to the Barnby Basin, bearing coal-laden barges and smoky little tugs pulling platforms of lumber and steel. The undergardeners couldn't visualize the long, light-filled, brilliant sheet of water that Daniel spoke about, or a day when a Hoyland family birthday might be marked by a nautical spectacular. But anyway, they did as they were bid and dug conscientiously within the marked-out area, striving to get the job properly started before the winter arrived and turned the earth to iron.

Daniel's priority had been to push through his plans before the family decamped to Glendonoch, but his powers of persuasion had been tested to the limit when he had first revealed his new scheme to Lady Netherwood. The king's car had barely turned out of Oak Avenue on the day of his departure before Daniel was seeking a meeting with the countess, unrolling his precious drawings in the morning room and pressing them flat on the table, a series of beautiful depictions of a garden quite unlike the one she had. She had looked at them long and hard before looking up and saying: "I don't quite understand."

"Understand what, your ladyship?"

"Well, Daniel, these drawings seem to bear no relation to my garden."

"These are my suggestions for how your garden could be."

"So this"—she traced with the tip of an oval, manicured nail the outlines of the proposed Grand Canal—"is a stretch of water where my lawns currently lie? And this"—again she traced a line, this time around the pared-down remains of her Japanese Garden—"is to replace my pagoda and goldfish pool?"

"This could be the most talked-about garden in the country," he said, deliberately evasive. "The most beautiful, complex, integrated, classical garden in England."

"Is that so?" She sounded peevish, still feeling irrationally bruised by his insistence on marrying Eve Williams.

"With your approval, of course, and your input," he said, the diplomat now.

"And with my money, more crucially."

He laughed. "Indeed. But look—it'll be Fulton House, writ large, and you know how widely admired that garden has been," he said. "If you look carefully at this scheme, you'll see a lot of the existing beds are all still in place. We don't need to change them; your planting's superb. But there are new ones here, here, and here, as well as a parterre across this area, and paths leading down to the wisteria tunnel and beyond. We can keep the goldfish, if you really can't bear them to go."

Her eyes followed his finger as it moved over the drawings. She could see the ambition of these plans, could visualize the glory for herself if Daniel pulled them off. But pride was making her snappish and mealymouthed, and though she nodded in apparent agreement with him, she said: "The pagoda must stay too. It's a particular favorite, much admired."

He looked at her, trying to gauge how bold he could be, how honest in his opinions. Not especially, was his conclusion.

"Och, well everyone has a pagoda, don't they?" he said. "But I was hoping you'd agree it's time for something new. Let's be the English garden with no pagoda. And if you miss it in the new scheme, we'll find a place for it, you have my word." The kitchen garden, he thought, with a wry private smile: a Japanese chicken house, perhaps.

"Hmmm. Why do I feel you're plying me with false promises?"

He placed a hand over his heart like a knight before his lady. "Never false, your ladyship. You have my word that the pagoda will be placed in safe storage until such a time that you accept that . . ."—he paused to smile at her—". . . I was right and you were wrong."

A moment stretched into two, three, four moments while the countess decided what she made of his playful insolence.

"Oh, you," she said, at last, waving her little hand at him in magnanimous exasperation. "I've given you too much freedom these past twenty years. Now you believe you may simply do as you wish. But go ahead. Let's see what you can make of our little corner of England."

And the digging had begun the very next day.

To the relief of everyone—for he really was very much loved by his friends and family—the earl had decided that, after all, he could accompany them on the shooting party to Scotland. He felt that, in fact, the break would do him good: that, and the company of the young people, whose high spirits were in such invigorating contrast to his own. Little Isabella was home from her holiday with the Suffolk cousins, and being reunited with his favorite had been something of a tonic: she adored her indulgent father, and this uncomplicated fact had done much to restore his equilibrium and soothe his injured pride. With his youngest child by him on the couch, or sitting on his lap, or taking his hand on a stroll through the grounds, Lord Netherwood began to feel almost heroic. He had been too long in the company of the excellent but severe Henrietta, who had coached him to accept her skepticism and exasperation as his just desserts. Isabella's company was restful and restorative by comparison.

But the principal reason for his decision to go to Scotland was the progress he felt he had made toward salving his own conscience; it would be a long job, but it had begun. The earl believed, since meeting William Garforth, that all the wrongs of the past—though they couldn't be righted—had at least been acknowledged and could now be used to inform his decisions and help prevent future mistakes. Harry Booth, the manager at Long Martley, had found that far from being sacked for disrespectful rudeness—and that in front of the king—he was in fact to be rewarded with the honor of presiding over the new Netherwood Collieries Mines Rescue Training Center. Mr. Garforth would be consultant to the project, and would advise on where in the pit yard to site the center and how to equip it. As at the West Riding Colliery, volunteers were being sought to form the core of a new highly trained rescue squad, and Henrietta had been absolutely right: hundreds of miners had so far applied to be considered and the earl felt humbled by their commitment to this cause. He wondered at himself, at his blindness to what mattered most to all these employees of his, at his own complacency that for decades had passed for benign liberal tendencies.

A great granite obelisk was to be erected in the center of Netherwood and engraved with the name of every man who had died in the explosion, as well as those who had perished in earlier days. Along with the rest, the stonemason would be chipping A. *Williams New Mill 1903* into the smooth gray rock, which was only right and proper: the death of one man in a pit must be honored in the same way as the death of eighty-eight. Meanwhile, an inventory of essential repairs in all three of the earl's collieries had been drawn up ready for immediate attention. The earl—facing head-on his new greatest fear: that he would perish beneath a pile of rubble in one of his own mines—had descended the shafts of New Mill, Middlecar, and Long Martley, and walked the roadways with his deputies, inspecting conditions underground, prodding roof supports and stooping to examine wagon tracks. There was talk of new equipment—electric coal-cutters to eliminate the perilous business of working under the seam, if the hewers could only be persuaded to use them, and hydraulic metal props to replace the wooden ones, if the men could only be persuaded that they were safer—and new iron winding gear was replacing the old timber structures at the three pits. Suddenly, and with remarkable speed, Netherwood's collieries were becoming pioneers: the best examples of the coal-mining industry's willingness to move with the times. The verdict of the inquiry was still to come—the affected area so badly damaged that it still wasn't safe for inspection—but here was Lord Netherwood, stirred out of complacency, whipping up a storm of improvements before any inspector had been able to demand it of him. With the zeal of the newly converted, the earl had even sent proposals to his three managers for pit head bathhouses, a modern phenomenon already in use in some parts of Europe, where miners sluiced off their filth and donned clean clothes before going home. But this was a step too far for the Netherwood miners: safety improvements were one thing, but where and how they washed was quite another, and nobody's business but their own. There was a hasty vote, and the handful of men who raised their hands in favor quickly sat on them again, resulting in an overwhelming "no" to a ridiculous notion that would make soft women of every man in the earl's employ.

"Thing is," said Harry Booth to Lord Netherwood when he reported back with the emphatic message. "We asked t'wrong folk to vote. We should've asked t'wives. I reckon they'd 'ave a different take on t'matter."

The earl had nodded earnestly, so keen to take seriously any suggestion for the better that he didn't realize Harry was only joking. This was how it was now: the earl so desperate to atone that he couldn't see the comedy in putting it to the women of Netherwood that their menfolk leave their muck at the pit head.

On the broad, shallow steps of Netherwood Hall's main entrance, Mrs. Powell-Hughes, Parkinson, and a hand-picked collection of their most presentable underlings formed a farewell party, so the family shouldn't have to leave their home with no one there to wave. It was the pleasantest of duties, thought the housekeeper disloyally. She really was pleased to see the back of them and if they decided to extend their stay in Scotland, you wouldn't find her complaining. For weeks now she and her girls had been run off their feet, and she knew the kitchen staff were feeling equally worn out after preparing breakfasts, luncheons, dinners, suppers, and who knew how many light snacks at eccentric, arbitrary points in time. The night before last, Sir Wally's bell had rung below stairs at two o'clock in the morning, when the last of the dishes from a long, late dinner had just been washed, dried, and stacked. They would have had every right to ignore it, being well past the time when anyone might be expected to answer; but Sally had trotted obligingly up there and had come back down—looking mortified—with an order for fried eggs on toast for Sir Wally and the Duchess of Knightwick, who was sitting up in his bed as bold as brass, her hair all mussed and the sheets pulled up to her neck to hide her nakedness. Mrs. Powell-Hughes was familiar with the ways of the world, but there were still rules to abide by, even when morals had gone to pot. So, what with bedroom antics, unreasonable demands, the king and all his entourage, the king's terrier treating the house like a glorified kennel, the dragging-on of the house party as everyone waited to see if the earl would accompany them to Scotland . . . it had all resulted in a house-keeper who was finally at the very end of her tether.

So when the convoy of cars and carriages had disappeared in its own cloud of gravel dust, Mrs. Powell-Hughes sighed feelingly and said, "Thank goodness they're gone," and in front of the parlor maids too, which was so unlike her that Parkin-son, shocked, dismissed them at once and caught the house-keeper gently by the arm as she made to leave herself.

"Are you quite well, Mrs. Powell-Hughes?" he said.

For a moment she looked at him, puzzled by his concern, and then the penny dropped and she laughed lightly. "Oh, don't fret, Mr. Parkinson. I haven't turned revolutionary. It was simply a mild expression of relief that we have the house to ourselves for a couple of weeks."

The demands had not yet been made on the butler that would compel him to utter—audibly at any rate—the words she had used. His own loyalty to the family seemed to know no limits, and of this he was proud. But he was a good man, and he did his utmost not to judge the housekeeper for her momentary lapse. She was tired. They all were. He smiled in a general, noncommittal way that he hoped demonstrated sym-pathy with her fatigue rather than with her views. She left him and returned to the house, and for a minute he stood alone on the steps, surveying the gardens with an attitude of grave ap-preciation and savoring the earthy, smoky smells of early autumn. A small shadow of concern crossed his benign features as he noticed that the recently departed wheels and hooves had left unsightly ruts and pockmarks in the pinkish gravel of the avenue. The driveway must be raked, all the long mile from the house down to the gates. This was well outside his remit, of course, but still he found himself hoping that Mr. MacLeod, immersed as he was in his Grand Canal scheme, would not overlook this small detail. For it was, thought Parkinson with pious, proprietorial satisfaction, the attendance upon such small details that made Netherwood Hall the glorious place it was.

Chapter 27

On polling day in Ardington, the Liberals and the Tories ran their supporters to the polls in gigs and carriages, and Anna made Amos laugh by cursing herself for not borrowing Sol Windross's rag-and-bone cart. As it was, they did their best, knocking on doors—again—to encourage their supporters to come out and place their cross by the name of Sykes for the Independent Labor Party. All the time, though none of the people he spoke to would have guessed it, Amos knew he would lose; this was valuable experience, but it wasn't going to make him an MP. He had known this even before the campaign began, and the weeks of hard slog had only confirmed it as a certainty. Mind you, he thought, it beggared belief that so many of these good working people would turn out in high numbers to vote for the wrong party. The previous member for Ardington had been swept into Parliament on a massive majority in the general election of 1900; he was a wealthy manufacturer, a Liberal, and pleasant enough, but with no interest in the town beyond its usefulness to him in gaining entry to the elite gentlemen's club that was the House of Commons. He had died of a heart attack—too much access to butter and cream, Enoch surmised—

and the Liberal candidate chosen to replace him was of the same breed: affable, arrogant, his belly asking too much of his waistcoat, his thoughts turning to luncheon the moment breakfast was finished. His name was Webster Thorne and he was just the sort of Liberal that Amos loved to hate: the sort of Liberal who, with a private fortune and a large house in London, had little interest in improving the lot of anyone else. They were a sorry lot, Amos said to Anna: trotting out reasonable, even thoughtful, political aims, but fulfilling none of them because of an innate and crippling smugness.

"Well, be fair. They're only in opposition," Anna said.

Amos snorted contemptuously. "All talk, no action," he said. "Every vote that might have some bearing on t'lives of ordinary folk gets dodged."

"Such as?"

"Such as a working wage for MPs. Now—that's summat that'd change t'very core of our political system, but time an' again, t'Liberals in Parliament duck that issue. And why? Because if they're honest, they don't think Westminster is any place for a workingman."

"And yet, here they come, these workingmen, to vote for Liberal Party," Anna said. They were standing outside the church hall, made into a polling station for the day, and they were forced to step back to make way for yet another carriage, which rattled up to the door and disgorged six more men for Webster Thorne. Anna shouted, "Vote Sykes for workingman!" and they looked a little startled. Three of them, all miners, greeted Amos as they passed. At least they had the decency to redden, he thought.

"See? It's nowt personal," he said to Anna. "Better t'devil they know. That's 'ow they see it, anyroad."

"Speaking of devils you know, it must be very hard for you at moment."

"What must?"

"Trying to keep hating Earl of Netherwood when he is busy with all his good works."

He raised an eyebrow at her and she raised one back: she was a regular thorn in his side, always poking at his principles to see if he might give them up.

"Long way to go before I'll doff my cap at 'im," he said, though she was right, in a way. He had nurtured his savage resentment toward Lord Netherwood for so long now that, in truth, it was more habit than emotion. Amos's dislike and mistrust of the earl went back years, but had been heightened and honed by a conviction that Lord Netherwood had somehow stood between himself and Eve—that his great wealth, his influence, his power to help her on her way had taken her out of Amos's reach. This particular beef had diminished into irrelevance since she'd sprung Daniel MacLeod on them all, of course. Still, there were plenty of other reasons to keep a nice level of antipathy simmering away on the back burner: iron winding gear and electric coal-cutters were all very well, but where did the benevolent earl stand on the eight-hour day? Where did he stand on sick pay and widows' pensions, on injury compensation and the right to paid holidays, on a minimum wage to guarantee every miner in the land a decent living? These questions were what stoked the fire at the heart of Amos's political credo; these questions—and the lamentable lack of satisfactory answers—were why he would rather lose as a Labor candidate than win as a hamstrung Liberal.

He looked at Anna, his diminutive, feisty foot soldier on the Ardington battlefield. "Come on," he said. "There's nowt more we can do 'ere. 'ow d'you fancy a glass o' milk stout an' a pickled egg?"

"How charming," she said with full Rabinovich hauteur. "I've walked until my feet bleed for pickled egg?" But then she smiled at him, and she couldn't have looked happier.

It was a mystery to Absalom Blandford that he had ever found Eve Williams desirable. Whenever he saw her these days—which was far more often than she realized—he was filled with an almost visceral revulsion; the same physical qualities that he had once convinced himself he wanted were now utterly repugnant to him. It was as if she emitted a repellent odor, the intimate origins of which were unknown to Absalom, but which radiated out from her toward his delicate nostrils whenever he was within range. He would watch her, unseen, and his face would contort with disgust. After these encounters he would have to bathe in the evening with extra care, scrubbing at his skin with a nailbrush so that the smell of Eve didn't revisit and torment him in his sleep. This phenomenon wasn't unique to Eve Williams, however; he could detect a different aroma around anyone who came into his orbit. This gift—or curse—was the latest manifestation of his personal fastidiousness, and like a bear or a bloodhound, he could sniff the air and know, without looking up, who had walked into his office. Jem Arkwright was filthy, unwashed; he carried the scent of horse manure and human waste. The earl, for whom Absalom had a cringing, obsequious respect, nevertheless bore permanent traces of the smells of engine oil, pipe tobacco, and smoked fish. But these various personal aromas had obvious, traceable outside sources. What disturbed Absalom about Eve Williams was that the source of her musk was hidden, tucked away somewhere in her folds of female flesh. He wondered that anyone could bear to be near her. He wondered that the new gardener, believing they were unobserved, could press up against her in his desperate, pitiful need without recoiling at once in horror at the stink.

Absalom watched her now. She had come out of the kitchen

and into the courtyard of the mill, where she seemed to have nothing better to do than trail around the tables and chairs with a half-smile on her face as if she were party to a joke that no one else had heard. She stopped at the fountain, bending at the waist to pick fallen leaves from the gristmill, and the dark shadow between her breasts was suddenly on display to him where he stood, closer to her than she could possibly imagine, in one of the hiding places he used for this sort of surveillance. He considered stepping out into the open, simply to startle her out of her complacent happiness, but rejected impetuosity in favor of the sensible option: remaining hidden from view, remaining vigilant, watching and waiting until his mental dossier on Eve Williams amounted to something incriminating. If it were in his power, he would collapse the trappings of her life around her right now. He would throw her out of the mill, withdraw the tenancy agreement of Ravenscliffe, reveal her to the world as the whore he knew her to be. But it wasn't in his power to do any of these things, because she was a cunning and dangerous prey: she had used her harlot's tricks to win the trust and affection of Lord Netherwood, and this kept her safe. But it would not always be so: this, Absalom knew.

He was back in his office, scratching at the ledger like a man with an itch, when Daniel MacLeod knocked on the door. He made the gardener wait for longer than was comfortable, then raised his head from his work.

"Come," he said with little encouragement, and the gardener entered, first kicking his feet against the step to dislodge the mud. Absalom pointedly studied his fob watch to indicate the relentless march of time and to make it clear, if it wasn't already, that whatever Mr. MacLeod's business, it was bound to be petty and tiresome compared to all the bailiff's other duties.

"Afternoon," Daniel said affably, his Montrose burr strange and startling to the ears of the bailiff, who didn't return the greeting. The rank mingled smells of rotting vegetation and potash invaded Absalom's extraordinary olfactory system and, resting an elbow on the desk, he casually covered his nostrils with the fingers of his right hand. Daniel was oblivious to this defensive maneuver. He had had no firsthand dealings yet with Absalom Blandford, though Eve didn't like him, he knew that much. She had described to him the bizarre occasion when the bailiff had dropped to one knee at the railway station and asked for her hand in marriage, having shown no previous attachment to her whatsoever. A supremely awkward moment, Daniel imagined, yet the fellow could hardly have been heartbroken at her refusal. A rash, ill-considered impulse, no doubt, but quite understandable; it amazed Daniel that he had found Eve before anyone else had claimed her, and the fact that the bailiff had once thrown his cap into the ring made Daniel more, not less, inclined to give him the benefit of the doubt.

"I'd speak to Lord Netherwood, but I gather he's away up to Glendonoch, lucky man," Daniel said. "No better place to be than a Scottish moor at this time of year."

There followed a stony silence relieved only by the monotonous tick-tock of the wall clock. Absalom had the unblinking gaze of a lizard, and he was never the first to look away.

"So, I'll get to the point," Daniel said, realizing immediately that he was not in the company of a pleasant man and fighting an urge to edge closer to the door. "We—that is, Eve and I—would be honored to accept the earl's offer of the use of the chapel on October the twenty-second. She wants Samuel Farrimond to officiate, though. He's the minister at Grangely. Would that be all right, do you think?"

Absalom stared. "I beg your pardon?" he said. His voice conveyed nothing of the outrage he was feeling on the earl's behalf.

Daniel laughed. "Should I repeat it all? Or just the last bit?"

"I heard you, in actual fact. I was merely expressing my amazement at your audacity."

"At my—?"

"Audacity, yes," Absalom repeated levelly. "You are either much mistaken or sadly deluded. The Netherwood Hall chapel is for the exclusive use of the Hoyland family and has been since the house was built almost two hundred years ago. Your mission here is simply preposterous and I must insist you leave."

"Now, just hold your horses, Mr. Blandford," said Daniel, more stunned than angry. "I'm not seeking your permission for anything. I'm merely informing you of a kind offer made to Eve by the earl, evidently without your prior knowledge."

The bailiff held up one hand as a barrier against Daniel's words.

"Mr. MacLeod," he said. "Your—intended—cannot possibly have been offered the use of the family chapel. It would be inappropriate in the extreme. A gardener and a cook? I hardly think so."

"Why, you miserable, jumped-up Sassenach bastard!" Daniel, all restraint and decorum abandoned, stepped forward and placed his two large hands on Absalom's desk, the better to hold a steady, hostile gaze. "I should knock your prissy wee head off your shoulders, except you're not worth the trouble it would cause me. But let me tell you something. Eve Williams and I will be wed wherever on God's earth we wish and if you have a problem with that, then I'm afraid you're going to have to swallow it."

He moved back, away from the desk, toward the door. Absalom, briefly alarmed for his own safety, relaxed marginally.

"Get out," he said, full of bravado now that Daniel was leaving. "Or I shall throw you out."

Daniel laughed. "I should like to see you try." He threw a final look of naked contempt in the bailiff's direction, then stalked out of the office, shoving open the door with such force that it swung violently back onto the brick wall outside, then slammed shut again with the momentum. Absalom shuddered. The man was an animal, with an animal's appetites and responses. He and the whore were well suited.

The Liberals took it, as everyone had known they would, but Amos was still the story in the following day's newspapers, because he had given Webster Thorne an extremely anxious few hours when a recount was ordered because the result was too close to call. In the end, Thorne's margin of victory was forty-five votes. The Tory candidate was never in the running, but everyone knew that it wasn't his votes that Amos had so audaciously poached. On the makeshift stage in Ardington church hall, Enoch raised Amos's arm in a victory salute and the small crowd of Labor supporters who'd stayed on for the recount—Anna among them—whooped and hollered their approval as if their man had been elected.

"Next time," Enoch shouted at Amos over the racket. "Next time." And a small part of Amos believed his friend might actually be right.

Chapter 28

By any normal person's standards, I'm an abject failure," said Henrietta cheerfully. "Even Isabella pities me, and she's only twelve."

Thea ceased her rowing, allowing the little wooden boat to temporarily pick its own course through the steel-gray waters of the loch. Henrietta had been coming here to this stretch of water on their Scottish estate since childhood; she was happy, now, to be sharing it with her friend. The day was cold, and Henrietta sat wrapped in fur with her back to the prow, but Thea had cast off her coat and her face was flushed with exertion.

"Well, snap," she said. "My parents have practically disowned me. It was their idea that I travel to England. They needed a break from the embarrassment I cause them."

"Did the Choates know what a flop you are?"

"The Choates are darlings. Much more freethinking than my folks. Caroline is all for girls learning Latin and math."

"Even so, I think she finds you a little wild."

"Oh, sure. And she'd much prefer it if I wore a girdle."

"Well, since you mention it, why don't you?"

"Why should I? I want to be able to move. You should

follow my lead and liberate your body." These last words she yelled, sending them out across the water so that they bounced back at them in duplicate from the hills beyond. Henrietta laughed.

"My mother's great fear, when she first met you in London, was that you were a suffragist."

"Was it?" Thea looked immensely interested. "And do you know, that's one thing she needn't have worried about at all."

"I'd rather like to be able to vote," Henrietta said. "I think if I knew I could influence the outcome, I might take an interest in politics."

"Couldn't much care either way," Thea said. "If someone gives me the right, I suppose I might. But I'm not waving a placard about it."

"Selfish girl," said Henrietta, but Thea just smiled at her and reached for the oars, which had, while they talked, lolled useless in the rowlocks. For a few moments they fought her, resisting her efforts to right them, but soon she had them tamed and began to draw them through the water. She was surprisingly adept at this, keeping a steady pace, cutting a straight and confident path back to the jetty.

"If I could just bring myself to marry," Henrietta said in a musing voice, leaving her unfinished statement hanging in the air between them.

"Have you been asked?" There was no malice or judgment in Thea's question, only genuine interest.

"Well, no. I seem to sort of stop would-be suitors from pursuing romance. When I sense it coming I start to talk loudly about mining or duck shooting. It's an affliction of mine, like an unfortunate birthmark or a nervous twitch. Quite beyond my power to cure it."

The boat glided smoothly alongside the jetty, and Thea leaned out over the side for the rope to haul them in and secure the vessel.

"Do you know that house on Netherwood Common?" she said.

Henrietta, surprised by this conversational about-turn, thought for a moment, then said: "Ravenscliffe, do you mean?"

Thea nodded. She looked directly at Henrietta, who thought what a startlingly wonderful-looking girl Thea could be, and was, in this light, in that blue dress, with a light bloom of perspiration on her face and her eyes the fathomless green of the sea in summer. Her beauty was of the quiet kind: hidden initially by its imperfections, it stole up on you by degrees.

"I saw it when Toby and I walked up there," Thea continued. "There was a woman outside, up a ladder, painting her own front door a beautiful shade of gray-blue, and I was so startled and—well, charmed, I guess."

"Probably Anna Rabinovich," Henrietta said. "Was she small and very blond?"

"Her hair was hidden by a scarf. But she seemed so capable. So independent. Imagine, Henry, taking up a paintbrush to change the color of your own door."

Henrietta shrugged. "Not sure I'm following," she said.

"No, Toby was kind of bewildered too. But to choose a color, any color you please, and apply it yourself, to your house—it seems to me the absolute epitome of freedom."

"I think Anna has to work jolly hard, to be honest."

"I don't mean the freedom to do nothing. I mean the freedom to run your own life."

"Ah, yes. Now there's a prize."

"We spoke for a while, Anna and I. She's painting the whole house just as she wants it, and she's making drapes for the windows. She seemed so . . ."—Thea hesitated, groping for the word that might adequately describe Anna's particular quality—". . . complete."

"And yet, so do you, to me," said Henrietta. "And you'll probably marry Toby, then you'll be complete to the rest of the world too. Whereas I, I'm Lady Henrietta Hoyland and five seasons have fruitlessly passed since I was launched in society, and until I marry I shall be forever considered half a person."

The boat was steady now, tied firmly by the rope onto an iron peg, but Henrietta and Thea sat on, looking at each other. Henrietta swallowed hard. High above them, a buzzard hung lazily, basking in a thermal current, keeping an eye on the water's edge.

"If I marry Toby," Thea said, "it'll be as much because of you as of him."

This statement was casually made and quite unexpected. Henrietta, who had believed her feelings for Thea to be a hopeless matter and quite doomed, didn't speak but let the joy of Thea's words blossom in the silence. She smiled, and Thea smiled too, and between them passed a moment of such magnificent understanding that Henrietta thought if she died now, in this cold, damp boat with the inhospitable waters of the loch all about her, she would die content. On land, behind them, a voice shattered the moment.

"There you are! We've searched high and low even though Dickie insisted neither of you were worth it and we shouldn't bother."

Tobias and Dickie had appeared on the shingle bank, having emerged through the tunnel of Scots pines that led to the edge of the loch. It was close-planted, this footpath to the water, almost enclosed, and it lent the loch an air of privacy, an air of a place where confidences, once shared, were safe. Dickie, smiling affably at his brother's blatant untruth, raised no objection and ambled along behind Toby, who jogged on to the jetty, his face radiant with the pleasure of finding Thea. He saw her, thought Henrietta, to the exclusion of everything else around him. Henrietta might as well not have been in the boat. He held out a hand, and Thea took it, returning his smile, matching his warmth.

"What were you talking about?" Toby said. "You looked jolly intense."

"Why, you, of course," Thea said smoothly. "Nothing else is half so interesting."

They linked arms and walked away from the boat, leaving Dickie to lend a steadying hand to Henrietta.

"They're pretty thick these days," he said.

"Yes, aren't they?" Henrietta smiled at Dickie, and she looked to him as though she was about to impart a secret, although she didn't. Instead she sighed with evident satisfaction and said: "I do believe dear Tobias is about to be reeled in."

Dinnertime in the banqueting hall, and the talk was all of ghosts. At Glendonoch Castle there were three regular visitors from the other side, all of them tormented in their individual ways. The Blue Lady ran about the grounds pointing in distress at the knife that had been plunged into her trachea; Little Jim, a young black boy, haunted the kitchens, and the weals of his regular whippings were clearly visible on his bare torso; and on the upper floors the ghost of the cowardly Earl of Storrey could be found in the oddest places, still trying to conceal himself from the Jacobite forces he was meant to be fighting. All the Hoylands, even Isabella, took an extremely equable view of their spectral housemates; it was an inferior Scottish castle that couldn't boast a regular haunting. Among the present guests, however, there was considerable consternation.

"Do you mean to say we shall see them? All three?"

This was Lady Hermione Hartwick, who was failing to conceal her agitation beneath the strenuously amused tone of her inquiry.

"Well, not Little Jim obviously," said Dickie mildly. "And

the Blue Lady never comes inside. But old Storrey—he's a regular in the ladies' bedrooms."

"Gracious heavens!" Alicia, the Duchess of Knightwick, had abandoned all pretense at sangfroid and was gaping unattractively at Dickie. "What an odious prospect."

"'Odious' being an extremely apt choice of word."

"Dickie dear," said Lady Netherwood. "We're still at the table."

"What on earth are you referring to?" Thea said, perplexed rather than alarmed. "Does the Earl of Storrey smell bad?"

"Rather!" said Dickie, enthusiastically. "He was beheaded—somewhat messily—for his treacherous cowardice, and he proved a coward to the end because everyone who's encountered him has picked up the distinct odor of—"

"Dickie! Desist!" Lady Netherwood glared at her son.

"Tell me later, Dickie," Thea said *sotto voce*, and winked at him. Vulgar girl, thought the countess. She shot a look at Teddy: a look that said, there—are you quite content with her? For although nothing had been announced, it was increasingly clear that it soon would be. Now that this battle was evidently lost, Clarissa unexpectedly found that Thea's evident unsuitability—her gauche manner, her idiosyncratic clothing, her unfortunate accent—made her existence easier to bear. She was as sure as she had ever been of anything that Dorothea Sterling was wrong for Tobias, but this belief, rather than reducing Clarissa to despair, gave her strength and a certain amount of satisfaction. Her own high standards of beauty, style, and good manners—for which she had always been renowned—would be set in sharp relief against the backdrop of Thea's shortcomings. In this, she found considerable solace.

"Are there ghostly visitations at Netherwood Hall? Or do you confine this particular sideshow to your Scottish home?" This was Sir Wally Goldman, whose voice dripped with skepticism, though if pressed he would have had to admit to some alarm at the prospect of a malodorous earl, long dead, lurking in the shadows of his room.

"No," Henrietta said. "Netherwood Hall is peculiarly free of lost souls."

"I expect Mrs. A will pay us the occasional visit now," Tobias said, and everyone laughed.

"Was she carried out of the house feet first?" said the Duke of Knightwick earnestly. "It's most important that she was, you see, because a soul can't return to a building if they're carried out with their feet pointing toward the door."

"Poor Mrs. Adams," the countess said vaguely, as she did whenever the cook's name was mentioned. She felt better disposed toward her, more able to mourn her inconvenient demise, now that Monsieur Reynard was installed below stairs.

"Well, if she's there, it'll be to keep an eye on the Frenchman," said Lord Netherwood, who was yet to be convinced that the new chef quite lived up to his reputation.

"He's awfully handsome, your *monsieur*, isn't he?" said the duchess. Her eyes widened, as if in anticipation of something delicious. "I went to the kitchens for a cold compress for Wally's croquet bruises and the Frenchman was wonderfully helpful, even though he had to leave his meringues. Do let me know, Clarissa, if you tire of him." Sir Wally flashed her a swift, injured glance, and she pouted back at him, playfully remorseful. Her husband looked tactfully away.

Archie Partington, Duke of Plymouth, had been following the conversation with his habitual expression of affable blankness. He had joined the Netherwoods in Scotland from his own neighboring estate, invited by the countess who always liked a peppering of eligible men at the table. Granted, he was rather elderly; but he was indisputably single, since his second wife had fallen off her hunter and died at the Boxing Day meet two years before.

"My cook at Denbigh Court," he said now, "organized her own replacement from her deathbed. The transition was seamless. Saved me all the bother of hiring."

"Don't you find," said Hermione Hartwick, "that one's staff seem indispensable when they're with one, and then they leave or they die, and one realizes they were perfectly easily replaced all along. A little like a favorite hound, in fact."

This seemed a singularly callous observation, though around the table there was neither the energy nor—in some cases—the inclination to contradict it. Silence fell, a dreaded conversational hiatus; Lady Netherwood jumped into the breach.

"Ladies?" she said, indicating the door, and Thea, entirely unready to leave the company of the men for the tedious chit-chat of the drawing room, said: "Oh, let's not withdraw tonight. Let's have some fun together."

This anarchic suggestion was greeted with enthusiasm by all but the countess, who felt woefully wrong-footed, and at her own dining table too. But the suggestion quickly gained momentum as everyone began calling out suggestions. Mahjongg, said Lord Netherwood, only to be laughed at for being too stuffy. He retreated into hurt silence while various parlor games were mooted, debated, dismissed. The two dukes were loudly insistent on their own favorites: Plymouth wanted riddles and enigmas—"Oh Archie," said Hermione Hartwick, "not all that 'Tis in the church but not in the steeple' nonsense"—and Knightwick longed for charades; he loved charades more than anything he said, and defied anyone to come up with anything more amusing, at which provocation his wife suggested sardines.

"More food? I really couldn't eat another morsel," Thea said, then she gazed in bewildered pique about the table as her companions roared with laughter. It was a game, Henrietta explained fondly: a sort of backward hide-and-seek, where one person hid, and everyone else hunted for them.

"And on discovery," said Sir Wally, in thrilling tones suggesting great intrigue, "instead of revealing the hiding place, you squeeze in there with them, until everyone but the last seeker is squashed into the same space—hence sardines."

"Well, that sounds extremely jolly," Thea said. "Just so long as smelly Storrey doesn't squeeze in too. I shall be the first sardine."

Tobias smiled at her. She was such a game girl. He wondered if she might tip him the wink as to her hiding place. Getting his hands on Thea Sterling had become just about all he could think about.

"Very good," said the earl. "However, I shall leave you to it, as my sardine-playing days are over. Instead, I shall nurse a fine Courvoisier in my library and look forward to hearing all about it."

"And I shall be in the drawing room," said the countess, her voice the very essence of displeasure and disdain. "Please do join me there when you've had your"—she paused—"fun."

Lady Netherwood rose, and the dukes—excessively disappointed at being denied enigmas and charades and disinclined to squeeze in anywhere with anyone—rose with her and accompanied her out of the room. Dickie adopted an expression of comical suffering.

"Oh dear," he said. "Wrap up warm. There could be a frost tonight."

"Oh pish," said the duchess. "An hour in the exclusive company of dreary Donald and awful Archie, and she'll be delighted to see us all again."

"Really, Alicia. You're too unkind," said Sir Wally, but he draped an arm cozily across her shoulders and he smiled as he spoke.

Thea, squiffy after two gin slings and wine with dinner, caught Henrietta's eye.

"As I haven't played before and I don't know the nooks

and crannies, let's break the rules and start with two of us," she said. "Henry?"

"Oh I say," said Tobias. "Surely you can find a hiding place without Henry's help?"

But his protest was futile, since the two young women were already on their feet and—since no one else objected anyway—Toby had to stifle his disappointment and remain with the seekers while Thea and Henrietta ran giddily out of the room.

Chapter 29

From the pit yard at New Mill up the track to the main road, it was one hundred and eighty-five footsteps, and from the main road to the edge of Netherwood Common it was a further five hundred and sixty-eight. Often Seth would leave the pit at the end of his shift and begin to count backward from seven hundred and fifty-three as he walked home; he liked this sense of the lengthening distance between himself and the colliery and he liked, too, the moderate challenge of keeping track of the numbers, coming as it did after nine long hours when his mental agility was not called upon at all.

Seth hated his work at the pit with a depth of feeling that was impossible to articulate: impossible, that is, if there had been a living soul he was willing to tell. As it was, he spoke to no one about the horrors of his day: the permanent cloud of dust too thick to see through, the ceaseless noise, the mindless cruelty of Mr. Oatley, the supervisor, the painful boredom—a physical ache, unlike anything he had ever experienced before—of the hours at the steel belt, sorting muck from coal. Mr. Oatley carried a long stick, which he periodically used to poke any lad who appeared to be slacking. "I'll chop out your kidneys and put 'em in a pie," he would say, over and over again, cackling demonically. Seth thought he was touched in the head. Opposite and beside him at the screens were boys he'd known at school, older boys who laughed raucously and shoved each other and seemed to find their work more than tolerable. They were happy to be out of the schoolroom, making their way in the world. But Seth, though he looked the same and sounded the same, felt like an actor playing a part. He played it well, though. He could hawk nastily and spit the dust out of his throat and onto the floor at his feet; he could stare sullenly ahead when the supervisor threatened to brain him for daydreaming; he could sit with his back against a brick wall and eat his snap, pretending not to care that his filthy hands left perfect fingerprints in the white bread.

But inside, where the real Seth resided, he wished with all his heart that he was still at school. He had always enjoyed it, but now, now that it was his past, he remembered it as bathed in a golden light, an idyll of indulgent pleasure: the pursuit of knowledge, the thrilling quest for swift solutions to hypothetical problems. Like all deep thinkers Seth understood just how much he still had to learn; but now he had willfully cauterized the steady flow of facts with which he had hoped to understand the world. Each day that passed at New Mill seemed a terrible lost opportunity. This tormented him. This, and the fact that his dad had loved this place, and yet he, Seth, loathed it. And so even his precious memories of Arthur were somehow tainted, all wrapped up in the misery of this new life that everyone had advised him against and yet he'd chosen anyway.

So it was a glum boy who walked slowly toward Daniel MacLeod as he stood waiting at the top of New Mill Lane; a glum boy, staring at the cinder path, ignoring all around him, silently mouthing his strange numerical litany. He only looked up when he saw a pair of boots ahead of him that clearly weren't going to move. When his eyes alighted on Daniel, his face registered first surprise, then embarrassment, and finally utter dismay. Still, he wasn't prepared to lose count.

"Five 'undred and seventy," he said, then again, "five 'undred and seventy."

"What's that?" Daniel said. "Five hundred and seventy what?"

"Doesn't matter. Just summat I do." He was determined now not to say another word.

"Fair enough."

They looked at each other for a moment. Seth held his silence, but he hadn't hurried on by, so Daniel took heart from this. He delved into a canvas bag slung over his chest and pulled out two terra-cotta pots, each bearing what looked to Seth like tiny palm trees. The pots were packed with rich black soil. So were Daniel's fingernails. He stared. The small leaves were sharply pointed and plentiful.

"What's them?" Seth said, tricked into speaking by his own curiosity.

"Pineapple tops, planted up just this morning in one of my hothouses. I thought you might like to try to grow them."

Seth looked at him suspiciously. He would very much like to try to grow them, but he didn't know how Daniel MacLeod might know that.

"Who sent you?" he said, and Daniel laughed.

"Nobody sent me," he said. "I thought, catch him on the way home and we can walk along to that allotment."

His voice was casual, though he was perfectly well aware of the various disastrous scenarios that might result from his precipitous action. It was just that he was thoroughly sick of playing this waiting game with Seth. If progress could be made before the wedding he knew how happy Eve would be. And when all was said and done, Seth was just a boy and boys' hearts could be unlocked, if you only had the right key.

"They don't grow 'ere. In our climate, I mean."

240

"Aye, they do, under glass and with a bit of care."

"I've no green'ouse."

"All right. Well, we can see about that. Shall we walk on over there and have a look?"

Seth said nothing. On the one hand, the possibility of cultivating exotic fruit in his allotment was truly interesting. But on the other hand, he'd vowed for the sake of his father to treat this interloper with chilly contempt. Clearly, these two positions were incompatible. But those little plants . . . they intrigued him. And had this maddeningly pleasant Scotsman just hinted at building him a greenhouse?

"Amos says you'd be soft to try and grow owt tropical in Netherwood soil," he said, attempting to remain unfriendly while at the same time prolonging the discussion.

"Och, well, Amos is quite right. Netherwood soil can't nurture pineapples into good health all on its own. But a skilled gardener like yourself can bring them on, in the right conditions."

It was no good. Seth had a brief, glorious vision of Percy Medlicott's face when the first crop of pineapples made themselves evident, and all resistance was lost.

"Right," he said. "Well, in that case."

"Good. C'mon then."

So they went together to the allotment, and though it was Daniel's first visit, it wouldn't be his last. They'd need a tan pit to warm the roots, he told Seth, and a sloping glass roof: a warm air flue too, if it could be managed. At Netherwood Hall they'd been growing pineapples since 1737, Daniel said; they knew what they were at down there. Keep the soil warm and keep away the mealybugs and the thrips, and there was more than a fighting chance that Seth would be cropping fruit next summer. Seth listened, intent. Occasionally he asked a question; how warm did the soil need to be, how many pineapples per plant? His animosity had dissipated into the clear blue sky.

They walked the plot and it didn't take long, up the brick path to the back wall, and down again. Daniel commented on the railway ties, deployed by Amos many months ago to make raised beds. Clever idea, that, he said. The willow trellis was beautifully done—was that Amos too? No, that was me, said Seth, and held up his hands: nimble fingers. What a team you've been, Daniel said, and he wondered, aloud, whether Amos would mind his being here, making suggestions.

"P'raps, at one time," Seth said. "But now 'e's that busy with union work, 'e doesn't get down so often." All the same, Daniel said, Amos should be consulted. Seth nodded, sagely. Men's talk.

For now, they placed the little pots under two large glass cloches, in a part of the plot where the autumn sun, when it shone, could still warm the soil. But there was room aplenty for a tan pit against the back wall, just a wee one, Daniel said, and he would build it as soon as he got the materials together. This was a fine plot, he said. Seth was a fine gardener. Maybe they could take a turn around the kitchen gardens at the Hall one day? Seth's heart beat a little faster at the prospect. Aye, he said, maybe.

The conversation didn't stray from the realm of the horticultural, but never mind. They were two gardeners, and two gardeners will never run out of something to talk about. Afterward they walked back together until Seth's path took him on to the common and Daniel's to Netherwood Hall, and they parted with no ceremony or words of farewell: a brief salute, a nod of the head, was all that occurred between them. And Eve knew nothing of it, except she noticed, when she came home from work, that Seth was reading the biography of John Tradescant: reading it intently, with a small frown of concentration, like a scholar.

Whittam & Co. was the new proprietor of Dreaton Main, barring a few legal loose ends and a signature or two. Hugh Oliver was in Netherwood with Silas now, the two of them acquainting themselves with their new venture, strolling about the pit yard in their Savile Row suits like Sunday visitors to a public garden. They were buying a going concern, so the Dreaton men were still at work, though Silas was already wondering if fewer men working a different shift pattern might not be more profitable. But these matters could wait until the colliery was properly theirs.

Hugh found Netherwood dreary after Bristol. And he couldn't ever live in a landlocked county, he told Silas.

"I feel hemmed in," he said. "No obvious means of escape."

Hugh attracted a good deal of attention. Somewhere back in his distant ancestry was an African slave girl and an English sailor: the result, two centuries later, was a Bristolian with skin the color of toffee and a head of jet black curls. People stared and made no apology for it: he was a wonder to behold in this town of pale, underground faces. Silas, aware of the impact his colleague was having, paraded him all over town: the Hare and Hounds, the Cross Keys, the newly reopened Hoyland Arms all played host to Hugh and Silas. And at Ravenscliffe, he was an instant success, the sort of man who—unlike Silas, his opposite in many ways but particularly this—wouldn't let a woman lift a finger if there was something he could do to help. Today he was holding the wicker basket for Anna while she unpegged washing from the line. It might have appeared unmanly, except he gripped the basket in one hand, and his arm was outstretched, so that he gave the impression of performing a feat of strength. The wind caught the sheets in Anna's hands and snapped them out and back again until she had grappled them into a manageable bundle.

"Good drying weather," she said, her voice swallowed by a gust. Her skirts were pressed flat against her thighs and her hair, missing its scarf, whipped becomingly about her face and caught in her mouth when she spoke. These things Hugh noticed.

"Good sailing weather too," he said. When he smiled, his teeth were startlingly white against his brown skin. "Those sheets of yours call to mind a clipper, sails full of wind. Makes me homesick."

"Pah. And how long have you been away from Bristol? Three days? Four?"

He sniffed the breeze. "It's the lack of salt in the air," he said.

"I only traveled once by sea and I hated it."

"Ah, your packet steamer," said Hugh, who had heard the story of her long journey from Kiev to Bremen and on to Southampton. "Stink and crush, I expect. I'm talking about tea clippers, racing each other back to England with the new season's leaves."

She shrugged, unconvinced, a landlubber to the marrow of her bones. She placed the tamed and folded bundle on top of the basket and they walked back toward the kitchen door.

"And our boats," he said, not discouraged by her evident lack of interest, "are very fine indeed. Steamers, admittedly, but they'd dispel in an instant your prejudice against them."

Anna said: "Not prejudice. Just a preference for dry land." Hugh, without so much as a dent in his enthusiasm, said: "We're going to turn heads, Anna, I can tell you. The new Whittam fleet will have only first-class cabins with every possible comfort. A ballroom, a dining room, a theater. In short, a grand hotel on the open sea."

"With bananas," she said.

She was merely stating a fact, hadn't intended to be funny, but he threw back his head and laughed.

Inside, Silas had pulled an armchair close to the range and was warming himself in a manner that Anna found shamelessly self-serving, but Eve seemed to find endearing. She ruffled his dark head as she stood by him, waiting for the kettle to boil. Seth was at the kitchen table, head in a book, his lips moving fractionally as he read, oblivious to the adults in the room. Hugh deposited the laden basket on the floor and sat down next to the boy.

"Good book?" he said.

"Aye, right good," Seth said, without looking up from the page. The muck of his working day had been sluiced off in hot water and his face was pink from it, his hair plastered to his forehead in flat spikes. He had worked his shift today and run to the allotment to check on the pineapple plants and found his tan pit already begun—the early foundations anyway, and a pile of bricks—though there was no sign of Daniel. Seth had paced out the footings to gauge the finished size and the joy he had felt at the possibilities of this addition to the plot was hard to bear alone. Three plots away, Clem Waterdine was turning a fork through compost with an expression of grim resignation and Seth had shouted across to the old man.

"Mr. Waterdine, I'm to 'ave an 'otbed."

"That right, lad?" said Clem, with fine-tuned impassivity. His head stayed down so that Seth was addressing the flat, greasy top of his cap.

"Aye. For pineapples and such like."

This, at least, provoked Clem into laying still his fork and looking directly at the boy.

"Tha'll nivver get pineapples," he said.

"We might. They grow 'em at Netherwood 'all."

"What does Amos Sykes 'ave to say about it, then?"

"Nowt yet," Seth said. "I 'aven't seen 'im. 'e's busy with 'is politics and that."

Clem had said nothing, but his expression spoke volumes.

Politics, pineapples—nothing to choose between them; both equally strange, both doomed to failure. Amos Sykes hadn't been elected to Parliament; pineapples wouldn't grow in a Netherwood allotment. Clem had picked up his fork and returned his attention to the compost, and Seth, feeling awkward now and crushed, had wished he hadn't bothered saying anything. This was why he hadn't told Anna about the scheme when he got home for dinner, or his mam when she came in from the mill, or Silas when he had turned up with Hugh. You just couldn't rely on adults to say or do the right thing, Seth had decided: better by far to limit what they knew.

"About this wedding," Silas said now, and Seth stopped reading.

"What about it?" Eve said. She sounded guarded. It wasn't long off now, but she still preferred not to talk about it in front of Seth.

"How would it be if I gave you away?" He spoke casually, though he rather hoped to move his sister to tears with his thoughtfulness. Disappointingly, she remained dry-eyed—beyond the dress and the venue, she had given little thought to the mechanics of the day and in all truthfulness, now that Silas had raised the issue, she wasn't at all sure that she needed to be given away by anyone. First time around, when she'd married Arthur, she had walked into the chapel with her father's brother, whom she barely knew but who had been tracked down in Bradford for the sole purpose of handing her over. Young as she was, and conventionally minded, it had still struck her as ironic that having managed for so long without the protection of a family, this stranger was entitled to both claim ownership and relinquish it, merely by dint of his surname. But this was Silas, long lost and much loved, so she smiled at him with good grace, grateful if not for the service he had offered, then for his kindness.

"Well, thank you," she said.

"No."

Seth's young voice trembled a little as he spoke out and all eyes were suddenly on him. He closed his book and looked at Eve, and she thought, Here we go again. But what he said was: "I should give you away, Mam." He looked at Silas. "If you don't mind, Uncle Silas."

Silas held up two hands as if to say fine by me, though in truth it rankled, having his thunder stolen so neatly. Eve, momentarily too shocked to speak, gazed at her son.

"Well," said Hugh, who had not the slightest idea of the pitch and swell of emotion all about him in the room. "You're the man of the house after all, Seth. Seems only right and proper to me."

"Yes, please," Eve said then, looking at Seth. "That'd be grand."

"Right you are," Seth said. He opened his book again and began flicking through the pages to find where he had left off and then, aware that his mother's eyes were still on him, looked up again.

"What?" he said, though he understood full well the effect of his words, and inside he glowed with the novel sensation of having done the right thing.

Chapter 30

At one end of the servants' dining table, Parkinson and Mrs. Powell-Hughes were eating egg-and-bacon flan and at the other, Claude Reynard and Sarah Pickersgill were eating *quiche Lorraine*, though their plates bore the same food. In the no-man's-land between them sat housemaids, footmen, and kitchen girls who didn't care what their dinner was called but were enjoying it almost as much as they were enjoying today's installment of the daily drama that was the butler's disapproval of the dashing chef. Perhaps because he was French, Monsieur Reynard seemed to lack the necessary antennae to pick up the nuanced chilliness of Parkinson's manner; much of the fun, for those in the ringside seats, was the chef's Gallic insouciance in the face of the butler's stern attempts at maintaining propriety in the dining hall, hierarchy at the table, discipline among the young members of the household staff. He raised an eloquent eyebrow now at Mrs. Powell-Hughes as Sarah Pickersgill, who had grown a personality since stepping out from the shadow of Mrs. Adams's bulky presence and into the sunshine of Claude Reynard's attentions, said to the table in general she'd heard that servants in other great houses had a bit of fun when the family was away.

"Fun?" said the housekeeper at once, not because she was unfamiliar with the concept—she had a lighter side, did Mrs. Powell-Hughes, though it was well hidden—but because Sarah appeared to be suggesting something illicit, of which the family might not approve.

"*Mais*, I think we have fun, Sarah," said Monsieur Reynard, feigning hurt feelings.

She smiled, and it was a little too arch for Parkinson's taste.

"This is your place of work, Sarah Pickersgill," he said, "whether the family is here or not."

But Sarah, the new Sarah, was less inclined to be put in her place. She continued on her theme.

"That's as may be," she said. "But when t'Knightwicks are away from Harradine Park, their 'ousemaids sometimes try on t'fine frocks and pretend for a day to be ladies."

"What arrant nonsense, Sarah," said Mrs. Powell-Hughes.

"True as I'm sitting 'ere. T'duke's valet showed me a photograph of 'em. All decked out in finery and posing on t'front steps."

"I saw it an' all, Mrs. Powell-'ughes," said Ivy Ramsbottom, made brave by Sarah's confidence and the fact that she had, indeed, seen a photographic likeness of four of the Knightwicks' upper housemaids clad in chiffon and large-brimmed hats adopting a pose of haughty indifference to the photographer on the steps of the ancestral home. "There were a little dog in it," she added, hoping this detail might dispel the skepticism on the housekeeper's face.

"Let me tell you now," said Parkinson, with heartfelt severity, "that if any one of you should be discovered in clothing belonging to her ladyship, or any other member of the family, for that matter, the result will be instant dismissal."

"With no character," said Mrs. Powell-Hughes.

"I was only saying," said Sarah.

249

"As is your perfect right," said Monsieur Reynard with silken tones and a wink, with which slight gesture he managed to somehow invest his words with a lascivious intimacy. The girls at the French end of the table smirked, and Parkinson wondered, with grave alarm, whether Sarah's virtue was in jeopardy.

"Anyway," said Sarah, defiant and breezy. "There's no wonder their staff lark about—look 'ow t'duchess carries on."

There was some truth in this, thought Mrs. Powell-Hughes, though she wasn't about to reward Sarah's sauciness by agreeing with her. In Parkinson's view, however, the moral tone of a household was in the hands of the servants, not the family, since for the idle rich temptation lay around every corner. His dander was up, and everyone—with the certain exception of Monsieur Reynard—knew it.

"The codes of behavior and standards of discipline that define an excellent body of household servants have always been understood and closely adhered to here at Netherwood Hall," he said, and his uncharacteristic pomposity was sobering to the younger members of the gathering; their smirks and smiles died on their faces. "I had thought, until recently, that I need have no concerns in this regard. However, of late this seems increasingly to have been a false confidence . . ."

He tailed off and looked pointedly at the chef, who had lit a cigarette and stretched himself languorously, amorously, in his chair: legs out, head tipped back, eyes closed, the better to enhance the sensual pleasure of his first inhalation. Unaware of the charge being laid—albeit obliquely—at his feet, he blew a lazy plume of smoke from the corner of his mouth, Sarah watching him furtively with hungry eyes. Parkinson, sad as much as affronted, longed for the bulky, uncomplicated presence at the table of Mrs. Adams. The appointment of Monsieur Reynard had been made in haste, and though the original thought had come from Mrs. Powell-Hughes, Parkinson had been very quick to endorse it; now, the butler lamented silently, he must repent at leisure.

Returned from Scotland and up early, the earl took a stroll through the stable yard to talk to his horses; they accepted his gentle endearments with bowed heads and modest eyes. It was a while since he'd ridden and there was some truth in the belief among the grooms that the earl preferred his motorcars to his mounts these days, but this had more to do with his stiffening joints than a diminishing love of horses and, anyway, whatever resentments the grooms might harbor, there was certainly no sign of reproach from the hunters this morning as they listened to him and nickered softly in reply to his murmured words.

Lord Netherwood was content to be back in Yorkshire. He was tired of company, tired of the sort of conversations that company made necessary, tired of traveling. He meant to remain here now until after Christmas, irrespective of Clarissa's plans; he would be impervious to her entreaties. Things to do, he thought, things to do. Hole in the roof of the racehorse stables where rain came in. Bally great hole in what used to be the main lawn, where Daniel MacLeod was creating a canal, of all things. Great changes afoot in the pits. All three of them needed a visit from him, but especially Long Martley, where Harry Booth had a great deal on his plate—the Crookgate district should be open again by now, and the rescue center would be up and running before too long. On which subject Booth must inform the newspapers; might as well nip in with a spot of good news before the Mines Inspectorate published their report. All of this ran through Lord Netherwood's mind in the time it took Absalom Blandford to trip-trap down the stairs from his estate lodgings and cross the courtyard toward his office, and the sound of his progress reminded the earl of another matter, equally pressing, which he'd been meaning to deal with ever since he heard Eve Williams was marrying the gardener.

"Absalom," he said, and the bailiff stood to attention at the threshold of his office, as pristine in his worsted and pin stripes as a soldier on parade. He all but clicked his heels.

"Your lordship?"

"I'd like to arrange an appointment with Mr. Jackson. Could you see to it?"

"But of course." Absalom Blandford had arranged his features into the expression he saved only for the earl, so though he longed to know what business Lord Netherwood might all of a sudden have with his solicitor, his curiosity was hidden by an obliging, oily simper.

"He must come here, however," the earl said. "Can't possibly be motoring off to Sheffield, what."

"No, your lordship, indeed not. So soon after your return. Quite impossible. Could I perhaps save your lordship's time even further, and conduct your business myself?"

For a tantalizing moment, the earl considered this, then: "Doubt it," he said. "I wanted to make over the mill to Mrs. Williams—wedding present, y'know. There'll be papers to sign."

This was said so casually that Absalom was certain he'd misheard.

"Make over . . . ?"

"The mill. That's it. Struck me some time back that she should have the business, lock, stock, and whatnot."

He was beaming at the bailiff, whose own face was losing the struggle, his smile reduced to a tight, thin line, white-rimmed and unnatural. Left to his own devices, he would have screamed and raged and hurled foul expletives into the October sky. By what dark art had Eve Williams wormed herself so effectively into the earl's affections? That she was to marry in the family's

252

chapel had been a blow of near-unendurable impact, so sure
had Absalom been that the brutish gardener was wildly, risibly,
contemptibly mistaken. The earl had confirmed the arrangement
with a casual apology for his forgetfulness—"I should have
mentioned it earlier, Absalom, but hey ho"—as if all he was
discussing was an overlooked detail, barely worth the mention.
But now here he was proposing an act of such wildly flamboyant generosity that it was surely Absalom's duty to prevent him.

"But, your lordship," he said, feigning calm professionalism.
"The business at the mill turns a tidy profit for the estate."

"Neither here nor there," said Lord Netherwood pleasantly.
"In fact, all the more reason to let her have it. Reward her
industry."

Absalom cleared his throat, wiped his brow, swallowed hard.

"I do feel, your lordship, that as your bailiff I should urge
you not to act rashly in this regard. The present arrangement
benefits all concerned."

The earl laughed.

"Why, Absalom! Are you defying me?"

It did appear so, and indeed the bailiff found himself unable
to refute the charge; his mouth worked to no audible effect and
he tugged at his collar as if it choked him.

Lord Netherwood, alarmed at his evident discomfort, said,
"Are you quite well, old chap? You look a little below par."

"I do feel somewhat unwell, your lordship," Absalom said,
thinking it was a wonder, in fact, that he hadn't vomited on
the earl's brogues.

"Well, look here, I have plenty to do and I don't doubt you
do too. A sentimental old fool I might be, but oblige me and
send that telegram to Jackson, what? Let me know when he's
coming."

"I just wonder if Mrs. Williams is worth the gift," the
bailiff said, reckless in his desperation.

"I beg your pardon?"

The earl sounded displeased now, and little wonder. Absalom flailed around inside his conniving head, desperately seeking some small fact to support his statement, knowing all the while that there was none. It was imperative, however, that this scheme be dashed to pieces before it gained momentum.

"I mean to say, that is, perhaps . . ."

The earl watched him struggle to frame a sentence, irritated beyond measure that his bailiff, previously unfailingly helpful and efficient in all matters, appeared to be attempting to thwart his wishes.

"—Perhaps the gift might look inappropriately generous to the wider world."

"Ah, the wider world," said the earl, in a deceptively measured voice.

"Yes, your lordship," Absalom said, encouraged. "One must exercise caution in regard to the giving of gifts to lower orders. People may jump to unfortunate conclusions about, shall we say, your relationship with the recipient."

Oh, how unwise was Absalom Blandford in his counsel. How rash and ill-advised were his words. He realized, too late, that in trying to gently show Lord Netherwood the error of his ways, he had merely succeeded in provoking in him a wave of profound indignation; it manifested itself in a dark red flush, which now rose rapidly upward from the earl's tweed collar.

"You have overreached yourself, Mr. Blandford," he said coldly and loud enough for an eavesdropper to catch every word. "I will not be swayed from my resolve by the frankly dubious threat of tittle-tattle among the locals. You surprise me. Surprise me, and disappoint me. Please do as you are bid, and do it at once. Thank you."

He turned, and in doing so saw Jem Arkwright, who was halfway across the courtyard, ruddy-faced and dressed like a farmer, his terrier bouncing maniacally at his heels.

"Ah, Jem," said the earl, relief evident in his voice. "A word, if you will."

He strode away from his bailiff, who stood immobile for a few moments, rooted to the cobbles by the weight of his shame and resentment, before stirring himself into motion and dipping, head bowed, into the sanctuary of his office. To his alarm, his body shook convulsively and his skin felt hot and damp, like a man in the grip of an ague. He sat down at his desk to steady himself and to think. The earl, whose reliance on Absalom's talents these past years had been the greatest joy of the bailiff's life, had turned on him like a viper, rewarding his loyalty and professionalism with a humiliating rebuke, an ignominious dressing-down. For all Absalom knew, the stable lads might have heard every word: they would delight in his disgrace, embellishing the incident in the retelling with vulgar additions and hoots of cretinous laughter. Oh God, Jem Arkwright may have caught the gist of it, too. The bailiff, pale and sweating, reached into his desk for a linen pouch stuffed with dried lavender flowers and pressed it hard against his nose and mouth, taking deep, fortifying inhalations of its calming scent. Slowly, his breathing steadied and his humiliation began to harden into a bitter determination not to be vanquished. He would apply his superior mind to this conundrum because Eve Williams must not triumph. The battle this morning may have been lost, but the war could yet be won. Hell had no fury like Absalom Blandford scorned.

Chapter 31

The wedding was to take place at ten o'clock in the morning, which meant that Daniel, waking early, had three clear hours to spend in his garden before sprucing up. He needed to occupy himself, needed to lose himself in physical labor, so that thoughts of Eve's body naked beneath him before the day was out didn't drive him stark raving mad at the eleventh hour and prevent the ceremony taking place. The enforced abstinence that Eve had infuriatingly placed upon them had certainly invested this day with profound significance, though for him it was carnal, not holy. He lay in Hislop's single bed—it was still Hislop's, to Daniel: never felt like his own—and indulged for a while in distracting fantasies, then with an effort of will he threw back the blankets and the cold dispelled his ardor in short order. Ducking to avoid cracking his head on the beams, he pulled on last night's discarded clothes and went downstairs. His escape from this miniature dwelling was coming not a moment too soon; any longer and he'd have had a permanent stoop. Also, it was an ill-lit place with too few windows, and those badly positioned. Daniel had never met his predecessor, but in his mind Hislop was more mole than man. He pictured him snuffling around this burrow in the half-light, scowling, when he ventured into the garden, at the brightness of the outside world. Daniel flung open the door now in spite of the chill, to let the gray dawn light into the kitchen while he made tea and buttered a slice of yesterday's bread. He would skip breakfast up at the Hall—the talk would be all spicy innuendo for a groom on his wedding day—and have a wee bit of time to himself on the banks of the Grand Canal. He smiled and let his mind drift to this work in progress. The project was storming ahead, the long, wide basin of the canal already almost dug. A complicated system of hydraulics was planned for the thousands of gallons of water that would be needed to fill it, but the area Daniel had chosen lay relatively low, and water from natural drainage as well as from the principal fountains in other parts of the grounds would feed into the new feature; great iron pumps, housed in their own brick buildings and hidden from view by the estate reservoir, were poised, ready to be called to duty. Lady Netherwood wanted a new fountain, this time a stone Neptune rising with sea nymphs from the center of the canal, but this, Daniel argued, would defeat the object and despoil the beautiful, glassy stillness of the water. This was their latest tussle: there was always at least one. The countess's tastes inclined toward rococo flourishes, while Daniel was for discipline and clean lines; they had been horticulturally incompatible for twenty happy years.

A rap on the low, mullioned kitchen window made Daniel jump, and he peered down to see the brown-toothed, sloppy grin of Stevie Marsh pressed up against it. Thirty-four gardeners beneath Daniel, and Stevie was bottom of the heap; if there'd been sixty-eight it would have made no difference.

"Mornin, Mr. MacLeod. Tha ready for thi nuptials?" he said slowly and stupidly; he couldn't help this, but it irritated people and this morning it irritated Daniel.

"Away and mind your own business," he said, and was instantly regretful.

Stevie stared through the glass. The open doorway was two feet to his right, but he hadn't the sense to find it.

"Tha what?"

"Och, it doesn't matter, Stevie. What is it you want?"

"Nowt really." He looked up at the sky, then back again. "Looks like rain," he said.

"Away you go then, and light that bonfire while it's still dry."

Stevie smiled a smile of fond recollection, remembering his mountain of leaves, the product of yesterday's labor. This was all he was really fit for—raking and sweeping—but he performed the task with unmatched thoroughness. No leaves were safe if Stevie was charged with the task of clearing them.

"Right you are," he said happily, then: "Mr. MacLeod?"

"Aye, what is it now?"

"Do you 'ave folk comin' to t'wedding?"

"Folk?"

"Aye. Fam'ly, like?"

"No, no. Just me. There's no one left in Montrose who'd trouble themselves to make the journey, I'm afraid."

"Poor do."

"Aye, I suppose it is." He honestly hadn't considered a guest list. He was a man with tunnel vision where this wedding was concerned.

"I might look in at t'chapel when you wed. Through t'window, like, not inside."

"Be my guest," Daniel said. "Come in if you like, take a pew."

Stevie shook his head emphatically.

"No. Tha dun't want an oaf like me in theer."

Daniel opened his mouth to contradict him, then thought better of it. Oaf, sadly, was about right. It would be altogether odd to have simple Stevie representing the groom's family.

"Right you are then, Stevie."

"Ta-ta then, Mr. MacLeod. I'll be off now."

"On your way, then."

Stevie loped away like a cheerful ape and Daniel let him make some headway before following him out of the door. He took a great lungful of crisp autumn air—the best kind, and nobody could persuade him otherwise—and smiled at nothing and everything. Stale bread for breakfast and no one for him at his wedding but the village idiot, but life was sweeter now than it had ever been, and was about to get sweeter still.

Eliza's dress was the most precious thing she had ever owned: no, ever seen. The most precious thing in the world, but it was hers. It was made from shot silk and was the same shade of deep pink as raspberry ice cream. It was snug in the bodice, full in the skirt, and there were layers of cream tulle beneath that made her feel like a ballerina, especially when she wore the cream satin slippers and pranced about her bedroom to the music, and before the audience, in her head.

"Oh, it's you. Thought there were an elephant in 'ere," Seth said, sticking his head around the door. "What you doin', anyroad?"

Eliza carried on dancing. "Dancing," she said. Seth could say what he liked this morning. Her happiness was inviolable.

"Should you be wearin' that yet?" he said.

Probably not, thought Eliza. It was only six o'clock and she hadn't washed her face or had breakfast. But obviously— really, truly obviously and who would say otherwise?—she needed to wear the dress for as long as she possibly could today. It was still unfastened at the back—there were twelve fiddly little silk-covered buttons that needed an extra pair of hands to manage—so it bagged out at the front, but still she felt utterly lovely in it. She ignored her brother's question and spun so that the skirt swelled around her like a full-blown rose.

"Show-off," Seth said.

Eliza's spinning slowed and stopped. She smiled at him.

"You can't be a show-off if you're on your own," she said, reasonably. "An' I was on my own till you poked your nose in."

"Tha'll be for it when Mam catches you," Seth said, but he left her to it. He thought she looked grand, actually, but he had never complimented Eliza in her life, and he wasn't about to start now.

By nine o'clock they were all ready, apart from Eve, who was still upstairs with Anna. The children were in the parlor, which was filled with the sweet scent of lily of the valley because a trailing bouquet had been delivered for Eve from Daniel earlier that morning, along with a note that she wouldn't let them read, because, she said, it was private. They had been instructed to wait quietly and on no account go outside to play; this last instruction was for Ellen and Maya, though. No mud pies, was the message.

Seth wore a proper morning suit, nipped and tucked to fit his skinny limbs. Eliza was now legitimately buttoned into her raspberry dress and though she'd stopped dancing, she still held herself regally and moved with a consciousness of an invisible audience. She stood straight-backed by the long sash window in the parlor like a ballerina awaiting her cue. Ellen and Maya were in cream cotton sateen with pink collars and sashes. They were uncharacteristically motionless, waiting side by side on the couch in the parlor; they understood that something special was going to happen and they had to stay clean, but that was all they knew. At least they had something to look at, because in front of them Seth paced the floor and bit his nails, overcome with anxiety at the role he was to play at the wedding. The glory of the offer had mutated into folly. He wished he could just sit in the chapel and watch, like everyone else. He wished he'd kept his trap shut when Uncle Silas first spoke up. And that was another thing—Seth had thought his uncle would have been here this morning, but he'd said not on your life, he'd see them at the chapel and he hoped Seth knew what he'd taken on, getting five women to the church on time, and rather Seth than him. His mam had laughed at the joke, but Seth hadn't. He felt he'd made a dreadful mistake and underestimated the burden of responsibility; its weight was making him feel very small.

Anna ran down the stairs and into the parlor and when she saw Seth she said: "Cheer up, it might never happen." She looked pretty, he thought. She'd almost run out of time to make herself something new to wear, but now here she was in a shimmery green frock, which changed color in the light, like a mermaid's tail. It was longer at the back than at the front so you could see the pale green shoes she wore and a hint of her narrow ankles. She wore a wide hat, too, which she'd decorated with leaves but it didn't look daft, it looked champion. Seth recalled a school pageant where the top class had dressed up as the seasons and Miss Mason was Spring. That's what Anna looked like. Spring, personified.

"Where's Mam?" he said. "It's time we went."

She smiled at him.

"Well, we can't go until cars come. We're not walking there."

He sighed in a weary, careworn way and sat down heavily next to Ellen and Maya so that they bundled into him helplessly, which was apparently hilarious. He scowled at them.

"All will be well, Seth," Anna said. "Really. You know what to do at chapel. We can practice again if you like?"

She had been so pleased with him for asking to give Eve

261

away at the wedding that she'd completely finished painting the tree on his bedroom wall and had added an iguana to one of the low-lying branches. This had been the one good thing to come out of his bigmouthed moment in the kitchen a few days back.

"No," he said.

"I go in and you wait for five minutes with your mam and girls. Then you give—"

"—a signal to t'minister an' just after t'music starts we walk in. I know."

"Well then."

"Well, I know what's meant to 'appen. But it's just, what if I trip an' fall flat on my face? All them folk thinkin' what a blitherin' idiot I am."

"You won't trip. When do you ever trip?"

"Be just my luck to do it today."

"If you race down aisle as if chasing tram, you might trip. But you'll walk down aisle at snail's pace. Have you ever seen snail fall over?"

From her imaginary stage by the window Eliza laughed at Anna, then gasped and said: "Oh Mam," and everyone looked at Eve, who was somehow standing in the room, though no one had heard her on the stairs. She was ready.

"Well?" she said to the assembly.

Eliza, who was seeing Eve's finished wedding dress for the first time, graciously and instantly conceded the spotlight.

"Mam, you look absolutely more beautiful than anybody in the world," she said.

Anna, creator of this vision, smiled with satisfaction at the finished effect. The dress was entirely from her imagination, and in it Eve looked ethereal, celestial, quite shockingly exquisite. Her hair was loose—no bun, Anna had said, not even a loose chignon—but it was held back from her face by a slender silver band onto which Anna had secured a row of perfect, waxy jasmine blooms. She wore no jewelery, no rouge, no lip color, but the dress and the simple adornment to her hair were together so lovely that on the couch the two little girls began to clap and cheer heartily, so Anna and Eliza joined in. Seth, who suddenly felt he'd never really looked at his mam properly before, found he had nothing useful to say and simply stared.

Chapter 32

S amuel Farrimond drove his gig as slowly as was possible without actually stopping. He wanted time to observe his surroundings and order his thoughts, so he kept the pony in check up the elegant sweep of Oak Avenue in order to delay his arrival at Netherwood Hall. He was not a man to be easily awed; indeed, he was an imposing presence himself. The Methodist ministry called, as in all things, for simplicity of dress, but within those boundaries Reverend Farrimond was never less than immaculately turned out: a handsome, silver-haired fellow with a carrying voice that served him well at the pulpit. But this rolling parkland, this immaculately swept driveway of dusky pink gravel, this fine, long, classical house with its windows lit as if by homecoming beacons—perhaps he had been too long in Grangely, he thought, for it seemed he had forgotten how arresting was the world inhabited by the very rich. It was his first visit to Netherwood Hall, for what business would a Methodist minister from an impoverished neighboring parish have at the sumptuous family seat of the local earl? None whatsoever, until life's unexpected twists and turns made it necessary, and it was indeed an extraordinary sequence of events that had brought him here today to unite Eve and Daniel in holy matrimony. Actually, he mused, as he kept a crawling pace past the classical portico of the south front, if it wasn't for him, none of this might have happened. Credit where it was due. It had been his idea, after all, that Eve should make a living from her peerless pies, and what a runaway success that had been. And now look—she had come so far that the Netherwood Hall family chapel was at her disposal, and the earl was sending a car to convey her to it. Fairy tales had been spun from less.

Ah, there was the chapel now: modestly proportioned, which was all to the good, and from what he could see through the open door, relatively unadorned inside. Well, perhaps the Hoyland ancestors had Methodist leanings, though from what he knew of the family, he had expected they would have thrown their money at God's house in the same way they threw money at their own. Now, now, Samuel, he chided himself, these are friends, not foe. And after all, they had shown real discernment and good taste when they took a shine to the lovely Eve, and her a poor Grangely girl, with a Grangely girl's traditional burdens: a hapless wastrel for a father and a mother so reduced by illness and poverty that she surrendered her last breath with a grateful smile. Samuel Farrimond knew this, for he had been there at the time and had gently closed Dinah Whittam's eyes, so that her children would understand she was gone. He had buried Dinah, and had feared for Eve, knowing her own resilience was all that would save her. And how she had risen! The minister had watched her progress through life with increasing joy, for she had truly flourished on the journey. No one was more deserving, of either her happiness or her success. She was a thoroughly splendid young woman. He hoped Daniel MacLeod was worthy of her; himself, he had hardly had time to form an assessment of the man's character, and that handsome face of his might blind a woman to other faults. One must look beyond the obvious to seek the truth; the longer he lived, the more he trusted the wisdom of this position. Good nature will always supply the absence of beauty, but beauty cannot supply the absence of good nature. Now who wrote that? He wondered if his faculties were beginning to fail, because time was when he would have had the source and the date off pat. In any case, it was a man of great good sense. Never a truer word.

The gig rolled eventually into the rear courtyard where the minister was obliged to stop, though he continued to stare, mesmerized still by the opulence of his surroundings, even here, at the business end of the house. If it wasn't for the horses and the stable doors, these outbuildings could pass for a respectable country manor: how many of his parishioners, he wondered, could comfortably be housed here?

"Ah, Reverend, splendid, splendid. Welcome sir, welcome."

He had expected a stable hand, not the earl, but there was Lord Netherwood striding toward him in mud-caked boots and a flat tweed cap and, in his hand, a shovel. This he flung to one side as he approached and it was instantly retrieved—so quickly it was almost caught before it fell—by a menial, who darted noiselessly from the shadows, then darted back again. Placing one steadying hand around the pony's bridle, the earl held out the other in welcome. The minister reached across and shook it, then sprang down from the gig in a surprisingly sprightly manner for a man who was the wrong side of sixty. He had met the earl on other occasions and found him likable enough, though Reverend Farrimond held a dim view of vast privilege—working tirelessly as he did among the very needy— and in his experience a person's capacity for spirituality diminished in direct proportion to their wealth. Only the poor could be relied upon to turn to God with constancy and humility, though they might have every reason to believe He had forsaken them. These thoughts were not written in his countenance, however, and he returned the earl's easy smile with what certainly passed for warmth.

"Very good of you to come, very good indeed, what," said Lord Netherwood. "I know what it means to the bride." He whistled, and from a stable came another young lad, falling over his own feet in his haste to respond to the earl, who silently handed over the minister's pony to be led away.

"Thank you very much," said Reverend Farrimond to the boy, rather pointedly.

The earl, oblivious to the veiled reprimand, went on.

"Best altogether to avoid the associations with sorrow at the Methodist chapel. Very understanding of you to come, we're much obliged."

"But it's entirely my pleasure, your lordship," the minister said, and if he sounded tetchy it was because the earl spoke with a proprietorial air, as if Eve's well-being was his concern alone. "Not to mention entirely appropriate. I've known her since girlhood."

"Quite so, quite so. Still, it's a fair trot out from your own parish, and I'm quite sure you have your work cut out there. Grangely, isn't it? An unhappy place, I gather?"

Piqued again, Reverend Farrimond said: "Ah, Grangely's fabled unhappiness. Please be assured our reputation for misery is much exaggerated."

In fact, misery was in the very air they breathed in Grangely, the water they drank and the muck they were obliged to walk in. But like the mother of a badly behaved child, the minister was immediately protective of his flock when an outsider dared to comment on its troubles. Especially when the outsider was a soft-bellied aristocrat whose closest brush with privation was doubtless nothing more severe than running out of creamed horseradish just as the roast beef was served.

Lord Netherwood hesitated, sensing at last a certain *froideur* in the minister's demeanor. Prickly fellow, he thought. Then: "Good show," he said, his all-purpose, fail-safe response that had served him well through the decades. "Good show."

Across the cobbles came two younger versions of the earl, with the same sandy hair and eyebrows, the same high complexion and the same amiable, ready smile. There'd be more of them inside too, depicted in oils and hanging on the walls, thought Reverend Farrimond. He was feeling distinctly peevish now, and he didn't admire it in himself. No harm had been done to him and any slight—if slight it could be called—had been delivered unintentionally. Best altogether to clear off, though, before becoming involved in an inconsequential conversation with these two scions of the Hoyland line.

"If you'll forgive me, your lordship," he said, though he was already walking briskly away, indicating with a wave the vague direction of the chapel.

"Of course, of course, make yourself at home, as it were. If there's anything you need . . ."

"Only the good Lord, thank you, and I imagine he's already there," said Reverend Farrimond. The earl and his sons watched him go.

"So who's that?" said Dickie.

"Methodist chappie from Grangely. Here for the splicing."

"Speaking of splicing . . ." said Tobias.

"Not now, Toby, not now," said the earl. "Let your mother absorb the reality of the engagement before we inflict an actual date upon her."

Toby's betrothal to Thea was official. The Sterlings had been informed, their permission sought by telegraph and joyfully granted by return—"Goodness," the countess had said, "how terribly eager"—and an announcement had been made in the *Telegraph* and *The Times*. Everyone was delighted, and the countess pretended to be. But now, Thea was back with the Choates in London and Tobias worried constantly that if he didn't push hard for a wedding date, his miraculous fiancée might yet slip through his fingers; she was a seeker of fun, and who knew what temptations were being laid at her feet?

"Before Christmas though, Pa," he said now. "A winter wedding."

The earl held up a silencing hand.

"I will not discuss further," he said, then to Dickie: "Marley still lame?"

Dickie nodded. "More so, if anything. He's with Maltravers now and he reckons it's chronic founder again. No chance he'll be fit for the cub hunt. I'll take one of your hunters, if I may."

They walked together toward the stables and Tobias, temporarily thwarted, pulled a cigarette from its case and lit up. Betty Cross appeared at the door from the kitchens and he watched her through the smoke of his first draw. Yesterday's girl, he thought. Seeing him, she lifted her skirts a little higher than was necessary and ran across the cobbles to the dairy. Not so long ago Tobias would have chased her there, and this thought passed through his mind along with the memory of the creamy swell of her breasts and the way she would boldly smile into his face while she guided his hand up her skirts. He could still have her, if he wished, and the thought wasn't wholly unpleasant, he had to admit. And yet he let her go. He knew where she was, if he needed her.

The motorcars couldn't negotiate the rutted track that led from the road to Ravenscliffe, so they waited for the little bridal party to pick their way down to them. Two yellow Daimlers. One for Anna and the girls, another for Eve and Seth. Would Amos be coming? Eliza had wanted to know, and Anna and Eve had looked at each other. It was a good question, but there was no simple answer to it, except to say no, which had prompted the perfectly reasonable subsidiary question, Why?

"We're 'oping he'll be at t'do afterward," Eve had said,

hoping this would satisfy Eliza. "The wedding part, well, it's just for fam'ly."

"But Amos sort of is fam'ly," Eliza had said. "I mean, Uncle Silas is comin' and we only just met 'im, really. But Amos, well—I really love Amos."

"And Amos loves you, sweetheart," Anna said. But he hates Lord Netherwood, she thought. And also . . . She looked at Eve, and Eve looked at Anna. That Amos had loved Eve was known between them, but never discussed. Did he still? Anna wasn't sure, and couldn't blame him if he did, because how would you stop loving her once you'd begun? She took her friend's hand and squeezed it.

"Be careful, this is uneven ground," she said.

"You can say that again," Eve said. And they smiled at each other, in perfect understanding.

Chapter 33

The congregation was very small. Eve had asked Ginger, Nellie, and Alice, and they were there, sitting right at the back because to be any farther forward seemed to them presumptuous. Also, Ginger had reasoned, they needed to be first out afterward, because the food wouldn't serve itself, would it? The three of them had been up at the mill since half past five, so the lion's share of the work was already done, but still, none of them wanted to be caught by surprise. Nellie had been marvelous: you wouldn't know she was suffering. It couldn't be easy for her, Ginger had whispered to Alice; other folk's weddings were bound to bring back memories of your own. Alice nodded, but thought Ginger was mistaken. This was nothing like her own wedding day, and if she hadn't been sitting in a house of God, she'd have been willing to bet that Nellie felt the same. It had rained when Alice married Jonas, and he'd worked the afternoon shift, leaving on the dot of one o'clock as if he couldn't wait to be gone.

Silas was there, up at the front, and Anna sat with him, though there was space for another two people between them, and they found nothing to chat about while they waited. The girls were outside with Eve and Seth, subdued into absolute obedience by the sense of occasion, waiting for their cue. On the other side of the aisle to Silas and Anna sat the earl and countess and their two daughters, Lady Henrietta and Lady Isabella. This was simply astounding to Alice Buckle, who couldn't take her eyes off the backs of their exalted heads. She knew she couldn't do what Eve was going to do, in front of people such as these; she would faint clean away and miss her own wedding. Ginger, beside her, was less diverted by the aristocrats than by the groom, who stood at the front in a full Scots rig-up, the like of which she had never seen before: tartan kilt, tweed jacket, garter flashes on long woolen stockings, stiff brown brogues. Ginger stared. A man in a skirt should, by rights, look like a right nancy, she thought: and yet he looked manlier than anyone in the chapel. When he shifted, even only slightly, the pleats on the back of his kilt swung and rippled like the surface of a pond when the wind blew across it. She was mesmerized. Nellie, catching the direction of Ginger's fixed gaze, gave her a nudge with a sharp elbow.

And then Wagner's "Bridal Chorus" struck up on the organ and all heads turned to the back of the church, because no one was too grand to want to see how the bride looked. The wooden doors had been flung open and she stood just inside the chapel on the arm of her son, whose face was endearingly grave. Lady Netherwood, who goodness knows had seen enough weddings in her time, felt the welling of unexpected tears: Eve was simply beautiful, and that gown! It was a masterpiece of couture: surely not the little Russian girl's work this time? The countess stole a glance at the groom, who had turned like everyone else and now seemed unable to drag his eyes away from the vision Eve presented. She didn't wear a veil, so the smile on her face was there for everyone to see, though at the moment it was directed only at Daniel. Henrietta, watching her progress, wondered how a gown could be at once magnificent yet entirely simple:

272

alluring yet wholly modest. Quite a feat, and with her long hair loose in that way and the band of white jasmine—she was a Millais or Rossetti made flesh. Simply divine. She wished Thea were here to share the moment. Then again, perhaps it was just as well she wasn't.

Anna, meanwhile, had tried to get a smile out of Seth but though he caught her eye, he held his expression of fierce concentration. Ellen and Maya were solemn too: shy suddenly, now that their big moment had come. Not so Eliza. She looked about to explode with joy. She beamed with the full force of her excitement, and Anna thought if she were allowed, the child would be turning cartwheels. Instead she adhered conscientiously to the slow and dignified step-together they had practiced in the entrance hall at home, but it was an effort of will, anyone could see that.

They reached the front. The girls slid into the pew next to Anna, Eliza with evident reluctance. Seth stepped away from his mother and she in turn moved to stand close beside Daniel. Samuel Farrimond cleared his throat and the couple looked away from each other and at the minister, but it appeared, for a long moment, as though he was lost for words and it's true that he was quite diverted by them, by the impression they made there, side by side. Never, he thought, had he seen a couple that looked so well together. He hoped that God would grant him the time to see for himself what these two might make of their union.

A cough—the earl's, quite deliberate—broke the silence, and the minister, looking up, was reminded of the task at hand. He was not a man to be perturbed by a brief lapse into reverie, however; a wedding service was a time for reflection, in his view, and life was lived already at too fast a pace. He paused a few beats longer, and then he began.

"We are gathered here today in the sight of God," he said, delivering the familiar words in his rich baritone, "to join together Eve and Daniel in holy matrimony. Who gives this woman to be married to this man?"

A long pause, then: "Oh, me. I mean, I do," Seth said. He reddened, thought he'd blundered, fluffed the one simple thing he had to say, but his mam, Daniel, the minister—they were all smiling at him.

"Thank you, Seth," Daniel said. Anna reached for her handkerchief.

They came out of the chapel to a guard of honor formed by the Netherwood gardeners, who stood in two lines with hoes and spades and forks raised high to form a tunnel. Stevie, who had known all about this plan yet still kept the secret, was at the farthest end with his seven-pronged leaf rake and a smile that would have lit up a dark room. Eve and Daniel ran through, and then the children had a go, and then Eliza went again, on her own. This, she thought, is how I want my life to be: silk frocks, laughter, an audience. Happiness bubbled away inside her at a constant simmer and her face ached with smiling, but she couldn't stop. Freed from the constraints of the service, she danced flamboyantly on the gravel drive until Anna shepherded her into a waiting motorcar.

"Mrs. MacLeod," said the earl, taking Eve to one side. It sounded so strange to her ears, and it would be weeks before she could answer to it without hesitation. Lord Netherwood enveloped her in an unexpected bear hug, which crushed her bouquet and left her breathless when he released her. "I couldn't be prouder of you if you were one of mine."

There was a tremor in his voice and Eve herself felt the threat of tears. She had so much to be grateful for, and most of it was due to him. He wasn't joining the gathering at the mill—Lady Netherwood felt that gracing the church service with her presence was glory enough for the happy couple: any more would be *de trop,* she said, a compromise of one's dignity. Her husband, while disagreeing heartily with her rationale, nevertheless had business to attend to at Long Martley and he supposed, also, that the wedding breakfast might go off with more of a swing without the inhibiting presence of the aristocracy. But there was something he had to say to Eve before she left; his wedding gift to her had to be explained.

"Now look," he said, and his face was suddenly serious. "I have something to tell you, and I don't want even a murmur of protest. It's my dearest wish that you should own your wonderful business in its entirety—no"—for she was about to demur, as he had known she would—"I will not listen to objections. Eve's Puddings & Pies will be just that—yours, my dear. This is my gift to you, on your wedding day. My bailiff has been asked to inform our solicitor of my wishes, so the paperwork should be ready to sign in the next day or so."

She stared at him, slow to absorb what he had just offered.

"Come to Mr. Blandford's office on Thursday. I shall be there too, and we'll get the ball rolling, what." He rubbed his hands together, gleeful at the prospect of giving away a gold mine. She found her voice at last, and though he had forbidden her to protest, she couldn't help it.

"Thank you, your lordship, but it's too much," she said. "My 'alf share in it is already more than I ever dreamed of. I don't need more than that. Really I don't."

"Alas, my dear, what you think you need and what I intend to bestow are two different things entirely." He laughed now, because she looked stricken. "The business shall be yours, I'm afraid, and you will have to take comfort from the fact that it gives me enormous pleasure to hand it over."

"Well," Eve said, her argument nothing against the might of his generosity. "In that case . . ."

"Believe me, I have given this due consideration—been

meaning to do it for a while, and then you went and got married, giving me the perfect opportunity, what." He paused to smile at her then, suddenly serious again, said: "I would ask one thing of you, however."

She looked at him hopefully. A condition attached might make her feel better.

"Use your new independence to think about expansion," he said. "New premises elsewhere—Barnsley, perhaps, or Sheffield, or farther afield. Even Bristol: why not? Your brother is no stranger to ambition, I think. Talk to him, seek his advice. You have a quite brilliant talent and a good head for business. Let's see where these assets might take you."

She smiled at him. "More Eve's Puddings & Pies?"

"Many more, I hope. Up and down England."

"You are so kind to me." She shook her head, wonderingly. "Too kind. I don't have t'words to thank you."

"Good. Lavish thanks are such a bore. But you do accept the gift, and the small condition I place on it?"

"I do."

"Excuse me, but didn't you say exactly the same thing to me just now?"

This was Daniel, who had sauntered up to join them. He grinned at his wife. The cat with the cream, thought the earl. Lucky, lucky fellow. Eve took her husband's hand.

"Let's go," she said. "I'll tell you all about it on t'way."

"Be happy," Lord Netherwood said. "And Mr. MacLeod?"

"Yes, your lordship?"

"You'll be doing something soon with that ruddy great hole over there, I presume?"

Daniel laughed. "Certainly I will. There'll be a regatta to plan by the summer months."

The earl clapped a hand to his head in mock despair. "Please don't repeat that to the countess," he said.

If guests had been a little sparse at the service, the reverse was true at the mill, where a throng had gathered by the time Daniel and Eve arrived. Anna and Ginger had swagged the upstairs dining room with long, lavish garlands, ivy from the walls of Ravenscliffe studded with white tuberoses from the greenhouses at Netherwood Hall, where there was no such thing as a season and any bloom was possible, at any time of year. The tuberoses gave off a heady scent, sweet and warm and faintly narcotic, though the less exotic smells of warm pastry and pork wafted up from the kitchen below to remind everyone where they were. When the bride and groom came up the stairs and burst into the room a great cheer went up, hollering and clapping and whistling: a joyful racket, joyfully received. Amos pushed forward to kiss the bride and shake the groom's hand, immediately redeeming himself for missing the service and dispelling Eve's fears of awkwardness between the man she'd turned down and the man she'd accepted.

"You look grand," he said to Eve, and to Daniel, "Look after 'er, or there'll be trouble," but it was said jovially, with a wink and a smile and Eve felt a wave of gratitude that he had come and that all was entirely easy between them. Anna caught Amos by the arm.

"She's happy you're here," she said as they stepped aside to make way for other well-wishers.

"I'm 'appy I'm 'ere an' all." He took a glass of champagne from a proffered tray, sniffed it, and pulled a face.

"She thought you might not come."

"Did she? Never a chance. Are they serving ale? This'll give me gripe."

"But you could have come to service too."

"And scraped and bowed to 'is lordship? Not on your life."

"Nobody scraped. Nobody bowed."

"Look." He put his untouched drink down on the nearest table. "I didn't much fancy it, that's all. Stately 'omes aren't my style. Stop trying to read summat into nowt."

Eliza danced up, all smiles and raspberry silk.

"Excuse me," Amos said to Anna. "I just need to ask this beautiful princess 'ere if she's seen Eliza Williams anywhere about."

Eliza squealed with laughter and gave him a twirl, then flung herself at him for a hug. Watching her, Anna wished she were at liberty to hug whoever she liked, whenever she wanted.

Chapter 34

You see, Tobias is a lost cause," said Lady Netherwood. "I can do nothing for him now." She was peeling a ripe peach with a filigree knife and an expert hand. Her husband was behind his newspaper, refusing thus far to come out. "And so," she continued, "I shall turn all my attention to Henrietta."

"Unlucky girl," said the earl. He had hoped for fifteen uninterrupted minutes with the paper before leaving for the colliery, and had been working himself up into an enjoyable lather at reports of pugnacious Russians firing at trawlers off Dogger Bank, having mistaken the east coast fishing fleet for the Imperial Japanese Navy. But such matters were nothing to Clarissa, who had sniffed him out and joined him in the morning room with this bee in her bonnet. She had sent the footman to fetch a peach from the hothouse tree, then had immediately begun on her theme: the urgent need to make a match for Henrietta. That was ten minutes ago and she was far from running out of steam.

"In any other family she would have been obliged to marry by now."

Stoically, the earl ignored her. Three fishermen dead and

others wounded in twenty minutes of hostile fire: Accident, my eye, thought the earl. We should blast the confounded Russian pirates to kingdom come.

"It's talked about, you know, and not kindly."

She waited. The peach was skinned; carefully, delicately, she sliced it from the stone, then dipped her fingers in a silver dish of warm water and dried them on a linen napkin. Teddy huffed behind his newspaper. She tried again, this time with a little more steel.

"It's an embarrassment and it reflects badly on us all. It reflects particularly badly on you."

He lowered his newspaper at last.

"Meaning?"

"You know perfectly well what I mean. You overindulge her independent spirit, and you support her refusal to take seriously any marriageable prospect."

"For which kindness I am to be reproached?"

"Indeed. It's no kindness to confirm her belief that she may simply gallivant through life, unfettered by the obligations of womanhood."

He began to laugh; he couldn't help himself. She looked so pained and long-suffering, yet there she sat with absolutely nothing to do for the rest of the day but eat a peach. Obligations of womanhood, indeed. It was barely half an hour after the wedding and clearly this event, plus the fact that she had little else to occupy her mind, had set his wife on this matrimonial one-note song. She was right, of course: Henry should be married by now. But so many supposedly eligible young men were blithering idiots and he could quite see why his daughter might prefer the company of horses, given the choice.

"It's so like you to laugh," Lady Netherwood said testily. She drummed her fingers on the side table by her chair, and the footman looked suddenly alert. Another peach, perhaps? It seemed not.

"It's so like you to find amusement in my concerns."

"Clarissa dear, I was amused by your choice of words, not by your concern for Henry," he said. "'Unfettered by the obligations of womanhood': splendid, quite splendid."

She looked at him, perplexed. How odd he could be! She was quite sure that when they married all those years ago he had been an entirely conventional young man. Now he seemed to be acquiring eccentricities with age, along with gray hairs and inches on the waistline.

The morning room door opened and Henrietta appeared, dressed for outdoors.

"Speak of the devil," said the earl. "Would you say, Henry, that you are unfettered by the obligations of womanhood?"

"Absolutely," she said. "Who wants to know?"

"Your mama. She believes it's time you were fettered, in fact."

Lady Netherwood gave a noisy, exasperated exhalation of breath. She glared at the earl and then at Henrietta. They would turn on her now, for sport: well, let them try.

"Where are you going?" she asked her daughter.

"To Long Martley with Daddy."

Lord Netherwood rolled his eyes heavenward: unfortunate answer, under the circumstances. Now Clarissa would forbid it.

"I forbid you to go," she said, right on cue. "Remove your hat and coat and come and sit down."

Henrietta stared at her, and then at her father, who cravenly picked up his newspaper again and opened it.

"Mama," she said patiently. "Daddy and I have an engagement with Mr. Garforth at the Mines Rescue Center. It won't be dirty or remotely dangerous, will it, Daddy?"

"Please don't appeal to your father against my word. He can do just as well without you. You have no business in a colliery yard. The very idea is preposterous."

"Daddy?" Her voice was indignant, not beseeching.

He considered his options, but only briefly. "Do as your mama asks, Henry. She makes a very good point."

"Thank you, Teddy."

Hands on hips, Henrietta all but stamped her foot in temper. If it weren't for her, there would be no Mines Rescue Center and now it seemed she was surplus to requirements. She glared contemptuously at her father, who had the good grace to look uncomfortable. He would have liked Henry's company, in fact, but to fly in the face of Clarissa's wishes would be impolitic, not to say disrespectful. There would be other occasions, and he tried to communicate this silently to his daughter. She was having none of it, however.

"Very well," she said. "Very well."

She removed her hat, pulled off her gloves.

"I won't join you in here though, Mama. You may enjoy your peach in private. I have a letter to write, as it happens."

"Good," said Lady Netherwood, thinking she had managed her wayward daughter very well. She cut a glance at the earl to share her satisfaction, but he refused to compound his disappointing performance by meeting her eye.

"Are you writing to Thea?" he said.

"I may, now that I have an entire day at my disposal. But first I have some business to attend to."

The countess, wary now, said: "Indeed? Of what nature?"

"Of a political nature."

Now the earl folded his newspaper and put it down. He looked extremely grave.

"To whom are you writing, Henrietta?" he said.

"To Mrs. Pankhurst," she said. "I feel it's high time we became acquainted."

Out she stalked indignantly.

"Bluffing," the earl said to his white-faced wife. "There's not a radical bone in her body."

Clem Waterdine had a fiddle and he struck up, unasked, with a Celtic jig that had Daniel organizing folk into a circle for the Gay Gordons. No one but him knew what to do, but he demonstrated with Eve, who picked it up quickly enough, shimmering in her ivory silk as they promenaded and polkaed on the polished wood floor.

"Look at Mam," Seth said to Amos. They were side by side at the edge of the room, each nursing a drink and swapping terse observations like a pair of old-timers.

"Aye," Amos said. "I'm looking."

"Never seen 'er dance."

"Nor me. I don't suppose there's much occasion to, generally speaking."

Seth looked away, down into his glass of dandelion and burdock. The sight of his mam in Daniel's arms made him suddenly uncomfortable. He didn't know much about sex beyond the mechanics of reproduction, but since starting work at New Mill he'd been forced to pretend he knew it all. To hear the other lads talk, you'd think they'd written the manual. They were dirty-minded buggers, too; Seth had taken a lot of stick from them when they got wind of his mam and Daniel. Times had been many that he'd wished he had a powerful right hook, but he was punier than any of the other boys on the screens. They'd pulverize him in moments if he started anything. He was due there later today—workingmen didn't get a day off for their mam's wedding—and the thought cast a little pall of gloom over his features. He looked at Eliza, dancing now with Silas, and he felt such longing for the freedom she had that his breath caught in his throat.

"Work all right?" Amos said, and Seth blushed furiously, feeling caught out.

"Aye," he said. He'd often suspected Amos of being a mind reader and there he went again, picking up on his precise thoughts.

"It's not though, is it?"

"No." No point lying if the man knew what he was thinking.

"So do yersen a favor and throw in t'sponge."

The sound of the fiddle and laughter, not to mention fifty-odd pairs of feet on the floorboards, made it hard to hear what Amos had said.

"Pardon?"

Amos leaned in. "I said, do yersen a favor and throw in t'sponge. Nob'dy wants you to be miserable, lad, an' it's not like your mam needs t'pittance they pay you."

Seth shifted in his chair. Was it as simple as that, then? He really didn't think it was.

"It's just . . . I'm Arthur Williams's son."

"Is that in dispute?"

"No. I mean my dad loved New Mill. If 'e were alive, 'e'd be proud to see me there."

"Your dad would've been proud o' you if you emptied middens for a living."

"It's like I'm carryin' on a family tradition, though. Williams men work at New Mill colliery, don't they?"

"Aye, they do if they 'ave to. And I'll admit, in your dad's case, that 'e loved that pit down to t'last nut and bolt in t'winding gear. But that were Arthur, and there aren't many men feel like 'e felt. There's plenty more drag their feet when they walk down t'New Mill lane."

"You didn't stop me going."

"Correct. Not my job, to stop you doing owt."

"Did you like it?"

"No, to be honest, Seth, I didn't. I never gave it much thought, mind; there was nowt I could do about it anyroad. But

284

now, well . . ." He sat back for a moment and thought about it. "Now I've realized I'm not by nature a subterranean creature."

"I don't think I am, Amos." Oh, thought Seth: the relief of saying that out loud. He hadn't been sent underground yet—wouldn't be until he was fourteen—but already he had begun to dread it. The trappers and water boys taunted the younger lads with what they had in store down the pit when their time came. A slow death of the soul in the pitch black is what it sounded like to Seth.

"There you are, then. Decision made. Get thi'sen back to school where tha belongs, lad."

On the makeshift dance floor Silas had cut in to dance with Eve. Close together like this, their likeness to each other was striking, even to them. He held her tight and smiled directly into her eyes, claiming an ownership of his own, different from Daniel's but no less binding.

"Look at us, Evie. How far we've come."

This was an enduring theme of his, but she indulged him, because—after all—it was true.

"And greater things yet to follow," he said. She wondered for a second if he knew about the earl's gift to her, but he was talking about himself. "Dreaton Main now officially belongs to me, as of yesterday."

"Silas! You never said. Congratulations! That's marvelous."

He inclined his head a fraction, accepting Eve's excitement as his due.

"I have to be back in Bristol tomorrow for a few days, then I shall return to Netherwood"—he leaned in conspiratorially, as if he was passing on state secrets—"to concentrate on coal." Ginger, beside them in the circle, gave Eve a shove.

"You're meant to be reeling," she said. Silas ignored her, but Eve smiled an apology and stepped to the right, making room.

"I plan to make an entirely new fortune," Silas said. "Coal, this time."

She flashed him an enigmatic grin.

"What?" he said.

"Me too. But from pies. Lord Netherwood gave me full ownership of t'business as a wedding gift."

He was so surprised that he stopped short and Ginger and her husband, Mervyn, cantered right into them. Silas pulled Eve out of the circle.

"Are you sure?" he said, still clasping her hands. "The building, the business—the lot? All yours?"

She nodded, a little bewildered by his intensity. Also, now she had told him, she wished she hadn't.

"But keep it to yourself," she said. "I don't want you raising a toast or owt."

"Our secret," he said. His face was lit up by the wonderful possibilities of life.

"And Daniel's."

"My God, Evie. My God! What a gift your earl has given you."

She shrugged, feeling uncomfortable; his hands on hers were too tight, he spoke too loudly—at this rate, the whole room would know her news. In any case, it had barely sunk in for Eve; her brother's reaction was quite out of kilter with the way she felt. Around them, dancers had begun to disperse because Clem had abruptly laid down his fiddle to go in search of pale ale. Amos, who still sat by Seth across the room, their backs to the wall, raised his glass at her and smiled. Anna, pink from dancing, appeared by his side and spoke to him, and whatever she said made him laugh out loud.

"Does he know?" Silas said, following her gaze.

"No! I told you, just you, me, and Daniel."

"So what he's been whispering about with Seth?"

"Vegetables probably. When to 'arvest t'beetroot."

"I don't trust him and his ilk. Not sure about her, either."

He meant Anna, and Eve felt something inside her plummet. She didn't reply, but stood looking at her friends and her son, who were now talking together. Seth looked up at Anna and told her something. Anna clapped twice, then bent down and hugged him. Eve watching, wanted to join them, but Silas spoke again.

"He's trouble, Evie. He doesn't have the best interests of this country at heart. He's out to bring down capitalists like you and me."

As usual his face was all smiles, and his voice was light enough. Was he joking? Eve wondered.

"Don't," she said. "They're my friends."

"And I'm your brother, and blood's thicker than water."

Still he smiled, then he kissed her on the cheek. "Let me find you a drink," he said. "We need to celebrate," then, seeing her face, he added, "discreetly."

She watched him weave an elegant path through the crowded room. Behind her, Daniel appeared and encircled her with his arms, pulling her backward into his chest. He dropped his face into her shoulder and kissed the warm hollow of skin there.

"Can we leave yet?" he said, too quietly for anyone but Eve to hear. He was pressed against her and she had to remind herself to breathe.

"Behave," she said. "We've only been here an hour."

His mouth found her ear: "Mrs. Daniel MacLeod," he whispered.

She turned in his arms to face him, and Silas was forgotten.

Chapter 35

Before she spoke, Henrietta had had no notion of writing to Emmeline Pankhurst. In any case, she had no idea how to go about it, or what she would say, or why she might bother. Naturally, she was well aware of the campaign for women's suffrage and, on an academic level, she approved of it. She had followed its emergence, noted its apparent lack of progress; she had formed opinions on the subject, which she aired with lively eloquence when called upon to do so. But to involve herself personally with the movement—well, this had simply never entered her head until, provoked by frustration, she had plucked the idea from her subconscious and flung it at her parents, specifically to sting.

And there it would have ended, an empty threat, nicely timed. Except that as she flounced from the room she heard her father's words—"bluffing" he'd said—and his unruffled confidence that he had her number turned indignation into anger. She paced the floor in her room, feeling a little ridiculous but too cross to settle to anything. She was twenty-three years old and yet she had no more control over her own life than Isabella. Perhaps she should marry, after all? Perhaps she should put names into a hat at the next church fête and have someone draw out a husband for her. At least then she might be mistress of her own household, if not her own destiny. But then an image of Thea rose before her and she dismissed all other possibilities. Like Tobias, she was besotted. In the lavender-scented sanctuary of Glendonoch's great pine linen press, they had silently positioned themselves side by side and Thea, with ingenious cunning and nimble fingers, had managed to pull and secure the double doors from the inside. Henrietta, whose imagination could supply her with nothing more intimate than this, had whispered an endearment and felt in the dark for Thea's hand, but was stopped and silenced when Thea had leaned in and kissed her, parting her lips with her tongue and running the tip of it along her teeth; she had wet a finger in her own mouth, then pushed it down the bodice of Henrietta's dress, finding a nipple and rubbing gently until it rose and hardened like a little nut under the caress, and Henrietta's breathing came fast and shallow; she had trailed a hand up under Henrietta's skirts, touching with fluttering fingers the soft flesh of her inner thigh above the top of her stockings. She had seemed to know exactly what she was at, and Henrietta felt at once weakened and empowered by the novelty of extreme desire. And then Dickie had galloped along the landing and flung open the doors of the press with a triumphant flourish and Thea, calm as you please, had beckoned him into join them while Henrietta had panted quietly in the scented darkness and attempted to collect herself.

She hadn't seen Thea since Glendonoch, but she thought about her almost all the time. Thinking about her now, Henrietta had to support herself, bracing her arms against the writing desk, light-headed with longing. No young earl-in-waiting, no young tweed-clad eldest son, no top-hatted young viscount had ever made her feel about to buckle at the knees.

The crunch of wheels on gravel brought her back to the

present and, looking up, she saw her father swaddled in tweed and wool, driving away from the house. Judas, she thought. If it wasn't for her, he would never have heard of Mr. Garforth, and now there he went, off to Long Martley to play the enlightened employer. Well, she would show him. Bluffing indeed. Votes for women! Why the blazes not? Full of purpose, she drew out the chair and sat down at her desk. A crisp, business-like letter to Emmeline Pankhurst, introducing herself and offering support: with this weapon, she would strike back at her infuriating parents, and if the cause of women's suffrage was advanced by the by, then that was all to the good.

She dipped her pen in the ink and with a steady hand she began to write.

In the pit yard at Long Martley, three men were performing chin lifts on an iron bar and another three were running back and forth between two posts with what looked like sacks of wet sand on their backs. A further four, stripped to the waist in spite of the cold, were lifting weights, raising the loaded bars in unison like a display team of strongmen. The earl felt over-dressed and not a little feeble. He whipped off his scarf and left it behind in the motorcar before crossing the cobbles to Harry Booth's office. Inside, William Garforth was holding a piece of breathing apparatus by its leather strap and he held it out to Lord Netherwood.

"New design," he said. "We're very pleased with the early trials."

It was heavy, and its weight took the earl by surprise so that he dropped it and had to retrieve it from the office floor.

"Quite a contraption," he said.

"Life saver," said Harry Booth. "Buys a man another hour in a smoke-filled tunnel."

"And how do men communicate when they're wearing it?" The earl hoped his question demonstrated his seriousness of mind and purpose. Poor show, dropping the mask, he thought. Puts a fellow at a disadvantage.

"Each man carries a horn," said Mr. Garforth. "One blast for safe, two for danger. No Lady Henrietta today?"

"No. I'm afraid she's indisposed." What a cad he felt, leaving her behind.

"Oh, what a pity. She'd be fascinated by the progress we've made. A remarkable young woman, if I may say so. Would you like to follow me?"

He was heading for the door, so the question seemed rhetorical. Outside, Mr. Garforth nodded at the weight lifters.

"Fitness training," he said. "The first requirement of an efficient rescue squad."

"Indeed." The earl wondered whether any of them should be mining for coal at this very moment, but anyway he saluted them as they passed. "Working jolly hard," he said.

"At any point they might be called upon to shovel many tons of rock, at speed, or to carry the dead weight of an unconscious miner on their backs. Strength and stamina, Lord Netherwood. Strength and stamina. Here we are."

They had reached a long, low-roofed building by the colliery headgear. It was windowless and, when Mr. Garforth ushered him inside, the earl saw a simulated underground roadway, faithful in every detail to the one at the bottom of the Long Martley mine shaft.

"We can fill it with rubble, pump it full of smoke, throw in a flood for good measure. It's remarkable, the terrors we can reproduce within these walls. Watch your head now, on the way out."

He smiled, stepped out again, and waited for the earl to follow.

"Do you know what I believe causes fifty percent of our underground explosions?" he said.

Lord Netherwood wished he could answer, crisply and authoritatively. Instead, he shook his head.

"Coal dust," said Mr. Garforth.

"Coal dust?"

"Coal dust. Bit of a problem, hmm? But I promise you, Lord Netherwood, that if you eliminate excessive coal dust from your underground workings, your collieries will be considerably safer."

"Eliminate coal dust from a coal mine?" the earl said. What madness was this?

"Where possible, yes. Or dilute its power with stone dust or chippings. Pure coal dust, at certain temperatures and in certain conditions, will explode into a lethal fireball. Might well have been the case here last month, but it won't say as much in the report. Is it out yet?"

"Imminent," said the earl.

"Coal dust," Mr. Garforth said again. "Don't underestimate it."

He set off toward the manager's office, and the earl followed in his wake. The leather soles of his Bond Street brogues had little purchase on the weathered stone-set pit yard and he walked gingerly, for fear of falling. Mr. Garforth, of course, had boots with a grip like Michelin tires. Why, thought the earl, did he always feel such a bally flyweight in the man's company? Ahead, Mr. Garforth was still talking.

"Doesn't need toxic gas to ignite it, you know. I've proved it time and again, back at my own colliery. But the only people who'll listen to me on the subject are the continentals. German collieries are years ahead. Years ahead. Well, here we are."

He stopped by the Daimler, which stood conspicuously yellow and incongruously clean among the coal wagons at the edge of the yard. The earl was pleased to see a little black Wolseley, however, tucked away in another corner: the fellow hadn't ridden here, then, on a white charger.

"Mr. Garforth," he said, "it's been instructive, as ever, and progress has been simply remarkable."

"Thanks to you, Lord Netherwood."

"Well, good of you to say but . . ."

"Your resources, my vision, and a loyal workforce. A winning combination, wouldn't you say?"

The earl hauled the crankhandle and blessed the patron saint of motorists when the engine sparked into life at the first attempt. He opened the door and climbed inside. Leather, walnut, chrome; this was his world, and in it, he began to relax.

"Until next time," he said. Luncheon: rare beef and a glass of claret. This thought cheered him further.

Mr. Garforth, straight-backed and soldierly, saluted him by way of a farewell. The car moved away, jolting on the uneven surface of the yard, and an arm emerged from the driver's side window, returning the gesture. Mr. Garforth smiled. He liked the earl. A willingness to learn was a rare commodity among the landowning class, in his experience. Not to mention a willingness to spend money on people other than themselves. Lord Netherwood hadn't even queried the last set of accounts, and he knew from Harry Booth that they were hefty. Guilt money, according to Booth, but this seemed ungenerous to William Garforth, who looked for the best in everyone he met and generally found something to admire. Respectfully, he waited until the Daimler had disappeared up the cinder track before he turned once again toward the manager's office.

Seth was free. When Eve and Daniel had left the party—one night away in a Sheffield hotel and Seth didn't want to dwell on the matter—he had seized the moment and walked straight to New Mill Colliery still clad in tailcoat and pinstripes, afraid that he if he turned up for the afternoon shift in work clothes he'd end up losing his nerve and be condemned to the screens for all eternity. Of course, the second he walked into the pit yard he regretted the strategy, but anyway he ran the gauntlet of hooting, taunting, and attempts on his dignity, and made it unscathed to the offices, where he stood for a moment, adjusted his waistcoat, then knocked at the door. It was opened at once by Sidney Cutts, who wasn't actually answering the knock, but merely exiting the colliery manager's office. He stopped though, when he saw Seth, and took a step back, the better to enjoy the spectacle.

"Don," he said, deadpan. "Little Lord Fauntleroy to see thi."

Don Manvers looked across at Seth.

"Bugger me," he said. Sidney and Seth switched places; the boy came in, the man left for the stores, and Seth could see him shaking his head as he went, as if he'd never seen the like. Mr. Manvers took a noisy slurp from a mug on his desk; tea, the color of dark terra cotta, furred the inside of his mouth. Unsmiling, unnerving, he said: "Well?"

"Sorry, Mr. Manvers," Seth said. "I came straight from my mam's wedding."

"Is that right? Well, tha looks a right idiot and no mistake. That's no getup for a working lad."

"I'm givin' notice, Mr. Manvers. I'm not cut out for t'job."

The pit manager sucked the tea off his teeth and stared at Seth. The lad had taken off the top hat, at least; he held it like a begging bowl, clutching the rim with his two hands.

"I could 'ave told thi that when tha came to ask for a place," he said, slowly and after an uncomfortable pause. "In fact, I think I did tell thi that. Or words to that effect."

"Yes, Mr. Manvers."

"Back to school, is it?"

"If they'll 'ave me."

"Go on then. Get gone. An' if them lads outside give thi an 'ard time, there's nob'dy to blame but thisen."

The boy walked backward from the manager's desk like a royal flunky. Don Manvers, hiding a smile, picked up a stack of timesheets and placed a pair of wire-rimmed spectacles on the end of his nose.

"Thank you, Mr. Manvers," said Seth at the door. It was done. He felt lighter, actually lighter; he felt like he'd just deposited a sack of coal on the office floor.

Mr. Manvers regarded him over the top of his lenses and said: "Does thi mam know?"

"No, Mr. Manvers. I'll tell 'er when she's back."

"Did tha buy 'er a wedding present?"

Seth colored. "No, Mr. Manvers."

"Well, tha won't 'ave to now," he said, then he took up a pen and resumed his paperwork, and Seth closed the door, then turned and ran pell-mell through the pit yard before anyone could get their hands on him.

Chapter 36

The earl, enjoying the drive home, had taken a spontaneous detour, running the motor up and around the narrow, twisting lane to the top of Harley Hill, where he got out and leaned on the bonnet, feeling the warmth of the engine through his coat. The scrubby green sward of the common rolled out beside him to his right and before him lay Netherwood, in a hundred shades of gray. At the center of the town the ground-work for the miners' memorial had begun. The plan had changed since its conception; it was to be bronze now, not granite, and not an obelisk but the figure of a miner carrying a lamp. Henry's idea, like so much else. A stone monument was imper-sonal, she had said, and not a fitting tribute to the men who had died in the earl's service. There was to be a granite plinth, however, and a great granite tablet bearing the names of the men claimed by the Netherwood mines. The mason had asked—politely, with no edge—should he leave space for other names, perhaps? No, the earl had said, we must assume the best, and in the event of the worst, then . . . tailing off, the earl had left the yard in the grip of a bleak reverie. The mason had reached P and already there were well over two hundred men and boys remembered there, in the stone. They weighed on the earl's conscience, these souls. Sometimes he saw them in his sleep.

In the distance the town hall clock struck half past twelve and the earl stirred himself for the homeward leg. Once again, he hiked the engine back into action, then slapped the wheel arch in an encouraging, friendly way—a horseman's habit that he had brought to motoring.

"Home, James," he said to himself, then climbed in and pointed the Daimler down the hill, releasing the throttle and letting the car pick up a bit of speed, just for the joy of it. He felt the rush of cold air in his face and allowed himself a short, conservative whoop of exhilaration, the thought crossing his mind that there was more of Tobias in him than he sometimes cared to acknowledge. He took one hand from the wheel and yanked at the earflaps of his leather hat, tugging them lower. Hawthorn whipped the sides of the car as he sped downhill. At each bend, he gave a blast on the horn, to announce his imminent appearance to anyone in his path, though he didn't actually expect to encounter anyone. A startled rabbit, perhaps, or a fat pheasant, running idiotically into his path instead of taking to the air; he'd certainly flattened a few of those in his motoring career. Damned waste it was too, when they'd been lovingly reared for the shoot.

"What's the difference," Isabella had asked him once, "killing them with the car or with a gun? Either way they end up dead." He had laughed.

"Dear child," he had said. "The difference is this; method one is an unfortunate accident: method two, a sporting assault, and a planned one."

"Not entirely sporting. The birds can't shoot back," she had said. Isabella had her mother's pretty pout and the same coquettish, endearing, irresistible way of conducting an argument. Henrietta, however—ah, she might learn a thing or two about womanly wiles from her mother and sister. She had stalked out of the morning room this morning with a face like a stormy sky, just as she had done since childhood. Henry's rages had always clouded her face and made her plain. The earl smiled at the recollection of her parting shot. Mrs. Pankhurst indeed! Clever old Henry; she had always known the precise weapons to use against her mother. He would find her the moment he returned and . . .

His mind emptied of all thoughts but that a pony, a gray mare, stood directly in his path and he was driving at speed toward her.

She stood as if rooted, her stocky little mass filling the space between the hedgerows, her head turned so that her eyes were fixed on the approaching vehicle. Lord Netherwood, anxious for the pony's welfare, careless of his own, swung the steering wheel violently to the left, though a small, rational part of him knew there was no escape from impact. The Daimler's front wing rammed into the pony's right flank, slicing into her solid flesh and inducing an instant reaction of wild-eyed panic. She reared to escape the pain and crashed down with her front hooves on the bodywork of the motorcar, producing a thunderous sound that the pony couldn't understand, driving her wilder still. He couldn't see what held her there, in the lane, though evidently she was unable to break free. If he had been able to stand, the earl might have calmed her; there were tricks of the hands and the voice that those who understood the language of horses could use to ease a frenzied beast. But, trapped in his seat, the earl felt stupid and helpless, pinned in by the heaving bulk of the pony, his arms wrapped above his head for scant protection. The motorcar's left front wheel was in a ditch and the vehicle listed hopelessly so that remaining upright in his seat, without his hands for support, was an appalling effort. The pony seemed intent on the destruction of either him or the Daimler, thrashing and tossing her head in an agony of pain and panic. Why couldn't she run? If he'd had a rifle, he would have shot her in an instant, for both their sakes; the mad whites of her eyes were close enough to put a bullet clean between them. But he had no gun, so he dropped his arms from their defensive position and attempted awkwardly to shift across to the passenger seat, away from the violent range of the pony's hooves. Again and again the creature reared, whinnying maniacally, baring long yellow teeth, smashing down with all her considerable might onto her tormentor.

For a split second they looked directly at each other, the earl and the pony, each eyeing their tormentor. Instinctively he shook his head as if to say, you have the wrong man; but he knew this was a kind of madness of his own. He tried to lunge sideways, his plan being to haul himself out of the motorcar and into the embrace of the hawthorn hedge on his left. The pony, foaming now, sodden with sweat, near exhausted from her own pointless exertions, hauled herself upright once again, rising on her hind legs and screaming with a kind of desperate, unearthly triumphalism. The earl, his legs twisted and trapped by the steering wheel, was nevertheless almost clear of her reach, but then she plummeted back down, and with entirely accidental accuracy she struck him a devastating blow to the head.

He knew nothing more. Senseless, he slumped sideways in the seat. The pony, with no sense of a battle won, continued to rise and fall against the Daimler. Her hooves, when they struck the earl, provoked no further reaction.

Seth, running home from New Mill Colliery, heard the crazed pony before he saw her, and he followed the sound, driven by curiosity rather than alarm. He approached the scene from the common, and at first the hawthorn hid the motorcar so that all he could see from the wrong side of the hedge was the old pit pony, the gray—a gentle mare, he knew her well—occasionally and desperately throwing herself upward, as if she was struggling to get clear of something. He jogged closer, looking for a way through the hedgerow, and then he saw flashes of yellow and chrome through the gnarled and knotted interior; one of the earl's Daimlers, no question about it. He couldn't, from this inadequate vantage point, see the earl, and he walked up and down quite calmly, looking for a gap large enough to squeeze through, and far enough away from the pony to be safe. She was tiring now anyway, the poor old thing. She must be fast on something. The driver of the car must have gone for help.

He was still in his finery. He placed the top hat carefully, responsibly, on a grassy mound, and then pushed his way— backward to protect his face—between the branches in a section of the hedge that seemed marginally less impenetrable than any other. The thorns dragged at the skin on the back of his neck and he cursed like a pit man as he emerged, backside first, onto the lane. And then, of course, he saw the whole picture: the pony, blood the texture of treacle oozing from a gash in her flank, a crudely made wire trap pulled tight around her left hind fetlock, her head and neck hanging low now over the badly dented bonnet of the Daimler, which lay at a tilt in the ditch. And in the car, Lord Netherwood, bleeding from the temple, lying at an unnatural angle across the front seats, making no attempt to speak or move.

Seth ran, powered by fear and the certain knowledge that alone he could do nothing to help. He pelted down the last leg of Harley Hill and, seeing no one to the right or the left, he flew over the road and burst into the taproom of the Hare and Hounds, where his startling appearance brought all conversation and a game of cribbage to an instant halt. He stood for a moment, panting extravagantly, scanning the faces before him, looking for someone useful, and his eyes alighted on Jem Arkwright, who stepped forward as if he had known he would be needed.

"Well, lad?" he said.

"It's Lord Netherwood. I think 'e's killed." The cribbage players—Sol Windross, Clem Waterdine, Percy Medlicott—carefully put down their pints. Jem started for the door.

"Where is 'e?" he said.

"Just up 'arley 'ill. There's a pit pony. And—"

"Show me," Jem said.

Seth began to run again, a fierce heat in his chest, his heart pounding, his throat tight and dry. At the foot of Harley Hill he began to flag, so Jem ran on ahead and by the time Seth reached the scene the land agent had already opened the driver's side door of the Daimler, and was tenderly lifting the earl out of the car. The pony was on her knees, and her eyes, though open, were clouded with distress.

"It's caught on summat," Seth said, his eyes full of tears now there was an adult on hand.

"Rabbit trap, by looks o' things." Jem had the earl in his arms as if he was no heavier than a child.

"Is 'e dead?"

"No," Jem said.

He set off down the lane and Seth stood by the pony, unwilling to leave her. Gingerly he placed a hand on her withers; her coarse hair was cold and damp and she shook under his touch.

"Mr. Arkwright! What about—"

"Fetch a gun an' shoot 'er," he said, without looking back.

"No," Seth said to the pony, not to Jem. "I shan't."

Jem carried the earl as far as Sheffield Road, where Sol Windross caught up to him with the rag-and-bone dray. He made a rudimentary bed from hessian sacks, and Jem placed Lord Netherwood onto these, then climbed up beside him, holding his head steady between his big hands and feeling, from time to time, for the faint beat of a pulse in the earl's neck.

And this was how he arrived back at Netherwood Hall; in the tender care of his land agent, on the back of Sol's cart. They drew up not in the rear courtyard but outside the great colonnaded entrance, and the footmen stood useless with shock as Jem lifted the earl and carried him into the marble hall, where Parkinson, alerted almost by instinct to the emergency, met him in his progress and led him up the sweep of stairs to the earl's private rooms, where Lord Netherwood's inert body was gently laid upon the silk counterpane of the bed.

Chapter 37

Word spread and the story grew, as stories do, in scope and substance, until Lord Netherwood had been crushed to a lifeless pulp under the merciless thrashing hooves of a rogue pony. Of course, only the earl knew the actual sequence of events, though Seth had a fair idea; he had pieced together the likely scenario while he knelt by the little mare and cut her free from the rabbit snare. The pony had blocked the lane, the car had smacked into her flank and veered into the ditch, the earl had taken a blow to the head from the pony's hooves. The car had taken a beating too; its long yellow bonnet was badly dented and the windscreen smashed. There was blood on the cream leather passenger seat. Blue blood, Seth thought, staring at it; but it was red, like his own. By now the pony was spent, defeated by her ordeal, her fear replaced by a passive indifference to her fate. Seth had run to Ravenscliffe and come back with a length of rope and wire cutters and, once she was free of the trap, he looped the rope about her neck and tugged gently to coax her to her feet. She was wary of the motorcar, wouldn't edge past it; he took off his tailcoat and covered her eyes and then her years in service underground began to tell at last, and she did as she was bid; they walked uphill for a short while until they came to a five-bar gate and then, passing through, they continued on home.

Anna, who had seen Seth come and go all in a tearing hurry, was looking out for him.

"What on earth?" she said, with some alarm. She didn't like the ponies. They came too close to her when she walked on the common and their proportions seemed all wrong: heads like stallions and legs no longer than a big dog's.

"She's 'urt. Jem said I should shoot 'er, but I think 'e was just mad because t'earl got knocked senseless."

As an explanation, this was hopeless.

"Tie pony on gatepost, then tell me again," Anna said. She stayed on the doorstep, watching from a distance.

"We need salt water for this gash, look," Seth said. "She might need stitching."

Anna thought of her needle and thread pulling in and out of the pony's flesh, and she shuddered.

"Not you," Seth said, seeing her. "Vet'nary."

He fussed a little longer around the mare, clucking and tutting until Anna, fatigued from the day, told him to look sharp and tell her exactly what had happened. He stayed by the pony but told Anna what he knew, and she sat heavily on the front doorstep, one hand at her mouth.

Seth said: "Oh don't fret. Jem'll 'ave 'im 'ome by now. Mark my words, 'e'll be right as rain." He sounded so sure of himself that Anna forgot that he was only twelve, and she believed him.

Doctor Frankland had been called to Netherwood Hall and was in attendance with the earl. Lady Netherwood, ashen and tiny, remained in the drawing room with her children about her. She had dismissed the footmen, preferring in this crisis to be unobserved, and they sat together, all of them silent, keeping vigil. Below stairs, at the great oak table of the servants' dining hall, the butler and the housekeeper sat quietly too. Parkinson had been arranging the luncheon table when Jem Arkwright had strode into the house, the metal cleats on the soles of his boots ringing out on the marble floor. An extraordinary sight, one man in another man's arms. He had followed the butler upstairs and placed the earl on the bed, not in a rush, with relief, as one might expect, but carefully, almost reluctantly, as if he would have preferred to keep hold. Parkinson tried to explain.

"He held him like this," he said, making a cradle of his arms. "As if the weight was nothing."

"We have hidden resources," Mrs. Powell-Hughes said. "We don't know how strong we are until we're called upon."

Parkinson nodded.

"Jem likely saved his lordship's life," she said.

Parkinson, who had seen the earl's injury and his pallor, couldn't reply. The great kitchen clock ticked on, filling the silence between them.

"I think I'll go up," Parkinson said.

Mrs. Powell-Hughes looked at him and nodded. It was as well to be on hand, she thought.

"See if I can be of any use," the butler said. "At least then I'll hear when . . . if . . . that is . . ."

The housekeeper said: "I know."

Daniel and Eve lay in bed. One night at the Royal Victoria Hotel in Sheffield was all the time away they could manage, and Daniel said they weren't going to spend it minding their manners in the dining room or taking afternoon tea in the drawing room. So they had gone to bed, even though it was only one o'clock and they had to draw the brocade curtains against the daylight. He was desperate for her; he undressed her gently enough, but he fell on her like a hungry man at a feast when, finally, she stood naked before him. Afterward he pressed her to him, rolling over so that he was underneath, and with his face in her hair he breathed her in. She traced a line with her finger from his shoulder to his elbow and laughed.

"What?" He spoke without moving his head and his voice sounded different, muffled.

"Your arm's pale as mine to here." She drew a line again, shoulder to elbow. "And brown as a berry to here." Elbow to wrist. Her nail drifting across his skin felt exquisite.

"And you," he said, rolling again so that now they were on their sides, face-to-face, "are cream-colored from head to toe. Every inch." He shifted his weight and lowered his head to kiss her. Tiny, fluttering kisses moving down her neck and over her breasts, beyond them to her belly, grazing softly against her thighs. He nudged open her legs, kissing her still, and she thought she should feel some shame at this intimacy; curtains drawn in daytime, respectability abandoned in the pursuit of new ecstasies. But there was no shame, not even a shred. Don't stop, she thought; oh, please don't stop, though she would have never said it out loud.

Daniel ordered cheese sandwiches and a jug of lemonade, standing stark naked at the table and dialing the big black telephone, speaking with a mysterious authority, as if he was used to hotel trysts and room service. It should be champagne, he said, not lemonade, but Eve was thirsty and anyway, she thought champagne was overrated. She watched him from under the covers, amused by his lack of self-consciousness.

"You'll put summat on, when t'food comes?"

"Might do," he said. He smiled at her and her heart flipped. "You look a wee bit tousled there, Mrs. MacLeod."

She blushed, and he laughed.

"It's fine," he said. "It's allowed."

"Perhaps we should show our faces downstairs, though. What'll they be thinking?"

He laughed again.

"Eve, it's a big hotel, they don't log our comings and goings."

"Still, though."

"Still nothing. You're staying right there on that bed. I'm not finished with you yet."

They grinned at each other.

"Do you suppose there's time, before the sandwiches?"

"Daniel!"

"No, you're right. A man can't work on an empty stomach."

She threw a cushion at him; they were dotted about the bed, plush red velvet, serving no purpose except to add to the opulence of the room. It was very fine, if a little overblown. She thought of Anna, moving through Ravenscliffe working her magic. Anna would pare this room back to its essential elegance. Where there was velvet, she would put muslin or linen. Where there was heavy flock paper, she would put paint in a soft, surprising color. Daniel hadn't seen the bedroom yet, the one they were to share at Ravenscliffe. Under Anna's influence, it was as if the sun shone in it all day long: palest yellow, cream, white, and then the bedspread was cornflower blue. When Eve had talked about it, in the kitchen up at the mill, Ginger had raised her brows and asked, wouldn't it be peculiar, the three of them up at Ravenscliffe; shouldn't Anna be moving out when Daniel moved in? Eve had looked up from her task, her hands suspended under warm, sudsy water in the sink.

"Why?" she'd said.

"Like I said, it might look peculiar." Ginger had sounded a bit uncomfortable. She hadn't meant to cast aspersions.

Eve had said: "I don't think so. Not to us, anyroad." She had pulled a saucepan out of the sink and begun to scrub at its insides.

"Well, you don't want to pay attention to what folk say," Ginger had said, and Eve had tossed her a look and said: "No, and you don't either," in a tone that signaled the end of the exchange. Anna's place in Eve's life was a given; certainly Daniel understood this, and it had never crossed his mind to question it.

Now he took a running jump and threw himself back onto the bed beside her. The bedstead rocked and the springs protested, but he just lay there, flat out with his hands behind his head, a great, contented smile on his face. She leaned across and kissed him chastely on the cheek.

"We've so much to look forward to," she said. "So much 'appiness ahead."

"We have," he said.

"I can hardly wait to be back. I mean, this is grand, being 'ere. But to be at Ravenscliffe knowing you're coming back at t'end of each day, waking up with you every morning . . ."

"I know. Waking up with me every morning—there's women would kill for the privilege." He winked at her and she pulled a face.

There was a crisp rap at the door.

"Hello?" Daniel said, still prone on the bed.

"Your refreshments, sir."

She looked at Daniel with startled eyes and he laughed.

"Och, all right then. Just for you, I'll pull my trousers on."

Doctor Frankland had been with the earl for almost two hours before the countess and her children heard his step on the stairs. Brisk and businesslike, thought Henrietta; the footsteps of a man coming to tell them that all was well, her father was recovered; he was sitting up in bed waiting to see them all.

The door was ajar and he pushed it fully open and entered the room. His expression was exceptionally grave. The countess stood.

"I am so very sorry," he said.

"Is my husband unwell still?" said Lady Netherwood.

"Mama," said Tobias gently, taking her arm, holding it tight.

"Lord Netherwood has passed away, your ladyship," said Doctor Frankland with infinite sorrow. He had never shirked from the difficult aspects of his profession, but to be the bearer of this news was painful to him. He knew this family intimately, all of them; the countess had suffered over the years from every fashionable illness and he had attended the births of all her four children; he had seen them subsequently through the ailments of childhood—had, on occasion, feared for their chances in the torrid grip of a fever. Their father, however, had rarely called on the doctor's services, and yet now he lay dead upstairs, victim of a strange and terrible twist of life's path.

"He never regained consciousness."

"We've lost him?" Henrietta's voice was cracked and broken, barely audible. The doctor turned to her.

"We have, Lady Henrietta. I'm so sorry."

She dropped aghast onto the couch and Dickie sank beside her. They held hands. Isabella fell to the floor, facedown on the fine Turkish carpet, screaming and screaming. Tobias, still supporting his mother, said: "Isabella. Please," but she continued on.

"May I see him?" said Lady Netherwood. Isabella's noise seemed not to register.

Doctor Frankland nodded and the countess gently pulled her arm from her son's grasp and moved toward the door.

"Mama, I—"

"No, Toby," she said, without turning. "No need."

At the top of the stairs she found Parkinson, though she passed him without a murmur. He watched her like a sad hound, suffering, longing for a kind word. He felt uprooted somehow, uncertain what to do, unprepared, in spite of years of service, for this awful eventuality. He would have liked to have stepped into his lordship's bedroom and pay his respects; reminisce, perhaps, about the years they had shared as master and servant; weep. But it was not his place to do so, at least, not yet. From behind the closed door of the earl's room, the sound of the countess talking softly to her husband threatened to undo him entirely. So he walked down the stairs. Mrs. Powell-Hughes was still unaware of Lord Netherwood's death. His heart was heavy at the prospect of burdening her with the news.

"Teddy?" said the countess.

Doctor Frankland had cleaned the wound on the earl's head, and bandaged it, and now the patient lay on his back under the counterpane, though he was still dressed in his motoring clothes.

"Teddy. Silly old thing, you still have your coat on."

He didn't answer. She sat by him on the edge of the bed, and gazed about her. Such a masculine room. She imagined the rooms of his London club looked much the same; men were so predictable, so easily pleased in these matters. It struck her that Doctor Frankland had closed the curtains, the thick green damask sinking the room into underwater gloom. Little wonder Teddy slept so deeply. She slipped from the bed—it was a fair drop, for her; once upon a time, in the early years, he had laughingly offered to provide a stepladder for her visits—and wandered over to the windows, dragging the drapes apart.

"Teddy?" she said, more loudly now, from where she stood. "It's time for tea and I do think if you stir yourself, you'll feel all the better for it. I hope you'll learn from this little misadventure, dear. Let Atkins drive. That's why we have him."

She walked back to him, lifted the counterpane, took his hand.

"Oh my! How cold you feel." She rubbed his lifeless hand between hers, then reached for the brass handle set into the wall by his bed. In the servants' hall a bell would ring, and someone would be here in moments. Meanwhile she would hold his hand like this, and chat to him while she waited.

Tobias went to find her. She looked at him when he entered his father's room and her face showed irritation, not grief.

"I thought you were Agnes," she said. "I rang. Your papa needs beef tea."

He stared. His eyes alighted on his father's body, still as stone, and he found himself unable to move or to speak. Behind him, just outside the open door, Mrs. Powell-Hughes arrived, red-eyed, responding to the swinging bell in the servants' hall, believing that perhaps the doctor needed assistance. She saw the earl on the bed; she saw the countess perched beside him, trying to warm his hand in hers; she saw Tobias, wordless at the threshold of the room. And immediately, she understood. She swept in, took control.

"Now, your ladyship, come with me to your room and I shall send Flytton to you. You leave his lordship to the doctor."

She had the countess by the shoulders and led her across the room as if she were a sleepwalking child. As she passed Tobias, the housekeeper placed a warm hand on his arm, lingering momentarily and giving him a look of such limitless sympathy, such comfort and reassurance, that it remained with him, pure and perfect, for all the difficult days to come.

Chapter 38

A t half past three on the afternoon of the day the earl died, the great bells in the two cupolas of Netherwood Hall were tolled thirty times, slowly and with a five-second beat between them. They told the county of a death in the great Hoyland line, and though word had spread that Lord Netherwood was mortally wounded, there were plenty of people who were stopped in their tracks in the street, in their kitchen, in the colliery yard, stilled and silenced by the sonorous, sorrowful chimes. The last time they'd rung in this way had been twenty-six years ago, when the fifth earl had died. Then, his end came as no surprise, the inevitable conclusion of a protracted illness: weeks and weeks during which his condition worsened by tiny degrees, the old man visibly shrinking in his bed, hovering between life and death, before finally releasing his fragile grip on consciousness and slipping away. But now—the death knell for the earl was unexpected, horrifying: he was hale and hearty, not yet fifty years old, and wasn't it only this morning that he'd driven to Long Martley in the best of spirits? This last was repeated again and again, as if his death defied all logic and the facts of the matter made it impossible.

"Everybody's alive until they die," Amos said to Anna the next morning. "Yet folk go on about 'ow they saw 'im looking right as rain. What do they expect? Grim reaper, following 'is car?"

Anna didn't quite like his tone. The town was in full mourning: schools, pits, and businesses closed, curtains drawn in the windows of every home, black-clad men and women in solemn huddles on their doorsteps or in their backyards, swapping what little they knew in somber voices.

"They're shocked, that's all," Anna said. "I am, too."

"Aye. Death's shocking, right enough, and we should know because it's a regular visitor to these parts." He knew he sounded bitter, resentful, so he left it at that, though she knew what he was thinking.

"Be careful, Amos," she said. "This isn't good time for you to rage against privilege. Think of his family. Grief is grief, however well you live."

He didn't want to upset her so he let it drop. But still, he thought, one less pampered aristocrat wasn't a cause for universal mourning. If the town closed down as a mark of respect every time a miner died in a Netherwood colliery, there'd be a good deal less money in the Hoyland coffers. Must Seth and Eliza believe their father's death was less significant than the earl's, because the school stayed open and the pits and the shops didn't close for business? It made him sick, that was the truth of it. But he'd save it for Enoch and the four walls of his office.

"Best be off," he said. He'd walked up to Ravenscliffe on his way to the station, though it was patently out of his way and both of them knew it. She was baking with Eliza on this unscheduled day of freedom, letting the child break the eggs into a bowl, then patiently picking out all the bits of shell for her. Seth was folded into an armchair, lost in a weighty-looking tome, chewing a finger as he read, a small scowl of concentration on his face. Making up for time wasted at the screens, thought Amos. He ruffled his hair as he passed, but the boy didn't even look up.

"Will you come later? Have a meal with us?" Anna's face, fresh and youthful, always gave him pause. He swallowed before he spoke.

"What time are they back?" He meant Eve and Daniel. He was long over his disappointment there, but he couldn't be sitting here at the table on their first night in the marital home.

Anna's face clouded. "I don't know. Soon, I think. It's dreadful—they know nothing about it."

"Aye, well." He turned to leave the room, then stopped. "Look, I'll tell you what, you come to me for a bite to eat."

She laughed, and he feigned indignation.

"Watch it," he said. "There's more to me than meets t'eye, young lady."

"Well, all right," she said. "But not today, because Eve's coming home. Tomorrow?"

"Tomorrow. Six o'clock. Bring an appetite."

"Can I come?" said Eliza.

Anna and Amos looked at her.

"I've only got two chairs," Amos said.

It sounded a poor excuse, and he knew it.

Daniel saw Eve home to Ravenscliffe and left her with Anna and the children, then half ran, half walked back to Netherwood Hall through streets that were eerily quiet for the time of day. They had driven into town in a hansom cab from Sheffield and both of them knew, instantly, that something was amiss. Eve had thought it was another rockfall, claiming lives, and she had sat catatonic with fear, unable to speak, until they reached home and she opened her front door and Anna took her coat, her gloves, her hat: it's Lord Netherwood, Anna said. Killed on Harley Hill by a pit pony—it's outside now, tethered to the fence. The absurdity of this statement detracted from the horror, but only momentarily. The earl was dead. Her benefactor. Her friend. She turned a stricken face to Daniel, who took her hand, holding it tight. He'd better go, he told them. He might be of assistance, somehow, to someone. He lifted her hand in his, and kissed it, then turned on his heel and left through the door, which was still wide open, letting the sharp October wind into the house.

Henrietta had risen early, earlier even than the household staff, so that when little Josie Morton arrived with her ash bucket and brushes to clean and relight the bedroom fire, edging into the room like a cautious mouse, dreading the possibility of disturbing her ladyship, she found her already gone. Her initial relief was followed immediately by anxiety over whether she should now leave the grate cold and empty and—perhaps more pressingly—whether she should report Lady Henrietta's absence to someone. Suddenly, in the space of just a few hours, life seemed to have lost all its certainty. In the end, she lit a fire, reasoning that Lady Henrietta might be glad of the comfort when she returned from wherever she had gone. But she didn't tell anyone that the bedroom was empty, because that anxiety was soon entirely subsumed by the bigger one of having now to enter the countess's rooms, a task she would have gladly paid a week's wages to avoid. The junior maids were all afraid of the countess's grief. They had heard she had run mad with it and, since none of them had seen her, there was no evidence to the contrary.

Henrietta's absence was easily explained. Sleepless with grief, restless with remorse, she had gone to the gardens to think. There was a place she was partial to, a favorite retreat from girlhood; an old weeping copper beech and beneath its sweeping canopy, the statue of a dog, a sitting Great Dane, faithful companion of an earlier Earl of Netherwood. When she was small she fitted snugly between his two front legs, and she would sit there looking out at the same things that he did. Now, though, she merely sat by him, leaning against his solid stone body and watching the trailing branches move in the wind, shedding leaves like tears.

She was sorry with all her heart that her last words to her father had been deliberately antagonistic: that their last conversation—out of all the hundreds of conversations they had had—had been ill-tempered. He had died believing her angry with him. And she had been. She had been angry because he had been a good and loyal husband, taking his wife's side against their headstrong daughter. Henrietta dipped her head onto her knees and wailed with the sort of noisy exhibition she detested in Isabella but which now, in this genuine crisis, gave her some sort of strange, cathartic release.

Belowstairs Monsieur Reynard, less affected than many in the kitchens, continued on as usual, though the breakfast he dispatched through the green baize door was returned an hour and a half later, untouched. Undaunted, he began preparations for luncheon; someone, at some point, would need to be fed, and he instructed Sarah Pickersgill to pull her weight.

"Life goes on, Sarah," he said. "And so we make beef consommé for the grieving souls."

She looked at him with damp eyes and he handed her a shin of beef.

"Run this through the mincer," he said. It wasn't that he was pitiless: just that there were tasks to be done. The earl is dead, long live the earl—that was Claude Reynard's view. There would be no lapse in culinary standards on his watch. When the family decided, in their own time, that they needed sustenance, he, their chef, would not be found wanting. It was an attitude that earned him, finally, a grudging respect from Parkinson, whose own sense of duty and obligation was proving greater than his sense of loss, profound though this was. He approved of the Frenchman's dogged professionalism, just as he disapproved of maids who openly wept on their way through the corridors of the house, or footmen who presented long faces to the world. None of them had known Lord Netherwood for as many years as Parkinson had, and had he given way to unbridled sorrow? No, he had not. He said as much to the assembled household staff, corraled by himself and Mrs. Powell-Hughes for an emergency meeting in the servants' hall.

"We have an obligation to the whole family, a duty to uphold the traditions of this fine house," he said. "This is not to deny our sadness at the earl's death; we feel it most profoundly." There were doleful sniffs and a general murmur of assent, and he paused for a moment to allow it to settle. "But our sadness, our distress, must not become an excuse for a decline in standards. Lady Netherwood is relying on us, more so now than ever before, as are her children. It does none of us credit if the smooth running of the household begins to falter. And it does no justice, either, to our memories of Lord Netherwood."

There was a small break in his voice at this point, and he paused again, as if—unthinkable notion—he might be unable to continue. He bowed his head, breathed deeply, and rallied.

"So. Let me see you carry out your duties with appropriate dignity and restraint. Mrs. Powell-Hughes and myself—and of course Mr. Reynard—will be looking to you all to help the family through this most difficult of times."

It was beautifully put, nicely judged; morale began to be restored under the butler's firm direction. And it was noted by all—and chewed over later—that the chef had been paid the compliment of a particular mention, even if Parkinson hadn't managed the French appellation. Credit where credit was due was one of the butler's abiding principles, and Claude Reynard had proved himself worthy of it. But nothing, nothing at all, would induce Parkinson to address him as *monsieur*.

"What did you do?"

This was Eve. She sat with Daniel in the quiet of the Ravenscliffe parlor. Her eyes were red, her face white, and she didn't look, or feel, like a newlywed. It was cold in the room without a fire, but the children were in the kitchen and she needed to talk, and to listen.

"Not much. I'd have liked to talk to the countess, pass on my—our—condolences, but there was no sign of her. According to the upstairs maids, she's been in her rooms with the doctor all day. Taken bad."

"She's not strong," Eve said. "In some ways, she's a child."

"Aye."

"Did you see any of them?"

"No. One of my lads saw Lady Henrietta, on the grounds by the stone dog. She looked like stone herself, he said. Poor girl."

"She was close to 'im. What about 'er mam, though—what becomes of 'er, now Tobias is earl?"

"The Dowager Countess of Netherwood. Doesn't suit her, does it?"

Eve shook her head no. "Will she stay at Netherwood 'all?"

"You're asking the wrong man. We'll all have to wait and see."

"It's such a shock. Such a terrible thing."

"There's a strange atmosphere down there just now. No lights lit in the windows, no comings or goings."

Eve thought of the household staff: imagined the dread silence in the servants' hall after Jem Arkwright brought the earl home senseless in his arms.

"Jem thought he'd live," Daniel said, as if he could read her mind. "They all did. But he never woke up."

"Poor Jem," Eve said. "'e'll take it bad."

They were quiet for a while, then: "What about the business?" Daniel said.

She flapped a hand, as if nothing was less important.

"No, Eve. He wanted to give it to you. You have to go and see Blandford. He'll be expecting you."

The thought of it, of walking into Absalom Blandford's office, the earl dead, everything changed, was dreadful to her.

"I'll see," she said, quite certain she wouldn't.

"I'll come with you, if you like. But you should go, Eve. The earl'd want it."

There was a tap on the parlor door and Seth came in, looking like a boy with something to say.

"Come and sit by me, love," Eve said, patting the couch, but he hung back by the door, feeling suddenly shy.

"Mam," he said.

"Yes?"

"I left New Mill. I left my job."

Abruptly, she stood, her hands to her mouth. She thought, he's safe, my boy's safe, and joy flooded her body and it didn't feel wrong, or disrespectful, not in the least. The world outside Ravenscliffe was one thing: the world inside, another. Seth smiled at her, a real, heartfelt smile such as she hadn't seen from him for many, many months.

"I'm so glad, Seth," she said, in a voice low with emotion. She walked to him and took his precious face in her hands and kissed his forehead. He was taller than she was, but he was her boy. He had come back to her, and she felt blessed.

Chapter 39

She had been so set against it, so determined to resist, but there she was anyway, making the lonely journey down Oak Avenue to see Absalom Blandford. It took her back, as she'd known it would, to the time many months earlier, when Anna and Samuel Farrimond had chivied her into asking the earl to invest in her business. She felt chivied again now: her instinct had been to let it lie, believing that if the earl intended her to have the business, he would have somehow made sure that she did. Nonsense, Anna had said. Lord Netherwood was dead. Yes, Eve had said, I know.

"Then you must go, as you promised earl you would, and see Mr. Blandford. Yes, yes"—Eve had been grimacing at the prospect—"he is horrible man. But what matter? You're there on business, not in friendship."

Daniel had agreed; it would be disrespectful to the earl, he said, to stay away. And Eve, stung by this suggestion, had capitulated. But she walked the mile down the tree-lined avenue with less confidence in her mission than either her husband or her friend. Daniel, at work somewhere on these grounds though she couldn't see him, had told her that she must look the bailiff directly in the eye, state her business, and sign whatever papers needed signing. And that would be that, he said. He'd offered to come with her, but she had declined; if she had to face Mr. Blandford, she would do it in her own right, as the late earl's business associate. I am Mrs. Daniel MacLeod and I have a perfect right to be here, she said to herself. It would have been a useful mantra, if only she had believed it.

There was a motorcar outside the hall, a little black two-seater with a drift of leaves at its right side, so it must have been parked there for a while. The doctor's car, perhaps. By all accounts Lady Netherwood was keeping him busy, now that there was nothing he could do for the earl. Eve wondered at the scene inside; Lord Netherwood laid out in his room, and life tiptoeing on outside his closed doors. When Arthur died, she couldn't have his body at home because it had been mutilated by the rockfall; it was a terrible admission, but she'd been glad of it. A corpse in the parlor was a bad custom, in her view, especially when there were bairns in the house. She shuddered. No cause to think of it all now.

Her boots on the ground announced her arrival in the courtyard behind the great house. A pall of inactivity hung over the stables. There must have been boys around, but there was no sign of anyone at all and the long row of stalls where the horses usually stood was empty. She crossed the yard to the estate offices and saw the pristine profile of Absalom Blandford; he was seated at his desk, though he appeared not to be working, but to be simply gazing ahead. The neighboring office, Jem Arkwright's, was empty, the door closed, the window shuttered. Eve faltered, losing heart, and she might have turned tail but for the fact that Mr. Blandford suddenly executed a swift and efficient turn of his head like a buzzard sensing prey and, propelled by his chilly gaze, she approached his door, knocked twice, and entered. For a disconcerting moment he held his position, scrutinizing the now-empty stable yard as if, after all, it had not been Eve who had caught his attention, but something else far more noteworthy. And then he looked at her and though he didn't speak, his expression invited her to explain her unwelcome presence here in the sanctity of his office.

"On my wedding day," she said, plunging in without preamble, "Lord Netherwood told me he wished me to 'ave full ownership of t'mill. I was to come to your office, 'e said, and see you. Lord Netherwood said that . . ."

Her voice cracked and her eyes brimmed. He continued to stare, coldly.

"Of course, 'e would've been 'ere too"—she reached for her handkerchief, wiped her eyes, struggled on—"if 'e was able to be."

"Really?" said Absalom, his voice laced with skepticism.

"I'm sure 'is lordship spoke to you about it, Mr. Blandford."

"Are you? How interesting. I fear you presume too much. I had no such conversation with the late earl. Certainly I would have remembered an exchange as remarkable, as . . . fanciful . . . as the one you describe."

She was silent. He continued to watch her, his mouth twisted with contempt. Could she possibly have misinterpreted the earl's words? she wondered. Caught in the hostile sights of the bailiff, she struggled to recall the exact conversation. Her thoughts swam. But no! He had mentioned a solicitor and papers to sign. There was no mistake, she was sure of it. She took a breath.

"Lord Netherwood told me you were to speak to 'is solicitor and that paperwork was being prepared. I wouldn't make up such a thing, Mr. Blandford. I can't believe 'e would make such an offer and forget to discuss it with you."

"No, indeed, we can agree on that much at least. The earl would never take such a step without involving me in the process. And try as I might, however strenuously I rack my brain, I can call no such matter to mind. So I must conclude, Mrs."—

there was a pause, while he appeared to be searching for the word—"MacLeod, that it didn't take place. Now, are we to continue with this entertainingly circular conversation, or am I to be allowed to return to my many business matters of a less fantastical nature?"

She looked at him, at his sneer, at his manicured fingers rifling through a bowl of potpourri, the only item on an otherwise empty desk, at his abundant hair oiled back into a sleek mane, at his cold, feral eyes; and she felt, for the first time in her life, the hot, unstoppable, incurable rush of pure hatred. It coursed like lava through her veins. She hated him, and would always hate him. There could be no forgiveness. He raised his eyebrows questioningly, as if mystified at her continued presence.

"You're a wicked man, Absalom Blandford," she said. "A wicked, wicked man. Lord Netherwood spoke to you, I know 'e did. I don't 'ave proof, but I know it. But I shan't fight you, because I've no cause to. I 'ave a life filled with love. You, I should imagine, have nowt: nowt at all, except for t'power to go against a dead man's wishes. Well, go on, and see if I care. Yours is a sad excuse for a life and I pity you."

He stood so abruptly that his chair crashed backward onto the floor.

"Get out!" His voice when raised hit a strange falsetto, quite different from his usual controlled, oleaginous tone. It was almost comical, but Eve didn't laugh. Instead she gave him a look so fierce, so direct, that he felt utterly exposed, entirely vulnerable, and then she turned and left, slamming the door behind her so that the glass in the window frames rattled.

Amos's rooms were at the nicer end of Sheffield Road, where the run of terraced houses overlooked not their mirror image, but a patch of open countryside to the west of Netherwood. He had a bedroom, a parlor, and a small kitchen, which he rarely used, since Ida Birtle, his landlady, provided dinner for her lodgers if they gave her enough notice and paid the shilling in advance. He had moved in here with his scant belongings and Mac the bulldog, each of them considering it a drop in their respective circumstances—"Backyard?" Mac had seemed to say as he stood bowlegged and bulky, looking at Amos with reproach in his brown eyes. They'd managed well enough, of course, and Amos had reminded the dog that there were plenty of landladies who wouldn't let a dog over the threshold, but still, it felt like a temporary measure. He didn't like to share a staircase with anyone these days, didn't like running the risk of meeting a fellow lodger on the early morning dash to empty his chamber pot. He didn't like Mrs. Birtle's habit of glancing pointedly at the hall clock whenever she saw him coming or going, as if his movements were suspiciously erratic, though he rarely altered the pattern of his days. And he didn't like the sound of snoring coming through the wall at night. Not only snoring, either: other noises, highly suggestive of a poorly stifled quest for solitary sexual ecstasy, emanated regularly from the lodger next door, a bank clerk called Trimble, with a furtive habit of dropping his eyes—as well he might—whenever he and Amos passed on the landing.

His little house in Brook Lane—the one he'd lost along with his job at New Mill Colliery—had been his entirely: his and Julia's, before she died, but then his own alone for the many years after that. He could walk, if he wished, stark naked from bedroom to kitchen, whistling as he went, and only the dog would be any the wiser. Amos had acquired Mac as a bit of welcome company, truth be told, when fate threw him into his path. One of a litter of six puppies he found in a sack in Milton Pond, the only one still with a chance of life. The tiny creature had managed to crawl up the pile of bodies and out

326

of its watery grave, so that when Amos gingerly untied the neck of the sack, the puppy had rolled out onto his hand, disconcertingly cold and hairless and with only the faintest trace of a pulse. Amos had kept him warm by his stove, then fed him drops of milk, little expecting the puppy to survive. But here he was now, a permanent, meaty fixture in Amos's life, breathing noisily with effortful concentration as he watched Amos preparing a shepherd's pie.

"Bitten off more 'n I can chew 'ere," Amos said to the dog. "You think it'd be simple, a shepherd's pie, but it's 'arder than it looks."

The lamb base hadn't thickened and it ran into the dish from the pan with the consistency of soup.

"Now 'ow am I going to get t'mash to sit on top o' that?" he said. He looked at Mac, who looked right back at him. "Let's 'ope she's not 'ungry."

With infinite care he began to drop spoonfuls of potato onto the meat sauce and watched gloomily as each one sank like a stone beneath the surface. He cursed himself for not just grilling a couple of chops. He had wanted to demonstrate the esteem in which he held her by making a meal that required a bit of effort. But he hadn't made a shepherd's pie in a long while: years, perhaps.

"Not a lot of point, fussing about wi' pies when it's just me," Amos said. "Well, and thee," he added, to Mac. "I expect you'd trough this in no time."

"Do you always talk to yourself?"

Anna's voice came from the parlor and Amos jumped as if he'd been shot by a dart. She came to the door and looked in at Amos and the dog.

"Ah, you're talking to Mac. That's all right then." She smiled.

"I never 'eard you knock," Amos said, and it came out sounding churlish.

"I didn't."

They looked at each other. She wore a coat of blue wool, tightly buttoned, and a blue felt hat shaped a bit like a bell, pulled down low. She always looked different from other women, Amos thought: the same, but different. Her clothes were always individual, though he couldn't have put his finger on why.

"Your landlady was there, in hallway. She said to come straight in, she said you were here."

"Aye, sounds about right," Amos said. "She'll be there when you leave an' all, accidentally on purpose."

"Stew and dumplings?" Anna said, looking at the shepherd's pie.

"Aye, sort of," Amos said. "Lamb stew and potato cobblers." He started to laugh, and she smiled at him.

"Pop it in oven then. I'm hungry as horse."

Amos looked at Mac. "Uh-oh," he said.

"I saw Mrs. MacLeod, leaving the bailiff's office," said Mrs. Powell-Hughes.

Parkinson was polishing the silver plate with a linen rag. He rubbed as if he might reveal another color altogether if only he worked hard enough.

"Can't Abel do that, Mr. Parkinson?" If indeed, she thought, it must be done at all.

"Not as well as I can," said the butler. "Anyway, he's needed in the cellar."

Truly, life goes on, thought Mrs. Powell-Hughes.

"I wonder what business she had there," she said. Parkinson looked up from his task.

"Who?"

"Mrs. MacLeod. Mrs. Williams-as-was. With the bailiff."

"There are all manner of possibilities," he said. "I suppose she's concerned for the business. His lordship was very involved."

"Mmmm. So many people affected. So many ramifications. Not just the immediate family, though heaven knows they'll feel the loss for years. That little girl . . ."

She meant Isabella, whose condition had now usurped her mother's as the principal cause for concern to Doctor Frankland.

"No improvement?" said Parkinson.

"None. Hysterical, poor mite. I wonder she has the energy to continue at it, wailing and carrying on. Maudie's been billeted in her bedroom to keep watch over her. Lady Henrietta's sharing Flytton."

Parkinson tutted sadly. Such upheaval. Lady Netherwood seemed to have rallied, at least, and to everyone's immense relief had stopped insisting that the earl was merely sleeping. Almost herself again, although still not quite; she had about her a disconnected air and she certainly hadn't risen to the challenge of the funeral arrangements, which were being managed entirely by Lady Henrietta, who sat in her late father's study as if she belonged there. Tobias, heir to the earldom, showed little interest in the proceedings. He had wanted the funeral to be held in London for reasons that Parkinson suspected were entirely selfish, and the moment his petition had been quashed by the rest of the family—not to mention the weight of tradition—he had grown petulant and obstructive, and could never be found when his presence was required. Parkinson knew that he must strive to correct his own tendency to opprobrium; it was not his place to judge the new master and find him wanting. But the butler deeply mourned the late earl. He was not ready, quite, to submit fully to a new regime. He had been in the room with Tobias, Henrietta, and Dickie when a London burial was mooted: so much easier for everyone to attend, Tobias had said. Parkinson, one hand frozen above the silver coffeepot, might have shocked everyone—including himself—by vehemently protesting, had Lady Henrietta not done so first. Disingenuous, she had said. Tobias mustn't use their father's death as a convenient excuse to see Thea. All in good time, she had said. She was little more than a year older than her brother, but she had spoken as an adult to a child. How safe the reins of Netherwood would have been in her hands: how very uncertain in her brother's. Parkinson allowed the thought to form, then instantly dismissed it. No good could come from insubordination, however private it might be. And he could take comfort from the fact that Lady Henrietta had triumphed, easily and swiftly, in the matter of a Yorkshire funeral. Anything else was utterly out of the question, of course. The late earl had always loved his Yorkshire home; Netherwood was his pride and his passion. It was absolutely right that he should rest in peace here, among his forebears, where he belonged. Tears sprang into the butler's eyes. He dipped his rag into the jar of paste, picked up another candlestick, and began to rub.

Chapter 40

"So you'll let it lie?"

"I shall, yes."

"Then you're a fool."

Eve gave Ginger a hard look.

"I'm sorry, Eve, but this business should be yours now, and you're lettin' that lizard get t'better of you."

"I can see 'ow it looks, but what am I to do, Ginger? Stand on t'town 'all steps and call 'im a liar?"

Eve banged down her rolling pin on the mound of pastry and sent up a small cloud of flour from the worktop. The pie lid could take the pasting she should have given Absalom Blandford. You weren't meant to bake when you were cross, but Eve was no longer convinced of the truth of this old wisdom; she was getting through these pastry lids like nobody's business, and the glorious smell of those already in the oven suffused the kitchen. As much as anything, she was cross that Ginger had so easily winkled out of her the cause of her ill humor. She'd vowed to keep it to herself—well, herself, Daniel, and Anna, and Silas was going to have to be told in due course—but Ginger had a sixth sense when it came to matters such as these, going after the truth like a ferret down a rabbit hole. Now that she knew, she'd been sworn to secrecy and Ginger wasn't known for spreading tittle-tattle, but it seemed to Eve that the more people she confided in, the more likely it was that soon everyone would know. Daniel had said: "So what? Where's the harm in folk knowing that Blandford's a treacherous bastard?" but Eve had shushed him; she felt differently about this. It was, after all, her word against the bailiff's, and while he wasn't much liked, he was also known to be a loyal foot soldier to the late earl. Also, the offer to her had been wildly extravagant—she'd been barely able to credit it herself, even as he insisted. What likelihood was there that anyone would believe her? There were enough people in Netherwood who thought Eve had already climbed too far above her station in life: she'd find little sympathy if she went around crying injustice now. No, she had said to Daniel; the earl's promise to her had evaporated when he died.

"Does your brother know owt about it?"

Ginger was a canny soul. She looked at a problem and saw its component parts, the numerous small difficulties that added up to the whole. Eve thought about her brother's feverish excitement at the wedding party, and felt dull dread at the knowledge that she would have to disabuse him.

"Only 'alf of t'story," Eve said.

"I see. Wrong 'alf, I suppose?"

Eve nodded.

"Well, I'll tell you this much for nowt, your Silas won't like it."

"No, well, if I can bear it, I'm sure 'e can."

Eve paused to drape a sheet of pastry over another dish of meat and potato. She crimped its edges, snipped the top twice, then pushed it to one side.

"Anyroad," she said, "it's not Silas's business, is it?"

"'appen not," Ginger said. "But 'e'll take a view." She left it at that, but her expression suggested she had more to say on the subject of Eve's brother.

"What?" Eve said.

Ginger opened her mouth to speak, then closed it again. "Nowt," she said.

The condolences were flooding in and everyone was so kind. Clarissa had written almost fifty restrained and elegant replies— "Your thoughts and words are such a comfort, yours in sorrow and friendship, Clarissa Netherwood"—in spite of the fact that Henry kept telling her there was no need. No one expects a reply to a letter of sympathy, she said. Perhaps not, her mother had said, but how lovely for them to know the value and beneficial effects of their letter.

This new Clarissa, the one that had emerged from the dark days immediately following her husband's death, seemed a veritable saint. Widowhood suited her—quite literally, since she wore black lace or charcoal-gray organza and her ethereal beauty was somehow enhanced by it. She had relinquished the reins of power gracefully, readily, allowing Henrietta and Tobias to argue over the details of what remained to be done, while she drifted about the house and grounds in a state of heightened sensitivity to kindness and loveliness. Daniel, overseeing the meticulous edging in local stone of the Grand Canal, had found he missed the cut and thrust of their old exchanges when she paid him a visit, swathed in sable against the late October day.

"Thank you for working so hard, Daniel," she had said. "Your progress has been quite remarkable."

He had been on his knees pegging plumb lines and hadn't heard her approach. When he stood, wiping dirt from his palms, she had said: "I'm so sorry to disturb you. You must think me an awful nuisance."

"Not in the least, your ladyship," he said. "I'm glad to see you."

She had looked about her and then down into the yawning chasm at her feet.

"How magnificent this will be. Such a grand and noble scheme."

He had looked at her sideways, suspecting her of sarcasm, but all he saw was an expression of serene joy.

"And how are you faring, your ladyship?" he had said. He felt some real concern for her; she seemed to him quite altered.

"Me?" she said, with some surprise. "Oh, quite well. Everyone is being so very careful with me, but I am quite well."

"A difficult time," Daniel said. "Your loss must be hard to bear."

Again, a look of surprise. "On the contrary, I find I can bear the loss of Teddy," she had said. "We were less and less in each other's company, though he was a dear thing and perfectly lovely over all the ruckus of the king's visit. But what I find unsettling, Daniel"—here she paused and lightly touched his arm—"is the uncertainty. One has always known one's place. Now I find myself unexpectedly adrift."

Their conversation had ended there and Daniel, who anyway had been rather lost for words, had watched her weave her way down through the grounds, away from the house. Now, in the kitchen at Ravenscliffe, he described the scene to Anna.

"Peculiar," he said. "As a rule she'd be berating my manners, my gardening, my dirty britches—you name it, she'd take issue. It was fine, mind; it was what I was used to. But today—I don't know. She doesn't seem particularly sad. Just different."

"I expect she'll be all right," Anna said, in a voice that invited no further discussion. She was out of sorts and she hadn't quite worked out why, but in any case, even in the best of humors she thought the countess a vain and silly woman. She'd only ever spoken to her once—and that a year ago, at the grand opening of the mill—but it was enough to form a poor opinion. It was possible, of course, that Amos's prejudices had squirreled their way into her mind and colored her own opinions, but she didn't think so. Any woman who wore pink chiffon flounces beyond the age of seventeen was of suspect character, in Anna's view. Daniel sensed stony ground and let the subject drop. He took a slug of strong, black tea and eyed her cautiously. Something was definitely up, judging by the way that iron was being handled. He watched as she shoved it back into the heat of the fire, then stood, her small foot tapping an irritable tattoo on the flagged floor as she waited for it to be ready. Daniel, who was really only waiting for Seth, considered pinning a note on the front door and heading off up to the allotment alone, but suddenly from down the hallway came the sound of the front door slamming shut and Seth, his cheeks ruddy with fresh air, barged into the kitchen like a small bull, shoving open the kitchen door with one shoulder so that it swung wide and slammed all the way back against the wall; the brass knob had already made a dent in the plasterwork from previous incidents, and Anna issued one of her loud Russian expletives, the meaning of which they could only ever guess at, since she always refused to translate.

"My 'ands are full," said Seth.

He was holding the slender shaft of his dad's old knur and spell pummel, and nothing else. She gave him a look.

"I mean, sorry," he said. He prodded ineffectually at the dented plaster and flecks of blue paint dropped off the wall onto the floor.

"Leave it be," she snapped. She seized the iron and slammed it down onto a gray school shirt, which lay stiff as cardboard on the ironing table, having dried to a crisp on a rack above the range. Seth grimaced at Daniel, who winked at him.

"I saw t'pony," Seth said to Daniel. "She weren't even lame."

"Well, there's one happy ending, then," Daniel said. The

335

boy had nursed the injured pit pony back to health without the assistance of a veterinary surgeon, for whom, anyway, Eve hadn't wanted to pay, feeling it a sort of betrayal.

Anna looked at the two of them, the iron poised in midair as if she might hurl it. "That pony is bane of my life," she said, her voice fraught with irritation. "Always there, looking for food. You must stop feeding it, Seth."

Seth dropped his eyes, his good mood ebbing inexorably away. Daniel took action.

"Come on, sonny," he said, "we've pineapple plants to tend."

Seth flashed him a furtive, grateful smile and they left, united against the injustice of feminine wrath. Anna, watching them swap significant looks as they sauntered off, banged the iron down once more into the fire because it was no sooner hot than it was cold again.

But this wouldn't do. This wouldn't do at all. She bent down again and, taking up a poker, knocked the iron away from the heat. Unceremoniously she dumped the remaining pile of ironing on the kitchen table, and, grabbing her hat and coat from a hook on the back of the door, she left the house. Eve would be home with the girls by six; Anna would be back before then, she was sure of it.

Amos was struggling with Engels and the development of utopian socialism. Enoch had reckoned it was easy reading, full of principles that Amos held already—"but better expressed, like"—but Amos was having trouble with it, reading and re-reading the same paragraph and never quite grasping its meaning. The result of this frustrating pursuit was not a greater understanding of Engels and the philosophy of socialism, but merely a heartfelt resentment toward Enoch. Amos closed the book, put it down, stood up, walked to the window, walked back to the chair, sat down again; he was edgy and restless, in no mood for mind-expanding political tracts.

"You're a bloody idiot, man," he said, to himself. "A bloody idiot."

Misery descended once again. He recalled, for the umpteenth time, his evening here with Anna, just yesterday. How lovely she was, how funny and clever and full of insight. How, when silences fell between them, he had failed utterly to tell her any of this. How, when she stood up to leave, he had nodded and seen her out, as if she was no more to him than a fellow campaigner. He feared rejection, of course he did; the last time he had offered his heart it had been kindly but emphatically declined. But was this past humiliation to mean that he was no longer man enough to face his own feelings? He groaned out loud and closed his eyes.

Outside, downstairs, someone rapped on the front door and he heard the click-clack of Mrs. Birtle's boots as she crossed the hallway. The murmur of female conversation, and then more footsteps. Someone was coming upstairs, and at quite a clip too. Mac, slumbering at Amos's feet, cocked an ear and opened an eye. Then a silence—whoever it was had come to a halt—and then a voice.

"Amos?"

Anna. On the landing, outside his door. He stood up.

"Come in," he said. He wished he had on a clean shirt. He wished he'd shaved.

The door opened and she stepped inside. Judging by her appearance, she'd run all the way from Ravenscliffe. Her small chest heaved and strands of blond hair clung to her face and neck. She stood just inside the door and looked at him, catching her breath, preparing to speak. And then: "Are you in love with Eve?" she said. Quite matter-of-fact and collected now, she had her hands on her hips and her head slightly cocked.

He gaped at her stupidly. He was thrown, totally thrown.

"I wouldn't blame you in least," she said. "But I'd like to know, just so that I can . . ." Here she faltered, and he took a step toward her, but she shook her head at him so he waited. "What is word?" she said. He shrugged, helpless. "Just so that I can . . . give you up. For my own peace."

There. She had finished. He walked to her and took her in his arms and held her for a long while, saying nothing. Tears coursed down his cheeks. He felt humbled by her frankness, ashamed of his own inhibitions, sorrowful that he had caused her anxiety and doubt; but more than all of this, he felt an upsurge of happiness greater than any he had ever experienced before in his life. He shifted her slightly within the circle of his arms, found her mouth, and kissed her. Two halves of the whole, united.

"No," he was finally able to say. "It's you. Only you, now and forever."

The hearse was prepared, a glass and gilt coach swathed in black crêpe, with four of the earl's black horses in harness ready to pull him on his last journey. Their bridles were trimmed with long, full ostrich feathers, which bucked and shivered in the wind, though the horses stood patient and steady. In front of the house, filling the terrace and steps, the black-clad servants and staff of the household stood together, heads bowed, perfectly still, as if praying. Before them, crowded in the park and grounds, the people of Netherwood stood to attention, young and old. The ardent and the faithful had begun to gather there just after first light, while the merely curious had turned up just in time to hear the great clock strike eleven. And as the last note sounded, out of the house came the mahogany coffin, mounted on a silver bier, lavishly adorned with roses of yellow and white, startlingly bright in the bleak tableau. The casket was placed carefully into the coach and slowly, slowly the horses began to move toward the private chapel.

The family walked behind. Tobias supported his mother at the head, and though both of them were grave, they appeared serene and collected; behind them, Henrietta and Dickie had Isabella between them, holding her by the hand. The child looked pitiful, ravaged by grief; the stoniest heart among the watchful crowds could not help but feel for her. Here was not a creature from another world entirely; here was a little girl who had lost her father.

Further mourners followed.

"That," said Anna quietly to Amos, "is Thea Sterling."

She pointed discreetly at a slender young woman, who walked alone directly behind the family. A glossy black astrakhan hat and jacket kept out the cold, but beneath it she wore a dress of exquisitely pleated blue-black satin short enough to show her ankles: on her feet were dainty black patent pumps.

"Next Countess of Netherwood," Anna said. "I know her. We chatted."

He put an arm around her shoulder, brought her closer to his side. She could talk him into anything at the moment, which was why he was here, feeling a bit of a fraud, though riveted by the spectacle in spite of himself. He wouldn't want Enoch to see him, mind.

"She liked color of our front door," Anna said.

"That right?"

Anna nodded.

"Well, there's some paint left in t'pot. You could let 'er 'ave it."

He was being facetious; even she—with her tendency, still, to be literal—knew it. But watching Thea walk a lone path on the fringes of the exalted family she would soon be joining, Anna wondered if she might not be exactly the sort of woman to take up a brush and paint her own front door, countess or not.

The earl's coffin was carried from the hearse and into the chapel. Next to Amos an old man said: "There 'e goes, then. End of an era, right enough."

"Aye," said Amos in reply and then, to himself: amen to that.

PART THREE

Chapter 41

The marriage of Tobias, Seventh Earl of Netherwood, to Miss Thea Sterling should have been the wedding of the decade. Instead it was a hole-and-corner affair, quietly conducted as if they were a pair of former adulterers trying to keep their names out of the newspapers.

This was Clarissa's story, at least. For their part, the bride and groom and the select group of eighty friends and family who attended the nuptials cherished their memories of a quite different version of events.

Of course, it had been rather restrained, as society weddings went. But they were still a family in mourning and, only six months after the death of his father, Toby was pushing the limits of acceptability by insisting on a spring ceremony.

"What's the tearing hurry?" his mother had asked brightly, as if she had no agenda of her own and was merely inquiring from polite interest. They were in the drawing room before dinner: Clarissa, Tobias, and Henrietta. Logs crackled in the hearth, the wall lights glowed soft yellow, and Parkinson offered sherry from a silver tray, but this mellow picture was deceptive, for the atmosphere was brittle.

"Thank you, Parkinson," Clarissa said, and then: "Goodness, Toby. People will think you have a vulgar secret. Wait until the winter, why don't you? Winter weddings can be very charming. Snow, berries, fur . . ."

"Out of the question, Mama," Toby had said. "Bad enough waiting until April. I'd marry her tomorrow if I could."

"Why?" Clarissa's voice was hard-edged. "Are you afraid she'll tire of you and slip away?"

Tobias had laughed. "Exactly," he said, cheerfully. "That's exactly what I'm afraid of."

"I would have thought Dorothea had too much to gain from this liaison to bolt. Certainly she has more to gain than you do. She's hardly overburdened with material wealth."

"She doesn't see life the way you and I do, Mama. She's a free spirit."

"How quaint."

"I wouldn't expect you to understand. But I won't be dissuaded."

"Importunate boy," said his mother.

Henrietta, who had listened silently to this exchange so far, said: "I don't believe Thea would flee."

"And how would you know?" said Clarissa, a little nastily, as if matrimony was one area where Henrietta's views were immaterial.

She colored, but remained composed. "Because I know Thea at least as well as Toby, and I happen to know she's in love."

"I'm in love with her, certainly," said Toby, missing his sister's meaning, as she had intended him to do. "Not always sure Thea's in love with me."

Henrietta smiled at him, though she didn't protest. In any case, Toby seemed not to mind either way; Thea's occasional indifference toward him didn't worry him in the least. Rather, he welcomed it, since it gave him license to please himself. Toby lived for the moment—always had. He couldn't be wasting time fretting about what the future held, when the present was so reliably and thoroughly entertaining.

The wedding took place on the seventeenth of March at St. Paul's Church in Knightsbridge and afterward at Claridge's, which had Elliot and Dorothy Sterling in raptures. They had arrived in London a week earlier, sailing into Southampton on a Cunard liner to great fanfare, courtesy of the Choates, on whom the Sterlings seemed to rely entirely for their position in society. There was bunting and a small brass band: by all accounts quite a party, dockside, to celebrate their inaugural steps on British soil. Joseph and Caroline Choate were themselves, in fact, preparing to return to the United States, their tenure in London having almost drawn to a close. However, the ambassadorial residence was still theirs for the time being, and they opened its doors warmly to their friends from New York City, whose gratitude and awe were seemingly limitless and never less than fulsomely expressed.

They were an amiable pair, well intentioned, if not—in Clarissa's view at least—well bred. In the minefield of English high society they frequently misstepped, and at every luncheon and soirée in the days preceding the wedding they managed to commit one frightful solecism after another, plunging Clarissa ever further into gloom. They struggled greatly with forms of address; the earl—whose name they invoked in sepulchral tones—was Sir Teddy, while she was Lady Clarissa, and occasionally, dreadfully, Lady C. Mrs. Sterling sometimes forgot to remove her gloves at dinner; Mr. Sterling ate every meal with a fork only, which he used like a small shovel in his right hand. During lunch at the Savoy Grill he went at his celeriac purée as if he was clearing a path through snow. Form dictated that he and the dowager countess were often seated side by side. "Quite the double act, Lady C," he became fond of saying. "We'll be running out of things to talk about at this rate."

If only, thought Clarissa. She sat glumly through these functions, feeling more and more like an observer than a participant. She had always regarded herself as a forceful person, a woman watched by other women and much admired by men. Now she could feel herself becoming colorless and insubstantial, as if all her magnetism and appeal had, in the end, been finite qualities from a source that was now quite empty. In her darker, less rational moments she took Thea for a witch with the power not only to enchant Tobias, but also to siphon off for her own use all of Clarissa's wit and charm. Certainly, the duller Clarissa felt she was becoming, the brighter Thea seemed to shine.

Her dress was ice-blue satin, created for her in Paris by the House of Worth. It had a twelve-foot train and she wore the palest blue tulle veil, which fell in soft folds from a coronet of diamonds. White and yellow gardenias, sent from the Netherwood greenhouses, formed her bouquet. A fleet of Teddy's Daimlers had been sent for the use of the bridal party, and when Thea drove with her father from the ambassador's residence, they drew back the roof and crowds collected along the edges of the sidewalks, although no one was sure who she was.

Mrs. Sterling wept copiously—"Tears of joy, folks!" she kept saying, "Tears of pure joy!"—before the bride arrived, and then stopped, abruptly, when she saw her daughter standing at the back of the nave, preparing to walk down the aisle. Shock, she said later, had taken the wind out of her; until that moment, she said, she hadn't fully appreciated the honor conferred on her daughter in marrying this particular young man.

This was a gracious thing to say, and it was a shame Clarissa didn't hear it. But there was no talking to her once the ceremony got under way: she simply became more and more cross. First of all Thea's arrival at church was announced by a rousing organ rendition of "Hail, Columbia," which had the small American contingent on their feet in a trice, soon followed by the rest of the obedient congregation. Clarissa was all for remaining seated, but Henrietta, catching her expression, lifted her surreptitiously but firmly by the arm and then, once up, she felt obliged to stay. But really! No one had insisted upon "God Save the King," and why would they? Because the English were secure in their Englishness and, unlike the Americans, they had no need to continually assert their national pride; this was what Clarissa hissed at Dickie when he handed over the ring on cue and joined his mother in the pew.

"I thought it was magnificent," Dickie said. "Very stirring."

She had missed Teddy then: missed his tendency to agree with her. One never knew what one valued about one's spouse until they were gone. Her eyes pricked with tears and she dabbed at them with a handkerchief and, from the other side of the aisle, Dorothy Sterling clucked and made a little moue of sympathy.

"You poor old thing," she said at the first opportunity. "Think of it as gaining a daughter, not losing a son."

She offered this gem with a finely timed vocal falter, as if it was an original thought, spoken aloud for the very first time at this, its moment of conception. Clarissa bestowed a chilly smile then looked steadfastly forward, determined to avoid eye contact, if possible, for the rest of the day. But the bride's mother was intent on forming a speedy alliance and it seemed she didn't need evidence of reciprocity; at the reception afterward she chatted brightly on, undiscouraged by Clarissa's frosty profile or glazed smile, forcing upon her all the unwanted missing details of her life in New York.

"We're on East Seventy-Second Street," she said, "not quite

Fifth Avenue, because who can afford *that* these days, but it's near enough. Anyway, those places on the park are enormous and as it is we're rattling around like two peas in a drum."

None of this meant anything to Clarissa.

"I suppose your house is pretty big?" Dorothy said. "You could probably fit two Fifth Avenue mansions into your Netherwood Hall. And to think, my little girl will be calling such a fine place home, after all these years of living on a budget."

"A budget?" said Clarissa. It was the first word she had spoken for fifteen minutes. "What exactly is a budget?" She pictured some kind of humble dwelling: waterborne, perhaps, like a barge.

Mrs. Sterling laughed. "Oh, you English with your famous dry wit! I must say, Lady Clarissa—" she leaned in confidingly— "I do admire your strength. The loss of Sir Teddy must be hard to bear, and yet, here you are, a picture of composure, when I know if I was in your shoes I should be just a mess. I'm always telling Elliot that if he goes before me I shall be mad as a hornet!"

To their absolute mutual horror, Clarissa began to cry. Dorothy, understanding intuitively that this thin, elegant, unremittingly grand lady would not welcome a matronly hug, waved a frantic arm at Henrietta, who registered the crisis, rushed to her mother's side, and swept her away from the party into the plush, upholstered interior of the ladies' powder room. Here they sat facing each other on chintz vanity stools, and Henry held her mother's hands, waiting for the sobs to subside. It was a most uncharacteristic display.

Finally, Clarissa was composed enough to speak.

"It's all too ghastly," she said. "Too, too ghastly."

"What is?"

Clarissa wafted a slender arm. "This is. This wedding, those people, the dreadful turn my life has taken."

"Oh, Mama," said Henry. Her voice was not entirely kind, and Clarissa withdrew her hands.

"Thank you, Henry, I would prefer to be alone now. Please leave, and send Tobias to collect me in five minutes."

"All right, but I'll come. Toby's busy. Everyone wants to talk to him."

"Send Tobias. In his father's absence, his place is by me."

Henrietta opened her mouth to respond, but closed it again. This was neither the time nor the place for a confrontation. In any case, thought Henry, there was more than one suffering soul in this powder room. She felt barely equal to the day herself; small wonder she had nothing to offer her mother.

"Very well," she said. She stood, and her mother looked her up and down.

"Your skin, in that gown, looks rather sallow," she said.

Henrietta turned and walked out of the room.

She found Toby and delivered their mother's message, then sought out Thea. She wasn't alone—she hadn't been alone since the day began—but anyway Henrietta touched her on the shoulder and said: "Could we talk?" and though Thea looked a little displeased, she made her excuses and left the conversation, following Henrietta to a mirrored alcove and sitting down next to her.

"What is it?" she said.

Her voice sounded impatient; she would prefer to be elsewhere, thought Henrietta, and she felt her heart constrict, as if it was held too tight in Thea's hand.

"I . . . I wanted you to know how very unhappy I feel," she said. She looked entirely bereft of the consolations and comforts of love. Thea softened.

"Oh, my dear one," she said and at once, Henrietta felt weightless with relief.

"I'm sorry," she said. "I shouldn't impose on your wedding day."

"Henry! Don't be humble. I can't love you if you're humble."

"Can't you?" Now her spirits plunged again, and even Henrietta could see how irritating it must be for Thea to have such power over the happiness of another.

"Oh, don't take me so seriously," Thea said. "And smile, for heaven's sake. Look, I can't be mooning around you, today of all days, can I? Whatever would people say? In any case, I'm rather enjoying being a bride, and dear Tobes is such a sweetheart."

"Yes, I know. He really is. And I hate the way I feel."

"Don't. You're my love too, just as much as he is. And soon I'll be permanently at Netherwood Hall and we can see each other every day."

"That's the thing, though. I don't want you to love Toby. I want you to love only me."

Thea laughed. "Greedy," she said. She leaned in so that her breath was hot in Henrietta's face. "I was yours before I was his," she said quietly and she kissed her tenderly on the cheek. Henrietta sat, rigid with suppressed desire. Thea smiled, stood, and wove through the room to find her husband.

Chapter 42

May Day, and the feast had come. Mysteriously, like a snowfall, it arrived in the night, so that when Eliza opened her curtains the next day the rides and stalls were laid out on the flat plain of ground where the common met the edge of town. She stared. It had missed two years in Netherwood—it always did, there were other towns in the West Riding of Yorkshire that were just as profitable as this one—but here it was, faithfully fulfilling its triennial obligation to thrill, to entertain, and to cheerfully fleece the pockets and wallets of the good inhabitants of Netherwood. Eliza counted back to May 1902. She was seven, then, the last time the feast came. Her dad had carried her around on his shoulders, and Seth had gotten lost for over an hour; she remembered the hot despair she'd felt at wasting precious time hunting for him, her mam and dad traipsing in and out of the attractions, calling his name. She'd been scolded by her mam for wanting to go on the Ferris wheel when Seth still hadn't been found, and her dad had said: "Hush, Eve, she's a bairn, she doesn't understand." All of this was clear as clear in Eliza's mind, and she let the words and pictures play out while she rested her forehead on the glass and waited for

351

signs of activity at the sleeping fairground. She was ten now, of course. Double figures. She'd be allowed to go about the feast with her friends, clutching her own money in her own purse. Seth had turned up in the crowd of men at a bare-knuckle fight; he'd ducked under the rope without paying to watch Lew Sylvester take on the feast's traveling champion. Their dad had hauled Seth out, lifting him by his collar and plonking him on the grass at their mam's feet. Then Seth had gotten a roasting for wandering off and getting into places he shouldn't, and had sulked for the rest of the visit, even when their dad won a coconut and cracked it open there and then for Seth and Eliza to chew on. Ellen had been too small, just a baby. Their mam had bumped her around the rough ground so that she bounced and laughed in the big pram, and that was all the fun she'd had. This year she was three. Big enough for the carousel. She could sit in a carriage, anyway. Not on one of the beautiful horses with their names painted on their saddles, though. Eliza had sat on one called Starlight, a dappled gray with a real red leather harness and reins. She rose up and down as the carousel turned, and you could imagine yourself galloping away over the common if you closed your eyes. In her imagination, Eliza had been riding Starlight ever since, whenever she wanted to leave behind the humdrum. She was keeping a diary of their travels in an old accounts book that she hid from Seth between her mattress and bedstead. She had turned the book upside down and was working her way through it on the backs of the used pages. *The Adventures of Eliza and Starlight* was its working title, though she thought she might change it to something more charged with mystery before it was published.

Downstairs, Anna was banging the gong. Shouting from the kitchen, as they'd done in Beaumont Lane, didn't work at Ravenscliffe. You could shout till you were blue in the face and still nobody would hear you. So Anna had come home one day carrying a brass gong with its own special wooden mallet. They kept it on the hall table and, tempting though it was to disobey, it was only ever to be struck when a meal was ready. Striking the gong just for fun was a deadly sin, Anna said. Eliza dragged herself away from the window, though there were men out there now, hauling tarpaulins off the stalls and drawing down the wooden shutters with long hooked poles. But ignoring the brass gong was also a deadly sin, and anyway, as ever, Eliza was starving.

There were eggs frying on the range and Daniel was slicing bread.

"Morning, beautiful," he said, as he always did when he was here to say it. He started work at the Hall so early in the mornings that Eliza usually missed him, but today was May Day, so everyone was here: Mam, Anna, everyone.

"Is Amos coming?" Eliza said.

"Later," said Anna. She was at the stove, flicking hot fat onto the eggs so the skin would bubble and brown over the yolks. Eliza smiled. What she loved best was when their kitchen table was so crowded that extra chairs had to be fetched in from the parlor and she, Seth, Ellen, and Maya had to crush up together on a bench that was only meant for three. Often, Amos was there, now that he and Anna were engaged to be married—a thrilling development, in Eliza's view, since she was once again to be a bridesmaid, though their flat refusal to set a date was a continuing source of frustration—and sometimes Uncle Silas came too. Very occasionally he would bring Mr. Oliver with him as well, and then they would be ten and it felt like a party.

"Daniel?" she said.

"Eliza?" he said.

"What's your favorite ride?"

Seth tutted. "Well, since 'e's never been to Netherwood feast, 'e wouldn't know, would 'e?" He spoke slowly, as if to a simpleton.

"Och well, they're all the same, wherever in the country they are," Daniel said. "There's always a carousel, a helter-skelter, a big wheel, a coconut shy . . ."

"My dad got banned from t'bell and mallet," Seth said. "Because 'e kept winning." This was a fact that Seth knew, rather than remembered: a family legend, kept alive by the retelling.

Daniel laughed. "Well, in that case I shall stay away from it, in case I make myself look a puny fool by comparison. I like the big wheel the best," he said, turning to Eliza, answering her question, "because from the top you can see the world from a different perspective. A bird's-eye view. The best thing," he said, sitting down next to her, "is when you get stuck for a while right at the top, with the seat swinging in the breeze. That's nice." He smiled at her, and she snuggled into his side.

"Will you take me on it?" she said.

"I thought you wanted to be with all your pals today?"

"Oh yes. I forgot." She looked a little flat now.

"Tell you what," Daniel said. "I'll meet you at the foot of the big wheel at two o'clock, for a ride on it together. Then afterward you can scoot off with your pals again."

"All right," she said, "I'd like that." Seth rolled his eyes; she was addled where Daniel was concerned.

Eve came into the room with Ellen and Maya. They liked to wear identical clothes these days, so whenever Anna made a new pinafore for one of them, she would have to make the same for the other. Today they were both wearing their dark red linen, not quite Sunday best, but almost. Saturday best, thought Eliza. Daniel stood to give Eve a kiss and pour the tea, and Eliza scooted along the bench to make room for the little girls.

"'ere we are then," Eve said. "May Day Feast, and this year it's right on our doorstep."

Anna said: "Mixed blessing, that." She wasn't keen on

354

fairgrounds, either the rides or the people that ran them. A motley collection of dwellings—some little more than covered drays—had laid claim to a patch of land that was too close for comfort, in Anna's view. She would dry the best linen in the house until the feast had moved on. There'd be no leaving the doors wide open, either.

"I wish Uncle Silas was 'ere," Eliza said.

A pause in activity among the adults, the merest shiver of tension: the child was oblivious, however.

"Uncle Silas said 'e'd take me to Bristol."

"Well, don't 'old your breath," said Seth. "Uncle Silas couldn't be much farther away if 'e tried." He was in Jamaica, in fact, overseeing operations there. Progress on the hotel had been sluggish, and if he was to advertise this summer, carry tourists there by December, he had to catch the slackers red-handed. This is what he'd told Seth. "Jamaicans—lazy buggers the lot of 'em," he'd said, flattering the boy with this adult talk. "Don't know the meaning of hard work." Seth, who had noted his uncle's pale, uncalloused hands and white-tipped nails, wondered exactly what hard work meant to Silas. Still though, you didn't become as rich as he had by sitting idle on your backside.

"There's a zoo," said Eliza, who wasn't done yet with Bristol. "They've an elephant called Zebi and she eats straw 'ats off ladies' 'eads."

Eve smiled at her daughter. She fancied a trip to Bristol herself, actually—Silas was always on at her about it, and she'd like to be able to picture him when he was gone. But now, it was awkward. She'd thought she could talk to Anna about most things: but not this, it seemed.

Silas had fallen foul of Amos, or Amos had fallen foul of Silas, depending on whose version of events you happened to hear.

Anyway, it amounted to the same thing; under the stewardship of Silas Whittam, the regime at Dreaton Main Colliery was undergoing a radical review. Timesheets had been scrutinized, wages and bills assessed. The manager and his deputy had been sacked, and in their place were two Bristolians, drafted in from Whittam & Co. to apply their accountants' minds to the boss's new venture.

"And what do they know about mining?" Amos had said: a dangerous topic, this.

"As much as they need to," Silas had replied, his voice pleasant, his eyes like steel.

"What they know about mining," Amos had said, directing his comment now to Anna, "could be written on t'back of a Penny Black." Anna, sitting across the table from him, had looked blank. "A stamp, then," he said. "A postage stamp. Oh, never mind. Fact is, they know nowt about owt."

They were all at Ravenscliffe, Silas too; he'd joined them for a Sunday roast before leaving for London, and Jamaica. A family gathering, Eve had said, and it had been lovely, until the children left the table and the talk had turned to Silas's plans for this latest business venture. He looked at Amos and feigned bafflement.

"What on earth can you mean?" he said.

"Clear enough, I would've thought."

"Not to me." Silas smiled, sat back in his chair, folded his arms. "Perhaps you could elucidate?"

Amos, his belly full of Eve's roast lamb, knew he shouldn't eat her food, then repay her by souring the atmosphere around her table. But it was hard to avoid and, anyway, her brother had no such compunction; he had fixed his sardonic gaze on Amos and was waiting for him to speak. So he did.

"You've sacked two good local men who're now struggling to feed their families, and you've installed in their place two

356

office clerks who wouldn't know a pick or a shovel if they fell over 'em."

Silas laughed. "You twist the facts, Mr. Sykes, to suit your own version of the truth. Perhaps you'd do very well as a politician, if only you could get yourself elected. What I've done at Dreaton Main—not that I feel obliged to account for myself, particularly—is remove two incompetents from their posts and appoint two men whose track records with regard to honesty, hard work, and business acumen are unblemished. I aim to make as much money from my colliery as possible. Now that might hurt your socialist sensibilities, but I make no apology for it."

There was an awkward silence, then Amos stood.

"Best be off," he said. His face was rigid with the effort of not speaking his mind.

"No, Amos. There's crumble," Eve said. It sounded silly, put like that, but she hated this growing animosity between the two men.

He made an effort and smiled at her. "Couldn't manage another morsel," he said, and moved away from the table. He was seething; they could all see it.

Eve looked at Silas, who smiled at her.

"That was delicious, Evie," he said. "As always." He looked perfectly relaxed; it was his speciality, to always appear entirely unruffled. In professional matters, it had often served him well. Anna thought it a deplorable trait. She stood too, and walked to Amos's side.

"I'll go partway with you," she said. "I need some fresh air."

She said this pointedly, as if the air at the kitchen table wasn't fresh, as if it oppressed her to stay put, then together they left the room. A silence descended in the kitchen. Eve looked dismayed, staring after them with helpless anxiety, and Daniel took her hand and squeezed it. He would take no one's side in this but his wife's, and in any case, both Amos and Silas had a point. They were grown men, when all was said and done; they must find a way of rubbing along together, in spite of their differences. He took a cigarette packet from his shirt pocket and offered one to Silas, who shook his head.

"You know me," he said. "Cigar man." Daniel shrugged and lit up. The familiar smell of a burning Woodbine filled the air. Eve stood and began to clear the table. Silas suppressed a yawn.

"I have absolutely no inclination to travel to Bristol after that wonderful meal," he said. "Perhaps I'll stay another night."

"T'money you waste at that inn," Eve said.

She carried a stack of dirty plates to the sink. It was Seth and Eliza's job, but they'd made themselves scarce and it was less effort to do it herself than to round them up. She turned and looked at her brother.

"You know you could stay 'ere, don't you?"

He shook his head. "Too chilly for my liking." They both knew what he meant.

"They're good people, Anna and Amos," she said.

"I don't doubt it," he said.

"Then can you try to be friends?"

"Certainly, when that fellow changes his tune."

"Well, that won't happen," Daniel said. "So perhaps you two could agree to disagree, and keep your differences of opinion to yourselves. Or at least, keep them out of this house."

He spoke mildly enough, but with considerable authority. Silas acknowledged the reproof with a curt nod of his head, without actually conceding any ground. He rather enjoyed goading Amos Sykes and had no intention of desisting; the man was, after all, so very easy to provoke—these soapbox orators usually were. Anyway, he thought, it was high time that someone took him on. He strutted around the pit yards like God's gift to the workingman, especially since the old earl kicked the bucket.

"So," he said pleasantly, "apple crumble?"

"Plum," said Eve.

"Even better. And all the more for us now."

Daniel flashed him a warning look.

"What?" said Silas, and to hear him you would have sworn that he meant no harm at all.

Chapter 43

Truly, this is a ridiculous country."

Thea paced the room, back and forth. Henrietta watched her, like a spectator at a tennis match.

"I mean, you're all so . . . so rigid. So stuck in your ways. So obsessed with the pecking order and so terribly, zealously vigilant about the detail."

"Well, perhaps," said Henrietta, anxious to placate but at the same time slightly needled. "But there's usually a good reason for the things we do."

"Oh, poppycock. It's all pomposity, a conspiracy to trap the uninitiated. If you don't know the rules, you can't join the club. Well, I don't think I want to be a member, thanks all the same."

"Oh, now Thea—"

"And you're a turncoat. I don't expect to be reprimanded by you of all people. Especially in front of an audience." Her dander was up, good and proper. She looked so adorable, thought Henrietta, flushed with annoyance like this: quite irresistible.

"All I said was it's not quite the thing to leap up and grab whoever you most like the look of."

"I don't see why." Thea stopped pacing and stood, hands on hips, facing Henry. "What's the point of being a countess if I can't do as I please?"

"Well, you can, most of the time. And you do. But if there's a duke in the drawing room you really mustn't gambol through to luncheon on the arm of Jonty Allsop. You made poor old Abberley look a perfect fool."

Thea laughed, in spite of her irritation. "Well, that isn't hard. Honestly, though, Henry. Who would you choose?"

"You, of course. But since I can't, I do what's expected of me."

This sounded a little prim, a little pious, a little reproachful. Henrietta had followed Thea to her room—recklessly, she felt, abandoning their luncheon guests, doubtless causing awkwardness—because she couldn't bear any bad feeling to exist between them: she had meant only to amuse with her remark, not to offend, and yet Thea's expression had frozen with displeasure. She had refused to meet Henrietta's eye throughout the meal and had leaped from her chair when the ladies rose, bounding upstairs instead of leading them to the drawing room. A very small part of Henrietta disapproved of such childish impetuosity: the rest of her longed to be back in favor with her beloved.

She was perched on the very edge of Thea's bed and now she leaned forward and reached out her hands. Thea stepped toward her and took them, though she held her ground when Henrietta tugged.

"Not that, Henry. Not now," she said. "I'm too cross."

Henrietta let go, immediately. She was so wary of making demands: so wary of pushing Thea away with the strength of her longing. She had realized in the course of the past few months that it was her lot to wait patiently for attention, and not to irritate the object of her infatuation by appearing to be, in fact, infatuated. This morning Henry had passed in the yard her father's devoted black Labs, Min and Jess, whose fate was now to sit and wait in the hope of a kind word or a soft hand; their situation, Henry had thought, was not so very different from her own.

"Your mother seeks to expose me constantly," Thea said. "She considers me gauche and ill-bred and she whispers about me to her cronies. You have no idea how it feels to be constantly judged and found lacking. And it's not just Clarissa. All eyes are on me all the time. I feel like a butterfly pinned under a microscope. Specimen A, the Lesser-Spotted Sterling."

Henrietta laughed. "Oh darling, this isn't like you at all. Usually, you don't give two hoots."

"I do, as a matter of fact. But I'm very adept at hiding it."

"Thea, you're absolutely all the rage—if anyone watches you, it's to copy what you're doing. Did you notice that scarf twisted through Mimi's hair? She didn't quite pull it off, admittedly, but she's desperate to ape your style, and she's not alone; you have a slavish following. I can't think of anyone who doesn't utterly love you. Except for Mama. But as for her, well, she's adjusting. It hasn't been easy for her."

Thea rolled her eyes and turned her back on Henrietta. No, it hadn't been easy for Clarissa, and, boy, didn't everyone know it. She might as well have gone the whole hog and worn black crêpe at the wedding: mother of the groom, the very image of fathomless suffering. She had been a good deal less distressed, in fact, at Teddy's funeral; then, when she might reasonably have been expected to grieve, she had drifted about on Toby's arm, relentlessly, winsomely, tirelessly charming. Well, Thea had her number all right; her mother-in-law was an artful creature and her vulnerability wasn't even skin deep.

"Thea. Please don't be angry." Henry's voice was wheedling, and it grated. Thea turned on her, as she sometimes did.

"Oh, just go! You'll doubtless be needed in the drawing room."

Yes, thought Henrietta, I doubtless shall, and my presence

here is clearly irksome. She stood to leave and risked a tentative smile, and—joy unbounded—Thea smiled back. Emboldened, Henrietta crossed the room. She took Thea's face between her hands.

"I'll make your excuses, darling. You mustn't come back down if you don't want to. We can manage without you." She leaned in and kissed Thea on the mouth, gentle and swift, not lingering, then she let her hands drop and walked to the door, though it was the very opposite of what she wished to do. If Thea had called her back with the seductive voice she occasionally used; if she had let her clear green eyes drop from Henrietta's face and roam slowly up and down her body—then all notions of duty and responsibility would have evaporated in the heat of a delicious pursuit of mutual pleasure. But not now: not today. Thea merely turned away in chilly silence, leaving Henrietta to return alone to the drawing room and attempt to explain to a wondering audience the extraordinary behavior of their young hostess.

For a long while Thea stood, just where she was, as if held there by the fibers of the carpet. She felt caged, hemmed in—ironic, in this vast house, but true. Soon they would be leaving Netherwood for Fulton House, and there, in the noise and the crush of the capital, she knew she would feel less constrained. But even while she anticipated a change of surroundings, her independent spirit resisted their reasons for decamping to London. They were going simply because everyone was going. They were going because it was May, the beginning of the Season, when the important families of England flocked like migrating birds to their London residences. And this was her life: predictability, the price of privilege.

She moved to the long cheval mirror and looked at her

reflection with a hard, appraising gaze. Thin, pale, a weakness at the chin—her father's chin—but wide, mesmerizing eyes—her mother's eyes—and lips that curved naturally into a charming smile. Hair: nothing special but beautifully cut. Bosom: flat. Derrière: flat also. Stomach: concave. She smiled at herself, then frowned.

"You," she said, "are a moaning minnie and you should snap right out of it."

She turned this way and that, admiring her silhouette in the oyster silk day dress, which swung with a fluid motion about her shins. This pleased her. Her lovely couture collection, growing ever larger, was a significant source of satisfaction and a not inconsiderable advantage of her new status. By the tiniest degree, her mood began to improve. In the mirror, the reflected Thea watched closely, as if awaiting instructions. All her life, her central and most dearly held tenet had been this: resist the predictable, the unexceptional, the inevitable. And yet here she was, apparently expected to make one of two choices: a solitary afternoon in her bedroom or a stultifying afternoon in the drawing room. She stood a moment longer, thinking, and then from outside, the sound of a motorcar filtered into her consciousness. Someone leaving already? Or an arrival, perhaps? A new guest might be just the ticket, stir things up a little, and with a further small lifting of the heart she moved across to the window and saw Tobias at the wheel of the Wolseley with Jonty Allsop and Dickie crammed in next to him. Instantly, Thea pushed up the sash window and yelled at them—"Hey! Where d'ya think you're going?"—and though her voice was almost certainly not audible above the engine, some sixth sense made Toby glance up at her window, whereupon he stopped the car at once and climbed out. "Thea, my dearest darling," he shouted, then: "Why aren't you with the ladies?" which made her feel cross all over again.

"Never mind that," she said sharply. "Where are you going and why aren't you taking me?"

"To the fair. And we did look for you, but you were mysteriously absent from the party. I assumed you were otherwise engaged." She loved this about Toby; if ever she wasn't where she should be, he hardly minded. It gave her the sense that within their marriage she was free. "My tropical bird," he had said to her once, before the wedding, when she was still to be convinced. "I would never try to cage you or clip your wings." It had inclined her toward marrying him, that promise, along—of course—with his sister's passionate intensity. It had seemed to Thea like a perfect arrangement and now, looking down at her husband, she smiled.

"Wait there," she called, and she darted away, appearing through the front door of the house not two minutes later. She had on a pea-green velvet jacket and a beret in the same fabric and color, set at a jaunty angle. He folded his arms and watched her approach, a smile of satisfied ownership on his face. Thea Sterling—for this is how he thought of her still—was his. She reached his side and opened her mouth to reprimand him, but he stopped her with a kiss.

"Gorgeous woman," he said then. "Simply gorgeous. You'll come with us then, I hope?"

"You make it sound as if it was your idea," she said. "You make it sound as if you weren't about to slink off with your cronies, leaving me in the drawing room crossing verbal swords with your mother."

He held up his hands in defense, the image of innocence wronged.

"You were nowhere to be found, my love. We searched high and low, didn't we, chaps?"

He looked back over his shoulder for support, and Dickie, from the car, said: "Get a move on, old thing. Thea can have my lap." He slapped his thighs with both hands.

"Must I?" she said, but she was laughing, and she didn't need to be asked twice.

A potent mix of mingled aromas assaulted Anna as she waited at the foot of the Ferris wheel; trodden grass, engine oil, frying onions. These were the sort of smells that clung to your clothes and hair: that seeped into your pores and followed you home. And the noise! She'd have her hands over her ears if she hadn't needed them to keep her purse safe in her pocket. Next to her, too close for comfort, an organ-grinder wound out an unmelodic racket, competing for precedence with a constant cacophony of shrieking from the thrill seekers; his monkey, sporting a tiny red fez and sultan's robe, bared its teeth at her and chattered menacingly. She suffered silently, the official keeper of the loose change and occasional holder of the coats, waiting stoically in the crush for the ride to slow and stop. When the children— laughing from on high, tousled and red-cheeked—caught her eye and waved, she smiled and waved back at them with an attempt at jollity, but it was a poor effort, anyone could see that.

"I don't have stomach for it," she said, when they begged her to join them on the merry-go-around or the cakewalk, and it was true. Even watching made her queasy. Eve and Daniel and all the children had ridden the magnificent new steam yachts, great painted boats that swung in a wide, sweeping arc, back and forth through the air, and Anna had had to look away. Now she stood with her back to the Ferris wheel because to watch its motion—smooth and sedate though it was—made her dizzy.

"You look as though you lost a dollar and found a dime."

Thea Hoyland stood before her in a covetable green beret, beaming.

"You remember me, right? Thea Sterling. Thea Hoyland

now, of course. Or am I Thea Netherwood? Never quite sure. We met weeks ago. This isn't your idea of fun, huh?"

Anna took the proffered hand, and shook it. "Not at all," she said. "Opposite of fun." She looked so glum that Thea laughed.

"You're kind of bad for business, I should think. Hey, what do you say we take a stroll, away from the mayhem?"

This was the new countess and all about them men were doffing their caps as they passed, but her manner was so completely informal that Anna saw nothing unusual in the invitation. However, she had Seth and Eliza's jackets tucked under one arm, and she indicated these with a gloomy expression, as if they presented an insurmountable obstacle to any change of plan. Thea smiled and said: "We'll wait for the Ferris wheel to stop, then. Gosh, he looks a malevolent little fellow."

She was talking about the monkey, who had shifted his attentions from Anna now and had hunkered down on his little platform as if preparing to spring at Thea instead. She beat him to it, lunging toward him and pulling a face, imitating his own grimace. The monkey shrank back, alarmed, and Anna laughed.

"Got to stand up to bullies," Thea said, then: "Look, here everyone comes." She nodded at the people spilling off the Ferris wheel and smiled at Anna. "You're almost free."

"Are you alone here?" Anna said, suddenly struck by the unsuitability of a lady, and a titled one at that, wandering unescorted around a fairground.

"Only by choice. I left my husband in a nasty little beer tent drinking flat brown ale. I'm to meet him by the coconuts at four, but I haven't yet decided if I will, or if I won't. He must take his chances."

Thea grinned and Anna thought, what a powerful, irresistible thing was a ready, engaging smile. "Here we are, about time too," Thea was saying, bright and brisk. She took the jackets and thrust them at Daniel, then she looped an arm through Anna's and pulled her away from the crowd. Eve and the children, joining him, followed his stupefied gaze as Anna, with a brief, apologetic backward glance, headed away up the common with the Countess of Netherwood.

Chapter 44

I'm so pleased to see you again," Thea said, the instant they were off. "I've thought a lot about you since we met."

"Have you?" Anna sounded skeptical. Surely the new wife of the Earl of Netherwood would have more to think about than their chance meeting on the common?

"I have. You were up a stepladder painting your front door."

"I was, yes. I painted whole house, in fact."

"Golly, did you really? May I see?"

"The house?"

Thea nodded. "May I? I'd love to view your handiwork."

Anna cut her a sidelong glance.

"You think I'm odd, I suppose," Thea said. "And I suppose I am."

She laughed, apparently delighted by her oddness, then was suddenly all seriousness again.

"Have you ever met a person with whom you feel an instant connection?"

"Yes, I have," Anna said at once. "Eve."

"Eve MacLeod, really? Right, because, you see, I met her

down at the Hall once or twice and while she seems very nice, I didn't feel it at all. But then that's the thing, isn't it?"

"Is it?" Anna was utterly perplexed.

"Chemistry. Here it works, there it doesn't, and not one of us can say who's going to spark it off. Do you agree?"

Anna had barely time to frame a response when Thea took off again.

"So when I met you, I just knew you would be significant to me somehow. There you were, the very spirit of independence, and I recognized something of myself in you."

"The very spirit of independence," Anna said. She was rather enjoying this conversation.

"Yes! So plucky and pretty, and capable. Who are you? I mean, you know—where are you from?"

They were at Ravenscliffe now—it really was very close—and Anna led Thea through the garden gate.

"Oh," she said, distracted by the house's sturdy presence. "This is something, isn't it?"

"It is," Anna said. "What you said about connections, I felt it here too. It can happen with houses, just as it happens with people."

"It can, yes it can," said Thea. She nodded her head vigorously. "And I don't have it at all with Netherwood Hall, which is a shame because I have to live there. Fulton House comes closer, but still . . . my favorite house in the entire world is a white clapboard beach house on Long Island. I spent every summer there until I was sixteen and I long to go back. So, you were saying?"

"Was I?"

"Yes, at least, you were about to. I want you to tell me about yourself. Where are you from—that accent, is it Polish?"

"Russian," Anna said. "Kiev."

"Kiev! How wonderful. Was it wonderful?"

"Not entirely," said Anna. She took out her key and turned

the lock, pushing the door open. The walls of the entrance hall were golden, rich and mellow, the color of hay in the August sun; they glowed with warmth. Anna's spirits always lifted when she entered the house, and they did again now. Thea, distracted once more from her interrogation, said: "This color—where did you find it?"

"I mixed it, from two other colors."

"You did? How did you know to do that?" She didn't wait for an answer but walked down the hallway until she reached a closed door. "May I?" she said, and Anna nodded. Thea turned the handle, opened the door, looked inside. Green, this time, but almost blue too, with a damask-style repeated pattern in silvery gray. Thea stepped inside and again her fingers traced the wall. I do hope they're clean, Anna thought.

"Did you do this as well?" Thea said. She meant the silver-gray; it was clear, on close inspection, that it had been applied by hand to the painted wall. Anna nodded.

"Easy enough, when you have printing block," she said. "There's place in Barnsley sells bric-à-brac: junk, really. But I found crate full of old blocks there, bought them for one shilling, cleaned them up. Good as new. I used this one in here, because it had traditional feel, you see?"

"I do see." Thea walked the perimeter of the room, examining the pattern, admiring its consistency. "And where did you learn to do this?" She expected to hear about a college in Kiev, intense instruction from fiery Russian artists, so when Anna shrugged and said: "Here. At Ravenscliffe," she stopped walking and stared in open wonder. She still had on her beret and jacket; I should take them, thought Anna, and offer tea, but Thea said: "Will you show me the rest?" so instead, she led her upstairs.

They toured the bedrooms—which could have been tidier, though who would have foreseen the need?—and Thea was enchanted. In Seth's room, gazing at the fantastical menagerie

371

revealed among the leaves and branches of the oak tree, she hatched a plan; she wanted Anna to redecorate her private quarters at Netherwood Hall. Anna must set a price per hour, and add to that the cost of whatever materials she needed. She wanted to take her up there at once to see the rooms, but Anna demurred; tomorrow would serve just as well, or the next day. Thea was all animation, full of excitement for the scheme; Anna was hesitant, cautious. It was one thing to daub one's own walls with a quirky mix of colors and styles: quite another to do the same for someone else, particularly when that someone else happened to live in one of England's greatest houses. But Thea would brook no objections. She had seen in Anna's work a wonderful way to make her own mark in the great ancestral home of the Hoylands. And why limit the scheme? Perhaps the drawing room or the dining room might be their next project? It struck Thea, bidding Anna a breathless farewell in the marvelous mellow glow of the entrance hall, that there might be no better reply to the dowager countess's hostility than to reinvent the principal rooms of the house in a style utterly her own. Well, utterly Anna's, at any rate. This thought, however, she kept to herself. She had the strong impression that Anna would refuse to set foot over her threshold if she felt she was a pawn in a power struggle.

"You'll come tomorrow, though? Please do—and then, when we all head off to London, you can get started in an empty house."

This was all so hasty, Anna thought, so impetuous. And what did this young countess know about her? Nothing, except that she could copy an iguana onto a boy's bedroom wall.

"I know this might seem crazy," Thea said, as if Anna had spoken out loud. "But I always follow my instincts. Gosh, why do you think I'm in Netherwood in the first place? I should be back in New York State, almost at the end of my freshman year at Cornell." She laughed brightly and her expression invited Anna to join her in marveling at life's unexpected twists and turns. However, Anna looked grave.

"There's much to consider," she said. "Practical matters to think about, other people's opinions to seek—so I can't say yes, I can't say no."

Thea's giddiness dissipated under Anna's sober influence and she clasped her by the hand. "But please do come," she said. "Give it some thought, by all means, but please do come in the end. Look, I'd better get back to Toby—I've been gone for so long that even he might be alarmed. But it's been such a pleasure, Anna. And such a revelation."

Anna said: "It's just paint, and imagination."

"It's a gift," Thea said. "Don't you forget it."

She stepped toward the door, and Anna hurriedly rushed forward to open it. It occurred to her that perhaps a little more ceremony might have been in order, but nothing about this woman invited it.

"I never offered you tea," she said, suddenly aghast.

"Oh pish," Thea waved a hand. "I'm awash with the wretched stuff. It's all anyone ever seems to drink down at the Hall." She leaned forward, confidingly, though there was no one to overhear. "Breakfast on my first ever morning, right? I'm at the long, long dining table munching toast and Parkinson leans into me and says"—she adopted the butler's fruity baritone—"'Darjeeling, Earl Grey, Pekoe, or Lapsang, Miss Sterling?' and I say, 'Coffee, please' and honestly, Anna, from the look on his face you'd have thought I had uttered an unspeakable profanity."

Anna smiled at her, a fellow foreigner in a strange land; when they parted, she felt she had made a friend.

The night was mild enough to sit outside, even now that the sun had long ago dipped from view, and Eve and Anna were side by side on the wide wooden seat of a swing, rocking almost imperceptibly back and forth and mulling over the ramifications of the countess's visit. The swing was Daniel's work—long ropes slung over a high, straight branch of an oak tree and a flat seat of cedar, sanded smooth—and it was a snug fit for the two women, though a perfect place for contemplation. It was quiet now that the fairground noises had finally ceased, though the rides were visible still, their hulking great shapes dark against the moonlit sky. Inside the house the lamps were burning and a soft glow from the windows pooled on the stone paths. Daniel was in the kitchen with a seed catalogue and a cigarette. Amos had been and gone, back to his lodgings and a pile of paperwork. The children were in their rooms, asleep at last after a rambunctious evening—fueled by the day's cotton candy and toffee apples—that had scuttled any chance of meaningful adult conversation. This was why she hadn't mentioned it to Amos, Anna said; this was why he'd gone home still not knowing that she'd been offered work by the countess at Netherwood Hall. Eve gave her a look.

"Right. Nothing to do with 'ow 'e might react, then?"

Anna was silent. Eve took her hand.

"I don't think 'e would stand in your way, really I don't."

Anna said: "Well, as for that, I wouldn't let him. But he has strong feelings about these matters. He might feel betrayed. I don't want to hurt him, Eve."

"No, of course not. But it's not betrayal; it's business. This is a wonderful opportunity for you, Anna. You must seize it, not shrink from it."

They looked at each other. There was something very familiar about this conversation and it struck them both simultaneously.

"Boot's on other foot now, isn't it?" Anna said. They smiled.

"It is," Eve said. "And if you hadn't badgered me into seeing t'earl, I would never have gone to London or met Daniel or moved to Ravenscliffe. So many good things came to me because I listened to you."

"And Amos was furious."

This was true. Amos had stormed in a rage from the little kitchen at Beaumont Lane, livid with Eve for taking Teddy Hoyland's money: for being bought so easily by the enemy's filthy lucre.

"Well, aye," said Eve, for there was no denying it. "But whatever Amos thought about it then, time's passed and proved 'im wrong. I'm quite sure Amos lives and learns like t'rest of us."

A pause and then Anna said: "She's very nice, you know."

"I'm sure she is. So was Lord Netherwood. I'm not sure Amos ever fully believed it, but he was a good man, in spite of all that wealth."

Anna nodded. She thought about Thea's words—"the very spirit of independence"—and she thought, too, about those fine, high-ceilinged rooms, flooded with natural light. This was a true opportunity: daunting, thrilling, full of promise.

"I shall go," she said.

"Good."

"And I'll catch Amos first thing, before I see her."

"Right."

"I shouldn't like to go without at least telling him."

"No."

"And then, at least he's been involved in my decision."

"That's it. Even if 'e's not best suited, you've talked it through."

"Yes. And he might think it a good idea, as I do."

"He might, yes."

They sat on for a while in silence, each of them thinking how very unlikely this was, but soothed by the gentle motion of the swing and the creak of the rope against the branch, until a chill finally began to steal up on them and they walked together back into the house for the inestimable comforts of the warm kitchen range and a pot of tea.

Chapter 45

Henrietta's mornings now followed much the same pattern as her father's had. She rose early, breakfasted alone with a pristine copy of the *Telegraph*, then retired to the study to deal with the day's business. The fact that this role had fallen to her and not to Tobias was questioned by no one, least of all him. It might have looked odd—indeed it did look odd—to the outside world that the heir to the Netherwood lands and title had no more to do with the running of the estate than thirteen-year-old Isabella; but to the family, the new status quo was perfectly natural. Even the dowager countess had stopped looking for suitors for her daughter, since marriage for Henrietta would necessitate her removal from Netherwood Hall and then where would they be? No, her place was now head of the family in all but name. Occasionally she needed Toby's signature; more occasionally still she sought his advice. But by and large, the family's interests were entirely in her hands, and this fact conferred upon her a new status that called for authority and respect. All of them understood that between nine o'clock and eleven o'clock in the morning, Henry mustn't be interrupted in the study unless the matter in question was so urgent as to be life-threatening. This rule didn't apply to Thea, of course, but then it was rapidly becoming clear that no rule applied to Thea, however sacred or ancient or downright practical it might be.

Henrietta had made the study her own in her six months of stewardship; she had added her own books to the shelves, altered the position of the desk so that it faced the fireplace, hung Sargent's portrait of her father on the adjacent wall, looking sternly out across the room from his gilt-framed canvas. Now it was quite her favorite room in the entire house, but even before her father's death, Henrietta had loved his study. It was small, relatively speaking, and with only one window it was a little dark, too. But these were the very characteristics that had drawn Henrietta here since childhood. Even in the summer the desk lamp had to be lit, and this gave the room a permanent festive coziness. The book-lined walls were a barrier to sound and, with the door closed, the household's comings and goings could be forgotten. Sometimes the young Henrietta would creep in here undetected and sit at her father's desk, crafting an imaginary letter, holding in her inexpert hands a prized goose quill, though never quite daring to dip it into the inkwell. It was only for show; he wrote with a fountain pen and had done so for years. But the quills were displayed on a shelf by the desk: goose, owl, swan, and turkey. They had belonged to Henrietta's grandfather, and they were at once worthless and priceless. She still sometimes stroked the soft fronds against her mouth and nose, inhaling the past.

No time now for such indulgences, however. The Mines Inspectorate had at last published its report into the explosions at Long Martley, and the detailed findings were on her desk, requiring her full attention. Head down, brow furrowed, she read of a catalogue of failings, laid ultimately at her father's door. Witness statements, site inspections, the regrettable number of fatalities: they all stacked up with grim relentlessness to make the case against the colliery owner. There was clear evidence, it said, of a fire which, though it had started many years earlier, had never been entirely extinguished; neither had it been effectively sealed off, and therefore it had remained a hazard, as evidenced by events on the morning of September 16, 1904. Tribute was paid to the bravery of the rescuers, but their operations were hampered by poorly organized systems, inadequate manpower, and a shortage of safety equipment. The management of the colliery—Harry Booth and his deputies— were exonerated of blame; they had done their best in difficult circumstances. However, the pit district where the explosion had occurred was unfit to be mined, being in dangerous proximity to the aforementioned fire. The inquiry had heard from four separate witnesses, including Mr. Booth, that the Earl of Netherwood, to their certain knowledge, knew of the risk of explosion but had failed to act on the information.

Henrietta stopped reading. She looked up from the dense type, rubbed her eyes with the heel of her hands. None of what she read was entirely surprising, except this last detail; she hadn't thought her father would willfully ignore a warning. Perhaps he hadn't fully understood the risks. She turned to look at his handsome, solemn face, gazing above and beyond her, but it revealed nothing. He had been a fundamentally good man, she thought, within the limitations of his generation and class. At least, he had been better than many. And yet he had failed the men whose lives depended on the safety of his collieries. Accidents, of course, would continue to happen; supports and props would continue to buckle under the weight of the earth; toxic gases would continue to ignite and explode; a pit could never be a safe place to earn a living. "But we have to be as sure as we can be," said Henrietta out loud to her father's portrait, "that at the final reckoning we are not found wanting."

She often spoke to him, here in the study, though it was rarely with this tone of reproof. She glanced back down at the document open on the desk in front of her and continued to read. The Long Martley disaster had claimed eighty-eight lives, and yet the Netherwood Collieries Company, while roundly condemned by the inspector, was not in breach of its statutory responsibilities; therefore no legal action would be taken against the owner. However, the Home Office would appoint a departmental committee to review mine rescue operations: specifically, the obligation of mine owners to provide efficient—and sufficient—rescue equipment.

She closed the report. Mr. Garforth would be interested to see it; she would request a meeting with him, perhaps at Long Martley, where the rescue training center was now fully operational. He had written to her, when her father died, a kind and generous letter of sympathy: *My heart goes out to you, Lady Henrietta. You will miss your father terribly, but be assured his memory lives on, and his reputation as a good man will endure the passing of time.*

He was entirely sincere, for he was not a sycophantic man. But he had only known the late earl for a few months, in which short time her father had striven with the zeal of the converted to improve the safety of his pits. He had achieved more than most colliery owners manage in a lifetime, but still, thought Henrietta, it was too late for the eighty-eight men and boys whose names were listed here at the end of the document. She read them aloud in a sort of impromptu, private tribute and felt the burden of their passing like a lead weight in the pit of her stomach; their deaths could have been prevented if her father had heeded the concerns of his men. What had he been busy with instead? she wondered. What pressing concerns had distracted him: a hectic around of engagements in London, perhaps, or the impending visit to Netherwood Hall of the king?

She stood and walked out of the study. She needed fresh air, and the company of an uncomplicated, guiltless man. She took the servants' staircase and rushed through the kitchens and out of the back door, and then she crossed the courtyard to the estate offices, from where Jem Arkwright was just emerging.

"Mornin', your ladyship," he said, tipping his tweed cap. "Is it me you're after?"

"Are you busy?" she said.

"Fences broken down by t'brook."

"May I come with you?"

"Aye. Long walk, mind."

He whistled and his terrier streamed across the yard, followed more sedately by Min and Jess, who were too old, or too dignified, to rush anywhere. Henrietta smiled.

"Do you think they miss him, Jem?" she said.

"More'n likely. I know I do, anyroad."

"Me too. Every day."

They set off through the courtyard. Oddly, Anna Rabinovich appeared, nodded politely at them, then rang the bell for admittance at the back door. Then they crossed paths with Absalom Blandford, who feigned distraction with a bootlace to avoid conversation. But for the rest of the morning they didn't encounter another living soul, which was exactly what Henrietta had hoped for. By the time they returned three hours later, her oppressed spirits had recovered almost entirely.

The Wire Trellis Inn on May Day Green served an exceptional pint of Samuel Smith's bitter and, since Enoch was buying, he had managed to persuade Amos to join him for half an hour away from the office. They could talk more freely here: neutral territory, said Enoch. At the Yorkshire Miners' Association people listened at doors, he said. He'd yet to catch anyone in the act, but he could sense these things.

"Too many conflicting views, y'see," he said. "We're all engaged in t'same mighty struggle, but there are myriad ways and means to achieve t'same end."

"You've been reading again, then," Amos said, doggedly unimpressed. He was out of sorts, and not much company. He would have done better to take a solitary walk, but Enoch wouldn't have it.

"Writing, actually," he said. "Fabian Society article on nationalization."

Amos looked at him over the rim of his tankard, though he said nothing.

"Nationalization of t'collieries, to be precise," Enoch said. "Premise being that coal belongs to t'nation, not to t'landowners."

Amos placed his glass carefully on the cardboard beer mat. There were dark rings where previous drinkers had set their pints and he lined his up on one of them with particular care, as if how and where he rested his beer were of utmost concern.

"Very nice," he said. "Let me know when I can claim my share." Out of sorts with Anna meant out of sorts with Enoch and, for that matter, with the Fabian Society too. Enoch took it mildly.

"Right you are," he said. "Will do."

"If you want to waste your time, that's none o' my concern. But I think there are other issues to tackle before we can give t'country's coal deposits to t'government."

"Aye, but Fabians like to indulge in a bit o' dreaming."

"First things first. Old-age pensions for them who can't work. Widows' pensions for them whose men are killed at work. Compulsory free schooling for every child up to t'age of fourteen. Decent health provision for everyone, whether or not they 'ave t'means to pay."

"Aye, but 'ow do you pay for all that? By nationalizing t'pits, that's 'ow. And while we're at it, let's nationalize t'railways an' all."

"Now you're talking soft."

Enoch smiled as if he knew something Amos didn't. They sat on for a while in the comfortable fug of the inn: cigarette smoke, beer fumes, damp wool. Then Amos said: "What would you say if I told you Anna was pally wi' t'countess?"

Ah, thought Enoch, now we're getting somewhere. "Well, and are you telling me that?" he said.

"Aye. All of a sudden they're like this," he held up two fingers, plaited around each other.

"Since when?"

"Beats me. First I 'eard was early today. She was on 'er way down to Netherwood 'all. Turns out t'countess's been to Ravenscliffe, wants Anna to do some painting for 'er. She said she wanted to ask me what I thought—as if it'd make any difference to what she does."

"Painting?"

"Aye. Decorating, like."

"So will Anna do it for nowt?"

"No, she'll get paid. But still . . ."

"Well, if money's changing 'ands, it's a professional arrangement."

"Not good, though, is it, what with me being a Labor candidate. Could be embarrassing, I reckon."

Enoch pondered.

"Will Anna do it?"

"Aye, she'll do it. She reckons she 'asn't made 'er mind up, but she'll do it."

"Well, then, we shall do what politicians 'ave always done—we'll turn it to our advantage."

"Right. Labor candidate's intended 'obnobbing with aristocrats. Pardon my dim wits, but I'm not seeing a bright side."

Enoch tapped the side of his nose knowingly and said, "'ave faith, my friend."

Infuriating little bugger, thought Amos.

"If your intended is an independent working woman with a mind of 'er own," Enoch said, "that reflects very well on you, I'd say."

Amos looked at him. Enoch was his political litmus paper: he detected acid, alkaline, and neutral in any given situation. Now, having issued his verdict, he returned Amos's look with mild eyes and an untroubled brow. Amos began to relax.

"Same again?" he said, nodding at Enoch's empty glass.

"That's my boy," said Enoch.

Chapter 46

Mrs. Powell-Hughes led Anna through the warren of servants' hallways that skirted the kitchens and up the back staircase. The housekeeper had kept her waiting in the boot room while the countess was located; Anna had detected a stony skepticism in Mrs. Powell-Hughes's face and voice when she heard that, while Lady Netherwood wasn't exactly expecting her, neither would she be surprised to see her.

"We had sort of arrangement," Anna had said.

"Sort of arrangement?" repeated Mrs. Powell-Hughes, unfamiliar with Anna's particular brand of English.

"Yes," Anna said, and left it at that. She saw no reason for lengthy explanations when she was certain that she would be vindicated. The housekeeper, impressed by the young woman's dress and demeanor, if not by her unscheduled appearance, had bid her wait, and bustled off. She came back, still flint-featured, not five minutes later.

"If you'd like to follow me, Miss . . ." and there she faltered. Anna had introduced herself but Mrs. Powell-Hughes had no memory for exotica.

"Mrs. Rabinovich," Anna said, slightly rolling the R for effect. She made conversation as they progressed through the servants' quarters, remarking on the sparkling condition of the copperware and the evident industriousness of the kitchen maids.

"Like beehive," she said. "Very busy. Do you enjoy your work here?"

The housekeeper was nonplussed. She didn't indulge in small talk with strangers as a rule, but no one had ever asked her that question before: indeed, she had never asked it of herself. Enjoyment was neither here nor there, though now, when required out of politeness to consider the issue, she realized the answer was a complex one: complex even before the late earl's passing, more complex still under the new order. However, she had to say something, so: "Indeed," she said, in a clipped voice intended to establish distance and repel further conversational overtures.

"I have always wondered," Anna said, entirely undiscouraged, "why all servants in great houses wear black. It is as if they're in permanent mourning." Silence. They reached the staff stairs but had to stand back for two bashful housemaids, who cascaded down toward them bearing long-handled feather dusters.

"Steady now," said Mrs. Powell-Hughes as they passed. "More haste, less speed."

Their words tumbled out in their anxiety—"Yes, Mrs. Powell-'ughes, sorry, Mrs. Powell-'ughes"—and slowed to a self-consciously sedate pace.

"Yet more black," Anna said.

"White aprons, mind you," said Mrs. Powell-Hughes, drawn into speaking. She felt unsettled and defensive as she set off up the stairs.

"Mmm, but wouldn't royal blue frocks be nice? Or mid-green."

The housekeeper sniffed. "And show every speck of muck. I don't think so. Here we are."

She pushed open the heavy green baize door and held it for Anna to come through. Thea rushed at them from apparently nowhere, spilling forth a warm welcome.

"Anna, you came, I am just thrilled, come, come, follow me, I'm so sorry you had to stand around, you should've come to the front door, next time do that, just walk on in and someone'll come find me, my—I just adore that jacket, is it really oriental or a clever copy?"

Unobserved, Mrs. Powell-Hughes winced. The young countess was so untutored in restrained elegance.

"Will that be all, your ladyship?" she said. Her tone was measured, by way of an example.

"What's that? Oh! Sure, Mrs. Powell-Hughes. Bye now."

Thea swept Anna away on the wave of her enthusiasm, whisking up the stairs, firing questions, which Anna answered with amused patience. Yes, she had made the jacket herself. Of course she could make one for the countess. No, she didn't have a carriage; she had walked here. No, she much preferred to walk; too much of her life was spent indoors already. Anna was older than Thea by only three years, but she felt like an adult answering the insistent questions of a child. It was endearing though, this avid interest in detail. Better, by far, than chilly indifference or tedious self-absorption. She tried, as she spoke, to take in her surroundings: richly patterned Turkish hall carpet, occasional tables bearing glossy pot plants, oil paintings, a series of them, all of hunting dogs in various stages of the chase. The walls and woodwork looked pristine, newly decorated. This puzzled her. Thea chattered on—such a long walk, thought Anna, to her bedroom!—about this and that and then she stopped, abruptly. The dowager countess stood ahead of them.

"Good morning, Clarissa," Thea said. Her voice had altered now, and a new, guarded tone was evident, even to Anna.

"Dorothea," said the dowager countess, by way of greeting. She turned to Anna and smiled graciously. "Mrs. Rabinovich, what an unusual pleasure."

Clearly, some explanation was in order. However, Thea looked at the floor, so Anna said: "We're on way to see how I can improve countess's rooms," and Lady Netherwood smiled.

"In what sense?" This was so plainly directed at Thea that she looked up.

"In the sense that I would like to put my stamp on them," she said. "I feel I'm living in a hotel."

Clarissa laughed in a show of disbelief. "But, my dear girl, they were redecorated not quite a year ago, for the king's visit. The whole house was redecorated. Are you proposing to fritter our money on something so fundamentally unnecessary? You surprise me. I had thought, with your background, that thriftiness would come naturally to you."

An unpleasant silence descended. The countess and the dowager countess locked eyes and Anna stood, supremely awkward, by the side of them. She coughed, and Thea said: "How rude we are, airing our private spats in front of visitors." She took Anna's arm, tucking it snugly against her own. "Come," she said, "I'm just down here, on the right," and she moved off, taking Anna with her. The dowager countess called after them.

"Before you run away, Dorothea—"

Thea stopped and turned her head, glaring at her mother-in-law.

"Thea!" she said. "I prefer to be called Thea."

"Yes, I know," said Clarissa, mildly. "Have you spoken to Monsieur Reynard this morning?"

Thea colored. "No, I forgot," she said. "But anyway, I've

no idea what to say to him. I don't care what we eat." She sounded very young again.

"I see. Then I shall have to see him at once. Goodness, Dorothea, how you overlook your responsibilities, and how fortunate for all of us that I don't."

She smiled, nodded at Anna, then glided away down the corridor. Thea and Anna watched her go, then, when she turned and began to descend the stairs, Thea flopped back against the wall. Her eyes had filled with tears, though she wasn't quite crying.

"Hateful crone," she said. "Just hateful."

"Should I leave?" Anna said.

"Absolutely not. She wouldn't expect you to, either—she's just taking a potshot at me. She never had a taste for blood sports until I married her darling boy. Now she goes for my jugular on every possible occasion."

"How very difficult that must be," said Anna. She thought of her own small battles with Silas; at least his visits were few and far between. To live permanently, like Thea did, with someone who thought so badly of you that she would humiliate you in front of another person—how could any amount of riches or material comforts make up for that? Anna felt a rush of sympathy for Thea.

"Come," she said kindly, "show me your rooms."

Clarissa summoned Monsieur Reynard to the morning room where they discussed the menus. She found this more of a tussle than it had ever been with Mrs. Adams. There was the language barrier for a start: he was dogged in his refusal to improve his spoken English, and often referred to cuts of meat or types of fish by their French names. Some of these had become familiar

enough to Lady Netherwood that she didn't bat an eyelid—
saumon was nice and easy, and *truite*—but this morning he had
proposed *petite friture* for the fish course at dinner and she
found herself quite in the dark. He had made no effort at all
to summon the English word, though Clarissa was certain he
must know. She had ended up saving face by pretending it had
just come to her—"Ah! Yes, of course, lovely"—so that now
she had no idea what she had approved. Quite ridiculous. It
was as well Teddy wasn't here to witness this rigmarole; long
after Mrs. Adams died he had continued to lament the absence
of her good, plain cooking. Pies and mashed potato were Teddy's idea of culinary heaven. Really, his palate had never developed beyond the nursery.

Also, Monsieur Reynard was dreadfully easily distracted.
His mind seemed to wander, mid-conversation. One might even
suspect he was bored. He had a way of lolling in the chair that
suggested he might nod off at any moment: a most unnerving
habit, which quite sapped the confidence of the speaker. He
lacked any natural respect for his superiors; indeed, Clarissa
wondered whether he in fact regarded himself as her equal. He
brooked no objections. What he said seemed to go. If she suggested other than he did, he simply shook his head and said
"non"—not rudely, but nevertheless emphatically. He made
Clarissa feel somewhat surplus.

But then, wasn't she? She was alone now in the morning
room, the chef having loped off with a—frankly—insolent smile
and what might have been a wink, though she couldn't be sure.
She sat at the oval table with her dainty chin supported in one
cupped hand, and allowed melancholy to steal over her again.
She had, she knew, been beastly to her daughter-in-law and
would—she knew—be beastly again. It came as naturally to
her as breathing. No part of her was ready to relinquish her

role in this family to anyone, least of all Thea Sterling, and every unkind word or dismissive gesture, every carefully enunciated "Dorothea," was Clarissa's way of continuing to assert her position. She was young still: only forty-four. She was not ready, not at all, to take a back seat. When her arrival had been announced at a small Chatsworth dinner last week as "the Dowager Countess of Netherwood," she had all but looked behind her, to see if Teddy's old mother had risen from the grave. Of course, by the time Teddy's father had died, his mother had been quite batty and harmless as an infant, confined to her rooms with a nurse and a bedpan; and earlier countesses had politely died, making the path as clear as possible for their successors. There had never been a Dower House at Netherwood Hall, because there had never been the need, not that Clarissa would have submitted to living in it, even if one existed. But here she was, beautiful, vital, full of health—if one discounted her migraines, and if she was entirely honest, they *could* be discounted—and yet she was expected to play second fiddle to the jumped-up, drawling daughter of a small-town American industrialist.

Clarissa sighed now, because her thoughts had drifted to Teddy—or, rather, to his absence. It was so maddening of him to get himself killed, and in such a silly, unlikely way, because look where it had left her—a reluctant member of the audience at the Thea Sterling show. Well, she thought, we are *not* amused. And could she bear to continue soldiering on here while Thea played at being a member of the aristocracy, stealing the limelight at every opportunity and charming everyone with her wild ideas and famously fun-loving personality? Clarissa shuddered. No, she thought. She really didn't think she could.

For a little while she sat on, deep in thought, and then all of a sudden she stood and crossed the room, with the purposeful aspect of a woman with a plan. She reached for the brass handle set into the marble surround of the fireplace and turned it vigorously, then waited for a footman to appear from the servants' hall. She would take a cup of coffee, and then, duly fortified, she would take control of her life.

Chapter 47

At the top of Market Hill in Barnsley stood the elegant stone edifice that was Butterfield's Drapery Market, the town's highly esteemed emporium of fine cloth, haberdashery, and other quality odds and ends. There was also a café—"Dainty Meals" promised the advertisement, "served in pleasant surroundings"—and this was where Eve now sat, with Silas, sharing a silver pot of Assam tea and a tiered platter of tarts and triangular sandwiches with the crusts cut off. She wasn't impressed.

"Yesterday's bread," she said. "And I don't know what this spread is, but it's not meat paste."

"Tastes all right to me," Silas said. "Mind you, after two months of fried plantain and curried goat, everything tastes ambrosial."

"What's plantain?" she said.

"Bit like a banana, but you wouldn't want to be eating it raw. It's not half bad, actually, the first couple of times. By the tenth time, you're going off it. By the twentieth, you'd rather eat your Panama hat."

"Well, fried plantain sounds better than goat. Smelly beasts."

"Mmmm. Again, quite palatable in small doses. Are you going to leave that?"

There was an abandoned egg and cress sandwich on her plate. She nodded and pushed it toward him, then picked up a lemon curd tart. She sniffed it cautiously, then nibbled at the pastry. Silas laughed.

"You eat as if you're tasting for poison," he said.

She put it down. "It's an affliction," she said miserably. "I can't enjoy food when I'm out. I always think I could do better at 'ome."

"And you most certainly could; which is why, dear Evie, you really should open up next door."

She took a sip of hot tea. "That's a nice brew, anyroad," she said.

"Well?" he said.

"Yes, I said I'd think on it, Silas. It's only been ten minutes."

"But it's perfect. There's good old Butterfield's here, with its delusions of grandeur, and Guest's down the road with their fine groceries. You'd slot in as naturally as the egg in that sandwich."

"Thank you, but I don't see myself as t'egg in anyone's sandwich."

"It's a pleasant building, currently empty, neither too big nor too small, in a part of town that passes for smart by Barnsley's standards."

"Now watch it," she said, wagging a finger at him. "No need to be rude."

"Well," he said. "It's all rather parochial, isn't it?"

She wasn't at all sure what he meant, but had no intention of showing it. She ignored him, and sipped at her cup of tea.

"I've always thought you should open up in Bristol. Clifton village would welcome one of your establishments with open arms. But I'm a reasonable man; I can see that might be a step too far for the moment. Market Hill, Barnsley, though . . . Close enough to Netherwood to keep a proper eye on, respectable establishments left and right"—he picked up her rejected sandwich and waggled it—"and an obvious demand for your food. What is there to think about? Apart from all the money you'll make. Now there's something to dwell upon, because you can raise your prices here in town, with no more expenditure on ingredients . . ."

She let him talk. He could talk the hind legs off a donkey, this brother of hers. He talked like a man who was used to being listened to, whether or not what he said was interesting, or even right. Hugh Oliver had told her that Silas held weekly staff meetings at Whittam & Co., assembling the workforce—packers, drivers, clerks, delivery boys, no exceptions—in the warehouse and detailing the week's profits, losses, triumphs, and failures, however small, however large.

"We're none of us allowed to speak while he does," Hugh had said. "Even I have to stand there mute, listening to the oracle. Woe betide you if you have to sneeze. Men have been sacked for less."

Eve looked at Silas now, still holding forth on the ins and outs of the catering trade, about which he knew next to nothing. Well, he might strike the fear of God into his own employees, but she was his big sister and could still put him in his place.

"Oh, be quiet," she said.

He stopped speaking and stared.

"I shall finish my tea, then go back and 'ave another look," she said. "I'm minded to take t'lease, but as and when I do, it'll be my idea, and not as a result of you blathering on."

"Charmed, I'm sure."

She smiled at him. "Do you remember coming here once, years ago? We stood in the doorway, too mucky to step inside?"

He nodded, though he was still affronted. He was out of the habit of being reprimanded; he had lost the knack of bouncing back.

"We wanted to see t'money whizzing back and forth on t'wires. Do you remember?"

"Of course I remember." It had been a rare trip to Barnsley, he thought. She can't have been more than eight; he would have been seven. How had they got there? He simply couldn't recall. He knew, though, that they had no money at all, and he'd wanted to lift a couple of pies from a market stall, but Eve hadn't let him, and then the lady behind the stall, seeing them whey-faced and pitiful, had said, "Now then you two, take a pie each, quick, before t'mister gets back," and Eve had told him, as they walked off clutching their booty, that God had rewarded them for being good. Silas had thought, what's the difference? Either way we get a pie. He still thought that, actually; one profits in life by whatever means possible. A stolen pie tastes just as good as a pie gained honestly.

"Those wires—do you suppose they save time?"

Silas followed her gaze. It was one of the wonders of Barnsley, this overhead network of slender cables carrying metal pots of money at thrillingly high speeds to a hidden cashier. Sent by a shop assistant, they flew across the shop and through a hole in the wall, then emerged a few moments later to hurtle back with a written receipt and the customer's change.

"Seems like an unnecessary palaver to me," he said. "But it's theatrical, and therein lies its value. I do believe people make purchases simply to watch the drama of the transaction." All those years ago they had stood outside, he and his sister, peering in as best they could, to watch the spectacle. They'd been shooed away eventually, and had gone instead to the open doorway of Guest's to inhale the exotic aroma of coffee beans, tea leaves, and cheese. You could feast on that smell if you were hungry enough.

"Listen to you," Eve said. "Did you swallow a dictionary?"

She stood, her tea finished and the remains of the food holding no appeal.

"Come on," she said. "Let's take a stroll."

They'd come to Barnsley together to look at premises, because Eve felt she had something to prove: not to herself, but to Silas. Absalom Blandford's treachery had festered for a while between them; his reaction, when she told him, had been a fury that was almost visceral in its ferocity. He had raged, not at the bailiff, but at Eve. She was weak. She was stupid. She was afraid of confrontation. She was inept in business matters. She had lost her chance at—

"At what?" she'd screamed at last, when she was pushed beyond her limits by his splenetic defamation of her character. "Lost my chance at what?" She was wild-eyed and furious, and he had calmed fractionally when, finally, she had matched his vehemence. "Lost your chance at real success," he had said. "Lost your chance at great wealth. Lost your chance to make your mark upon the world."

"Well, so be it. What should I do? Put a gun to t'bailiff's 'ead and force his 'and?"

"Have you spoken to the earl's solicitor, at least?"

"No, I wouldn't dream of it." She was aghast. "I have no idea who 'e is or what I'd say."

"Evie, for God's sake, take control of this situation!"

"Silas, I swear we shall fall out if you keep this up. I wish I'd never told you in t'first place. If Lord Netherwood truly meant for me to have t'business, wouldn't 'e have written it into 'is will? But 'e didn't. It was a rash promise, made on my wedding day when 'e was in a sentimental mood. For all we know 'e might have changed 'is mind if 'e'd lived."

"What rot. That business, that building should be yours."

"No, there's no 'should' about it. There are other ways— better ways—to succeed than being 'anded everything on a plate. And I'll tell you something else. Absalom Blandford can stew in 'is own juice and watch me triumph without gifts from Lord Netherwood. I've 'ad enough favors already. The rest I'll manage on my own."

Silas, thwarted and—a novel experience this—temporarily humbled, had fallen into silence. But in the weeks that followed, whenever he reappeared from Bristol, he was like a dog with a bone, returning again and again to the topic. Whichever way he looked at it, it seemed to him that a life-altering chance had slipped through his sister's fingers and he found he could hardly bear it. His own existence had been transformed by just such a gift from a benefactor; it seemed right, to Silas, that Evie be elevated too. The prospect of it excited him: he and his sister proving to the world that they were as good as many and better than most. Without her knowledge he rooted out the name of the Netherwood estate solicitor in Sheffield, a Mr. T. B. Jackson—they never progressed to first-name introductions—who was little inclined to speak to a stranger about the late earl's wishes, but was prepared to confirm, however, that he had been summoned by Absalom Blandford to the estate offices in October last year, although the meeting had been cancelled by the bailiff soon afterward. There was nothing untoward or unusual about this, Mr. Jackson had said. However, his tone and expression implied that there was something extremely untoward and unusual about Silas Whittam's questions. Mr. Jackson showed him the door; he knew nothing, he said, of the matter to which Silas alluded.

Silas, walking away from the solicitor's fine Georgian office in Paradise Square, cursed himself for bothering. He was too busy for all this, he thought. There were any number of other matters demanding his attention and here he was, fighting a battle for his sister that she didn't even want to win. Of course, he knew exactly what had rattled him: the parallel with his own story was too extraordinary to be disregarded. He remembered with perfect clarity the morning that Walter Hollis, facing Silas across the boardroom table, told him that as of this day, he was a very powerful young man. Sir Walter had placed a fountain pen on top of the paperwork, slid it over to him and smiled.

"Consider it payment for services rendered," he had said. "Your just rewards for hard work and exceptional loyalty." He had spoken as if his protégé might protest at his generosity: far from it. Silas's signature was on the dotted line before you could say Global Steamship Company, and the ink had barely dried before he was moving forward with his own ambitious plans. Yes, he knew very well what it meant to benefit from a miraculous stroke of great good fortune; and he wanted it for Evie, too. It seemed utterly dreadful to Silas that it had been promised to her, then snatched away. And her serene acceptance of this body blow was, to him, inexplicable. They resembled each other in looks alone, he had concluded; inside, they were chalk and cheese.

They walked along Shambles Street, then back along Peel Parade and into Peel Square. In the sunshine the town looked bright and prosperous, and even Silas, whose prejudices against Barnsley were entrenched, could see a certain gritty charm in the cobbled streets and proud shop fronts. There was an integrity and authenticity to this place and these people, he thought; civic pride was a wonderful phenomenon. At the Central Café in Queen Street Eve made him wait while she watched customers come and go. She studied the menu in the window—sixpence for crumpets and a pot of tea, a shilling for Yorkshire pudding with roast of the day, one and six for ham, egg and potatoes, and a pudding—and she suddenly wished she'd come with Ginger instead of Silas, because she wanted the benefit of her sharp mind and plain speaking. These meals at these prices—they'd be hard to beat. The cost of all the alterations and refurbishment to the place on Market Hill would have to be taken into account, and the rent there would likely be higher than Queen Street. She looked at Silas but he was admiring his own reflection in the plate glass. He caught her eye and smiled without turning.

"Done?" he said.

"I want to go back to Market 'ill," she said. "But I want to go in this time, so let's talk to t'agent, see if we can take t'keys."

She set off walking at a brisk pace, taking him by surprise, so he had to jog along to draw level with her.

"You're going to take it, aren't you?" he said.

"Might do."

He grabbed her and kissed her flamboyantly on both cheeks, and a passerby gave an indulgent smile, taking them for a courting couple. Eve shoved him away.

"Folk are staring," she said.

"Today, Barnsley," he said, too loudly for comfort. "Tomorrow, the world!"

Eve said: "Don't be soft," though there was something about Silas's enthusiasm that was catching and she smiled as they walked on, arm in arm in the June sunshine, a handsome couple, turning heads as they went.

Chapter 48

Enoch Wadsworth's rented room was miserable enough with the lamps lit and a fire burning, but more often than not he forgot to do either. The carpet was worn through to the backing in places, and the horsehair stuffing was emerging like fungus through a hole in the couch. There were antimacassars along its back, which seemed like an unnecessary refinement, given the scarcity of visitors to sit on it and the state of the room in general. A narrow single bed, still unmade from the night before, occupied most of one side of the room and at the other was a drab little desk, textbooks open all around its outside edge, the day's newspapers spread on the floor at its feet and a ream of paper in the very center, at which Enoch scribbled furiously with an erratic old fountain pen, which either ran copiously with ink or dried up unexpectedly for a moment before releasing a new flood. But he was used to its habits, and he persisted patiently, stooping close over the paper in the gloaming, the better to see what he'd written. Soon it would be too dark to see anything at all, and then he would remember to light the wick of his oil lamp, giving himself a few more hours at the task in hand before he finally accepted the need to sleep. He had on the shirt, tie, and tweed suit that he'd worn all day at work, but had added an oversized woolen cardigan and a scarf, wound twice around his throat, the loose ends thrown over his back to keep them out of his way. His pipe, lit but for the time being forgotten, rested on a saucer on a window ledge that was just within arm's reach. Soon it would go out, and when he picked it up for a comforting puff, he would find it unresponsive and would have to coax it back into life with a succession of Swan matches. A scattering of them, blackened and spent, already littered the floor around him.

It was an unedifying tableau: the dwelling of a man whose mind was too cluttered with concerns for the outside world to worry about the condition of his own small place in it. He never felt the lack of creature comforts; his own degraded version of the trappings of domesticity was absolutely all he needed. He simply didn't see the threadbare carpet or the tattered lining of his curtains; if the cold seeped into his bones, he donned another layer of wool and moved the pen a little more vigorously on the page. It was only when others strayed into his domain that its shortcomings became apparent, and even then only fleetingly. He would register their ill-disguised dismay, their furtive glances at the unmade bed or the soot-streaked window, but never for long enough to do anything about it. Anyway, visitors had only ever been very few and far between, and these days, apart from the once-weekly knock from his landlord— whose quarters across the landing were no more salubrious than his own—it was really only Amos who had the dubious privilege of crossing the threshold.

So, here was Enoch, at nine o'clock on a Monday night, holed up in his room on Racecommon Road in Barnsley, engaged, to the exclusion of all other activities, in the tireless pursuit of social justice. Always, always, there was work to be done: he was never idle. Often he had letters to write or an article for the Fabians, or a newly published tract to read.

Tonight, though, he was writing a speech, and this was what he loved most: putting into Amos's mouth the best and most powerful combination of words from the infinite supply that he held in his own head.

He saw great possibilities for Amos, possibilities far beyond the constituency boundary of Ardington, but first he had to get him elected. The euphoria following the by-election last year had swiftly evaporated when it became clear that Webster Thorne wasn't quite the waste of space they'd believed—and hoped—him to be. Thorne had perhaps himself been shaken by the close brush with defeat; he had rented a house on the fringes of the town and, on weekends and during parliamentary recesses, he could often be seen in one of the local inns or at church, singing lustily with the choir. He said all the right things, too: seemed conscious of the realities and difficulties of an ordinary working life. It worried Enoch that the Liberals, particularly the younger branch of the party, were developing an increasingly collectivist platform: that, and a tacit acceptance by the Labor Representation Committee of the practical advantages of cooperation between the two parties. In February, at Caxton Hall in Westminster, the LRC had signed an undertaking not to oppose parliamentary candidates endorsed by the Trades Union Congress, many of whom would be standing on the Lib-Lab ticket. This was a retrograde step, in Enoch's view, and not one that the Independent Labor Party had any truck with. He'd said as much to Ramsay MacDonald, buttonholing the Labor grandee outside Caxton Hall, undeterred by the man's powerful bearing and stellar connections. We shouldn't be playing up to the Liberals, Enoch had said; we shouldn't be encouraging this kind of reciprocity.

"Who are you again?" MacDonald had said. He was secretary of the LRC and was standing for Labor in Leicester, and Enoch could see that he had the look of a winning candidate about him, but it didn't mean he shouldn't be kept on his toes.

"Enoch Wadsworth," he had said, and they had shaken hands. "I'm with Amos Sykes, your Ardington candidate. And we're campaigning on a strictly independent Labor platform. This cross-pollination's a curse and a hindrance."

"Hardly cross-pollination," MacDonald had said, but he had taken a card from his pocket with his London and Leicester telephone numbers on it, and told Enoch to keep in touch.

"Interesting times, Mr. Wadsworth," he had said. "Interesting times."

The next day, back in Barnsley, Amos had listened to an account of this brief encounter.

"You'll be all right then, when I'm beaten by Thorne again next time around," he had said. "You'll be sittin' pretty in MacDonald's office in Westminster, openin' 'is mail, brewin' 'is tea."

"Aye, well," Enoch had said. "Think on."

When Amos arrived it was past ten o'clock.

"Sorry, sorry, sorry," he said, nipping in with an apology before the sour expression on Enoch's face got translated into words. "Got caught up wi' summat. Bloody 'ell man, this room's like a cave. Let's 'ave some light."

It was gloomy; Enoch realized that, now that he wasn't alone in the room. He stood, a little stiffly because his legs were protesting at being so long in a sitting position. He struck another match and lit the lamps, though the half-hearted glow improved things only marginally.

"Them globes are sooty," Amos said. "You want to trim your wicks."

Enoch looked at him over the top of his spectacles.

"Any more domestic advice, or shall we get on?" he said.

"Go on then, what 'ave you got for me?"

Enoch picked up the top four sheets of paper from his desk and handed them to Amos, who began to read.

"I want you to steer clear of local concerns this time," Enoch said. "I want you to tackle wider, national issues, international ones an' all. Free trade versus protectionism, nationalization of industries, taxes on t'rich for t'benefit of t'poor, a universal 'ealth service."

Amos ignored him and for a while continued to read, then he looked up. "Fancy language, this," he said.

"You need to sound more like a statesman."

"As opposed to what?"

"Don't get pouty. All I'm saying is that, from time to time, you need to speak like a parliamentarian. It's all well and good being a man of t'people, but you 'ave to show 'em that as well as being like 'em, you're also different from 'em."

"But I'm not different."

"You are, though. You've got ambition and passion and t'power of oratory; you 'ave words at your disposal—my words, sometimes, admittedly—to articulate what they think, but can't say."

Amos held up the pages. "No good if they don't understand what I'm on about," he said.

"They'll get t'gist. Look, folk don't want a man in power who's just like they are. Folk want a man in power who 'as a quality that sets 'im apart."

"You've been thinkin' about Ramsay MacDonald again, 'aven't you?" Amos said in the mock-injured tones of a jealous lover. Enoch laughed.

"Well, aye, since you mention it. MacDonald's a man with t'common touch who nevertheless leaves nob'dy in any doubt that 'e's destined for 'igh office. Did you 'ear Keir 'ardie when he campaigned for Merthyr in 1900?"

Amos shook his head. "Too busy mining," he said.

Enoch ignored the barb and plowed on with his point. "Well, it were t'same thing. A workin'man addressing t'workers, but using this inspired rhetoric, words that send you off to t'polls to put a cross by 'is name."

Enoch's heroes: that he had them still was one of the things Amos liked so much about him. Time, experience, and the relentless grind of life hadn't inured Enoch to the magic of his old enthusiasms; for a Yorkshireman, he was surprisingly uncynical.

"Anna reckons I should be campaigning on women's suffrage," Amos said now, changing tack.

Enoch sat back in his chair and gave this new thought a moment's consideration.

"Adult suffrage," he said, "not female suffrage. Female suffrage is just a distraction."

Amos whistled. "Don't be saying that to Anna."

"Why not? Adult suffrage includes adult women. Why should disenfranchised women take priority over disenfranchised men?"

"Because Anna says so," Amos said. He was only half joking.

"I've seen them Pankhursts in action," Enoch said. "I reckon they see Labor as a shortcut to winning t'vote."

"And what's up wi' that?"

"We 'ave one principal aim, Amos: to get more workingmen in Parliament. This Labor movement doesn't 'ave firm enough foundations yet to go championing every so-called good cause. You stand up in Ardington and start shouting 'Votes for Women' when there's still one in four workingmen who don't qualify, and you'll look like a right crackpot."

Amos sat down on the couch. Unused to regular service, its springs complained. "We should steer clear altogether then." He yawned, widely, convulsively.

"That's not what I'm saying," Enoch said. "I'm saying

there's iniquities in our voting system that need tackling. One vote per 'ousehold is patent madness when you 'ave maybe three grown sons still living under your roof. I reckon that's an issue that could be a vote winner for you around 'ere. And I'll tell you what, there'd be no danger of a Tory win, or even a Liberal one, if every working-class man 'ad t'right to vote. Amos?"

There was no response.

"Amos," Enoch said, more loudly, and Amos opened one eye. "I'm jiggered," he said. "Dog tired," and he closed it again.

"Well, if you will turn up so bloody late. Where were you, anyroad?"

Again, no response. Enoch sighed heavily, like a disgruntled wife at the end of her tether. He stood and fetched a blanket from a wooden chest at the end of his bed, and draped it over Amos, pushing him sideways at the same time so that he ended up prone on the couch. This maneuver was accomplished none too gently, though Enoch tucked him in, huffing and tutting as he did so. A night sleeping in his good suit and tomorrow he'd wake up stiff and cross, berating Enoch for the lack of fresh milk for his tea. He stood for a moment looking down at Amos, who had surrendered to sleep still wearing his cap. Best leave it on, Enoch thought; it'll not be getting any warmer in 'ere.

He went back to his desk, sat down again, and began to write.

407

Chapter 49

Amos should have been with Enoch by eight o'clock, and if he'd done as he'd planned, if he'd followed his diary and kept life simple, he would have made it comfortably. Union meetings at New Mill, Long Martley, and Middlecar had taken him to half past five, and he could have then popped home for a plate of Mrs. Birtle's Monday night bubble and squeak before catching the half past six train from Netherwood to Barnsley. Instead, he'd taken a left turn at the top of Middlecar Lane and walked three miles to Dreaton Bridge. He'd bought a pie and a pint from the Bridge Tavern—poor fare, the pie cold, the beer warm—and had then continued on to the colliery on the southern outskirts of the town; he had no appointment, it was outside his geographical remit and—as such—it was absolutely none of his business. But he'd gone anyway, propelled by an impulse to see for himself just what Eve's brother was up to.

Silas had been quick to assert himself: that much was clear without even walking the cinder path to the pit yard. A glossy new sign had been erected declaring Dreaton Main to be under the ownership of Whittam & Co., Avonmouth, Bristol: Managing Director Silas Whittam Esq. There was a crest of some description, an emblem, painted alongside the company name. Amos squinted at it, trying to make it out. Waves, by the look of it, and a banana palm. He laughed; if that didn't sum up the absurdity of this situation, he didn't know what did.

The pit yard was fairly quiet; the doors to all the surface buildings were closed and the few men he could see paid him no attention. Amos stood at the center of the yard and looked around in a leisurely way like a man in a gallery, admiring the exhibits. Collieries had never inspired odes to their beauty, but Dreaton Main wasn't a bad-looking place. It was filthy with smoke and coal dust, and the slag heaps were as dispiriting as they were anywhere, but the workshops were built from mellow gray stone with slate roofs, as if someone years ago had actually given more than a second thought to their appearance and striven for something better than the habitual motley collection of outbuildings, whose cheap construction gave them the impermanent, higgledy-piggledy look of a failed frontier town. The headstocks and pulley wheels were in the old style and made of wood, but they looked in good order; better, at any rate, than the ones Amos had trusted his life to for thirty years at New Mill. The general impression was of a well-maintained place of industry: newly tarred weatherboards and freshly painted woodwork, the same nautical shade of blue as the sign at the top of the track. It was a surprise to Amos, this well-kept yard, and an unwelcome one; he had hoped for something less.

A lad appeared, head down, leading a pony, and Amos hailed him.

"Now then, son, I'm 'ere to see t'gaffer. Who's on today?"

"Mr. Long," said the boy, immediately taken in by Amos's bluff.

"Frank Long?"

409

"No." The boy looked confused. "Eric Long. There is no Frank Long."

"My mistake, much obliged. And what do they call you?"

"Edward Wakefield." He fidgeted, scuffing the toe of his clogs on the stones; his eyes darted left and right.

"Morten Wakefield's lad?"

"Aye."

This was a stroke of luck. Amos knew Morten Wakefield from his knur and spell days: a cheerful bloke, with an endearing willingness to stand a man a pint, which singled him out in these parts.

"Is 'e about then?"

"No, 'e's on days." The pony chucked his head in a mild display of impatience, and the boy, clearly beset by anxiety, said, "I'd best get on, mister."

"Right-o, Edward, but do your father a favor and give 'im this."

Amos delved into his capacious jacket pocket and produced a YMA pamphlet, red ink on white paper: "Minimum Wage for Miners," it said; "The Time Is Now."

"Arcadian Hall, Barnsley, next Wednesday, everybody welcome, tell 'im."

The boy shrank back as if he was being handed a ticking bomb, and Amos laughed.

"Go on, it won't bite," he said.

"No ta, you're all right," the boy said, but Amos stood there anyway, holding out the leaflet, so he took it. He didn't look at it, though; instead he shoved it hastily out of sight. By now he looked profoundly uncomfortable, and Amos felt a pang of pity for him, crippled as he was by youth and timidity. He nodded kindly at the boy, who clicked his tongue at the pony and moved off, just as, across the yard, a door opened and a man—smartly dressed, well groomed—looked out.

"If you're after work, we're not hiring," he said. He wore a three-piece suit and a gold fob watch and these, with his southern vowels and milk-fed complexion, gave him away as one of the Whittam imports.

"Eric Long?" Amos said, crossing the yard.

The man looked affronted at this unexpected familiarity. "Indeed. And you are?"

"Amos Sykes, area organizer for t'Yorkshire Miners' Association." He smiled and held out a hand.

The man gave a bark of incredulous laughter. His own hands were pushed into his trouser pockets and that's where they stayed.

"You have some damned cheek." He spoke authoritatively, but he couldn't have been quite thirty, thought Amos. He had a spot of high color on each cheekbone and an unfortunate, halfhearted beard; if its purpose was to hide the jutting chin, it had failed. Amos smiled genially, as if nothing could be pleasanter than this chance encounter.

"You're a Bristol man, Mr. Long?"

"None of your bloody concern. What's your business here?"

"Oh, nothing sinister. Just wanted to introduce myself, open up t'lines of communication."

"You're wasting your time. We have a non-union policy at Dreaton Main."

"So I understand. That's a very backward-looking attitude, Mr. Long, if you don't mind me saying."

"I mind very much, as it goes. We'll run this colliery as we see fit and we won't be taking advice from your sort." He sniffed.

Getting up his nose then, thought Amos. Behind him, across the yard, the winding gear began to move and a few men had begun making their way down the track from the village. It was an odd time for the shift change to start. At every pit in the vicinity the shifts—days, afternoons, and nights—began and ended at the same time. Half past five in the morning. Half past one in the afternoon. Half past ten at night. You could set your watch by the activity of the winding gear. Here, though, it was half past six, and the present shift was just coming up; either the men were working shorter hours, or longer ones, and Amos would have bet the contents of his wallet on the latter.

"Are you a mining man yourself, Mr. Long?" he said.

The man gave him a cold stare. "I am now," he said.

"Then you'll know that miners endure t'worst working conditions of any section of our society."

"Not here, they don't. Now, I'm about to close this door and get on with my work, so you might prefer to leave, if you don't want to look a fool in front of this lot." He indicated the men who were now gathering outside the time office.

"Oh, don't you worry about me," Amos said. "It's your own reputation you should be tending." He glanced backward at the miners in the yard, then back again. "Bit early for t'night shift?" he said, but the office door closed in his face with chilly finality. Amos shrugged and wandered over to the men, who fell silent at his approach. This didn't perturb him in the least. Miners were a suspicious breed, even at the pits where he was a regular visitor; here, his face was unknown.

"Amos Sykes, YMA," he said, to the gathering in general. No one spoke. "Is anybody 'ere interested in a fair deal?"

Silence.

"Anybody 'ere thought about union membership?"

Again, silence. One of the men looked beyond Amos to the offices, then looked swiftly away. Amos turned. Eric Long was standing at the window, watching closely. His arms were folded and he had on his face an expression of objective interest, as if he was observing a fascinating experiment. He caught Amos's eye and held his gaze coldly. It was the closest Amos had come to feeling unnerved in a very long time, standing here in this pit yard, scrutinized by the manager, surrounded by silent men. Suddenly, though, someone began to talk.

"Thing is, we'd all rather 'ave a job than not, in't that so?"

Amos spun around to join the conversation, but it was impossible to tell who had spoken. Then the voice started up again.

"There's not one man in this pit yard who'll 'ave owt to do with t'YMA. That fella's wastin' 'is time."

It was a miner at the very fringes of the group. He had his back to Amos and was, ostensibly, speaking to a colleague. But he spoke loudly, and there was no doubting his intention.

"If that fella 'as our best interests at 'eart, 'e'll walk out of this yard and not come back. Them among us wi' union membership were sacked. Rest of us are contracted not to join."

Amos walked a short distance away from the group of men. They had begun to move now, through the open door of the time office, and a new group of miners were clattering down the steps from the bank, with the shattered look that all miners had at the end of a shift. Amos, in his suit, clutching his leaflets, felt suddenly like a lesser being. Still, he thought: in for a penny. From a distance, he began to speak.

"One day, it'll be illegal for Silas Whittam to prevent you from joining your union, or to sack you for being a member. On that day, I shall be back. And if any of you want to exercise your freedom to do as you wish in your own time, there's a minimum wage meeting at t'Arcadian Hall in Barnsley, a week Wednesday, seven o'clock."

There was not even a flicker of interest. It was as if he couldn't be seen or heard. The miners were simply going about their business, clocking in, collecting their brass checks for the

413

descent, moving on to the lamp room. Amos, with a slightly desperate air, went on: "The YMA will not rest until every miner in t'kingdom has a fair minimum wage—boys as well as men. Every single one of you should know you 'ave a set amount of money due to you every payday. We'll fight for this right with or without your support and cooperation, because we believe it to be t'very basis of a civilized society."

Behind him someone laughed, and he turned to find Silas standing a mere arm's length away from him. Amos, visibly startled, took a step backward, and Silas laughed again, without humor.

"Talking to yourself, Amos? First sign of madness."

Amos felt wrong-footed, good and proper. Silas must have walked down toward the pit while he, Amos, was in full flow. They stood for a moment eying each other, then Silas said: "You're trespassing and you're harassing my men."

"I've said my piece," Amos said.

"I could detain you if I could be bothered. I could have you before the magistrate."

Now Amos laughed. "You're a strange man, Silas Whittam. Your sister doesn't know t'half of it."

Silas's expression darkened and he looked at Amos dagger-eyed.

"Get off my land. If any man here has engaged with you in any way at all, he'll be sacked. Your presence risks their livelihoods, do you realize that?"

"This industry's full of bullies like you," Amos said. "Wielding your big stick over 'elpless men. But it's all going to crumble beneath you, and if you weren't so puffed up wi' self-importance, you'd see t'signs."

"Start walking, Sykes, or I'll set the dogs on you."

There was no sign of dogs, but he was the sort of man to keep them. He was almost snarling himself, his handsome face twisted into a mask of loathing. Amos performed an elaborate, ironic, courtier's bow and took his leave; but as he walked away, he was trembling and his heart hammered in his chest. It was anger, not fear, but it didn't stop until he boarded the train for Barnsley.

Chapter 50

These days, Monday to Friday, Lilly Pickering walked from Beaumont Lane to Ravenscliffe with her ragged assortment of younger offspring trailing behind, before and about her. She would arrive at ten past eight, by which time Daniel would be long gone, Eve would have left for the mill, and Seth and Eliza would have gone to school. Anna would be waiting for Lilly, who on arrival would go immediately to the big kitchen and warm her backside on the range, however brightly the sun might be shining outside. Too thin, Daniel said: no flesh to warm her bones. Anna would then take off for Netherwood Hall to wield her paintbrush in the countess's suite of rooms. Lilly held the fort at Ravenscliffe—a little washing, a little cleaning, a few stolen moments on the swing in the sunshine— until Anna came back at four in the afternoon, unless Eve managed to get home sooner, in which case Anna would walk not into the riotous assembly of Pickering infants, but into a calm, orderly house with tea in the pot and warm scones on the table.

The arrangement suited everyone. Lilly had real, regular paid work; a weekly pay packet, the first she'd ever had. Her children ate a cooked dinner every day, prepared the night before by Eve or Anna. Maya and Ellen had four new playmates—the best kind: clueless and easily led, happy to fall in with orders from the two little generals. And Anna was released from domestic duty for the first time since she'd come to live with Eve, in those dark days when the loss of Arthur was still an open wound and Anna was a foreigner in Netherwood.

Anna's walk to Netherwood Hall took her each morning past the new miners' memorial, and every day she would pause and lay a hand on the lamp that the bronze miner held out before him as if he was following its light down a tunnel. She kept this little ritual to herself, but it had become important, and passing by without this moment's pause was now unthinkable. She had never known Arthur Williams, but she felt he had somehow granted her the right to step into the life he had left behind, and for this she would always be deeply grateful. When she stood before the bronze statue, she imagined Arthur like this: a noble bearing, his shoulders broad, his arms sinewy and strong, his eyes warm in a careworn face. She saw Amos, too, of course. Her own Amos, who through gritted teeth had given his blessing to this new venture of hers, and who could see—indeed, had admitted—that the happiness it seemed to bring her made his own qualms and concerns immaterial. She was more than halfway through the job now. Thea would be back at the end of July, and her rooms would be ready for her. She had given Anna carte blanche to complete the work as she saw fit—"surprise me with something wonderful" had been the instruction, daunting in its simple optimism—and this had included the freedom to hire some help for the donkey work. Cue Jimmy and Stan, seconded from the only firm of painters and decorators that had adequately fulfilled Anna's scrupulous list of requirements: cleanliness, thoroughness, and affability in adversity. She was a hard taskmaster, and she didn't like her instructions to be questioned.

They were waiting for her this morning; overalls laundered, obliging smiles on clean-shaven faces. They never made a start without her, and they never finished until she said they could. Something about her made them anxious to please.

"Morning, boys," she said now, walking past them in the courtyard, collecting them in her wake.

"Morning," they said in unison, like nicely behaved school-boys. They followed her into the house, whose passages and doors she knew now as well as she knew Ravenscliffe.

"Cup of tea before you get going?"

This was the housekeeper, who had spotted Anna's progress from the boot room past the kitchen.

"No, thank you, Mrs. Powell-Hughes, best crack on," Anna said.

The housekeeper smiled. She liked this young woman very much. It had taken precisely one working day for Anna to win her heart, and she hadn't even really been trying. When the family was absent, the great house was always cleaned with the sort of dedication to infinitesimal detail that wasn't possible when they were in residence. There were 612 chandeliers in Netherwood Hall, and each one would be washed, one crystal drop at a time. Curtains and pelmets would be removed, beaten, brushed, and replaced. Pictures would be taken down from the walls and their frames carefully cleaned with stubby little sable brushes whose bristles penetrated every cranny of the elaborate gilt. With all this to accomplish, the very last thing Mrs. Powell-Hughes needed was decorators traipsing in and out of the house, so she was very much minded to take umbrage when she had entered the countess's rooms at the end of Anna's first day there, fully expecting mess and mayhem. Instead, she had found Anna on her knees with a dustpan and brush, cleaning the carpet. The two lads seemed to have gone, the dust sheets were folded in a tidy pile by the door, and the pots of paint and brushes were stacked in a wooden crate. Two long stepladders had been laid on their sides along the skirting boards. Anna had looked up from her labor.

"I'm just about done," she had said, not apologetically, but with satisfaction.

"But aren't you back tomorrow?" said Mrs. Powell-Hughes.

"Oh yes," said Anna. "But tomorrow I don't want to arrive to yesterday's mess." She had stood and with a gesture of her hand directed the housekeeper's attention upward. "I cleaned chandelier. I hope you don't mind. It was a little bit dusty, and I was up ladder and . . ." She tailed off and shrugged.

Mrs. Powell-Hughes looked up. The myriad glass droplets were pristine in their brass surround. She looked about her. In the housekeeper's mind, the memories were still painfully clear of the pandemonium caused during the last lot of renovations: paint on the stair runners, builders' rubble in the bathrooms, turpentine fumes accompanying her all day long on her arounds. Redecoration meant disruption. And yet, here was a room in better order now than it had been before Anna arrived. She looked about her, at the walls and the ceiling. Nothing much seemed to have changed, except that on the long section of wall between each of the three sash windows, she could see the sketchy outline of what appeared to be birds in flight. Anna, following the direction of the other woman's gaze, said: "Just ideas, nothing final."

Mrs. Powell-Hughes, her eyes still fixed on the birds, said: "Years ago, Lady Henrietta drew on the drawing room walls in charcoal." She looked away now, at Anna. "There was such a rumpus."

"A rumpus?"

"Fuss, you know? Lots of shouting and crying—well, Lady Henrietta cried, when her pictures were washed away. They weren't half bad, actually."

419

"What were they?"

"Horses. She was mad for horses as a little girl. Still is, of course, though she seems to have less time for them now."

The housekeeper looked sad, Anna thought; lost among her recollections.

"You've known Lady Henrietta for a very long time?"

Mrs. Powell-Hughes nodded. "Almost all her life. She was a babe in arms when I took this position. And Master Toby—the earl, I should say—was just walking. They were delightful."

There was a brief silence, almost awkward. Anna said: "They must be very fond of you," and the housekeeper seemed to come to, returning to the present from the past.

"Well," she said, briskly now, "I'd best crack on." She smiled warmly at Anna, who returned the compliment. "See you tomorrow Mrs. Rab . . ."

"Anna," said Anna. "It's so much easier."

This was when she first began. Now, five weeks into the job, they were as thick as thieves. Anna—endearing, engaging, entertaining—had tapped a maternal vein in Mrs. Powell-Hughes, who found the details of Anna's life quite fascinating by comparison with her own rather uneventful history and, for her part, Anna enjoyed rediscovering the lost luxury of a motherly ear. Her brief marriage to the poor, sick Jewish boy; the rift this marriage created with her family in Kiev; her love now for a firebrand former miner; her surprising, modern views about a woman's place in the world: all these matters were aired over refreshments at the kitchen table, and the older woman had found that Anna, young though she still was, had a surprisingly wise head on her shoulders. There was no giddiness about her, no flightiness; she had all the best qualities of Mrs. Powell-Hughes herself, without her tendency—

acknowledged, to her credit, by the housekeeper herself—to judge too swiftly or too harshly. Furthermore, as Anna wasn't a member of staff, she could be accepted as an equal, and this had proved an unexpected and wonderful bonus, because while hierarchy must always be respected, a housekeeper's life could as a result be a little lonely. Constantly vigilant, ever on the lookout for wrongdoing or shoddiness, Mrs. Powell-Hughes was no one's first choice for a companion at the tea table, except sometimes for Parkinson, who suffered just as she did from the inevitable and necessary dearth of friends at the top of the household's pecking order. In Anna, however, she had found a confidante, and today, having failed to tempt her at the beginning of the day, Mrs. Powell-Hughes caught her instead as she left.

"I have a jug of lemonade here, Anna," she said. "Can I pour you a glass?"

Anna hesitated. She preferred to go home, not to linger here, but she was parched, and there was ice in the jug too, crowding the surface of the lemonade and frosting the glass. She said: "Yes, please, Mrs. Powell-Hughes," because although she was always Anna, the housekeeper's Christian name was not for public use; it simply hadn't been mentioned, and the moment for asking had now long passed. Anna pulled out a chair from the table and sat down. The backs of her hands were flecked with white paint, and she scratched at it absently while the housekeeper poured a drink.

"Still coming along well up there, is it?" Mrs. Powell-Hughes hadn't been in since that first day; Anna had asked if the door could remain locked, so that the countess, when she returned, would be the first person to lay eyes on the finished work. To the astonishment and dismay of the upstairs maids, the housekeeper had agreed, and since the key to that room hung from the iron ring on her belt loop, no one so far had managed so much as a peek.

"Mmmm." Anna took a long drink. "Oh my," she said, "that's so good," then: "Do you ever have anything to do with Mr. Blandford?"

"The bailiff? Not much. He likes to see the household accounts, though what business it is of his I'd like to know."

"I need to give him this." Anna pulled an invoice from her pocket. "Bill for my materials."

"Well, his office is just across the way there."

"Yes, I know this. But I wondered, could you give it to him?"

This seemed an odd request and the housekeeper looked at her askance. Anna shrugged.

"I don't like him," she said. "I'm sorry if he's friend of yours."

Mrs. Powell-Hughes laughed. "He's no one's friend," she said. "The only person I ever saw him smile at was the late earl. He's an odd one, but he's a good bailiff, I will say that."

Anna placed the bill on the table in front of her.

"So, will you give this to him? I'd rather not have to do it myself."

"Of course I will, dear. I'll send it across with the next set of accounts." She studied Anna for a moment, then said; "I must say, you don't seem the type to be frightened off by a stern face."

"He's bad man," Anna said. "I prefer not to deal with him."

"Bad?"

Anna nodded vehemently.

"Is there something we should know?" said the housekeeper. She spoke gently, picturing a dreadful physical assault in the shadows of Netherwood Common; occasionally, her preference for gothic novels invaded her common sense.

"Well, it's business matter, between him and Eve," Anna said.

"Oh, I see." This didn't seem half so interesting, but she prodded again. "Well, evidently it's upset you very much. What exactly has Mr. Blandford done?"

Anna considered for a moment. Many months had passed, much water had flowed under the bridge, but still, Absalom Blandford's treachery rankled in Anna's loyal heart. She took another draft of lemonade, then told the housekeeper the full story.

Chapter 51

ᕫᖾᑎᐢ

Henrietta had written to Emmeline Pankhurst all those months ago in her fit of pique, but it had been Christabel who replied. Her mother was temporarily indisposed, she had said, but she had thanked Henrietta for her letter and her support and included a long list of dates. These were of meetings of the Women's Social and Political Union, to which Henrietta was cordially invited. All were in Manchester and Henrietta had attended none of them. Indeed, after her father's death, she had felt so ashamed at what then felt like her childish defiance that she had burned Miss Pankhurst's letter as an act of atonement, fancying that she could feel the late earl's approval and relief as the sheet curled and blackened and, finally, disintegrated in the grate. However, there had been a pamphlet enclosed with the letter too, and this Henrietta had kept: *The Rights of Women: A Plea for Suffrage*. In it, Christabel Pankhurst set out her case so passionately, fluently, and altogether admirably that Henrietta found that she couldn't in all conscience destroy it. Instead, she had pushed it to the back of her bureau and from time to time she took it out and read its contents. She found herself very drawn to this cause, although there had been a time when, influenced by her parents—in particular her mother—she had taken the opposite view: that politics was a male domain for good reason, and that a woman's qualities, while no less valuable than a man's, were better employed in the home. Of course, these days Henrietta was responsible, by default, for the smooth running of three collieries and an estate of twenty-five thousand acres. It was impossible to believe or to argue, either to herself or anyone else, that she lacked the particular acuity of thought or vision to make her own mind up about whom she would like to govern the country. And Christabel Pankhurst's words, set out so forcefully in her pamphlet, perfectly articulated this burgeoning belief and fixed themselves in Henrietta's mind as her own strongly held principles.

However, she had yet to contribute anything practical toward the cause. And then, one warm Saturday in June, as she strolled through Kensington Gardens with Thea on one arm and Tobias on the other, their attention was drawn by a gathering just inside the park by the Albert Memorial. A crowd had collected around an elegant young woman who appeared to be haranguing not the gathering in general, but one gentleman in particular. Her voice was raised and her color was high, and although she had no podium or pedestal, she drew the eye and dominated the little scene.

"And you believe, sir," she was saying, "that womankind falls into the same category as infants?"

"In terms of the law of the land, madam, I do." The man's voice was reasonable, in contrast with her own, which was distorted by indignation.

"A woman may be a taxpayer, a homeowner, even—merciful heavens!—a queen, and yet we're still unworthy of the right to vote?"

"Thank you, madam, you state my position most succinctly." He smiled, and looked about him at the faces in the crowd; someone laughed, though most people avoided his eye as if they weren't yet quite ready to pledge their support either way.

"Then, sir, you are a fool."

This was a new voice. It came from the back of the crowd, and it was Henrietta. Tobias and Thea gauped at her in utter astonishment, and the collection of spectators turned to face the newcomer to the debate, parting slightly so that the man at the front, who was now at the back, could see the foe. "What do you fear will happen if women are enfranchised?" she said. "Do you think we will cease to be wives and mothers? Do you think we will stop loving our children, stop caring for our family members, simply because on polling day we have the same right as you to place a vote?"

She had a clear, clever, rational voice, and the man, a tall, bewhiskered, professional-looking chap with a silver-tipped walking cane, seemed rather taken aback. He rallied, however.

"I think, madam, that loving your children and caring for your family is the greatest service a woman can perform for society," he said, and in the crowd there were nods and murmurs of approval. "And a dignified woman will always submit to her husband's or her father's judgment in all other matters."

"Or her brother's," Tobias chipped in merrily, and Thea jabbed him hard in the ribs.

"I denounce your assertions."

This was the first woman again, and everyone turned back to her. Her eyes blazed and she spat out her words with contempt for his position.

"It is false dignity if it is earned by submission. True dignity for women lies in revolt. We must shed the slave spirit and stand as equals with men, shoulder to shoulder."

"Women of the British colonies are citizens and voters," Henrietta said now, seizing the stage before he was able to interject. "But they haven't ceased to be wives and mothers.

Instead, they have shared with their menfolk the democratic right to elect a government."

"A woman's democratic rights are expressed through her husband, madam. This is the civilized way." The man brandished his cane at Henrietta, not to threaten her but to emphasize his point. "I will never concede this point of principle."

"Then, sir, you are to be pitied," Henrietta said. "Women will fight their way into every sphere of human activity and you and your kind, like the dodo and the dinosaur, shall become extinct. However, your demise will not be regretted, but celebrated."

Across the crowd, the other woman, the first speaker, began to applaud. Toby and Thea joined in and this seemed to signal the end of the entertainment, so the spectators started to drift away. The man with the cane hissed "traitor" at Toby as he passed, stomping out of the park onto Kensington Gore. Toby laughed with delight.

"I say," he said. "You're a dark horse, Henry. How did you manage to come up with all that?"

She didn't answer, but instead walked over to her fellow combatant, who smiled warmly.

"Eva Gore-Booth," the woman said, and held out a hand. She was tall and slender, with a beautiful mass of golden hair.

"Henrietta Hoyland," said Henry. She judged, in that moment, that her title might be distracting.

"You were quoting Christabel, I think?" The young woman's voice was cultured and well-bred, like Henrietta's own.

Henrietta laughed. "I suppose I was, though it's hard to know where her views end and mine begin."

"Well, it's a pleasure to meet you, Miss Hoyland. Will you perhaps join us this evening? A few like-minded souls in discussion: nothing too seditious." She delved into a bag and produced a scrap of paper onto which she scribbled an address. She handed it to Henrietta, smiled again, then took her leave. She had a meeting at the House of Commons, she said; this un-scheduled public debate had drawn her away from her princi-pal purpose and made her late.

Henrietta, Thea, and Tobias watched her go.

"Well, I never, Miss Hoyland," Toby said.

"What a blast," said Thea. "Shall you go?"

Henrietta looked at the address. "Fetter Lane," she said, and looked at Toby. "Any the wiser?" He shook his head.

"Not my beat," he said. "The City, I think. You absolutely can't go though, old thing."

Beside him, Thea said, "Do what you like, Henry," and then, to Toby: "She can do what she likes. False dignity lies in submission, Tobes. True dignity lies in revolt." She punched the air and shouted her words upward, into the sky.

Samuel Stallibrass, the family's coachman in London, didn't much like the idea of Lady Henrietta spending the evening in Fetter Lane; in his view, Holborn was one of those perfectly respectable quarters of London that at nightfall changed, mys-teriously and entirely, almost beyond recognition. Without the daytime activity of lawyers and journalists, without the profes-sional, purposeful bustle of besuited, white-collared gentlemen, the narrow streets seemed somehow narrower, the shadows darker; menace hung in the air. Tonight, although it was mild, a steady rain fell on the cobbled streets, and twice one or other of the horses lost their footing, a hoof skittering across the wet stone, making Mr. Stallibrass anxious for Lady Henrietta's safety. The address was Neville's Court, an Elizabethan building in a turning directly off Fetter Lane. He drew up as close as he could to the entrance—which was not close enough, in his opinion—and dismounted. He was a tall man, well built and lavishly whiskered, and his face bore a permanently forbidding expression, though a kinder-hearted fellow you wouldn't find in all of London. His top hat glistened with rain. He opened the door of the carriage but his bulk in the doorway prevented Lady Henrietta from climbing down.

"This is an unlikely place we've come to, m'lady," he said, "and I don't mind telling you I'd rather we drove right on by."

He spoke with the authority of a guardian and, indeed, this was the role in which he cast himself every time he sallied forth with a family member. He was particularly protective of the females, but still, times were many when he'd quite literally yanked Tobias or Dickie off the pavement or out of a club and into the safety of his carriage. His special gift was to turn up just as drunken jollity deteriorated into belligerent unpleasantness. Now he stood, immovable as Nelson's Column, in Henrietta's way.

"I don't intend to linger in the dark, Samuel," she said. "And you may accompany me to the door, if you wish."

"That's the very least I shall do, m'lady. Having accompanied you to the door, there I shall remain until you reappear."

She laughed. "In the rain?"

"In the snow, if the temperature should chance to plummet."

"Then I shall feel dreadful all evening, picturing you wet in the street."

"And I'm sorry for that, m'lady, but it can't be helped. Those are my terms if you insist on this scheme."

"Oh Samuel," she said, leaving her seat so that he was forced to take her hand and help her down. "You sound just like my mother." He raised a huge black umbrella and held it over her head, and then together they hurried toward the entrance to Neville's Court, where a mildewed porter opened the door a crack and peered suspiciously at them.

"Hello," Henrietta said, more brightly than she felt. "I'm here at the invitation of Miss Gore-Booth."

The porter hesitated. "What number?" he said.

"Open this door at once. This is Lady Henrietta Hoyland and she shall not be kept waiting." Mr. Stallibrass boomed his instruction to good effect. The door was swiftly pulled back and Henrietta stepped into a communal hallway, from which a variety of doors led into individual apartments and a dark winding staircase led to other, numerous floors. It was not a welcoming entrance hall: rather, it was one where leaving was surely more pleasant than arriving. The distinctive smell of damp pervaded the atmosphere; the fungal, fertile smell of untended furnishings, though it could also perhaps have emanated from the porter, who looked very much as if he needed an airing. Mr. Stallibrass, looking in from the doorstep, grimaced. He had been heartened at first to see the building was staffed, but he saw now that this lifting of his spirits had been misplaced. Henrietta, however, was undaunted.

"Thank you, Samuel," she said and then, to the porter, "Number fourteen please," and the door was closed on the coachman, who called out that he would stay precisely there, on the step, until she emerged. Henrietta smiled apologetically at the little man on whom she now relied, and he smiled back, though hesitantly, as if he was out of practice. He had a limp, she noticed; his left foot dragged behind and made progress up the stairs rather slow. However, they presently arrived outside a door much like all the other doors, on which was painted in black the number fourteen and there he left her, with a nod of encouragement to go ahead and knock, which she duly did. There was a delay of some moments before someone answered; she could hear the hubbub of conversation, a smattering of laughter. It struck her, rather late in the day, that she had no idea what she meant by coming here this evening. Certainly she was motivated more by curiosity than conviction. To whom did all those voices belong? She hoped she wouldn't be asked to address the meeting, or write a pamphlet of her own.

At this point, just as her confidence was failing, the door was swung wide and—relief unbounded—there stood the young woman from Hyde Park.

"Miss Hoyland!" she said, pleasure and surprise lighting her attractive face.

This was so awkward, thought Henrietta. Miss Hoyland sounded like another person entirely, but then perhaps this was just as it should be, in this dowdy building in a strange part of London, among people she didn't know. Certainly, she had no inclination to correct Miss Gore-Booth's form of address, so she merely smiled and took the proffered hand, shaking it warmly. To her confusion the door opened immediately onto a room; there was no antechamber to hang one's coat or hat, no opportunity to improve one's disheveled appearance. There were six people in the room, seated around a hearth in which a fire burned rather sulkily, more smoke than flame. They ceased their conversation and turned interested faces toward her and one of them, a bearded man in a shapeless, tweed three-piece suit, stood and removed himself from the circle. He had an intense gaze, though a kind one, and it settled on Henrietta.

Eva said: "This is Henrietta Hoyland. We met in the park in the most marvelous of circumstances."

"You're very welcome, young lady," said the man in a mellow Scots brogue. He held out a hand. "Keir Hardie. Can I make you tea?"

Chapter 52

The effect of the Grand Canal was to make this section of the gardens appear infinite. The glassy surface drew in the trees and the sky, reflecting them back at the world. Standing at the edge of the water looking down, it was as if an identical landscape had been revealed, stripped of color and fathoms deep. It was mesmerizing. Six York stepping-stones, perfectly level pedestals that rose only a fraction higher than the surface of the water, allowed a person to walk out into the center of the canal, though the stones ended at this halfway point so that if you wished to travel the length in a boat, there were no insurmountable obstructions. Before the canal was filled, the stepping stones had looked like six useless brick chimneys rising from the bottom of the basin. Now the slabs of stone appeared to float on the water, light as lily pads. They were farther apart than a grown man's comfortable stride, so that to reach each one safely, a sense of adventure was required, a leap of faith. For Anna, the journey to the middle required real exertion; she had to collect herself before each jump, then on landing had to quickly regain her balance to avoid a drenching. On the sixth stone she turned to face Daniel, who was standing on the edge of the canal, laughing at her. She panted extravagantly and clutched her sides.

"What an achievement," Daniel said, and he clapped. She lifted her skirts and curtsyed.

"But now I must come back."

"Would you like a piggyback?"

"Not on your nellie," Anna said. This latest phrase had been overheard in the kitchens of the hall, and was redeployed for the first time now. She watched his reaction, to be sure she had the context, but he merely smiled and said: "Come on, then, let me at least give you tea in the hut before you go."

She leaped back across the stones, red-faced with exertion, and they set off toward Daniel's old dwelling, which he now used as an alternative to the servants' hall when he fancied a brew. Now that he didn't have to live there, he'd grown quite fond of it; like a summerhouse, or a potting shed, it was a place to sit, smoke, and reflect. Anna, seeing it through her designer's eyes, would have liked to empty it of furniture and give it a new start. The walls around and above the fireplace were streaked with woodsmoke, the ceiling was stained yellow after forty years of Hislop's pipe, and now Daniel's daily Woodbines were contributing to the grimy palette. Rather than look at it, Anna sat outside while Daniel made the tea. There were two old steamer chairs strategically positioned in a sun-trap by a bed of fragrant catmint. The chairs had been saved from the scrapheap by Daniel; he had sanded off the lichen and fixed a slat here and there, planning to take them up to Ravenscliffe for use in the garden. But for the time being, here they had stayed, and in this midsummer warmth they were pressed into action on a daily basis. He came out with two mugs and handed one to her.

"Cheers," he said.

"Cheers. So, what's next, if your canal's finished?"

He laughed. "Och, a few months of steady maintenance, I

reckon. I feel I've lost the countess's interest. The dowager countess, that is."

"But new earl and countess, aren't they interested?"

"Not that I've noticed. And I don't criticize them—gardening's not for everyone. But the dowager countess is—was—a superb plantswoman, with a passionate regard for her gardens, here and in London. It all seems very different now."

"Well, she still seems to live here." Anna's voice lacked sympathy.

"Aye, she does and she doesn't. She can't seem to connect, do you know what I mean? She's sort of vacant. I thought she'd love the canal when she saw it completed—there's nothing like it in any garden in Britain. But it barely registered."

If Anna could feel no sorrow for Clarissa, she did at least feel sorry for him: his great vision realized, but roundly ignored.

"You need to stop looking to her for approval," she said. "When they all come home again, make beeline for new countess. It is her you work for now, and new Lord Netherwood. Tell her your canal is finished, and they must celebrate its fineness."

He looked at her. "You know what, Anna? You're absolutely right."

"This I know," she said. "Also, you must paint these chairs blue, then they'll be perfect."

"You'd paint me, no doubt, if I sat still for long enough." He smiled at her fondly. He had a lot of time for Anna: her way of making sense of the world, her kindness, her love for Eve. All these things recommended her to Daniel, but especially the last.

"Are you almost done with the great work down there?" he said now.

"Another week, perhaps a little more."

"You've enjoyed it, haven't you? The work, I mean."

She nodded. "Loved it," she said.

"You've a prodigious talent, Anna. You've turned Ravens-cliffe into something extraordinary."

She smiled, sipped at her tea, but didn't answer. Ravenscliffe was always perfect, she thought. She had simply adorned it. And then he said: "When you marry, where shall you live?" and as if responding to a stage direction, the sun went behind a cloud.

There were miners from twenty different collieries at the Arcadian Hall on Wednesday night. The place was packed to capacity, and men spilled into the street through the double doors, which were propped open to ease the stifling heat caused by the crush of bodies in a confined space. The mood among the men was an odd mix of expectation and agitation: not wholly pleasant, though not mutinous either. But there were stirrings of discontent during the speeches, an air of dissatisfaction with the progress—or lack of it—made by the YMA and the wider organization, the Miners' Federation. It was high time something tangible was done was the general feeling: something that actually improved members' lives, rather than merely promised improvement.

Amos was up at the front, arms folded, cap at a jaunty tilt, sitting on a raised platform assembled for the speakers. He looked out over the crowded hall and his heart was full: this union had come so far, so quickly, whatever the mutterings of discontent among the men. He felt a great sense of satisfaction, a quiet, sustaining confidence that this movement toward social justice had achieved a steady, unstoppable momentum. In front of him, addressing the serried ranks of miners, was John McAllister, a deputy at Berrow Colliery and a rising star of the YMA.

He had shunned the sartorial conventions of the managerial classes and worn baggy britches and a black wool waistcoat over his collarless shirt. I am one of you, was his message: we are equals in this struggle. Dangerous approach that, thought Amos: could come across as patronizing. Still, the man had the gift of the gab and no mistake. He was a vigorous speaker, using his body as well as his voice; under his arms were two dark, damp circles of sweat, though even these he seemed to carry like badges of honor, outward signs of his commitment.

"We workers of Yorkshire will not rest satisfied until a minimum wage is agreed for miners across the length and breadth of this kingdom," he said, drawing his speech to a close after fifteen passionate minutes. "This moment has been a long time coming and our wait has been painful and arduous. But I say to you tonight that our time is now. The honest workingman and boy will know the security of drawing a fixed sum every pay day—*will* know it, I say: not *should* know it. We all understand and agree the need for this step—that is no longer under discussion. Let tonight be the point at which we can look back in years to come and say to ourselves: 'That's when the tide turned in our favor: that's when justice was finally and for ever handed down to the workingmen of Britain.'"

He was a Scotsman, and the Scots had a way of holding a crowd, in Amos's experience: there was a natural, lilting lyricism to their polemic. The audience clapped and whistled, and John McAllister returned to the empty chair next to Amos.

"You might 'ave put some vim into it," Amos said. "You came over as a right wet lettuce."

John grinned. "Away you go, then; show me how it's done."

Amos stood. He had no speech in his hand; what he wanted to say was all in his head, and in his heart. Experience had taught him a few tricks of the trade: have the confidence to let the crowd settle; collect your thoughts before you open your mouth; lower the voice as well as raise it, for quiet words could be more powerful than words spat out in fury. This last tip was stolen from Webster Thorne, his Liberal opponent in Ardington. Amos listened to him speak as often as he was able, and the man was too damned good for comfort. His public-speaking ability spoke of years of practice: a good grounding at Eton—there was still something of the schoolboy debater about his appearance—three years as a star of the Oxford Union, then on to the peerless finishing school of the House of Commons. There really wasn't much Webster Thorne didn't know about the power of words. Still, Amos thought now as he drew breath to speak, he wasn't half bad himself.

Afterward, when the resolutions had been moved and passed, all of them unanimously, Amos stepped down into the melee and looked about him for someone to talk to. He was missing Enoch, who had taken off to London for one of what he called his "Fabian forays." As a rule, he attended every public appearance Amos made, and never lost any time telling him how he could have been better, stronger, clearer. Tonight Amos had had the audience in the palm of his hand, and he wished Enoch had been here to witness it. In the corner of the hall a trio of doughty women were serving tea from an urn and Amos made his way over there, not so much out of a desire for tea as a desire to look purposeful in this hiatus after the event. A pint of mild would have been more like it, but the Temperance brigade, always in evidence at miners' meetings, were out in force, dispensing Typhoo Tipps and custard creams as if they were all a man could want.

"Sugar, love?"

"Sweet enough already, thanks," Amos said. He took the

tea, then turned away from the trestle table, and there stood Morten Wakefield, so close that the cup and saucer in Amos's hand only just fitted in the gap between them.

"Now then, Morten," he said, with a mixture of surprise and pleasure. "You made it. That's grand." He took a step back as he spoke, so that they weren't so uncomfortably close, and he held out his free hand in friendship. Morten Wakefield's reply was a swift, brutal left hook; it caught him on the cheekbone underneath his right eye and sent him crashing to the floor. His cup and saucer sailed disastrously upward, anointing his face with hot tea as he fell. One of the ladies at the urn screamed and another one said: "That smashed crockery'll 'ave to be paid for," which, even through the fogged confusion of semiconcussion, struck Amos as funny.

He pushed himself up on his elbows, but didn't risk standing. Gingerly he touched his cheek and felt something warm and wet, though whether it was blood or tea, he didn't know. His vision swam and the right side of his face throbbed and tightened. In front of him, two men had Morten pinned by the arms, though he made no struggle, so their efforts at restraint looked hammed-up, like a pantomime arrest. For a moment, victor and vanquished looked at each other, then Morten said: "My lad's lost 'is job because o' thee. Sacked for pocketin' your stupid fuckin' pamphlet. It were my good fortune that I weren't on afternoons wi' 'im, else I'd 'ave been tarred wi' t'same brush."

"Morten, good God man, that's criminal." Amos, still ignominiously prone on the wooden floor, struggled to his feet with some difficulty. His head felt implausibly heavy on his shoulders and his right eye was almost closed.

"Aye, well. You came where you shouldn't 'ave come. What did you think? That Whittam's all 'ot air? That you can do as you please?"

There was pain in Morten's eyes. He was a decent man, a

peaceable man: Amos knew this. His captors on either side pulled at his arms as if to frog-march him off the premises.

"Let go," Amos said to them. "'e's done nowt wrong." Then, to Morten, he said: "I'm sorry. If I can mend it, I will."

Morten's face was unreadable but his words were unambiguous enough. "If you set foot in Dreaton pit yard I'll fuckin' kill you," he said. Around them, the crowd was entirely silent, transfixed. Amos hung his head and Morten began to move away toward the door.

"Nob'dy saw," Amos called out, suddenly. "There was nob'dy there when I talked to your Edward."

Morten turned. "Whittam lined up every man in t'pit yard and 'ad 'em searched. Our Edward 'ad your leaflet shoved in 'is jacket pocket. Do you know what's funny? T'lad can't even read." And he walked out of the silent hall and into the night.

Chapter 53

Breakfast at Fulton House. In attendance: Clarissa, Toby, Thea, Dickie, Isabella, and a newcomer—a friend of Isabella's named Bryony, whose mother and father were in the throes of a marital scandal and who had placed their daughter in the temporary care of the Hoyland household in order to give full vent to their emotions at home. The presence at the table of an outsider, young and harmless though she was, had a beneficial effect on the assembled company; small ceremonies were carefully observed, small kindnesses politely acknowledged. Beneath the surface, of course, familiar tensions and resentments still flowed freely, but Bryony, to a large extent, was protected from them. She was the youngest child of the youngest son of an obscure branch of the Chester-Moreleys, a Midlands family whose fortune had been made in tea a long time ago, but not quite so long ago that it no longer mattered. "She's one of the lesser Chester-Moreleys," Clarissa tended to say when asked about Bryony and her circumstances. That she had welcomed this little nonentity into the hallowed halls of Fulton House—and a nonentity who now had the whiff of social disgrace about her—was the closest Clarissa had ever come to an act of real charity. She was pleased with her own conduct in the matter; she enjoyed the role of benefactress and felt that the child's chances in life could only be enhanced by an association, however brief, with one of England's finest families.

"Bryony," she said now. The girl peered up through a thick, black fringe. "Bryony, please help yourself to more eggs."

This sounded rather like an order, and Bryony made to stand.

"Bryony, sweetie, only if you actually want eggs," said Thea.

"Well, naturally," said Clarissa. "I shouldn't want you to have more eggs, Bryony, if you didn't want them. I shouldn't want anyone to have more eggs on my account."

"In all my life you've never encouraged me to have more eggs."

This was Henrietta, late to the table. She looked different, thought Toby, though he couldn't quite say why. She took a plate from Munster, the lugubrious London butler, and worked her way along the hot buffet.

"Yes, well, I'm sure you understand why that might be," said Clarissa.

"Late night, Henry?" said Toby.

"Not madly so." She took her place at the table and began to eat. All of them, except Bryony, waited for Clarissa to begin the interrogation: Where had she been? With whom had she spent the evening? What time had she returned? But the moment for asking arrived, bloomed, then passed, undisturbed. Clarissa cut splinters from a semicircle of pineapple and ate them delicately, one by one. Her children swapped guarded looks. Here was their mother, undoubtedly: but where was her waspish insistence on propriety? It had increasingly begun to seem as if she didn't much care what any of them did anymore. She was interested in Bryony, in the way that a person might display enthusiasm for a new hobby, but her own offspring were getting away with murder.

"And was it an instructive evening?" Toby seemed to relish this situation. It amused him to discover just how far his mother could be pushed before she finally tuned into the meaning of their conversation.

"Very. Perhaps you should come next time. Open your eyes to what's happening in the world."

Clarissa snipped at a bunch of grapes, taking only three for her plate. With a small sharp knife she cut one into four sections and, spearing them with a fork, she ate each tiny segment with a preoccupied air.

Toby laughed. "Women's suffrage? I hardly think so."

Everyone—except Bryony—looked at Clarissa, but still she sat and sliced and nibbled, and on her face was a beatific smile. Clearly, she was elsewhere. Henrietta could have stood on the table and demanded votes for women without provoking more than a yawn. She smiled across the table at Toby.

"I believe I'm a naturally combative speaker. I learned this about myself last night. Among other things."

He shrugged. "Really?" he said. "I learned that about you a long time ago."

Henrietta had been drawn into the circle the night before by Keir Hardie, who introduced her to the rest of the gathering. She barely heard the names—her mind was swimming with the novelty of this situation—but as well as Eva Gore-Booth, there was Sylvia Pankhurst, her young brother Harry, a woman called Teresa something-or-other, and a slightly later arrival who slipped into the room soon after her: a tall, thin, owlish man whose name escaped her entirely. Space was made for her, a chair drawn up. The accommodation was humbler than a servant's bedroom at Fulton House: one room, shabbily furnished, its separate functions delineated by smoke-stained curtains, strategically placed where a wall should be. Mr. Hardie offered to make her tea, which she accepted, but then watched with some misgiving as he spooned leaves into a saucepan, added cold water, then set it to boil on a small griddle over the open fire. It reminded Henrietta of the outdoor adventures she'd had as a child on the grounds of Glendonoch. The brew, supplied to her in an enamel mug, was black and bitter but she sipped at it politely, and listened to the discourse. Teresa was confident and argumentative and her upper lip had an unsettling habit of curling upward on one side, giving her an expression of great contempt for the rest of the world. Sylvia seemed a more comfortable creature, although her long, heavy face made her look rather sad. Henrietta warmed to her, though: her ardent convictions were tempered by a willingness to listen, especially to Mr. Hardie, who sat close to her, smoking a pipe. Henrietta wondered if the famous Miss Pankhurst might be a little in love with the charismatic Scotsman. He seemed solicitous of her, too: they were familiar with each other, clearly.

For the first hour of the evening Henrietta sat, endured her tea, and nodded here and there to show she was paying attention. The conversation was wide-ranging: the injustice to women of being deprived a voice in the government to which they paid taxes; inequalities between the sexes in the labor market; the iniquities of the divorce laws. Henrietta felt daunted by how much she didn't know. Even the boy, who couldn't have been much more than sixteen, seemed well versed in the rhetoric; he shared the floor equally with his adult companions and drew regular agreement from Mr. Hardie, who paid him the compliment of listening gravely to each new point. For all that the themes were injustice and inequality, it was a harmonious assembly, but for the man in the round, wire-framed spectacles, whose role seemed to be devil's advocate; however forthright,

443

informed, or intimidating the speaker, he remained implacably opposed to the principle of women's suffrage.

"When workingmen lack a vote, middle-class women must wait their turn," he said, then sat back in his wooden chair and watched the gathering combust. Then, when the dust settled, off he went again: "Really you should ask yourselves if it's democratic freedom you're after, or self-aggrandizement." Once more, he sat placidly while eloquent abuse rained down on him. He was a Yorkshireman, thought Henrietta, with a Yorkshireman's stubborn streak, and recognizing the type gave her the confidence to speak.

"You think, do you, that men are more deserving of the vote than women?" she said, and all faces turned to her.

"Not exactly, no," he said. "But pragmatically speaking, if t'vote is granted to all working-class men, all t'changes you're seeking will follow on."

"Then women must wait patiently with the lunatics and criminals until such a time as you men deign to pay proper attention to our plight?"

"That's about t'long and t'short of it, though I wouldn't phrase it that way in a pamphlet."

"Ignore Enoch, Miss Hoyland," said Eva Gore-Booth. "He's a Fabian, and their record of support for the cause is patchy, to say the least."

"I don't see you lot campaigning for t'vote for all womankind," Enoch said. Like Mr. Hardie, he had a pipe, and he puffed contentedly at it, entirely unperturbed by his minority position in the room. "Just middle-class women, like yourselves. Women of property. The iniquity of that strikes me as very troubling indeed."

Henrietta shifted in her chair. She thought of Fulton House and Netherwood Hall and wondered what this collection of activists would think of her if they knew from where she had sprung. For the rest of the evening she held her tongue, feeling humble in the face of their erudition and commitment. However, she told herself as coats were fetched at the meeting's end, she had made a start. True, she had the comforts of a vast fortune, the delights of three elegant homes—one of them palatial—and a combined staff of more than two hundred and fifty servants to ease her passage through life, but she had made a start.

"Lady 'enrietta 'oyland, I believe."

She jumped at the voice, which was deliberately low and discreet. The owlish man was just behind her, and he had her coat in his hands. He held it out for her and smiled.

"Enoch Wadsworth, district organizer of t'Yorkshire Miners' Association. I recognized you when I walked in. Fancy you fetching up 'ere."

"Have we met?" She tried not to sound supercilious, though she was aware that her high-born vowels made this a possibility.

"Not likely. But your family's quite well known in our parts." He said this with an ironic smile and she felt foolish.

"Of course," she said. "I suppose I should have corrected Eva when she introduced me, but she just assumed . . ."

"Aye, well, she would. But there's no shame in a title, y'know. You inherited it, just as some folk inherit poverty."

"Indeed," Henrietta said. "And I've never considered it a difficulty until very recently."

"Well, for what it's worth, and knowing what I know of your suffrage pals, they won't 'old it against you."

She really didn't know what to make of him. Here was a man who, were she in Netherwood, she would expect to doff his cap as she passed—not, she told herself sternly, that he should have to. Yet he was so casually self-assured, so entirely unfazed by her rank and title; sympathetic, even, as if he was sorry for the burden she carried.

"Thing is," he said, "it's what you do that counts, not who you are."

She nodded. She remembered how, in the week before he died, when she still imagined her father would be always there, Teddy had quoted an English philosopher at her—an attempt to express his own new *modus vivendi*. She couldn't remember the philosopher, but she could remember the words.

"I have always thought," she said, "the actions of men the best interpreters of their thoughts."

"John Locke," Enoch said at once. "A fine mind." They smiled at each other, and then he said, "I shall be seeing you, then, Miss 'oyland."

"You shall, Mr Wadsworth. And thank you for your discretion."

"Anytime. If I were you, though, I'd nip out quick before they all spot that liveried coachman waiting for you on t'doorstep."

Now, eating kedgeree and drinking tea poured from a china pot, not a saucepan, Henrietta felt buoyed by possibilities and purpose. A new world had presented itself last night: a world where she might become someone else and, by so doing, be more herself. Thea, next to her at the table, placed a bold, proprietorial hand on her shoulder, caressed her neck, trailed her fingers down her back. These were the actions of a lover, but here in the dining room, under the unsuspecting eyes of the family, their significance was lost.

"Will you come to my room?" Thea said. "I need your undiluted company."

"Oh, pardon us for spoiling things," Toby said.

"Pardon granted," said Thea. She stood and held out a hand. "Henrietta?"

"Not now," said Henrietta. She smiled, though Thea looked

stunned, as if she'd been slapped. "I'll join you presently," Henrietta said, gently.

"Very well," Thea said. "Though I may be gone."

"Oh?" said Toby. "Anywhere interesting?"

She glared at him. "Would you like an itinerary of my movements?" she said.

"Dorothea," said Clarissa, looking up from her grapes. "Before you leave, there's something I have to say, and it may as well be now."

Everyone turned to her. Thea sighed, as if inconvenienced beyond belief.

"I am to be married. I shall wait until next year for the sake of form, but then I'm to be married."

The silence was almost comical, and indeed a bubble of nervous laughter floated up from somewhere inside Bryony; she clutched her hand to her mouth, appalled. Beside her, Isabella took immediate refuge in tears, though they had no impact on anyone, least of all her mother, who popped the last morsel of grape into her mouth and smiled benignly at the table in general.

"Mama!" said Henrietta. "Who to?"

"Archie Partington." Clarissa wiped her fingers fastidiously on her napkin and set it carefully down beside her plate. "He has been kind enough to propose and I have been"—she paused, searching for the right word—"generous enough to accept."

Again, silence. The older siblings looked at each other for enlightenment, but found none.

"You don't mean the Duke of Plymouth?" said Henrietta at last.

"I do, as a matter of fact. And furthermore, I find your tone impertinent."

"Sorry, Mama. But you must permit me to at least show surprise. He's rather . . ."

447

She tailed off, daunted by the challenge in her mother's eyes.

"Ancient," said Dickie. "Archie Partington is ancient."

"He's sixty-two, in fact," said Clarissa. "But, yes, rather older than I am."

"I say, Ma," said Toby, "you'll be a duchess."

She smiled at him. "Darling boy," she said. "I knew you'd understand."

Chapter 54

Anna, walking along King Street on her way home from Netherwood Hall, saw Hugh Oliver before he saw her. He was strolling in his characteristic, unhurried fashion, but he was looking down rather than ahead, so that when she said, "Good evening, Hugh," he jumped and she laughed.

"You have paint in your hair," was the first thing he said to her and then: "Forgive me, good evening, Anna," which made her laugh again. It was months since he'd last been in Netherwood and she'd forgotten how much she liked him. He offered his arm and she reminded him that until they'd met, he had been walking in the opposite direction from her.

"But aimlessly," he said. "For want of anywhere to go."

"Then you must come back with me to Ravenscliffe," she said, and he nodded his approval at the suggestion.

"I should be at Dreaton Bridge," he said as they began to walk. "I should be staying this evening at the Bridge Tavern."

"And yet here you are."

"Indeed. Have you ever been to Dreaton Bridge?"

She shook her head.

"Never have I seen a bleaker place," he said.

"It can't be worse than Grangely," she said. "Grangely is worst place I've ever seen. I lived there, you know, with Leo, when Maya was born. Grangely killed my husband, though everyone said it was tuberculosis. I was lucky to leave when I did, or Maya might have been next to die."

She looked so pale and grave and his heart went out to her. He had thought about Anna a good deal since leaving Netherwood for Bristol. Her spirit and her confidence had remained with him, and from time to time he had heard her voice in his head, her very particular way of speaking. Occasionally and—he told himself—irrationally, he had imagined a life in Bristol with her by his side. Nothing that had occurred between them in his last visit had given him encouragement, but he needed no more, it seemed, than what he'd had: lively conversation, shared laughter, and the surprisingly stirring sight of Anna in the wind, bringing in sheets from the washing line. This chance meeting now was serendipitous, perhaps: Lady Luck had diverted him from Dreaton Bridge and directed him instead to King Street in Netherwood. Thus ran the dialogue in his head as they walked out of town toward the common, talking back and forth in friendly fashion. Only when she asked why he had come did the mood—inexplicably, to him—alter, and not for the better. He was back from Bristol, he told her, because Silas had returned to Jamaica and there were concerns about the smooth running of Dreaton Main. His function, he said lightly, was simply to cast the shadow of management over the pit yard to be sure everything was as it should be. Beside him, Anna stiffened and withdrew her arm, and he stopped in surprise.

"What is it?" he said.

"You do his dirty work, then," Anna said.

"I don't see it that way. I'm second-in-command, after all."

"You know he sacked that young boy?"

"For breaking colliery rules, yes."

Anna laughed bitterly. Hugh, anxious to swing the conversation back to its pleasant beginnings, said: "Look, it's just business. Tell me what you've been up to, to end up with blue paint in your hair."

She ignored him. "Silas sacked Edward Wakefield to hurt Amos Sykes," she said.

"Well, yes, it was partly to teach a lesson to all concerned." Hugh, desperately underinformed where Anna's love life was concerned, sensed no danger.

"Amos was attacked, did you know that? Attacked by Edward's father. This, too, was because of Silas."

"Well, yes, indirectly. But if Sykes had stayed away, it wouldn't have happened." Hugh's voice was level, reasonable; what he said couldn't be denied, and even Anna—after the event, when she first saw his damaged face—had wondered at the sense of Amos walking into the lion's den of Dreaton Main, courting controversy and confrontation with Eve's brother. But still she bridled at Hugh's calm assessment; he had no notion of the complexity of the situation, no understanding of the welter of emotion. Amos may have been rash and ill-advised, but he was a passionate, principled man, driven by a desire to fight injustice. She was proud of him and would defend him, always. With her silence now, she hoped to convey this. Hugh, silent too, watched her warily.

They were at the gate to Ravenscliffe now, and Anna wondered if she could withdraw her invitation to come inside. Then the front door was flung open and Eve was there, all smiles of surprise and warm greetings for Hugh, offering him dinner and a bed for the night, and there was nothing to be done but to follow Eve into the kitchen, where the children, seeing who accompanied her, fell into a tumult of excitement at the unexpected arrival of the charming, affable, handsome Hugh Oliver. There was roast chicken just out of the range, and a salad so fresh from the allotment that Ellen triumphantly plucked a caterpillar from the underside of a lettuce leaf and Maya began

451

to clamor because she didn't have one too. It was a merry scene, and Anna's anger subsided under the relentless balm of Hugh's warm, good-natured conversation. He had the children rapt with a story of a cargo of animals sent in crates from Africa; they were unloaded at the Avonmouth docks and a crowd gathered to see the spectacle. In the first crate, he said, was a zebra.

"But when they opened it the poor beast was almost dead," he said. "It couldn't support itself and when the sides of the crate fell away, it simply slumped to the ground."

Eliza, eyes instantly full of tears, stared at him.

"What was wrong with it," she said. "Was it seasick?"

Seth tutted and said, "Dehydrated, I expect," and Hugh nodded at him. "Correct," he said. "The zebra was thirsty. A young man from the zoo knelt by its side and dripped water into its poor, dry mouth."

"Poor zebra," said Ellen.

"Poor zebra," said Maya at once.

"And did it do t'trick?"

This was Eve, as engaged as the girls by the zebra's fate. Hugh nodded.

"Eventually, though it lay there for a long while first. There was a camel too, and a pair of lions, male and female. All on the dockside, not in cages, not even tethered."

Seth said: "Too weak to attack anyone, were they?"

"Indeed. Nearly dead, all of them. The shipping company loaded them up in the hold in Africa, then practically forgot they were there."

"Are they in trouble now?" Eliza said.

"No, since all the beasts pulled through. Poor show, though."

"I want to see t'docks at Bristol," Seth said. It sounded to him like a place where reality met fantasy.

"Did you know Anna's getting married?" Eliza said, in the

way she had of taking a conversation and making it her own. Hugh put down his knife and fork and the smile left his face, only for a second, but long enough for Eve and Anna to register the meaning.

"Are you?" he said, steadily. "To whom?"

"Amos," Anna said.

"I'm to be bridesmaid again, aren't I, Anna?"

"You are, Eliza, yes."

"Anna," Hugh said, after a moment's pause. "I wonder if you'd mind coming outside with me for a moment? I need your advice on a personal matter."

Eve and Anna glanced at each other across the table.

"Of course," said Anna, for, with the children all about them, there really wasn't much else she could say.

He held open the door for her and they stepped out into the garden. He walked toward the gate, as if he meant to go out onto the common, but she stayed put on the doorstep, arms folded, so he came back toward her. The June evening was warm and light and the scent of roses—Amos's roses, planted last summer—was all around.

"I'm sorry," he said. "If I'd known, I wouldn't have spoken about Mr. Sykes as I did. The last time I was here, I don't think there was even a suggestion of romance between you and him."

She raised her eyebrows; what did he know of the secrets of her heart? She remained silent though, letting him speak.

"Is the date set?"

She shook her head, no.

"Then I shall take that as my one, slender hope that I haven't yet lost you."

She was shocked now into speaking. "You cannot lose something you didn't have," she said.

"In my mind, and from a distance, you were becoming mine," he said. "You sprang to mind so often, so clearly, that I began to think of you as part of my life in Bristol—at least, to imagine that you could be part of my life there. Anna . . ."

He faltered, searching for the words. He had been thrown into crisis by her news; vague and pleasant thoughts of a growing mutual attachment had turned in a moment to an urgent need to press his case. She held up a hand as if to stop his words, but instead he seized it with both of his and went on: "Anna, I do believe with all my heart that I have never and will never meet anyone so perfect for me as you are. I do understand that this alarms and startles you, because we were friends, not lovers, last time we met. But I know I could make you and Maya happy, and you would make me the happiest man alive if you would allow me to."

His eyes beseeched her to give him encouragement and it struck her how very odd this was, to be suddenly and unexpectedly wooed by a handsome man of business, in his suit and handmade shirt and soft leather shoes that were made for city streets. He still had her hand clasped in his. He smelled of sandalwood soap and his fingernails were as perfectly white-tipped and oval as her own. When Amos held her hand, she could feel the lines in his skin and his nails, even now, a year after leaving New Mill, were never clean. She opened her mouth to speak.

"Anna?"

The familiar voice was full of trepidation. Amos stood at the fence that separated Ravenscliffe's garden from the common and his face was stricken: truly stricken, as if he gazed upon the scene of a terrible disaster. He began to shake. At once, Anna dragged her hand from Hugh's grasp.

"Amos," she said. "It's all right."

He cut an alarming picture. The swelling around his right eye had diminished but an ugly purple and yellow bruise had bloomed across his cheekbone; the affected eye was bloodshot and still not fully open. Hugh, sleek and exotically beautiful, turned to look at his rival and then back again at Anna.

"Him?" he said. "Are you quite sure you want him?"

Amos seemed unable to speak. He might have raged: thrown himself in furious self-defense at the challenger. Instead he stood like a dumb animal and watched what he thought was his future unraveling. But he kept his eyes on Anna and saw that she ignored Hugh's question and walked past him to the gate, which she opened and passed through. Transfixed, Amos's gaze never left her and now she stood before him.

"It's all right," she said again. "Really it is." She stroked his head softly, then let her hands rest at the back of his neck and kissed him carefully, again and again, on all the unbruised parts of his face, so as to cause him no more pain. Tears fell down his cheeks and he felt not shame, but profound relief, as if he had just stood at the brink of hell, felt the heat, seen the horror, then been granted a reprieve.

When she stopped kissing him and looked back at the garden, Hugh had gone inside. The door to the house was closed.

Amos didn't come in. Within the walls of Ravenscliffe lay a grave threat to his peace of mind and he didn't much fancy maintaining a front of studied neutrality for the sake of Eve and the children. So they walked up the common from the house and sat for an hour or so on the long, gnarled trunk of a fallen oak. He looked shocking; Morten Wakefield had a damaging fist for an affable man, and had split the skin, as well as bruised it. Amos had gone home to Sheffield Road after the event, in the belief that the worst might be over by the time Anna had to see it, but in this he was much mistaken. Mrs.

Birtle hadn't helped, applying iodine to the cut, which had stained his cheekbone a lurid shade of orange, and the following day when the bruising presented itself fully, the variety of blues and yellows was marvelous to behold, from an objective point of view. Anna was used to it now, a few days on, but she could see what an unlikely beau he must have appeared to Hugh. She smiled.

"What?" Amos said.

"Nothing. I was just thinking how handsome you look."

He cut a rueful glance at her, not yet quite ready to laugh. She took his hand and laced her fingers through his.

"We should be married, Amos."

"That's t'plan," he said.

"Soon, I mean. Let's not wait till after election. Let me fight it with you, as your wife."

He smiled at her, and winced.

"When, then?" he said.

She leaned in toward him and kissed his good cheek. "When it doesn't hurt to smile," she said. "When both sides of your face match."

"And where shall we live as Mr. and Mrs. Sykes?"

This was a large question, the answer to which he hardly wanted to hear. Ravenscliffe had a powerful, talismanic significance to Anna and to Eve, he knew that. But she didn't hesitate, not for an instant. "Anywhere. Ardington's nice."

He looked at her gravely. "Will you be sorry to leave Ravenscliffe?"

She shrugged: a gesture so familiar to him and so dear. "I made it for Eve," she said. "My home is where you are."

Chapter 55

The noble ears of Archie, Duke of Plymouth, must have been burning for quite a few weeks after Clarissa made her announcement: again and again he was discussed, and not always—in fact, rarely—in a flattering light. Isabella—who, although she was assured she had met him, couldn't call him to mind at all—formed a mental image entirely from the conversations she overheard among her siblings. That he was vastly rich was a given, and not particularly reassuring or interesting. That he was as old as the hills was a worry, since at only thirteen she supposed she had many years ahead of being obliged to call him Papa. That he had a pronounced limp and needed a stick was alarming, since Isabella detested physical imperfection and felt not pity but loathing for the afflicted. That he had a house in the South of France was, at least, quite glamorous, but that he used it in the long English winters to ease his arthritis was humiliating, and detracted entirely from any potential cachet of being able to casually claim familiarity with the French Riviera.

"I know she doesn't love him," Isabella said to Bryony.

"Well, obviously not," Bryony said. "They're both far too old for that."

They were side by side on the train, traveling back to Netherwood from London. They had been allowed a carriage to themselves—bliss—with their own hamper full of crab-paste sandwiches and lemon cake—double bliss—and the privacy to discuss quite openly the intriguing matter of Clarissa's engagement to Archie Limp, a name chosen by Bryony and embraced wholeheartedly by Isabella. Bryony's stay with the family had been wordlessly extended beyond the end of the Season; divorce proceedings had now begun, vile accusations cast by each party. Bryony, as yet, was ignorant of this detail, but her paternity was being called into question in the most insulting terms, and it was true that the black-haired girl looked very unlike her fair-haired father. Clarissa feared for her; the Chester-Moreley name might not be much, but it was all the child had. Meanwhile, Bryony was happy as a lark that her tenure in Isabella's comfortable nest had been extended, and for her part Isabella found Bryony an entertaining and instructive companion, if—occasionally—a little too sure of herself.

"I don't think Mama's too old to be in love," Isabella said now. She paused, and considered for a moment, then added, "And she's very pretty."

"Prettiness is neither here nor there and love doesn't figure in these matters anyway. It's all about status."

Isabella was stumped by her friend's easy command of the adult world. Bryony was fourteen—only six months older than herself—and yet she was terrifically in the know. She was a dark horse, too. In company, thought Isabella, Bryony could seem as quiet as a clam. But what she was doing when her hands were clasped in her lap and her eyes were dipped to the floor was listening; she listened closely to everyone, stored up their words, then used them to express her own opinions in a most impressive way.

"You see," Bryony continued, "as wife of Archie Limp,

458

she'll be a duchess, not dowager countess. And since Thea is only a countess, your mother will take precedence."

"But Mama, married to Archie Limp." Isabella grimaced. "Imagine, Bryony. Do you suppose they'll . . . ?"

Bryony shook her head firmly. "They won't bother with that side of things," she said. "At least, not with each other. In any case, once men are over the age of fifty, they lose the urge and turn to other pastimes. That's why the shooting season's so long."

Isabella fell silent. For a while she distracted herself from the subject by trying to deduce, from the view through the window, exactly which part of the country they were in. This proved too dull, and impossible, so she closed her eyes and pretended to doze. Bryony's worldliness could be unsettling at times; Isabella's very real and understandable concerns about the future were nothing to a girl who had spent half her life being buffeted like a falling leaf in the emotional maelstrom of her parents' disastrous marriage. Isabella was glad to have Bryony for company, but sometimes—now, for instance—her pearls of wisdom made Isabella feel sad. She rested her head against the window of the carriage and thought that perhaps if she pretended hard enough, sleep might actually come to her and she could forget that her mother was taking her to live in a place called Denbigh Court with an old man whose stick, when he made his way across a wooden floor, sounded like a third leg.

There were motorcars to meet them at Hoyland Halt, and a carriage for the dowager countess. Atkins took Toby, Thea, and Dickie; a junior chauffeur, Phillips, took Isabella and Bryony; and Henrietta, out of kindness, rode with her mother in the landau, which looked increasingly like a museum piece amid the fleet of motorcars garaged in the stable yard at Netherwood Hall. Toby's love of the motorcar exceeded even that of his late father: since the earl had died last October, three further Daimlers had been added to the collection and a plan had been hatched to hold speed trials on the grounds. Toby was hoping to make a circuit incorporating the oak and elm avenues and Thea was to have driving lessons with Atkins so that she could take part. September, they thought: shooting and racing. She had returned from London in high spirits. Clarissa's shock announcement had done Thea a power of good—she couldn't have hoped for better news—and she bounced up the wide stone steps of the house on her husband's arm, smiling warmly at the household, which was gathered in tidy formation to welcome the family home, with Parkinson and Mrs. Powell-Hughes at the helm. Parkinson bowed respectfully at the earl and countess, but it was the dowager countess for whom he reserved a special, dignified twinkle. She returned it, stopping by him as she mounted the steps with Henrietta.

"May I say, it's extremely good to see you again, your ladyship," he said.

"Dear Parkinson. So much more handsome than Munster," she said, and they laughed. "Is all well here at Netherwood?"

"Everything is as it should be, your ladyship. Tea will be served in the drawing room in half an hour."

She smiled again and moved on. To Henrietta she said: "They do all seem very dear, now that I shall be leaving." And Henrietta said, "They *are* all very dear, Mama, whether you're leaving or not. I think they'll miss you tremendously."

"And shall you?"

"Need you ask?"

"Evidently, yes."

"Nothing will be the same without you, Mama."

"What a clever answer, Henry," said Clarissa. "If you ever

460

tire of the mining industry, perhaps you could consider the diplomatic service."

This made Henrietta laugh out loud.

"Actually, I was thinking of a career in politics," she said.

"Super," said Clarissa. "One way or another I'm quite sure you'll be notorious." She moved away and Henrietta watched her go. She didn't think she would miss her mother at all, was the truth of it, although she liked her better now that she seemed to have washed her hands of her. Clarissa had announced on the train that she planned to spend September at Denbigh Court, in order to establish what must be altered there before she moved for good. It was as if none of them mattered very much anymore: or, rather, she had done with them what she could, and now she could do no more. Except for Isabella, of course. Isabella was still Clarissa's great hope. Henrietta had denied her the vicarious pleasure of a triumphant season, a brilliant marriage, an exalted son-in-law. Isabella, Clarissa was sure, would prove more obliging.

"Henry!"

Thea's voice rang down the staircase to the marble hall where Henrietta still stood. She began to walk up the stairs and could see Thea at the top, her face lit with excitement.

"Henry, Anna's here, we're about to see my room. Will you come too, take a look?"

Thea's redecorated quarters didn't hold much immediate appeal for Henry, who longed for a few very specific comforts after the journey home: Maudie's deft fingers unbuttoning her traveling gown and brushing her hair, the particular luxury of a warm bath in daylight hours. But it would have been churlish to say no, so she followed Thea along the wide landing to where Anna Rabinovich—summoned by Mrs. Powell-Hughes when she had known for sure what time the countess would arrive home—stood outside the locked door to Thea's private rooms. Anna held the key.

"If you don't like, please say," she said to Thea. "In any case, I will know, whether you say or you don't."

Thea winked at Henrietta. "Thrilling, *n'est-ce pas?*" she said and then, to Anna, "Go on then, open up."

Anna turned the key and pushed open the door, and Thea walked in. Facing her, painted onto the wall and almost filling it, was a white clapboard house, set into a permanently sunny day on a Long Island beach. The blue of the sky extended onto the adjacent walls, fading into paler hues the farther it was from the focal point. Seabirds wheeled about the room; one appeared to perch on the wide shelf of a window surround, others seemed farther away, twisting in the sky, reveling in flight. The house had a porch and steps that ran down directly onto the sand, and its door was wide open; warm colors spoke of comfort and hospitality inside. The wooden slats of the house seemed to possess an extraordinary texture, blues and grays giving shade and depth to the white. At the windows of Thea's room, curtains of white silk had replaced the pink damask, and they were tied back in soft folds with plain blue cord. They looked like summer clouds against the blue walls. Thea moved across the room to the painted house and touched it. She still hadn't spoken.

"Golly," Henrietta said. She looked at Anna. "This isn't redecoration, it's art."

"Same thing," Anna said.

Thea turned; she was smiling, but there were tears in her eyes.

"How did you know?" she said.

"You mentioned it once, remember? Your perfect house? Of course, I don't know yours—I had to use pictures in books. I hope it's something like."

"It's perfect," Thea said. "It's utterly perfect. It feels like home."

Clarissa sat at her mirror. Behind her, Flytton moved efficiently around the room setting out nightclothes and bundling discarded linens into a chest for removal to the laundry.

"What do you make of the Great Work?" Clarissa said. She meant the painted walls of Thea's room, which Flytton immediately understood. The maid pulled a face: noncommittal, though erring on the side of disapproval.

"Quite," said Clarissa. "Rather *de trop* in my view, though perfectly fitting for Dorothea, who is rather *de trop* also. Could you unpin now?"

Flytton immediately ceased her tidying and came to stand behind Clarissa, running expert hands over her head, pulling out the pins that held her hair in its elegant twist. Released, it fell down her back. There were streaks of gray now, quite distinct from the dark blond that had been Clarissa's natural color all her life, and it had a coarser texture than the blond. She lifted a hand to a strand of the new shade and looked at Flytton in the mirror.

"How ghastly," she said.

"Hardly, your ladyship. And when it's up, none of it shows."

"I was thinking of a cut. The chignon looks a little *passé*, don't you agree?"

"If you mean out-of-date, then no, I don't. It shows off a slender neck like nothing else."

Clarissa tilted her head to one side and then another. Her neck was slender, certainly. But she had seen the way Thea's hair swung when she moved and though nothing would drag a compliment from Clarissa's lips, she wondered if, as Duchess of Plymouth, she might be at liberty to cut a more modern figure than she had as Countess of Netherwood.

"You'll come with me, of course," she said to Flytton, omitting the question mark.

Flytton looked at her, puzzled. They had been discussing hair.

"To Denbigh Court," Clarissa said. "I can't go without you."

"Oh, your ladyship, I'm sure you could manage perfectly well with the duke's household," said Flytton.

Clarissa gave her a hard look. "You do know that isn't true, I suppose?"

And Flytton did, though she thought she might not capitulate immediately. There were very few occasions in life when she had found herself in a bargaining position, but this was certainly one of them, and the Duke of Plymouth, she had heard, had very deep pockets indeed.

Chapter 56

The study door was closed and, as in the late earl's day, this was an unequivocal sign that the occupant shouldn't be disturbed. Three months' absence from Netherwood meant there was a good deal of business to be seen to, and Mrs. Powell-Hughes knew as well as anyone that Lady Henrietta would have enough on her plate without being further burdened. But the housekeeper still hadn't shared with anyone the story told to her by Anna all those weeks ago, and it had begun to feel like a guilty secret. The injustice done to Eve MacLeod was somehow compounded by the fact that Mrs. Powell-Hughes knew all about it yet had done absolutely nothing. This, it should be said, was how the housekeeper saw it: Anna had no such complaints. She had sought nothing but the satisfaction of revealing Absalom Blandford's true nature to a wider audience, but Mrs. Powell-Hughes, having heard the sorry tale, felt a responsibility to her new friend to take action. In the subsequent weeks she had kept a close eye on Absalom and had even, once or twice, crossed the yard with the intention of challenging him directly. But in his years as bailiff he had cultivated an aura of such remote and unapproachable self-sufficiency that she hadn't quite found the nerve. She was afraid of him, that was the truth of it, and his position seemed unassailable. He had not a single friend in the world, and yet no one openly spoke ill of him, unless it was to comment—more in wonder than in criticism—on his unrelenting professionalism, his dedication to the duties of bailiff, the seriousness of mind that was always evident in his expression and his bearing.

So Mrs. Powell-Hughes had abandoned all thoughts of heroically grasping the nettle. Instead, she had temporarily turned her back on the many tasks of the day yet to be accomplished, and had knocked at the closed door of Lady Henrietta's study. There had followed an unnerving silence. Behind her, Agnes had appeared from the morning room with a tray of used china and whispered, "Is everything all right, Mrs. Powell-'ughes?" for which she had received a withering nod and a dismissive flap of the hand.

"Come in."

Lady Henrietta's voice had a distracted quality, and indeed she seemed deeply engrossed in paperwork when the housekeeper entered the room, looking up only when her eyes reached the end of the document that was laid on the desk before her. Surprise registered on her face when she saw Mrs. Powell-Hughes, though she politely and swiftly replaced it with a smile of inquiry.

"I'm so sorry to disturb you, Lady Henrietta," said the housekeeper. "I know how busy you must be and I'm reluctant to add to your long list of concerns, but I find I must turn to you on a matter of some great delicacy."

"Goodness," said Henrietta. "How alarming."

She set down her pen and gave the housekeeper her full attention.

Secure in his orderly office, blissfully unaware of any impending disruption to his peace of mind, Absalom Blandford followed a list of figures in his ledger with the nib of his pen, his agile mind calculating the sum total as he went. These were the monthly accounts from Eve's Puddings & Pies: clear profit again, half of which he was excessively pleased to say still belonged to the estate. Not once in the difficult weeks and months following Lord Netherwood's death had Absalom had cause to question his actions in protecting the family's interests. Not once had he wavered in his certainty that he had done entirely the right thing, and because he was blessed with the happy knack of self-delusion, he now believed—truly believed—that he had been motivated not by an unhealthy hatred of the scheming Mrs. MacLeod, but by a pure and noble loyalty to the family he worked for. The facts of the matter had been manipulated in his mind to present a more satisfactory version of events in which his own role was above suspicion. When the dear late earl's natural generosity wandered into the realms of foolhardiness, his able helpmeet Absalom Blandford had stepped into protect not only Lord Netherwood's reputation, but also the fiscal interests of the estate.

This wasn't to say that his loathing of Eve had diminished in any way. On the contrary, it still burned with white heat at the core of his being, and as far as he was concerned it always would. Being a man of limited emotional range, Absalom had always kept a tenacious hold on the few feelings that did thrive in his near-barren soul. But his success in thwarting Eve's progress on the road to financial independence had purged some of the poison, and he found he could deal with her accounts with something approaching equanimity, even though it was her own despised hand that had entered the figures he now studied. He had cured himself, too, of the habit of watching her. There seemed to be less need, since some sort of revenge had been exacted. Absalom was quietly proud of this self-control. His superiority over lesser mortals was never much in doubt, but it was nice anyway to have it confirmed.

All of these thoughts were running in a contented loop through his mind when Lady Henrietta rapped on the door of his office and entered. He jumped at the sight of her, lost as he had been in his private world. She closed the door behind her and for a moment simply stood and stared at him in a manner he found profoundly disturbing. A flush began to spread upward from his neck and he reached involuntarily for the potpourri. Then, a little late, he remembered the protocol and stood up, though she at once ordered him down again, making him feel as if he was somehow bungling a perfectly simple situation. This, in turn, made him defensive, so that by the time she began to speak, he was already thoroughly rattled and all of his expertise was required to maintain a front of unruffled calm.

"I have just been told a most extraordinary thing," she said, getting immediately to the point in the interests of a swift conclusion. There were few people in Henrietta's world who made her feel uncomfortable, but Absalom Blandford was certainly one of them. "I have just been told that you defied my late father's wishes and denied Mrs. MacLeod his gift to her."

There it was: the charge, laid squarely at his feet. But without evidence, it was merely hearsay and tittle-tattle. And there was no evidence.

"If you mean Mrs. MacLeod's insistence that she was promised the business in its entirety, then I must protest my innocence," he said. "I have always discharged my duties with irreproachable efficiency, but I received no instructions to that effect from your late, lamented father."

"Forgive my bluntness," Henrietta said. "But I think you did."

He blanched, then flushed again, but his eyes never fell from her face. Calm, he told himself. Calm, calm.

"I think my father made his wishes absolutely plain to you," she went on. "But then he was taken from us, and you saw this as your opportunity to defy him for your own mysterious reasons."

His face assumed an expression of injured innocence.

"Your ladyship, you do me an injustice," he said. The sound of his own voice, steady and grave, was almost enough to move him to tears of righteous indignation. "My purpose here is to serve the estate, and I hope I have always done so with the utmost rigor and attention to detail."

"Mr. Blandford, your purpose here is to do as you are bid. Did my father instruct you to make a gift to Mrs. MacLeod of her business at the mill?"

He looked at her, and his silence eloquently expressed his sadness at being doubted.

"He did not, your ladyship. Had he done so, I would have carried out his wishes to the letter."

"Mr. Blandford, please don't be hasty." She moved closer, close enough to lean with both hands on the desk. He could only imagine the mess her fingers would be leaving on the polished mahogany. "Please think carefully before you answer so unequivocally. Could you, perhaps, be mistaken?"

For a fraction of a second, he wavered in his confidence. Something in her manner unnerved him. Then he rallied.

"There is no mistake, your ladyship, except that of Mrs. MacLeod in spreading this lamentable misrepresentation of my character."

"Mrs. MacLeod has never spoken to me of the matter. From what I understand, she has no wish to seek justice, preferring to expand her business at her own expense and without recourse to you. However, I have been told a story this morning by a trusted individual. I am minded to believe this individual because although I barely know you, Mr. Blandford, I knew my father very well indeed."

She paused. Still, he held her gaze.

"My father held Eve Williams—Mrs. MacLeod—in very high esteem. He admired her independence, her industriousness, her business acumen, and, more than likely, her beauty, because, after all, he was only human. To present the business to her as a wedding gift seems to me exactly the sort of thing my father would have done."

The bailiff's face twitched visibly under the effort of remaining impassive.

"And yet," he said, "he didn't."

"And so," she said, as if he hadn't spoken, "I did something I have never done before. I took my father's journal from the shelf."

Absalom's mouth dropped open and he snapped it shut again. Here, indeed, was an unforeseen difficulty.

"I have it still, back in the study, open at the page in October last year when he notes in his meticulous fashion that he spoke to you regarding his plans for Eve. How odd, then, that you have no such recollection."

The bailiff opened his mouth again to defend himself but found himself, for once, lost for words. Henrietta watched his face closely, and was satisfied; the trap had sprung and he was caught. He closed his eyes. To continue to protest his innocence remained an option; whatever the earl may or may not have written in a journal was evidence of a sort but, still, it would hardly be upheld as definitive in a court of law. And yet in the face of Lady Henrietta's clear-voiced case for the prosecution, Absalom Blandford, master of the cutting rejoinder, was powerless to respond.

She was in his office for ten minutes. Mrs. Powell-Hughes knew it, because she had noted the time when Lady Henrietta left the house through the kitchen door, and noted it again when she returned. It was hardly time to boil a kettle, she remembered thinking, hardly time to make a pot of tea. Lady Henrietta had gone back to the study to resume her business there and Absalom Blandford, the housekeeper couldn't help noticing, had left his office shortly afterward and had climbed into one of Lord Netherwood's Daimlers. Phillips had been driving. They were gone for half an hour, and later, when Mrs. Powell-Hughes had engineered a chance encounter with Phillips, he told her he had been asked by Lady Henrietta to drive the bailiff to Mitchell's Mill. No, the young chauffeur had said; he had no idea what Mr. Blandford's business there was. Mr. Blandford, said Phillips, was not the sort of chap to welcome cheerful inquiries about the whys and wherefores. This, conceded Mrs. Powell-Hughes, was incontrovertibly true. She had returned to the house resigned to the fact that though something was clearly up, she had no idea what it was. Yet.

They were busy with the lunch service at the mill when Absalom Blandford entered the kitchen and asked for a private word with Mrs. MacLeod. She was absorbed in making a batch of puff pastry, a labor of love requiring cool hands, a pound of best butter, and a patient temperament. Ginger stepped in front of her as the bailiff approached, and Nellie, who was tenderizing a batch of beef shin, stepped forward too with the wooden mallet still in her hand. Between them they might have pulverized him, but Eve looked up and saw from his face that he was already altered. The perpetual sneer was missing, and the arrogant tilt to the chin. He looked shifty rather than threatening, so she showed him through to her office, though she left the door wide open just as a precaution. In his hand he held a thick file of papers and in a curiously gauche and childlike gesture he thrust this at her the instant they were alone.

"What's this?" Eve said. She held the file gingerly, as if she couldn't trust it.

"The deeds to Ravenscliffe," he said, the words coming out in a rush in the end, though he'd been sure in the car on the way from Netherwood Hall that he would be unable to utter them. She stared at him, uncomprehending.

"It's yours," he said. "Lady Henrietta wishes you to have Ravenscliffe, rather than to continue to pay rent on the house. She asks me to wish you much joy, and she asks that you accept this gift as a formal apology from the estate, for failing to carry out her father's wishes with regard to the business."

Eve looked down at the bulky envelope, then back at the bailiff.

"Her father's wishes," she said, faltering a little, "were thwarted by you, Mr. Blandford."

He closed his eyes briefly, as if her words caused him pain. When he opened them again she was watching him steadily.

"Indeed," he said.

Still she watched him, waiting—perhaps—for an apology.

"The deeds to the house," he said, speaking carefully, "are recompense for last year's unfortunate misunderstanding. We understand you would prefer the business to remain a joint concern for the time being. However, we trust you will accept the house as a gesture from the family, in the late earl's memory."

It wasn't contrition, but it was as near as made no difference. But though Absalom clearly thought his ordeal was over, Eve had other ideas. As he made to move out of the office, she stepped smartly between him and the open door.

"Not so fast," she said. Ginger and Nellie, out in the kitchen, made ready to snare him should he bolt.

"Last October you told me Lord Netherwood never meant

472

to give me t'business. You made me feel very small, Mr. Blandford, and very, very foolish."

Almost imperceptibly, he nodded. There was no emotion
in his lizard's eyes, but his bearing betrayed discomfort, at which
she silently rejoiced.

"Are you telling me now that I was right and you were
wrong?"

He looked at her and something of his old contempt seemed
to color his features as if, having been forced to abase himself
before her, he took heart from the fact that he could fall no
further. Indeed, the journey back to full-blooded superiority
had already begun.

"The only thing I am telling you," he said, "is that Ravenscliffe is now yours. That, Mrs. MacLeod, is the end of my
business here. Good day."

He left then, sidestepping Nellie and Ginger, and beating a
hasty retreat through the courtyard. Behind him, in place of
a visiting card, he left an astonished silence.

There was no journal, never had been. Teddy Hoyland had
been the sort of man who was too busy living his life to spend
any time writing about it. But Henrietta had realized, as she
looked into her bailiff's cold eyes, that some sort of evidence
must be produced to shock him into a more confessional frame
of mind: that, and a direct threat of the termination of his
employment. Do not think, she had told him, that you are
unassailable here. Do not think that the years of service you
have given this estate give you, in return, the power to flout
my wishes. Unless you right this wrong, this will be your last
day as Netherwood bailiff.

Absalom Blandford had thought, just for a moment, that

perhaps dismissal would be preferable to the alternative. But a glimpse of a future stripped of his status was a terrifying thing, and was not to be borne. He was the Netherwood bailiff, and that was all he was; there were no other layers, no other strings to his bow or facets to his personality. He was useful to the estate, certainly: but the estate was essential to him. So he would survive this blow to his pride—had survived it; already it was history—and he would rise again. By midday he was seated once more at his desk and only the keenest observer of his habits and appearance would have noticed an occasional facial tic that now and then broke the surface of his composure; a sort of incomplete wink of the left eye, which came and then was immediately gone. A sign that beneath his habitual expression of haughty disdain lay a positive tumult of carefully suppressed yet conscientiously nurtured bitterness.

Chapter 57

The gentlemen of the press had been invited to view the new fleet of passenger liners, and since champagne had been mentioned, attendance was high. There were three new vessels, larger than their older siblings but bearing a distinct family resemblance: silver-gray hulls, buff-colored stacks with a broad navy band and a thinner band of red immediately below the blue. They were distinctive ships, the most easily identifiable of any sailing under the Red Ensign. Silas had named them for constellations—*Cassiopeia, Orion,* and *Pegasus,* romantic names with popular appeal but touched by greatness. Silas and Hugh, immaculate in evening dress, stood at either side of a gangplank, welcoming their visitors like society hosts at a London club. Up on deck an orchestra played the "Britannia" overture and vigilant waiters—the dining room staff that had been hired by the company for the inaugural voyage—offered flutes of Dom Pérignon to each new arrival and immediate refills when glasses were drained. The journalists were decked out in dinner jackets too, though Wilberforce Trencham wore tweed, as he always did. A professional assignment was no place for dress shirt and tails, in his view. He eschewed the champagne, too; with a glass in one hand, how was one to take notes? He badgered the hosts with questions, not about the fine marquetry ceiling of the ballroom or the inlaid marble floors of the bathrooms, but about fuel consumption and tonnage and the relative merits of comfort over speed. How many knots, he asked, would *Cassiopeia* make? A ship this size must surely be forced to keep under twenty knots to avoid the massive incremental increase in fuel?

"Thank you for your concern, Mr. Trencham," Silas said. "But please rest assured that we have coal aplenty in our own Yorkshire colliery." There was an appreciative titter from the champagne-fueled audience.

"And so how many knots would you expect your liners to make? Forgive me for repeating myself, Mr. Whittam, but I don't believe you answered my question."

"Our commitment is to luxury, not speed," Silas said. He smiled at the journalists collected around him. "The ship does not exist that betters our fleet in the quality of its accommodation. First class only and, waiting for them in Jamaica, a first-class hotel."

"Yes, yes, but how many knots will this vessel make?"

This was how it was with Wilberforce Trencham. His head could not be turned by the trappings of luxury on the new Whittam liners when all he wanted to know was how fast they would sail.

"Sixteen knots," Silas said, though he had hoped to evade a direct answer, for reasons that were immediately exposed.

"Quite slow, then," said Mr. Trencham. "Slower than Cunard's vessels. Awfully long journey to Jamaica."

"We're not after the Blue Riband, Mr. Trencham."

"Happily for you." The journalist sniffed and pocketed his notebook, as if he'd seen all there was to offer and was sorely disappointed. Hugh, who had been silent until now, said: "Mr.

Trenchham, our aim is to provide our passengers with a voyage they will wish to prolong, not one that they long to be over. These ships will redefine first class." A low buzz of agreement emanated from the crowd, though Mr. Trenchham didn't add to it.

"And how much has the Colonial Office put forward to support the new venture?" he said. This was an impertinent question, and both Silas and Hugh ignored it, instead steering the pack away from the ballroom where they currently stood and up the magnificent central staircase to the upper deck.

"Irritating bastard," Silas said *sotto voce* to Hugh.

"Next time he asks a question, just answer it," Hugh said. "You make it appear we have something to hide. Who cares about knots? Or, for that matter, how pally you might be with Alfred Lyttelton and the Colonial Office. The paying passenger doesn't. Stop being so evasive."

Silas took the point, but grudgingly. He rubbed his temple, where a headache threatened. The strain of the past few months had been immense: the *Pegasus* would set sail at the end of September and all the cabins were fully booked. Two weeks later the *Cassiopeia* would leave harbor, and then, two weeks after that, the *Orion*. And yet the Whittam Hotel, when he had left it at the end of his last visit, still lacked shutters at its windows and mosquito screens at its doors. It was highly possible that he might have to accommodate his passengers in the Mountain Springs Hotel, though it would half kill him to have to admit defeat and ask. The Whittam staff, all recruited locally—a prerequisite of the deal with the Colonial Office, otherwise Silas would certainly have recruited in London—persisted in an insolent refusal to appear in any way helpful. They lolled about the hotel as if Silas had built it for their own leisure. That, or they weren't to be found at all. One could be forgiven for thinking that the cheerful ping of the brass bell on the reception desk was a signal to the staff to lie low. It was all a source of immense concern. He thought he might yet have to sail ahead of the *Pegasus* to reassure himself.

"I hear there are difficulties with the hotel." This was Mr. Trencham again, settling with uncanny accuracy on the least welcome of questions. He was so close that Silas could see the hairs that sprouted unchecked from inside the journalist's ears.

"From whom?" On his other side, Silas heard a hiss of irritation from Hugh, which he ignored.

"I never reveal my sources, Mr. Whittam, but your answer confirms my suspicions. They do say that only the Americans can manage the Jamaicans. Apart from anything else, they're a sight closer to the island than you are."

"Can't fault your geography, Trencham. But do tell your spy from me that the Whittam Hotel will be a flagship resort, and the Americans are welcome to watch and learn."

The journalist laughed. He so enjoyed needling Silas Whittam. There was no spy, in fact; but something was troubling the man, and since the ships looked quite remarkably beautiful, he had surmised that the hotel must be the problem. He delved for his notebook and scribbled a few words, glancing up to see Silas rub once more at his temple. Mr. Trencham smiled. There was nothing personal in his satisfaction; he had no grievance against Silas Whittam at all. But in his experience, life never ran smoothly for anyone for as long as it had apparently run smoothly for Whittam. Wilberforce Trencham just wanted to be there, notebook in hand, when the great man fell.

The town hall office was festooned with pink roses; the blousy, wanton kind that spilled forth their petals and their fragrance with wild abandon. Frederick Sidebottom, the registrar, raised an eyebrow at the sight. All very well, he thought, but who'd be sweeping up the mess when today's comings and goings had knocked petals and leaves all over the floor? Not the bride and groom, that was for sure. Mind you, he thought, the room looked grand, all trussed up with flowers like this. Most of the civil weddings he presided over were drab affairs, a quick in-and-out, ring offered and accepted, register signed and a forced smile for Mr. Mainwaring and his box Brownie, then on their way. Today, though, Mrs. MacLeod had come first thing with armfuls of blooms and foliage and had spent a good two hours stringing them up on the walls and the backs of the chairs. Then her husband had come in with a trellis affair, a metal arch, which he'd stood at the head of the aisle between the rows of chairs, and then watched as his wife twisted flowers and leaves through that as well. She'd sprayed them all with water so that tiny droplets still hung on them now like morning dew, giving them a freshly picked appearance. They'd taken liberties, strictly speaking, and Mr. Sidebottom would have been well within his rights to ask them to take their flowers elsewhere, but although he wasn't the most romantic of individuals, some small neglected corner of his heart softened at the effect, and he held his peace.

He cast an eye over his desk. Polished to a high shine, with his name nailed to it on a brass plaque. Mr. F. J. W. Sidebottom. Many were the times he'd had cause to silently thank his parents—long departed now, of course—for their wisdom and ambition in giving him three fine Christian names, a string of initials to elevate him in his chosen field and confer upon him gravitas and import. Plain Fred Sidebottom couldn't have ever been a town registrar; Fred Sidebottom would have had to be a coal merchant or a chandler. But Frederick Jeremiah William Sidebottom—now there was a man who was destined to preside over a register of births, marriages, and deaths, the solemn rituals of a town's population.

He walked to the double doors at the back of the room

and flung them open with aplomb. A collection of guests had assembled in the galleried entrance hall, and their animated chatter subsided at the sight of Mr. Sidebottom, big-bellied and broad-chested, imposing in a pinstriped three-piece suit. He scanned the gathering and his eyes alighted on the Countess of Netherwood and Lady Henrietta Hoyland, whose presence at the town hall was so remarkable that Mr. Sidebottom momentarily forgot himself and stared at them in a foolish, around-eyed manner. The striking of the clock's bell on the hour brought him to his senses. He took command once more, reordered his features into a dignified half-smile, and without words but with a considerable flourish, he invited them into his inner sanctum.

"Did you think of asking Eve and Daniel here today?"

Hugh and Silas were still on the *Cassiopeia*, but they were alone now. They reclined like overdressed holidaymakers in two cream canvas deck chairs on the upper level of the ship. On the floor between them stood an open bottle of Dom Pérignon which Silas reached for now and, holding it to his mouth, took a copious swig.

"Indeed I did," he said. He belched, handed Hugh the bottle, then leaned back in his chair with his eyes closed. "Not only did I think of it, but I also acted upon the thought. Invited Evie, the gardener, Seth, and the girlies. However, they declined."

He looked rather sorry for himself, Hugh thought: Silas was full of arrogant confidence and pride, but he was also a younger brother who wanted his sister to see what he'd achieved.

"Shame," Hugh said. He lifted the bottle to his mouth and took a swig too. "Another time, perhaps. What kept them away?"

Silas looked at him and grimaced. "The wedding of Anna Rabinovich to that dreadful union agitator. What she sees in him I do not know. Mind you, she's a handful herself. Just as well they marry each other. Spare some other poor devil the fate. Hugh?"

Hugh had stood up, apparently in some agitation, and was now standing at the rail, gripping it hard and staring at the row of warehouses on the dockside.

"What have I said? Don't tell me you wanted to go to the wedding."

Silas laughed, but Hugh, when he turned, looked grave.

"I proposed to her," he said.

Silas gaped at him. "To the Russian?" he said.

"To Anna, yes."

There was a silence. Gulls wheeled overhead and threw obscene cries into the empty sky. Silas and Hugh looked at each other, neither of them knowing what to say.

"I had no idea," Silas said at last.

"No. Neither did I, really. But then I saw her again on that last visit and . . ."

"Lucky escape, old chap. She's a willful little harpy who thinks far too much of herself."

"Stop it." Hugh's voice was harsh. "She's a better person than you and me, that much I know."

Silas gave a skeptical laugh. Hugh glared. He felt, in this moment, that Silas Whittam might benefit from a good old-fashioned thrashing. He didn't look like a man who had ever taken a punch, or thrown one; his perfectly regular features had an almost womanly delicacy, and Hugh imagined the pale skin splitting like a peach as his fist drove into the beautiful, mocking face. He turned away again, to keep himself from temptation.

"I was going to sail back to Kingston," Silas said, moving instinctively into safer territory. "Soon. Before *Pegasus* leaves harbor. I thought I'd stay until the first guests arrive, just to be sure they get what we've promised. But you could go in my place. What do you think?"

"Fine," said Hugh. "As you wish." He didn't turn around.

There was very little ceremony in the event, in spite of all the roses. Anna and Amos met with a smile on the town hall steps and waited together until the small collection of friends and family were seated inside. She wore a cream two-piece, which she'd made from a Butterwick's pattern, adapting the unadventurous cut of the skirt to give it more swish and flair. Amos surprised everyone by appearing in a new, rather well-made suit in dark gray wool, which he wore with a white waistcoat and a navy-and-white-dotted necktie. He carried a soft gray Homburg.

"Nice," Anna said, when she saw him.

"You expected my old tweeds and a flat cap, didn't you?" Amos said. "You're not t'only one with a bit of an eye, you know."

He took her hand and pressed it to his lips in a moment of silent communication. Then, still holding hands, they went side by side into the room, down the short, carpeted aisle, and under the bower of blooms. There, with the utmost simplicity and economy of words, they pledged their love for each other and became man and wife.

Chapter 58

fterward, at Ravenscliffe, they all gathered in the September sunshine and ate as if they'd spent the morning in hard labor. The spread consisted entirely of Russian delicacies: *pirozhki*, *blinis*, caviar—which had arrived by train from Fortnum & Mason—potato salad, pickles, smoked fish, and borscht, ladled into tiny cups and served with dark, grainy bread. The health, wealth, and happiness of the bride and groom were toasted with vodka, poured again and again from bottles that Anna had packed into an ice-filled tub. Mrs. Powell-Hughes, knocking back her third, had an uncharacteristic flush to the face and a marvelous, inexplicable sense of well-being. She had manipulated the staff rota to give herself a half-day holiday, and to feel part of this merry band of well-wishers was beyond price, as unfamiliar a sensation to her as the particular saltiness of the black fish roe on her tongue or the rush of heat in her throat as the vodka slipped down.

"Are you having fun, Mrs. Powell-Hughes?" Anna said, slipping an arm through hers and giving it a squeeze.

"I certainly am, dear. I've eaten enough to sink a battleship, but I couldn't name a single thing." She laughed brightly, full of the joy of the unpronounceable.

"This is food of my childhood," Anna said. "It makes me think I should perhaps go back—to visit, I mean."

Mrs. Powell-Hughes, who had traveled—just once—from Netherwood, to her sister's boardinghouse on the East Yorkshire coast, nodded sagely.

"You do that, dear. Take your husband. Travel broadens the mind." She hiccupped twice.

"Bit hair-raising in Russia at the moment."

This was Henrietta. She had come with Thea to the wedding because Tobias had refused, on the grounds that he knew neither bride nor groom from Adam. "Have you read the papers? Sounds rather brutal. I should wait until things pipe down."

Anna said: "Things never pipe down in Russia."

"Still, though," said Henrietta, "I don't suppose it's always quite as alarming as it is at the moment. No need to take unnecessary risks."

Mrs. Powell-Hughes, who didn't have the first idea what they were talking about—show her a housekeeper with time to read the newspapers and she would show you a housekeeper who wasn't doing her job—said: "Don't the girls look lovely," and the three of them turned their attention to Eliza, Ellen, and Maya, who were prettily handing out further titbits, though it was hard to know who was going to manage any more. Eliza privately thought this wedding a bit of a disappointment, though she was careful not to show it in her face. She was happy for Anna and Amos, but unhappy for herself. There were few enough chances in life to shine in front of a captive audience and yet she had been required only to sit patiently in the town hall and then take Anna's flowers from her when the time came to put on the wedding ring. She was beginning to think direct action might be needed on her part, and she wondered if she might ask for dance classes. She had seen a sign in Barnsley when she went with her mam to see the new shop: it hung above the high windows of an old cotton mill. *Mademoiselle Evangeline's School of Dance*, it said. *All levels, beginners welcome.* Eliza had felt an immediate connection with Mademoiselle Evangeline, even without clapping eyes on her. She was sure that within those austere and unlikely walls lay her destiny. She made a graceful pirouette at the thought of it, and the blinis she carried spun off the plate. Amos's friend Enoch bent down with her to help collect them up again.

"Pop 'em back on t'plate," he said. "Nob'dy'll be any t'wiser. Nowt wrong wi' a bit o' muck." He winked at her and she smiled.

"You 'ave one, then," she said, and he laughed and took one from her.

"Now then, 'ere's Lady 'enrietta, see if she'd like one an' all."

Eliza held out the plate to Henrietta but felt compelled in the presence of grandness to confess. "They've been on t'grass, your ladyship," she said, dipping into a little curtsy, and Henrietta said, "In that case I'll have two," so everyone laughed. Eliza moved on, collecting smiles, spreading happiness. Henrietta turned to Enoch.

"I think you've been very discreet, Mr. Wadsworth," she said.

He blinked at her from behind his around lenses.

"In what way?" he said.

"You don't seem to have breathed a word to anyone," she said. "Unless they all know and are waiting until I leave to poke fun."

He shook his head. "Nowt funny about it, your ladyship. I admire you, if you really want to know. Not many ladies of your social standing spare a thought for owt beyond their social calendar."

"Harsh, yet probably true," she said. "Well, anyway, I'm grateful to you. Not that it's a secret, of course . . ."

"But neither is it common knowledge. Understood." He tapped the side of his bony nose.

"Look at those two. Thick as thieves," Amos said. He and Eve were standing together a little distance away from the main gathering. Amos looked grand, Eve thought: statesmanlike in his tailored suit, and glowing with pride and pleasure. Constantly his eyes sought out Anna, as if he was making sure she was real.

"It's that vodka," Eve said. "Unless they actually know each other. Do they?"

"Doubt it. Mind you, Enoch'll talk to anybody."

Eve smiled. "Bet you never thought you'd 'ave t'Countess of Netherwood and 'er sister-in-law at your wedding."

This was risky, but he took it well.

"Aye, strange," he said. "But what's to be done? Anna likes 'em, they like 'er. Thing is, she sees no difference. I look at 'em and see nowt but privilege, whereas Anna, she's more open, like."

"Well, it's a changing world, Amos."

"Aye well, it can't change fast enough for me."

For a while, they were silent. Then Amos looked at her and said: "You made t'right choice y'know. For me, and for you."

"I think I did, though I was sorry to 'urt you."

He nodded, acknowledging the hurt: no point pretending otherwise, when it had been so plain to see at the time.

"Now, though, I feel blessed," he said. They both looked at Anna, who was laughing with Seth, holding the back door open for him as he crept with extravagant care into the garden bearing a large platter of pineapple pieces—his own, the first harvest.

"You are blessed," Eve said. "You both are."

"Get on with you," Amos said. "You'll 'ave me in tears."

The time to leave was drawing near and Anna withdrew from the party, responding to an emotional pull from the house that she no longer tried to resist. She had never shied from change, and she didn't now, but her assertion to Amos, oft repeated, that she would be happy with him anywhere had been as much to convince herself as to reassure him. She felt assaulted by conflicting emotions. Excitement, happiness, sorrow, gratitude, anxiety: all these feelings fought for precedence and she felt worn down by them. Life would seem simpler, she thought, when they left. Some little distance was required for a clearer head. She and Amos had planned four nights in London—Maya was to stay here—and then they would begin a six-month let on a sturdy Victorian villa in Ardington, from where they would be well placed to campaign when a general election was called. This, Anna longed for. The by-election had given her a taste for the fight. Webster Thorne, she thought, should be quaking in his boots.

She had packed earlier, before the wedding, and open on the bed was her small suitcase: brown leather, scuffed at its corners, scarred by former travels. It had once belonged to her father, and she was certain that when he had flung it at her, telling her to take her things and not return, he hadn't intended it as a farewell gift. Nevertheless, she was pleased she had it because it was all she had now from her Russian past: this, and a collection of memories of variable and dubious clarity. When she thought about her life in Kiev, which was rarely, it was as if she looked at events through a window of frosty glass, the images blurred and distorted through patterns of ice. She hadn't really meant what she said to Mrs. Powell-Hughes about wanting to go back. That was just the borscht and the blinis and—doubtless—the vodka, taking her to a time when she'd thought there were no limits to her parents' love. She was glad, though, that their blind prejudice had forced her away: glad, too, that she'd loved Leo and that he'd known the joy of Maya before he died. Through another person's eyes, perhaps, her recent life might appear dragged down by turmoil and tragedy, but she saw it differently. She had never wished for a settled existence. Her parents had expected her to marry a merchant's son: to grow fat and complacent and, ultimately, unhappy, as they had. But her girlhood dreams, vivid and startling, were always of escape: birds freed from nets, butterflies released from jars, a dancing black bear breaking free from its shackles. And in the end, she had fled too. Now she stood on the brink of change once more, and this new turning in the road was simply another stage of the same journey: the adventure, continued. This was how she looked at life.

She moved over to the bed and closed the case, snapping the brass clasps to secure it. A tap at the door and Eve came in. She smiled.

"You look serious," she said.

"Serious business."

"Right enough. Can I 'elp?"

Eve indicated the suitcase, but Anna shook her head.

"All done."

"Good," Eve said.

They looked at each other.

"You'll come and visit? Stay sometimes?"

"Of course. A lot, if Maya has say in it."

"And Ardington isn't far, is it? Two stops on t'train."

Anna nodded. Two stops on the train. How often had they repeated that to each other?

"And with t'new shop in Barnsley—"

"—we'll see each other often."

There. They even finished each other's sentences, so eager was each to convince the other and so frequently had they tried. Then, as they stood swapping smiles of reassurance and en-couragement, Eve gave up the fight and began to cry. One of them had to, because just as this was the beginning of something, so it was also an ending, and this had to be acknowledged, respected, honored. Anna rushed across the room, wrapped her arms around Eve and gave way to tears too, and for a while they abandoned themselves to their sorrow like Ellen and Maya, luxuriating in the relief of it.

When the tears abated, they clung to each other for a little longer and then sat down on the edge of Anna's single bed feeling limp and weary. Eve looked at Anna and laughed.

"Look at t'state o' you. What's Amos going to think?"

"If I look as bad as you, he'll wonder why he married me."

"Not likely. I've never seen a man more smitten."

"Daniel?"

"As smitten, maybe. Not more smitten."

They smiled. Eve pulled a handkerchief from a pocket of her skirt and blew her nose, then offered it to Anna, who did the same.

"Remember, won't you, that you always have a home here? This house is yours as much as mine. In fact, if it wasn't for you, Blandford would have thrown us all out at t'end of t'tenancy."

"I think even he couldn't have argued with another twelve months' rent in cash," Anna said.

"You don't know 'ow much 'e loathes me. I think loathing me is what gets 'im out of bed every morning."

Anna laughed.

Eve said, "It's not right though, Anna, that you're leaving. Ravenscliffe was your idea, remember?" She switched into Anna's accent, pitch perfect: "Kitchen big enough to dance polka."

Anna gave her a shove. "And so it is," she said. "When you're out at work, that's what I do."

"Ah, that's why t'washing never gets done," Eve said.

They leaned into each other, propping one another up, and were quiet for a little while. The sounds of conversation and laughter drifted up from the garden. They should go downstairs,

Eve thought, before they were missed. But when she spoke, what she said was: "Look. About Silas."

Anna nodded, understanding Eve's impulse. He was always between them these days; the only subject they had ever failed to see eye to eye on, the only thing they hadn't ever been able to discuss. Could they be friends, Eve asked now, her voice fragile with tremulous hope. Anna, gentle but direct, said she didn't think that was very likely. They were too different, she said: Silas felt the same, she was sure of it. And how could she set aside her own qualms, now that she was married to Amos?

"No, I know," Eve said. "It's not easy. But if everybody could just try . . ."

"Perhaps if Silas could relent, and give Edward Wakefield his job back?"

"Perhaps if Amos could apologize fully to Silas?"

"Perhaps if pigs could fly across Netherwood Common?"

They laughed, but ruefully.

"Y'know, Silas really isn't all bad," Eve said.

Anna shrugged. "Perhaps not. But neither is he all good."

"No, 'appen not. But he's my brother. To 'ave 'im back means a lot to me."

"I know this," Anna said. "And I don't belittle it. But you must just accept that Silas means different things to you and me and Amos."

Eve looked troubled, melancholy. Watching her, Anna wished she could say what Eve wanted to hear. She sought for something else instead, some other kind of solace to offer.

"Eve," she said. "This must never, ever come between us."

Here was something they could hold on to.

"Never," Eve said. She took Anna's hand and clasped it vehemently in her own, keeping it there for a moment. Then she released it and smiled, though a little too brightly. She doesn't believe, Anna thought, and she, too, was wondering—

490

behind her smile—if their friendship would survive the influence of Silas Whittam. Between Eve's blindness and Amos's hatred lay an ocean of potential for grievous harm.

"Come on," Eve said then. "You've got an 'usband waiting downstairs. Best be off."

They both stood. There was a lingering awkwardness between them still, a sense of a difficulty unresolved. Time, perhaps, would erase it. Certainly, time would tell.

"Leave that suitcase," Eve said. "Seth'll fetch it. I know 'e'd like to."

"What did you think of his pineapple?" Anna said. Eve wrinkled her nose, dropped her voice. "Awful," she said and suddenly they were laughing again, rocking silently with shared mirth because the fruit really had been dreadful: under-ripe, woody, quite without flavor. Daniel had tried to dissuade the boy from presenting it, promising a better crop next year, but there was no telling Seth anything, once his mind was set. Still, thought Eve as they walked downstairs together now in good spirits, the pineapple had done them a favor in the end.

Chapter 59

September passed, October and November followed in rapid pursuit. Parkinson wondered aloud where the time was going, so swiftly did the days spin by. It's because we're so busy, Mrs. Powell-Hughes told him, it's because the work never ceases, and she was right. The house was alive with comings and goings; as one set of guests left with merry farewells, others would arrive with boisterous hellos. When the dowager countess left for Denbigh Court in September—taking Isabella with her and therefore, unavoidably, Bryony too, to whom Tobias had given, unkindly, the nickname Barnacle—the young Lord and Lady Netherwood had flung open the great doors of Netherwood Hall as if her absence was all they'd been waiting for. There followed a near-constant stream of visitors. The speed trials in early September—"A triumph," said Parkinson gloomily, "if only in the sense that no one died"—brought forty guests to the house, and twenty-five motorcars to the stable yard. For two days no one was safe on the avenues, since when contestants weren't racing, they were practicing, and there was no peace to be had until it was all over. Wally Goldman took the title in his Ford Model A, managing an average speed of twenty miles an hour, even accounting for a couple of hair-raising bends where the avenue met the lane. Tobias, in a Daimler Wagonette de Luxe, had to settle for second place, and Thea, in a brand-new Daimler Phaeton, came in fifth overall and was crowned motoring queen at the last-night banquet. There were riotous scenes when the chair she sat in was lifted high by four young men and carried in a lap of honor around the table. Parkinson spent more time in the cellars fetching wine than he did in the dining room. Henrietta began to feel old.

There followed, in the subsequent weeks, four shooting parties, a point-to-point, and a fancy-dress ball, the theme of which was The Hunt: all the ladies were foxes, all the gentlemen were hounds or masters of the hunt. The chase—a wild career through the ground-floor rooms of the house—ended when the foxes had all been caught and corraled in the library. Three of the hounds went too far and had their foxes pinned to the floor as if they really did intend to tear them limb from limb, so Tobias, magnificent in white breeches and red jacket, clambered onto the Chippendale library table in his riding boots and gave a blast on his huntsman's horn to break things up. Footmen watched with impassive faces. The ladies were saved but the Chippendale table was not.

More and more, Henrietta absented herself from these hedonistic entertainments and even Dickie, who was game for most things, declared them "a bit much" and took himself off to the Italian Riviera with an old school chum. Thea and Toby reigned supreme in the palace of high jinks. Henrietta remembered with fondness the days when a dinner party would conclude with cards and music in the drawing room, and no one wished for anything more. She was no prude, but wantonness and impropriety in private was one thing: in public, quite another. And yet the boundaries of what was and wasn't acceptable were being constantly pushed, as if a life lived quietly was no life at all. Henrietta, increasingly drawn by her high-minded and earnest suffragist friends, found herself less and less dependent on the attentions of Thea. Thea, in turn, filled her empty hours by planning party after party as autumn turned into winter, the pinnacle of which was a Fireworks Spectacular—her response to a startlingly persuasive plea from the head gardener that the Grand Canal should be officially opened in some way commensurate with its grandeur. Daniel had requested a meeting, not in the morning room where generations of countesses had always conducted their business, but by the side of the canal itself from where he had invited her to join him on the farthest stepping stone, this being the vantage point from which the water looked its most dramatic.

"What you have here, your ladyship, is the largest uninterrupted stretch of water of any private garden in the kingdom," he had said. "Just be still for a few moments and consider this fact."

His tone wasn't quite that of gardener to countess, but Thea's sense of social superiority was not what it would have been had she been born to this life. She still had a habit of smiling at the footmen and asking them how they were, and she had asked her new lady's maid to call her Thea (which the maid declined to do—the very idea made her feel faint). So, standing there on the square gray stone, she had taken no offense at the slight reprimand in Daniel MacLeod's voice and had done as she was bid. She gazed out across the water and as she did so she felt she looked at the canal for the first time, though of course no one could fail to miss it. It lay there before her, magnificent, glassy, and reproachful, and she had turned to Daniel and said: "Fireworks, do you think?" which was, of course, the perfect answer.

So fireworks it was, and such fireworks that the county had

never seen. Locals gathered on Harley Hill and Netherwood Common to watch the spectacle from a distance. Pyrotechnicians came and arranged their wares around the water's perimeter, sending thousands of pounds' worth of explosives squealing into the black winter sky, releasing red, blue, and white lights above the vast mirror of the canal. Afterward, on the main terrace, kitchen staff—noses blue with cold—served beef bouillon in enamel mugs, hot baked potatoes with butter, and toffee apples. Thea, mastermind of the whole affair, felt heady and powerful with the success of it. She sought out Toby and tilted her face up to his. She knew she looked adorable, cheeks rosy with the cold air and the hot broth. With her eyes on his, her fingers found the buttons of his greatcoat and she opened them, then snuggled into the folds of the coat with him. He stooped to kiss her.

"You taste beefy," she said. She slipped a hand deep inside the waistband of his trousers and felt the shocking contrast of his warm flesh against her cold skin. He gasped, then moaned into her hair like a helpless animal. He pulled the coat tighter around and submitted to her skillful attentions: tiny movements, adroitly placed. In seconds she brought him shuddering to a silent climax and then she brought out her hand, wiped it, deft and efficient, on his tweed waistcoat, and slipped away. He lost sight of her almost at once; it was dark, and the terrace was crowded with friends. His wife had as many tricks as a seasoned whore and this should probably trouble him, he thought: for the life of him, though, he couldn't do anything but smile.

Denbigh Court would do very well, Clarissa thought. It was older and more distinguished than Netherwood Hall: begun in the sixteenth century and completed in the seventeenth, it had been designed by a student of Inigo Jones and had all the free and fanciful hallmarks of the Jacobean age. Netherwood Hall, by comparison, was quite flat and dull. Archie Partington would do well enough too, though Clarissa had made it plain, in terms that couldn't be misunderstood, that their relationship would not extend into the bedroom. His face had fallen, but she had stood firm. It wasn't as if he lacked an heir; he had offspring from both of his previous marriages. And she presumed that, if he still felt the urge to seek physical pleasure, then he must have some arrangement already in place. There was no earthly reason for his marriage to Clarissa to alter the way they both lived. All of this she set out with no more emotion than a lawyer, adding that if Archie should predecease her, she must insist on inheriting, in her name for the duration of her own life, his Park Lane mansion. She would not be forced to hole up with his oldest son, Henry, and his fat wife, whose name she had been told countless times but which continued to elude her. Archie listened to all of this and when she finished, he said: "Very well, my dear. Received and understood," and then he gave her a bracelet of emeralds and she felt almost sorry that she'd been so stern.

"How do you like the duke?" she said later to Isabella. "Shall you be able to love your new papa?"

"Shall I be expected to?" Isabella asked, with some surprise. "I don't see why I should if you don't."

Clarissa had chided Isabella for her insolence, but half-heartedly. After all, she made a perfectly good point. However, she must remember, said Clarissa, that through the Duke of Plymouth, great connections could be made. He dined with the king whenever he was in London, she said, widening her eyes significantly, as if to suggest that Isabella might reasonably hope to throw her cap at a prince. Isabella was skeptical: wasn't royal blood a requirement in the bride of a prince?

"Depends," Bryony said in the bedroom that night. "One of the younger ones with no chance of the throne, perhaps. You're the daughter of an earl, and you'll be stepdaughter of a duke. Quite the aristocrat. I, of course, can hope for very little, especially now my parents have brought disgrace upon me. I shall be free to marry for love, however. I shall live a passionate life with a man who cares nothing for material wealth."

She sounded jubilant, not tragic, and Isabella was silent. She didn't know what to say. The older girl seemed to have the knack of deflating Isabella's spirits while affecting to buoy them up. She wondered if she might have Bryony sent back to London.

Claude Reynard had given notice. César Ritz was building a new hotel in Piccadilly that would open in spring next year, and Monsieur Reynard simply couldn't resist the glamour, the cachet, or—perhaps most significantly—the promise of working once more among compatriots. This Yorkshire kitchen had lost its appeal; he wished to bark orders in French and have them understood; he wished to sit, eat, and behave how he liked, free from the baleful gaze of an English butler; he wished never again to be asked to provide a crowd of unruly inebriates with fifty baked potatoes in place of dinner. At home in Bordeaux, *pommes de terre au four* was what his grandmother had fed to the pigs, and they did not require an Escoffier-trained chef to produce them. Sarah Pickersgill, given the bare bones of the news by Mrs. Powell-Hughes, dropped like a stone onto a kitchen chair and looked at the housekeeper with damp and wounded eyes.

"Why?" she said.

Mrs. Powell-Hughes said: "He has his reasons," which meant she wasn't entirely sure herself.

"I believe he's had a better offer," said Parkinson. "The London Ritz wants him, and if you ask me—"

"I haven't asked you, Mr. Parkinson," said Sarah, made bold by her grief and disappointment. "And I don't want to 'ear it."

She stood and ran from the room, her pinafore at her face to catch the tears. The butler looked at Mrs. Powell-Hughes in indignation, but she wasn't in the mood to join him.

"Let her go," she said. "She'll come to her senses before long."

There was a pause, during which Parkinson wondered when, exactly, it had become acceptable for an undercook to dish up insolence to a butler. For now, and while he still could, he blamed Claude Reynard.

"The sooner the Frenchman goes, the better," he said. "Good riddance, I say. He has his merits, but I'm afraid I just don't like him."

"Well, Mr. Parkinson, you surprise me," said Mrs. Powell-Hughes. "You've done such a good job of concealing it."

He was polishing the plate as she spoke and something in her tone made him stop and look up from the task. The house-keeper had turned away to busy herself with table linen, but Parkinson got the distinct impression that her shoulders were shaking with laughter. For a little while, he watched her, hurt and indignation battling in his breast, but soon enough the shaking stopped and she began to hum lightly as she folded the linen glass cloths and placed them in tidy piles in a cupboard drawer. But he felt unsettled. It seemed to him—and it had done now for quite some months—that the ordered surface of his existence was starting to craze with hairline cracks, and the sight of the housekeeper's private mirth was yet more evidence of a creeping deterioration in standards of behavior. It was disorienting; he was surrounded on all sides by the familiar, yet by tiny increments the world was altering, and not for the better. It was a measure of his distress that he found himself wondering who was butler at Denbigh Court and whether the dowager countess might insist he be replaced by her own dear Parkinson.

Chapter 60

On December 4, the prime minister, Arthur Balfour, surrendered the seals of office, driven out by dissent in his party over tariff reform, and the shrewd Scotsman Henry Campbell-Bannerman stepped up to the breach with a minority Liberal government. There'd be a general election within weeks, and Enoch was worried. Balfour's game plan was to maneuver the opposition into office, dragging all the old Liberal disagreements into the spotlight and ushering in an easy Conservative victory at the next election. But his tactics were wrong, said Enoch to Amos.

"Dead wrong. Campbell-Bannerman's a canny bugger. Look at 'is Cabinet. Asquith, Gray, Haldane—it's stronger already than t'last lot. All Balfour's done is given t'Liberals a chance to shine."

"Aye, I reckon you're right," Amos said. They were in their office at the YMA, but union business lay unfinished on their desks while bigger themes enjoyed their full attention. This was how it was these days: hard to concentrate on minor amendments to this or that motion when the nation was in a state of limbo and every day the newspapers promised that an election was imminent. "Webster Thorne's walking around Ardington like 'e's lost a penny and found a shilling. Thinks there's a place for 'im in t'Foreign Office, by all accounts. Pal of Gray's from a long time back, apparently."

"Balliol," said Enoch, glumly. "That lot all know each other, one way or another."

"It's what you know that counts in Ardington, not who you know," Amos said. He smiled. "Anyway, we've got a trump card now."

"Oh aye?"

"Anna. She's on first-name terms wi' t'mayor, she's making a new set o' curtains for t'miners' welfare. Butcher saves t'best cuts o' meat for 'er. Greengrocer lets 'er know when 'e gets Savoys in. You'd think she were born and bred."

It was true. Anna had lived in Ardington for just two months, but already she was part of the local furniture, familiar and welcome. Molly Jenks, who for the past thirty years had sold an unchanging range of strictly serviceable balls of wool from her shop on the main street, was now stocking bolts of cloth and reels of ribbon so that Anna would go in more often. She sat on the Poor Relief Committee, the Miners' Welfare Committee, and had been asked to join the school board when the new term began in January. Twice a week she and Maya took the train to Netherwood, and the stationmaster wouldn't let the train go until they were safely on it, even if—as sometimes happened—Maya refused to run and they were five minutes late.

"Don't get complacent," Enoch said now. "It'll take more than Anna to send you to Parliament." He was in a black mood. Just days, in all likelihood, before an election was called and the Liberals were looking like the future.

Amos looked at him across the desk.

"It will," he said. "But if she was married to Webster Thorne—perish the thought—we should be worried. So think on."

501

The house they had rented had a number, not a name, which struck Anna as rather sad, since it was such a characterful dwelling in every other way. It was an old weaver's cottage, built during the Barnsley linen boom in the eighteenth century, so the basement was high and cavernous, having been built to accommodate the looms. Outside, a long flight of stone steps ran up from the pavement to the raised front door. From the parlor, passersby could be heard but not seen. A good house for a flood, Amos said, should the Dearne and Dove canal ever burst its banks. It had a good-sized kitchen, a second small parlor as well as the larger front one, three bedrooms upstairs, and no bathroom.

"Tin tub and outside privy," Anna had said when they first looked at it.

"Just like t'old days. Can you face it, or shall we look elsewhere?"

But the fact was, she liked the cottage and in any case there wasn't much indoor plumbing to be had in Ardington. So she settled for what she'd once been grateful for, and Maya, whose only memories were of Ravenscliffe and night-time trips along a dark landing to a lavatory whose hidden pipes clanked and groaned monstrously, thought the chamber pot a fine invention.

There was still an old loom in the lofty basement: a cumbersome beast, with trailing strands of warp thread hanging from the heddle. A spindle-backed chair was positioned at its center and there were foot pedals to work the shuttle. This basement was to be Anna's workroom, and though Amos had offered to chop the loom up for kindling, Anna had insisted that it be left in peace. This morning she had cleaned it, wiping away the dust of decades and now she sat down on the chair and pushed hard on a pedal with her right foot. The loom, woken from its long sleep, lurched into noisy activity and she drew back at once, in some alarm. She tried again, more gently this time, watching the mechanics of it, trying to understand and interpret its movements. She wondered if she might try to make her own cloth. She wondered where to buy flax for linen. She wondered who had once sat here, making from the warp and the weft something useful, or even beautiful.

Outside on the street the sound of a motor—a rare thing in Ardington, where the horse and cart still reigned supreme— interrupted her reverie, followed by footsteps, quick and purposeful, up the steps, from the pavement to her door. Mac barked at their approach. A sharp rap and then Maya's voice came from upstairs—"Mam," she shouted from her post at the parlor window, "there's a lady." Anna left the loom, climbed the basement steps, and opened the front door to find Thea Hoyland, all smiles, incongruous in a bolero jacket of gold sable and a matching fur headband. On the street Atkins stood beside the motorcar. He nodded when he saw Anna, and touched his cap. She waved.

"Wonderful," Thea said. "I was worried you might be out and about. Can I come in?"

Anna smiled. "Of course," she said, and she opened the door wide, hoping as she did so that Amos wouldn't come home to find the countess in the house and a Daimler outside.

Tobias was in bed reading *Horse & Hound* when Henrietta found him. His bedroom had been the last place she looked, given that it was already almost lunchtime, yet there he was, tucked up and smiling at her, a little sheepish; he could tell from the way she was dressed and the flush to her cheeks that she had just come in from outside, and even Toby wasn't insensitive to the glaring contrast of their respective situations.

"Hello, sis," he said. "You find me in *déshabillé*, old thing. I feel somewhat at a disadvantage."

"I've had enough, Toby," she said, and he sat up a little straighter against the duck down.

"Look here," he said. "Give me half a mo' and I'll sling on some clothes. I meant to be up in time for lunch anyway."

"I'm going to Manchester for a few days to stay with a friend there. You'll find the diary on the desk in Daddy's old study—you remember where that is, do you? Two doors down from the gun room, if that helps."

Her tone was distinctly cold. He wished he was in the armchair, at least.

"Not quite sure what you're driving at, Henry. Of course I know where the study is."

"Good. Then you can make your way there after lunch and acquaint yourself with what has to be done over the next week or so. There are meetings at all three collieries, and Mr. Garforth is coming over to Long Martley from Altofts tomorrow, so it's especially important that you're there to see him. There's a contractor coming to conduct a drain survey at Home Farm. Jem knows all about that. Be sure to speak to the bailiff at least once, doesn't matter what about, it's just that he's been left to his own devices for too long and needs reminding that he isn't a law unto himself. Someone should address the matter of hiring a new cook. Sarah Pickersgill might do, though she's rather young for the job. Where's Thea, by the way? I can't find her anywhere. Honestly, Toby, you look quite ridiculous, gaping in that way."

He was sure now that she was having fun at his expense, and he put on a high-pitched comedy voice to show what a sport he was. "Mr. what? Drain survey? Who's Sarah Pickersgill? Have you gone stark raving mad?"

"On the contrary, I believe I've come to my senses. I shall

be in Manchester until next Wednesday, after which you, Thea, and I will sit down together and talk sensibly about how the multitude of responsibilities attendant on our privileged existence here may be shared equally between the three of us."

"Who do we know in Manchester?"

Now he whined rather than spoke, and his question was hardly to the point, but she answered patiently enough.

"You don't know anyone," she said. "I have several friends there, but I shall be staying with Eva Gore-Booth. I'll leave an address, for emergencies only."

"Look, you've caught me by surprise here," he said, adopting a third voice, this one his sensible man of the world. "Let's reconvene in the dining room at one. Yes?"

"No, I shall be on my way by then. I'm lunching on the train. Cheerio, Tobes. And don't look so glum. Say good-bye to Thea for me, will you? Did you say where she's gone?"

"Why would I know? She pleases herself."

"Whereas you are the embodiment of altruism," she said, and she stalked out of the room, leaving him to wallow in his own injured feelings. His sister was such a brute, always had been. She spoke to him as if he was a perfect idiot. Two doors down from the gun room indeed. He reached for a cigarette from the box on the bedside cabinet, lit it, took a long, restorative drag, then, with the cigarette hanging from the corner of his mouth, lay back against the pillows again, his hands behind his head, his eyes closed. He breathed heavily through his nostrils, in and out, again and again, and the sound he made was curiously soothing, curiously effective at banishing unpleasantness. Betty Cross popped into his mind, unbidden but not unwelcome. He conjured an image of her, her bodice untied to the waist, his hands up her skirts, and from there it was an easy step to wondering idly if she was still in the Netherwood dairy or whether some other young lord had the pleasure of her these days. And in the end it was this thought, rather than the diary on the study desk or any of the estate matters awaiting his attention, that got him out of bed.

When Amos walked in at just past six o'clock, Anna and Maya were sitting together at the kitchen table playing pairs. She was only three years old but there was no beating her at this game: once seen, always remembered. Anna, on the other hand, found the opposite was true: once seen, instantly forgotten. Maya thought this was hilarious. "No, Mam, that's t'kitten," she was saying, though she spoke with some difficulty, on account of her merriment. Anna was quite glad of the interruption.

"Come and sit," she said. "Help me find yacht."

"We're on," Amos said. "Campbell-Bannerman's dissolved Parliament."

She stood up, since his tone and his news seemed to merit it.

"Good. At last," she said. "Tea?"

"I'll make it," he said, and so she sat down again, watching him. So this was it: the beginning of the campaign, the end of the wait. Amos picked up the kettle and placed it on the range. On the worktop was a sheaf of papers of various sizes, each headed with a different address. He picked them up and flicked through.

"Thea Hoyland brought them," Anna said to his back. He turned and looked at her. "They're letters from friends of hers who want me to work for them."

He looked back down at the papers. Antley Hall, Warwickshire. Canbrook Court, Wiltshire. Pemberton House, Belgravia. Wetherton Manor, Derbyshire. He looked up again.

"We've a general election to fight," he said. His expression was dark.

"I know. And when it's over, I shall either be wife of an MP or not, but I shall be free, either way, to work if I wish."

"You've said no, though? You can't work for all these damned toffs," he said. "It's not fitting for t'wife of a Labor politician."

She left unsaid the obvious, that he might yet lose.

"I didn't say no, I said thank you, and I said I'd think it over. And if I decide to do it, I'd like your blessing, but I don't need it. In any case, where will our money come from, when—if—you're elected?"

This was a good question. There was no weekly wage for an MP. Keir Hardie and the small handful of other Labor men in the House of Commons took donations from well-wishers and unions, and small salaries from the ILP, but Amos was by no means sure how deep that pot was, or how full.

"We'd manage," he said though, stubborn and infuriating. "Anyroad, that's of no account. I just don't want you mixing with their ilk. I thought Netherwood 'all would be t'last of it."

He didn't raise his voice in the least and his conversational tone—maintained for Maya's benefit—belied the challenge in his eyes. Beside him, the kettle started to whistle, but he ignored it.

"Where's the disgrace in it?" she said.

"Can't you see 'ow it'll look to my detractors? Don't be naïve, Anna."

She was trying hard to stay calm, but he was making it very difficult.

She swallowed hard. "I'll fight every waking moment to get you elected—to give you what you want," she said. "And then we'll talk about this—about what I might want." They looked at each other, both of them miserable now.

"Amos?"

This was Maya, down from her chair and tugging at his trousers. He bent down and picked her up.

"Now then, sunbeam. What is it?"

"Kettle's whistling."

"So it is."

He put her down and pulled it off the burner.

"Thank goodness for you," he said to her. "Wherever would we be without you?"

Anna said, "I thought of something today. Invite voters to come to you here, in the house, with issues that are important to them. You can listen, I can give them tea and cake, they go home thinking what a good Member of Parliament Amos Sykes would be." She smiled at him, and it was as if the cross words had never been spoken. This was like her: to dispel ill feeling before it took root. She was a wonderful woman, he thought.

"You're a wonderful woman," he said.

She stood up, crossed the kitchen, and kissed him.

"Best of luck," she said, and kissed him again.

Chapter 61

"The cat's among the pigeons now, good and proper."

Daniel waved the day's edition of the *Daily Telegraph* as he walked into the kitchen. Eve was sitting in the armchair, her feet up on a wooden stool. She looked pale, he thought. He sat on the broad arm of the chair and opened up the newspaper.

"Listen to this. You'll never believe it." He cleared his throat. Eve waited, watching him. Then he began to read.

"'Suffragists caused pandemonium at Manchester's Free Trade Hall yesterday, when Winston Churchill, the Liberal candidate for North-West Manchester, addressed the packed assembly. Mr. Churchill, who recently left the Conservative Party to join the Liberals, is known to sympathize with the suffragist movement, and yet his views did not protect him from constant interruption as he tried to deliver his address. In some exasperation, Mr. Churchill invited one particularly vehement heckler onto his platform to put her views 'in a civilized manner.' Lady Henrietta Hoyland"—Daniel paused here for effect, and indeed Eve was suitably astonished, eyes wide, hands at her open mouth—"'Lady Henrietta Hoyland, the eldest daughter of the late Edward Hoyland, Sixth Earl of Netherwood, proceeded to berate Mr. Churchill and the party he now represents. When she left the platform, Mr. Churchill announced that nothing would induce him to vote for women's enfranchisement after the disruption she and her cohorts had engineered. Later, Mr. Churchill admitted he still had some sympathy with the cause, but that he "would not be henpecked." After the event, Lady Henrietta spoke to journalists outside the Free Trade Hall. She condemned the Liberal Party for "professing to champion political freedom while consistently blocking any progress for the Women's Franchise." She went on to say: "If the Liberal Party will not promise to give votes to women before the election, they will certainly not do it afterward." Lady Henrietta is rapidly becoming known as one of the leading and most vocal members of the Women's Social and Political Union.'"

Daniel put down the paper and laughed. "Can you credit it?" he said.

Eve said. "Manchester. Whatever is she doing in Manchester?"

"Up and down there all the time, they say. The servants' hall was in a proper lather about it this afternoon. You'd think she'd brought disgrace on Parkinson personally. He's walking about the place like he's following a coffin."

"Poor thing. What about t'family?"

"Cheerful enough, from what little I've seen. The new guard takes modern life pretty much in their stride. Not sure about her mother, though."

He thought of the dowager countess and her old preoccupations: pagodas, peaches, palm houses. She had never given a thought to the wider world, the world outside the perimeter walls of Netherwood Hall or Fulton House. Now her daughter was harassing MPs and government ministers, dragging the family name into the newspapers, bringing politics and polemic

510

to the drawing room. It was, as Amos would say, a strange turn.

Daniel put the paper down and ran a hand through Eve's hair. "How're you feeling, love?"

"Weary," she said. "I went to 'ave a look at Ginger in Barnsley, and ended up behind t'counter for a couple of hours. She was run off 'er feet."

"Then take on another girl. Don't be running yourself ragged."

Eve yawned. "I've asked Sarah if she wants to go. It's easier to find somebody new in Netherwood than to start looking for staff in Barnsley."

"And does Sarah want to go?"

"She's got to ask Nellie first. She won't do owt that might worry 'er mam. Nellie likes Sarah to be where she can see 'er."

For a little while they sat on in silence. The kitchen was always the warmest part of the house, and today Eve had stoked up the range and lit a fire against the January cold. It had been a mild winter so far: too mild, really. There was spring blossom on the trees and the wrong flowers unfurling their tender petals in the garden. But suddenly nature had had a change of mind and when Daniel had left the house at half past five this morning, the common had been white with hoar frost: cobwebs, blades of grass, the tangle of hawthorn and blackthorn branches in the hedgerow, were all transformed into works of intricate art. He had almost turned back to wake Eliza so that she could see the glory. He had crunched on, though, through the carpet of frost, leaving perfect footprints in his wake, the first of the day, as if he was the only man walking through this white world.

"Are the bairns with Lilly?"

Eve shook her head. "They're at Anna's. Went straight to Ardington when school finished."

"Ellen too?'

"It would've taken a stronger woman than me to try and stop 'er. She went with Seth and Eliza. We should go ourselves before too long. I told Anna we'd be there for t'count."

"Are you sure you're up to it? It could be a long night."

He placed a gentle, proprietorial hand on her swollen belly. Four months to go, and then they would see who was in there.

"I'll be fine. I was on my feet from morning till night when I fell for t'other three. Look at me now, feet up by t'fire like Lady Muck."

He smiled. "Right-o, your ladyship. I'll just shrug off these work clothes and then we'll be off."

He kissed her on the head, then left the room and went upstairs. She closed her eyes. On the fire, a log shifted and the movement made it fizz with new life. In the small of her back, where it had started to ache, she had pushed one of Anna's cushions, a patchwork of velvet in as many blues as she had been able to find in the remnants bin at Butterwick's. Anna was all over the house, still. She was in the colors on the walls, the rugs on the floors, the fabrics on the chairs and at the windows, and even in the particular arrangement of the furniture. It was a comfort, thought Eve, but she still missed her every day she didn't see her. Anna—slightly cavalier about mealtimes and bedtimes, always more interested in what someone had to say than whether their shirt was clean or their hair was brushed— had countered Eve's domestic excesses: shown her that she could delay the cleaning or the washing and the world would not come crashing down around her. Once, when bright rays of sunshine broke through a pewter sky and a perfect rainbow had arched over the common, Eve had said she couldn't come to look because she was busy. Anna had marched through the house, manhandled the broom out of Eve's hands, and pushed her bodily up the hallway and out into the front garden. "See?" she had said, pointing upward, and the rainbow had been spectacular, every color bold and clear against the next. "In seconds, it will be gone. The kitchen floor, however, will still be there."

The Labor campaign in Ardington had been as good as it could be, and if Amos didn't take the seat it wouldn't be for lack of trying. He and Enoch had been given leave by the YMA to put their union duties on hold for the duration, though the old Liberal traditionalists who formed the hierarchy there made it perfectly clear that their money was on Webster Thorne. Anna's idea of inviting the electorate into their home had been a masterstroke. Amos had sat behind a desk in the front parlor listening to their concerns, noting them down; Anna had plied them with currant buns. True, some people came more than once with patently trumped-up excuses, and other people came, blatant and unapologetic, only for the buns. Eve had had to lend them Alice Buckle to keep up with the demand. Alice had stationed herself in Anna's kitchen and baked with ferocious intensity, like a revolutionary in a makeshift bomb factory, stockpiling grenades for an oncoming battle. Toward the end of the campaign Keir Hardie had come, graciously stopping off at Ardington on his twelve-hundred-mile tour of the country to personally endorse the Labor candidate and air his own manifesto at a packed meeting in Ardington church hall. He was a bit too radical for around here, Enoch thought, but on the other hand, he was a national figure, a Labor legend, the pit boy who won a seat in Parliament and rode to the House of Commons on a wagonette while a lone trumpeter played the "Marseillaise."

"Very best of luck, Mr. Sykes," he had said, shaking Amos's hand at the end of the evening. He was at the tail end of his national tour and heading back that same night to his own Merthyr constituency. "I shall see you in the House of Commons before this month is out."

"Wish I 'ad 'is confidence," Amos had muttered to Enoch, after the great man had gone. "And 'is constituency, for that matter."

"It was 'ard graft won Merthyr Tydfil in 1900, just as 'ard graft will win you this one," Enoch had said. He was proud of his man, and proud of himself for spotting his potential. True, Webster Thorne had upped his game, reinventing himself since the by-election as a Liberal reformer with a newfound passion for social housing and old-age pensions. He'd lost that potbelly, too, Enoch had noticed, and by all accounts had turned teetotal in his quest for serious-mindedness. A mistake, Enoch and Amos agreed: you couldn't trust a man who stood at the bar with a glass of bitter lemon in his hand.

Anyway, it was all over now. The votes were cast and the ballot boxes were in the hands of the council officers, whose job it was to count the crosses. It was a three-man race in Ardington, though an unwinnable one for the Conservatives. This was the case at the best of times, but in this contest, thrown into disarray by Balfour's resignation, the party had hastily selected a candidate who knew neither the constituency nor the county and had made his way to Ardingly by mistake. By the time he had got himself from Sussex to Yorkshire, no one could take him seriously. This, although it had been the cause of much hilarity at the hapless man's expense, was a worry to the Sykes team: there were few natural Tory voters in Ardington, but those there were might very well turn Liberal for want of a serious candidate of their own. What they wouldn't do, as Amos never tired of telling Enoch, was vote Labor.

At the back of the polling station—the church hall on any other day—Eve had arranged two wooden chairs so that she could sit down with her feet up and not be in anyone's way.

Anna sat next to her, though she was up and down constantly, always in demand. Anyway, conversation was effortful, such was the throng, Liberal and Labor supporters trying to outdo each other in robust stoicism as the evening dragged on toward night. Maya was fast asleep on Eve's lap, facing forward, her little body curled like a cat over the bump. Ellen and Eliza, frenzied by fatigue, made circuits of the room, galloping like giddy thoroughbreds, neither of them able to remember why they'd started, neither of them willing to stop. Seth stood with the men, listening to their talk, affecting their expressions of preoccupied gravity. A miasma of smoke, added to constantly by their pipes and cigarettes, hung above their heads.

Anna looked at Eve: there were shadows under her eyes. Her hands were laced protectively across the sleeping child, but Eve looked like the one in need of sleep.

"Should I take her?" Anna said. "Is she heavy?"

Eve shook her head. "She's keeping me warm."

"You could wait at our house, though. It'd be more comfortable." She was full of concern for her friend; this seemed no place for a pregnant woman.

"Not likely," Eve said. "And miss t'moment? Anyway, I'm right as rain, as long as I can sit down."

Anna nodded. Then she said: "Daniel tells me you might be looking for new waitress."

"Aye, that's right. Do you know one?"

"Well, yes and no," she said. "Does it have to be girl?"

Eve considered. "No," she said. "I don't suppose it does. Are you thinking of summat for Amos, if tonight doesn't go 'is way?"

Anna laughed. "No, but I know someone who needs work." The boy your brother sacked, she thought, and though she didn't say it, Eve understood immediately.

"Edward Wakefield," she said, and Anna nodded.

"And if I took 'im on, might Amos bury t'atchet?"

Anna didn't answer directly. "I just want to him to make amends with Morten, truth be told," she said. "They'll be missing that boy's pay packet."

"Nice of you," Eve said. "Morten Wakefield made a right mess of Amos's face."

Anna shrugged. "He's forgiven," she said, "but Edward is still out of work."

"Well," Eve said, "Sarah Kaye was all fingers and thumbs when she first started, and now she's a grand little waitress. If Nellie lets 'er go to Barnsley, there's no reason why we couldn't give Edward a chance, if you think 'e'd like it." She smiled. "We could get 'im a frock coat. Put 'im on t'door, like at Fortnum & Mason."

At the front of the room there was a significant hubbub, a scraping of chairs and a clearing of throats. Someone called Anna's name and she looked at Eve with something akin to panic in her eyes. Eve took her hand and squeezed it.

"Come on," she said. "This is it."

Anna lifted Maya into her own arms. The child stirred, but didn't wake.

"Anna! Up 'ere."

This was Seth's voice, carrying across the hall from the makeshift stage at the front. He was there with Enoch and Amos, and they all three mimed at her to get a move on, which she did, pushing her way through the melée. Eve followed in the path she created.

"Mam!" Eliza shouted. "Mam!"

The child's face glowed with the thrill of it all. She reached for Eve's arm and pulled her into the middle of the family huddle, to keep the bump safe from other people's elbows. Seth had jumped down to join them too; he chewed his thumbnail and watched the men on the platform with anxious intensity. If Amos lost, he wasn't sure he could bear it. Anna handed him the sleeping Maya as she passed, and Seth, having taken her,

516

immediately gave her to Daniel, who already had Ellen on his shoulders. She leaned down and tapped Maya smartly on the head so that the younger girl awoke and opened her eyes in surprise. Daniel, fearing noisy tears at the crucial moment, kissed her on her hot plump cheek, and she yawned at him, then smiled. In front of them, Anna had made it to the platform and though there were wooden steps on either side, Amos reached down with one arm and pulled her up.

"Are you all right?" she said, and he said, "I am now," though he looked, to her, to be taut with nerves, unlike Webster Thorne, who occupied his space on the platform with the un-ruffled, worldly air of a man whose attendance here was a mere formality. If anything, he seemed a little bored. He arranged his face into a genial smile and offered a hand, which Amos shook, mistaking the gesture for cordiality.

"Prepare yourself for disappointment, Sykes," Thorne said, *sotto voce.* "My man's been on the door all day, and his esti-mation is a solid Liberal victory."

Amos opened his mouth to reply but the returning officer had stepped forward and the crowd, suddenly silent, turned avid eyes upon him. Anxiety churned in Amos's gut. He looked away from Thorne and ahead into the crowd and his eyes found Eve, who sent him a smile so replete with warmth and faith that Amos felt suddenly steadier. He smiled back. Ellen, from her perch, waved at him flamboyantly with both arms and cheered as if he'd already won. Beside him, Anna reached for his hand.

"Here are the results of the election contest in the con-stituency of Ardington."

The returning officer was Lester Moorhouse, chairman of the parish council; a Liberal, Amos thought resentfully, though there was no clue in his neutral expression as to what was written on the piece of paper in his hand. He was milking the moment, though: his pause was a little long, a little theatrical, and his voice, when he spoke again, was loaded with self-importance.

"Mr. Webster Thorne, Liberal Party: two thousand, seven hundred and eighty-five votes."

A hum of urgent conversation waxd and then waned. Amos and Enoch looked at each other, knowing without speaking that they shared the same thought: Thorne had polled well. Their anxiety had been well founded.

"Mr. Vincent Camberley-Brook, Conservative Party. Eighty-three votes."

Someone sent up an ironic hurrah and earned a ripple of laughter, but it was of the nervous, distracted variety, and offered no real release from the tension.

"Mr. Amos Sykes, Independent Labor Party."

In the pause, Amos heard only the pounding of his own heart. His hand, in Anna's, was cold and his mouth was bone dry. He felt he stood on the edge of a precipice; he hadn't realized, until now, how very much he wanted to win.

"Two thousand, nine hundred and forty-two votes. Mr. Amos Sykes is duly elected as the Member of Parliament for Ardington."

These last words in Mr Moorhouse's moment in the spotlight were lost in the animal roar of victory from Amos's supporters. Thorne and his agent exchanged stunned looks of abject confusion. They stood immobile, trying to comprehend the loss while pandemonium broke out all about them. Like a shot, Seth was back on the platform, hooting with ecstatic triumph. Eliza clambered up too and threw herself joyfully into the mayhem. Enoch, tears streaming down his face, joined Amos and Anna in a tight embrace and the three of them swayed there, heads together, quite undone by emotion, unsteady with relief and disbelief. When they finally pulled apart, Thorne was gone from the platform and the Liberal supporters were trailing out of the hall like guests ejected from a party. Vincent Camberley-Brook, entirely unsupported in the crowd but gentlemanly in defeat, waited politely for the victory speech; when there is no hope of winning, neither is there disappointment at losing. And in front of the platform an expectant, jubilant, giddy crowd of Labor voters shouted for their man. He stepped forward and they hollered their approval, clapping and clapping, stamping their boots on the wooden boards. Amos waited, let them settle, and then he spoke.

"Today, my loyal friends, you have put your trust in me, and I make this pledge to you now: I shall not let you down. There is much work to be done, but I shall not rest until there is no child hungry in Ardington, no workingman without fair pay, no widow without t'means to support 'erself and 'er family. It's an honor, a privilege, to represent you, and I shall endeavor always to justify your faith in me." Here his voice cracked and faltered and he looked down at his boots. A swell of cheering rose to fill the moment, giving him time to collect himself. Anna moved closer and he reached for her, pulling her tight to his side. Someone shouted, "Three cheers for Amos and Anna Sykes," and Amos looked at her, and then out across the hall, and he laughed out loud, warm and flushed with happiness. This was his world, and it was a place where anything was possible.

For an authentic taste of

Anna's homeland,

try your hand

at these traditional

Russian delicacies.

Anna's Recipes

Pirozkhi

Ingredients
16 fluid oz warm milk
1 tablespoon sugar
1 tablespoon yeast
2 tablespoons melted butter
1 egg
1 teaspoon salt
1½ lbs flour
Half a cabbage, finely chopped
6 hard-boiled eggs, chopped
Salt and pepper to taste

Method
Pour a little of the warm milk into a bowl and add the sugar and yeast. Set aside until it foams—about 10 minutes. Pour the rest of the milk into another bowl and to this add the melted butter, the egg, the salt, and 4 oz of flour. Stir, adding the yeast mixture. Then continue to mix in the flour, about 4 oz at a time, until the dough comes away from the sides of the bowl and doesn't feel sticky on your hands. Cover

with a linen cloth and set it in a warm place for about an hour, during which time it should almost triple in size.

While the dough rises, cook the cabbage in butter until it wilts, then stir in the chopped eggs and cook until the cabbage begins to turn golden brown at the edges. Season with salt and pepper. Set aside to cool.

Tip the risen dough onto a floured surface and form into a long sausage, about two inches wide. Cut into one-inch pieces and roll into balls. Flatten the balls, place a small spoonful of filling in the middle, then fold the circle in half to enclose. Pinch the edges together tightly to seal. Brush the upper surface with beaten egg.

Put the pirozkhi on baking sheets, leaving room between them to spread, and bake in a hot oven for about 20 minutes until golden brown and puffed up.

Blinis

Ingredients
3 oz buckwheat flour
9 oz strong white flour
1 teaspoon salt
1 teaspoon dried yeast
6 fluid oz milk
5 fluid oz sour cream
2 eggs, separated
1 oz butter

Method
Sift the flours and the salt together in a large bowl and sprinkle in the yeast. Gently warm the milk and sour cream in a small pan—do not overheat. Add the egg yolks and whisk together, then pour this into the flour, whisking again until you have a thick batter. Let the bowl stand, covered, somewhere warm for about an hour, then whisk the egg whites until stiff and fold into the batter. Cover again and let stand for another hour.

To cook, melt butter in an iron pan and drop a generous tablespoon of batter into the pan. When the upper surface begins to bubble—after about a minute, perhaps less—flip the blini over and cook on the other side for thirty seconds. Transfer to a cooling rack then repeat the process until all the batter is used up, adding butter to the pan when necessary. This recipe is for about 20 blinis.

Serve warm with thick sour cream and caviar.

Ukrainian potato pancakes (*deruny*)

Ingredients
6 potatoes, peeled and grated
1 large onion, peeled and grated
2 eggs, beaten
2 tablespoons flour
Salt and pepper to taste.

Method
Mix the grated potatoes and onion together. Add the beaten eggs, the flour, and a twist of salt and pepper.

Heat oil in a flat skillet and drop a large spoonful of the mixture into the pan. Fry until browned on one side, then flip over and brown the other side.

Serve warm.

Borscht

Ingredients
1 large onion, sliced
4 large beetroot, 3 peeled and diced, 1 grated
1 carrot, diced
1 stick of celery, diced
1 bay leaf
1 large potato, peeled and diced
Half a cabbage, finely shredded
2 pints excellent, gelatinous beef stock (the better the stock, the
    better the soup)
2 tablespoons cider vinegar
1 teaspoon honey
Salt and pepper to taste

Method
Soften the onion in butter in a large pan for a few minutes, then add
the diced beetroot, carrot, celery, and bay leaf to the pan and stir well
to coat everything with butter. Cook for 10 minutes over a low heat.
Add the grated beetroot, the potato, and the cabbage, cook gently for
a few minutes, then pour in the stock and simmer until the vegetables
are meltingly tender. Add the vinegar, honey, and salt and pepper to
taste.

Serve with sour cream and chopped dill.

Bibliography

Bailey, Catherine, *Black Diamonds: The Rise and Fall of an English Dynasty* (Penguin Books, 2008).

Barstow, Phyllida, *The English Country House Party* (Thorsons Publishing Group, 1989).

Black, Clinton V., *History of Jamaica* (Longman, 1999).

Elliot, Brian, *South Yorkshire Mining Disasters*, volume II (Wharncliffe Books, 2009).

Elliot, Brian, *Pits & Pitmen of Barnsley* (Wharncliffe Books, 2006).

Elliot, Brian, *Yorkshire Miners* (The History Press, 2009).

Fraser, Bryan, *The West Riding Miners and Sir William Garforth* (The History Press, 2009).

Holman, Bob, *Keir Hardie: Labor's Greatest Hero?* (Lion Hudson, 2010).

Howse, Geoffrey, *Around Hoyland: A Second Selection* (Sutton Publishing, 2000).

Parsons, R. M., *The White Ships: The Banana Trade at the Port of Bristol* (City of Bristol Museum and Art Gallery, 1982).

Phillips, Melanie, *The Ascent of Woman: A History of the Suffrage Movement* (Abacus, 2004).

Pugh, Martin, *The Pankhursts: The History of One Radical Family* (Vintage, 2008).

Russell, A. K., *Liberal Landslide: The General Election of 1906* (David and Charles, 1973).

Reading Group Guide

The first chapter of *Ravenscliffe* shows Anna's emotional response to the house on the common. How significant do you think buildings are to our state of mind? And how symbolic, for Eve and for Anna, is the move from Beaumont Lane to Netherwood Common?

Eve's son, Seth, plays a significant role in *Ravenscliffe*, particularly in the first two parts. Does his anger and resentment prevent him from being a likable character? Or is it entirely understandable? Do you think the adults in his life handle him well?

As well as the fictional characters of *Ravenscliffe*, there are also real historical figures such as Edward VII, Keir Hardie, and Sylvia Pankhurst. How successfully do you think the author weaves them into the narrative, and what effect does their presence have?

Before his untimely death the Earl of Netherwood seems to be reevaluating his life and his priorities. How genuine did you feel this impulse was, and how far might it have gone? Do you think his response to the colliery disaster reflected well on him, or badly? Was it too little, too late?

How does the earl's death alter life for his family? Do you think Henrietta's character would have developed in the same way if he had lived?

When Thea marries Tobias do you consider her a force for good within the Hoyland dynasty, or the opposite?

What evidence is there in *Ravenscliffe* that British society—and the world at large—was on the brink of great political change?

If the cast of characters were transported to the present day, who among them do you think would be best equipped to cope with modern life? Who would fare worst?

Conversely, if you were transported to the world of *Ravenscliffe*, how would you cope and at which level of society would you find a place?

Why do you think, in the twenty-first-century, we are still so drawn to the Edwardian era? Does what we know of this period in history—and what we know happens as the century rolls on—influence our understanding and interpretation of fictional events?

Q&A with Jane Sanderson

Ravenscliffe has a large cast of characters and storylines—how do you organize your writing to give them all the right amount of space?

That's a good question, because one of the things I worry about is forgetting someone after the first few chapters, so that they appear once, then never again. It has very occasionally happened to me as a reader, and I do hate to be left wondering what on earth became of so-and-so. How I avoid this is to write everyone down on an increasingly long list as and when they appear—it sounds fairly obvious, but it's really helpful to be able to scan the list from time to time and remind myself of what I called the housemaid or the groom, or some other bit part who might need another mention. Equally, the list is useful to remind myself of loose ends, those smaller storylines that remain unresolved or that have been temporarily lost in the bigger dramas. One of these days—when I have a free week or two and a very large sheet of paper—I might make a Netherwood family tree, with everyone on it, and their connections to one another.

Do you have a clear picture in your head of the town's geography?

Yes, I do. It helps, of course, that I'm thinking of my old hometown of Hoyland when I visualize Netherwood, but I think it's actually quite important that I can picture, for example, the route from Ravenscliffe to Netherwood Hall that Daniel and Anna take, or Seth's journey from Ravenscliffe to New Mill Colliery, or the earl's fateful drive from Long Martley up to the top of Harley Hill. Perhaps when I get around to doing that family tree I could also do a map of Netherwood with all its principal landmarks, like those maps of Earthsea at the front of Ursula K. Le Guin's books that I used to pore over as a child.

Do you know where your stories are heading when you start, or do they evolve as you write?
Yes and yes, I would say. That is, I have a fair idea of where I want everyone to end up, but I don't know exactly how they're going to get there. Before I start writing the books I prepare a fairly detailed outline for my editor of what's likely to happen, so the structure of the stories—the bones of them—are in place at the very beginning. But it's perfectly possible for new ideas and solutions to present themselves, or for individual characters to develop in surprising ways. I didn't know, for example, that Absalom Blandford was going to deny Eve her gift from the earl until I got well into the writing of *Ravenscliffe*, although I had always known he would wreak some sort of revenge on her for spurning him in *Netherwood*. It would be very dull for me, as the writer, if I knew down to the very last detail exactly what was going to happen. I often sit down without knowing at all what I'm going to write, and then surprise myself with the way the story goes.

Have you got a favorite character?
Oh, that's a tricky question to answer, and I think I would have to say no. There are things about all my characters that I like: even the reptilian Absalom is interesting to me for his nastiness. His meanness makes him fun to write—I don't know anyone remotely like him, but he sprang fully formed into my imagination. Of course, among the cast are a few that stand out for special mention: Anna is terrific for her resourcefulness and loyalty, and Amos is fantastic for his integrity and his sense of humor, and his engaging awkwardness in matters of the heart. Henrietta, too, is

such a strong individual, so uncharacteristic of women of her class. And the lovely Eve will always have a place among my favorites, because she was the start of it all. I've enjoyed the way that the children have emerged in *Ravenscliffe* too: Eliza has come out of the shadows and Seth has grown in an interesting and—I hope— satisfying way. This next generation of Netherwood inhabitants could be the ones to take the story on, up to and beyond the First World War, perhaps.

How do you get started on your books?
With some trepidation initially, then with increasing confidence as the words start to fill the page. In fact, I think find it more difficult to finish a book than to start one. There's something so significant, somehow, about those final sentences. Giving them weight and interest but steering clear of sentimentality is my goal.

Could you see your books on the screen?
Yes, I really could—but I suppose I would say that, wouldn't I? Nevertheless, I think both *Ravenscliffe* and the earlier *Netherwood* are extremely televisual, and I'd love to see them brought to life. I'd be hoping for an old-fashioned thirteen-part series, though, not one of those two-parters they like to give us these days, where everything gets condensed into too small a space and entire characters are chopped from the action.

Your female characters tend to be very strong: does your writing have a feminist theme?
There's no agenda, though I can see why you might ask that question. Eve, Anna, Henrietta, Thea—they're all independent-minded women with a strong seam of resilience running through them. And of course Henry is drawn to the suffragists, whose vociferous campaign for the enfranchisement of women was certainly a milestone in the long fight for equality of the sexes. But I think the key word there is "resilience." I grew up around strong women who, while they probably wouldn't have described themselves as feminists, led independent and—in my grandma's case—self-sufficient lives, and did their best with the hand they were dealt. I wouldn't say there's a specifically feminist theme to

my writing but I certainly do salute the women in my corner of Yorkshire who knew what they wanted and worked hard to achieve it.

Did you have a house in mind when you pictured Ravenscliffe?
No, it was purely imaginary, unlike Netherwood Hall, which was based very specifically on Wentworth Woodhouse, a stately home near my own hometown. Netherwood Common is imagined, too, but I liked the idea of Eve and Anna and the children making a home in a big old house, with open countryside all around them, and the freedom and space to be themselves. It's a symbolic move away from the confines of the miners' terraces.

Are your characters based on anyone you know? Are you in the book?
One of my friends says that I'm definitely Amos. If I am in there it's because you can't help, as a writer, deploying your own values or your own sense of humor, although these things don't emerge in one individual but are scattered among the characteristics of the cast. Similarly, there are elements of people I know now, or people I used to know as a child, in various characters in the books—though I'd say this is more true of the working classes than the aristocrats, since there's no blue blood in my family!

How easy is it to write the Yorkshire dialect?
Not very easy at all, to be honest. I had to tone it down from the way that I know Yorkshire folk talk because it becomes too much of an obstacle to the uninitiated. As it is, the dropped aitches and the *t'* instead of "the" are quite difficult to sustain and can look daunting on a page where there's a lot of dialogue. But I felt it was important to distinguish between the working-class locals and the other characters, and also I wanted to be faithful to my own Yorkshire roots. I sometimes think the books should come with an instructional DVD so that everyone knows how to "talk Tyke."

How long did it take you to write *Ravenscliffe*?
About a year, six months less than it took me to write *Netherwood*, although *Ravenscliffe* is about twenty thousand words longer. Of course I had a deadline this time around, and I must admit this made me more disciplined about my writing. I didn't let a day go by without adding to it, even if it was only a couple of hundred words.

If you weren't a writer, how would you like to make a living?
Naturally, I'd bake fabulous pies and sell them.

BOOKS BY JANE SANDERSON

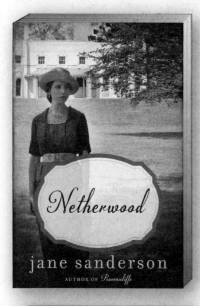

NETHERWOOD
A Novel

Available in Paperback and eBook

Netherwood has all of the upstairs/downstairs drama of the best *Downton Abbey* episodes—the setting for high drama, forbidden love, and families fighting the changing of the world. Above stairs: Lord Netherwood keeps his considerable fortune ticking over with the profits from his three coal mines in the vicinity. It's just as well the coal is of the highest quality as the upkeep of Netherwood Hall, his splendid estate on the outskirts of town, doesn't come cheap. Below stairs: Eve Williams, is the wife of one of Lord Netherwood's most stalwart employees. When her ordered existence amid the terraced rows of the miners' houses is brought crashing down by the twin arrivals of tragedy and charity, Eve must look to her own self-sufficiency, and talent, to provide for her three young children.

RAVENSCLIFFE
A Novel

Available in Paperback and eBook

Yorkshire, 1904. On Netherwood Common, Russian émigré Anna Rabinovich shows her dear friend Eve Williams a house: a Victorian villa, solidly built from local stone. This is Ravenscliffe, and it's the house Anna wants them to live in. It's their house, she says. It was meant to be. As Anna transforms Ravenscliffe, an attraction grows between her and union man Amos. But when Eve's long-lost brother Silas turns up in the closely knit mining community of Netherwood, cracks begin to appear in even the strongest friendships. Meanwhile, at Netherwood Hall, cherished traditions are being undermined by the whims of the feckless heir to the title, Tobias Hoyland, and his American bride Thea Stirling. Below stairs, the loyal servants strive to preserve the noble family's dignity and reputation. But both inside the great house and in the world beyond, values and loyalties are rapidly changing.